She was haunted by dreams—dreams of a place she'd never been to, of a time long faded from the face of the earth, and of a man she'd loved more than life itself...

A hawk called and circled overhead.

Flickering memories, vague and unsettling, darted through her mind. She looked up, and the man before her faded into nothingness. She stared at the space where he had been, waiting for something.

A soul-searing pain ripped through her.

Loneliness.

She was agonizingly alone. Separated from that which completed her.

Her heart ached with overwhelming intensity. Deep despair racked her body. Her soul cried out, "Where are you?"

No answer came.

The anguish was so excruciating that she began to weep. A deep keening wail ripped from her throat. "Where are you?"

A hand fell on her shoulder.

"I'm here," a voice said softly.

Joy leapt in her heart as she savored his nearness. "I couldn't find you."

He laughed. "Did you look for me?"

"Everywhere. I've been so alone without you." She smiled and touched his cheek—but the hand she saw was unfamiliar—changed from her visions.

Dazed, she looked around her at the ancient ruins of a lost civilization, then at the man she barely knew—who was tightly wrapped in her arms. "Ram?"

"Yes, love?"

She grabbed a handful of his reassuringly modern shirt front and buried her head against his shoulder. "What's happening to me? I think I'm losing my mind."

"Are you all right?"

"Would you be all right if you thought *you* were losing your mind?"

He smiled. "Probably not."

It was the beginning of a great adventure...

If you liked this book, be sure to look for others in the *Denise Little Presents* line:

MOONSHINE AND GLORY by Jacqueline Marten	(0079-1, $4.99)
COMING HOME by Ginna Gray	(0058-9, $4.99)
THE SILENT ROSE by Kasey Mars	(0081-3, $4.99)
DRAGON OF THE ISLAND by Mary Gillgannon	(0067-8, $4.99)
BOUNDLESS by Alexandra Thorne	(0059-7, $4.99)
MASQUERADE by Alexa Smart	(0080-5, $4.99)
THE PROMISE by Mandalyn Kaye	(0087-2, $4.99)
FIELDS OF FIRE by Carol Caldwell	(0088-0, $4.99)
HIGHLAND FLING by Amanda Scott	(0098-8, $4.99)
TRADEWINDS by Annee Cartier	(0099-6, $4.99)
A MARGIN IN TIME by Laura Hayden	(0109-7, $4.99)
REBEL WIND by Stobie Piel	(0110-0, $4.99)
SOMEDAY by Anna Hudson	(0119-4, $4.99)
THE IRISHMAN by Wynema McGowan	(0120-8, $4.99)
DREAM OF ME by Jan Hudson	(0130-5, $4.99)
ROAD TO THE ISLE by Megan Davidson	(0131-3, $4.99)

Available wherever paperbacks are sold, or order direct from the Publisher. Send cover price plus 50¢ per copy for mailing and handling to Penguin USA, P.O. Box 999, c/o Dept. 17109, Bergenfield, NJ 07621. Residents of New York and Tennessee must include sales tax. DO NOT SEND CASH.

DREAM OF ME
JAN HUDSON

PINNACLE BOOKS
KENSINGTON PUBLISHING CORP.

PINNACLE BOOKS are published by

Kensington Publishing Corp.
850 Third Avenue
New York, NY 10022

Copyright © 1995 by Janece Hudson

All rights reserved. No part of this book may be reproduced in any form or by any means without the prior written consent of the Publisher, excepting brief quotes used in reviews.

If you purchased this book without a cover, you should be aware that this book is stolen property. It was reported as "unsold and destroyed" to the Publisher and neither the Author nor the Publisher has received any payment for this "stripped book."

The P logo Reg. U.S. Pat. & TM Off. Pinnacle is a trademark of Kensington Publishing Corp.

First Printing: May, 1995

Printed in the United States of America

*For all of my very special friends and fellow travelers:
Nancy Royall, Linda Van Dyck, Gloria DesRoche,
Ahmed Abdelmawgood Fayed, and the rest.
To dear Bill and Elsie Sechrist
and other Egyptians,
present and
past.*

▼

Author's Note

Because ancient Egyptians wrote in hieroglyphics and modern Egyptians write in Arabic, there is considerable variance in the English spellings of Egyptian names, places, and other words. I relied heavily on Elias's *Practical Dictionary of the Colloquial Arabic,* which is often considered the definitive authority on Egyptian Arabic, for common words and endearments. Also it seems that not even Egyptologists can agree on dates or on the exact translations of early writings left on papyri, monuments, and tomb walls. When I have used any of these in text or quotations, I have opted to use either the most commonly accepted versions, the ones used by the author/translator in some of the quotes I chose, or the ones that best suited my purpose.

At night I often feel
The stars reaching through my flesh
Their soft fingers of light
Coiling around my heart
With a lover's embrace and the promise
That such love will outlast even
These endless sands that are my home . . .

                        Bedouin poem

Prologue

He came to her from the shadows, mist still clinging to his form and obscuring his features so that only his deeply penetrating eyes were distinguishable. This time they were blue, an arresting blue like pale crystal shot with fire.

A familiar love for him swelled and filled her with an inner glow. She smiled and held out her arms to him. He brushed her temple with his lips, then kissed her softly. His presence cloaked her in a surreal splendor as their spirits blended, like two souls meshing into one to form a timeless unity. When he drew back, she was filled with sadness and a wrenching longing to hold on to him forever.

She sensed his smile, an ephemeral flood of warmth that spread through her like sunlight. As he placed a pendant around her neck, a magnificent golden falcon suspended on a gold chain, his features seemed to materialize, forming high cheekbones, a strong jaw, and a dark mustache.

"It's time," he whispered. "Come to me. Come to me." The words echoed in the mist as he disappeared among vague stone shapes in the shadows.

Sitting upright with her right hand clasping the pendant and the other hand extended toward the disappearing figure, Meri Vaughn awoke with a start. Her right hand clutched nothing but air, and the left one was making a dramatic entreaty to the Victorian hat rack in the corner.

Although she was quite alone in her bedroom, she felt extremely foolish about her performance, even if it was a dream.

She tried to laugh it off and go back to sleep, but she was too unsettled to sleep. The dream bothered her more than she would have admitted to anyone. She'd been having a variation of the same theme for years, more frequently in the past few months. But the nocturnal drama was becoming more real and the man more defined. Traces of his scent lingered in her awareness, and his touch seemed imprinted on her skin. This was the first time her phantom lover had spoken. What could it mean?

After wiggling and shifting and turning and pondering for another half hour, Meri gave up trying to sleep. She fixed herself a cup of camomile tea and sat in her bedroom rocking chair. Pulling her knees to her chest, she tucked her flannel nightgown over her toes and rocked, sipping tea and mulling over the dream.

She firmly believed that dreams meant something, especially emotional, recurring ones. But what? She didn't buy into Freud's idea that all dreams are sexual. Well, the dream was sexual . . . sort of . . . but it wasn't merely *sexual*. She knew instinctively that there was more to it than sex.

Sitting alone in the dimness of her bedroom, she worried over the scenario with the strange man who seemed so familiar. Finally she decided that the man was obviously a part of herself, her animus or masculine side, urging her to follow his lead.

Yes, that was it. Her animus was telling her that it was time to be bold, assertive—to go for it.

But go for what?

She rocked and sipped her tea until the answer came like the proverbial lightbulb clicking on in her head. Rising, she went to her desk in the spare bedroom and picked up a packet of papers. The moment her hand touched the envelope, a sense of rightness sent a rush of excitement through her.

The bundle contained bid papers—the key to a much brighter professional future. She was a photographer, not exactly the easiest business to be in for someone just starting out. When the invitation to bid had arrived earlier that day, she'd almost trashed it, thinking that the scope of the proposal was beyond her abilities. Now she decided to look at it again, to think bigger and bolder.

A brilliant idea came to her as she thumbed through the pages—one that would give her fledgling business an edge on her competitors. For once her mother would be proud of her.

"Hot damn!" she said, laughing and clutching the papers to her breast. "This is *mine.*"

Snatching up the phone, she called her partner in Paris.

One

Concerning Egypt I will now speak at length, because nowhere are there so many marvelous things, nor in the whole world beside are there to be seen so many things of unspeakable greatness.

Herodotus
Fifth Century B.C.

Pushing her way through the babble of Arabic in the teeming, narrow alleys of Khan-el-Khalili bazaar in Cairo, Meri Vaughn felt as if she'd been transported in time to another world. Smells—of leather, spice, and roasting meat mingled with ripe fruit, riper bodies, and donkey dung—were surrounding her, almost smothering her. Fighting for breathing space, she squeezed through a group of German tourists—bargaining over lizard bags at one of the stalls—and dodged a Saab beeping its way through the crowd.

She'd promised to buy some brass for her mother and ship it back to Dallas, but how in the world could she compete with the throngs of shoppers? It was her first outing since she'd arrived in Egypt the evening before. Wishing that she'd followed the concierge's advice and used a guide, Meri twisted and turned in the rabbit warren of alleys and hoped to hell she wouldn't get lost.

But the truth was that she was lost. She had been lost since she'd made her first turn off the main street a half hour before. Lost or not, she was determined to buy her mother's blasted brass before she worried about it.

Spotting a likely shop, she elbowed her way through leather-faced men wearing long, flowing *galabiyahs* who hawked their wares to tourists in western garb. The dimly lit shop, which smelled faintly of polish and sandalwood, was an oasis of quiet after the cacophony outside. The proprietor, a spare, elderly gentleman in a striped robe and skullcap greeted her warmly.

"I'm looking for brass," Meri said.

"Ah, an American. Come this way. I have fine brass, the finest in Cairo."

He did indeed have fine brass, but the prices seemed high. Recalling from a guidebook that she'd read that merchants expected some dickering over their wares, she tried the bargaining skills she'd learned on border excursions to Mexico. After a few minutes of spirited haggling, they settled on a reasonable compromise for the several pieces she bought. He even agreed to ship her purchases to Dallas and charged everything on American Express.

She was about to leave when something in the glass case beside the register caught her eye. Her breath left her, and she froze.

The light glinted off the pendant in a peculiar way and cast a surreal glow onto the outstretched golden wings and the smooth stones clutched in the falcon's claws.

When her breath returned and she could speak, Meri said, "May I see that necklace in the case?"

"Ah," the shopkeeper said, picking up the pendant and offering it to her. "The pectoral. My finest piece. Exquisite gold. Very old. Very beautiful." He quoted her an outrageous price.

The falcon warmed her palm as she held it, and the chain spilled through her fingers like a golden cascade. She was almost overwhelmed by a feeling of *déjà vu*. An eerie awareness encapsulated her in a cocoon of timeless, spaceless sensation, and the air around her hummed with some sort of strange emanations.

Was she dreaming again? She was sure that her trip to the market had been real, but perhaps she was asleep. She pinched herself and it hurt. But dream or no dream, the experience was unnerving.

She shook her head and handed the pendant back to the proprietor, impatient to be rid of it. "Too much."

He smiled and held up his hands, palms out, refusing to take it. "No, no. It is yours. A gift."

She frowned. "A gift?" The pendant cost ten times as much as the brass she'd bought, and she'd already observed enough about Egyptian marketing strategies to know that his behavior was highly suspicious.

The shopkeeper glanced over her shoulder and nodded.

Meri turned to look behind her. The blood drained from her face. A tall, dark man stood in the doorway. She'd never met him in her life, but she immediately recognized his eyes. His unearthly blue eyes.

He was the man from her dreams.

Her heart began pounding, and her mouth went as dry as the Sahara. Either she was dreaming or she was going mad. She closed her eyes tightly and shook her head. When she looked again, no one was there. The hair on the back of her neck prickled.

"Who was that man?" she demanded, clutching a wad of the shopkeeper's sleeve.

"What man, miss?"

"The man who was standing in the doorway. He was very tall, with blue eyes."

"I saw no one, miss."

Either the proprietor was lying or she was seeing things. Maybe it was jet lag. Feeling dazed by the experience she left the shop and walked several blocks, trying futilely to make sense out of the events.

"Meri Vaughn, get hold of yourself," she muttered, clenching her fists.

When something sharp bit into her palm, she was startled to discover the falcon pectoral still in her hand. Turning, she retraced her steps, determined to take the necklace back to the merchant.

But she couldn't find the shop. She could have sworn that she'd returned to the right place with the perfumery on one side and the ironmonger on the other. Either the shop had vanished into thin air, or she had been mistaken. Mistaken, she was sure. Getting lost in the bazaar was easy. Hadn't she been lost almost from the moment she entered the crowded maze? What was she going to do with the pendant? The idea of keeping it made her uneasy.

A small girl with rumpled hair and a dirty face tugged at the leg of Meri's jumpsuit, held out her hand shyly and asked, *"Baksheesh?"*

Sure that providence had answered her question, Meri dropped the necklace into the child's palm. "There you go, sweetheart." Glad to be done with it, she decided to put the entire episode out of her mind.

She'd taken no more than two steps when she stopped dead in her tracks, mouth agape, as she saw *him* again. Or at least she thought it was the same man. Leaning against the weathered food cart of a street vendor half a block away, he was casually eating a pastry. He wore the same light-colored slacks and white shirt with sleeves rolled up to his elbows and the top buttons undone. His tie was loosened and his suit coat was slung over one shoulder. She was too far away to see his eyes, but she could swear it was he. Perhaps not, she persuaded herself. In a country where most men had dark hair and mustaches, it was easy to be confused. But he was a head taller than most of the other men.

As she stood rooted to the spot, staring at him, he smiled, toasted her with his tart, then started toward her. As he neared, sudden panic assailed her.

She turned in the opposite direction, pushing her way through the crowds and running down the street. Chest heaving, she twisted and turned through the alleyways, doubling back and weaving an uneven pattern. When she could run no farther, she ducked into a doorway and plastered herself against the wall of a small coffeehouse. The few patrons looked at her strangely, then shrugged, shook their heads, and continued sipping their espressos.

A waiter approached. "You want coffee, miss?"

"A taxi," she gasped, splaying her hand across her chest to hold in her heart. "Where can I find a taxi?"

Carefully following the waiter's directions, she got lost twice before she finally emerged from the labyrinth of the bazaar onto a normal city street filled with traffic and exhaust fumes and busses packed with people.

She flagged a passing taxi and directed him to the Mena House in Giza.

When she arrived at her hotel room, she flung herself on the bed and vowed that she wouldn't stir until her friend and partner Welcome Venable arrived.

She tried to busy her mind and forget her experience in the bazaar, but it crept into her consciousness again and again. Thinking back, it occurred to her that she'd overreacted to the situation. Just because a blue-eyed man had appeared when she was looking at the pendant was no reason to get upset. Just because a man—the same man she was *positive*, tried to approach her was no reason to turn hysterical.

The whole thing was simply a strange coincidence. There were probably hundreds of pectorals like the one she'd seen, replications of some ancient relic, hanging in most of the shops in the city. After all, rag-tag kids and grubby street vendors peddled "genuine mummy beads" from every corner. And there were certainly plenty of blue-eyed men in the world. She'd heard that Egyptians liked blondes, and the man had simply misinterpreted her casual American ways.

Of course. That was it. The man in her dreams was a figment of her imagination. He wasn't *real*. She'd gotten spooked and overreacted to nothing.

Laughing at her silly behavior, she rose and freshened up in the bathroom. She didn't have time to waste if she wanted to check out the Pyramids and the Sphinx before Welcome arrived. The trip to Egypt was for working, not playing tourist or hiding in her room like a frightened mouse. She and Welcome had a tight schedule to maintain to get all the photographs for the travel brochure. Their new company had been darned lucky to be chosen—even with the added enticement that Welcome, who was a top international model, would pose for the layouts.

A few minutes later, with her camera slung over her shoulder and her hands thrust into the pockets of her turquoise jumpsuit, Meri walked alone down the palm-lined drive of the Mena House Hotel toward the Pyramids.

A strong breeze ruffled the ash blond tendrils that escaped her loose topknot. The April sun was pleasantly warm against her skin. It seemed to draw tension from her as she made her way through the brightly colored gardens.

In the distance a loudspeaker echoed the voice of the muezzin as he called the faithful to noon prayers. The haunting sound raised chills along her spine as she stopped and breathed in the smells of newly cut grass, flowers, and warm sand mixed with antiquity. She moved on through the lush grounds of the hotel toward the towering structures at the edge of the desert.

She couldn't stop staring at them. The Pyramids of Egypt stirred her spirit and prompted strange, unnamed longings to well up inside of her. All her life she'd been teased about her strange Egyptian name, Meritaten, and she'd tried to ignore her secret fascination with the place where she'd been conceived by young lovers in a carefree moment. But something about this area spoke to her, called to her, beckoned her as if it held her destiny.

Destiny? Did she believe in destiny? She was such an odd amalgam of her father, an aging California flower child, and her mother, a tough Texas businesswoman, that sometimes she wasn't sure if she believed in karma, or self-determination.

As she neared the edge of the grounds, a small ragged boy waving postcards ran to meet her.

"Hello, beautiful lady! Where are you from?"

"I'm from the United States, from Texas."

"I like Americans. Welcome to our country." His impish grin split the dirty face as he scampered along beside her. "You want some postcards? All these for one dollar. You need a guide to see the Pyramids? I, Ahmed, am the finest guide in all Cairo."

Meri stopped and laughed as she noted the grimy bare toes that peeped out from his striped cotton robe and the black eyes that danced with mischief. "In all of Cairo?" she asked in mock disbelief. "How old are you to be such a fine guide?"

"Nine, beautiful lady, but I have been a guide for many years," he answered, puffing out his thin chest. "You want to ride a camel to the Pyramids? My cousin has the finest. Come, come," he said, as he grabbed her arm and pulled her toward the animal stalls, "I show you."

After they settled on a price for his services, the boy scurried away to one of the camel drivers and held an animated conversation with him. In a few moments he returned with an elderly man and a large ambling beast. The gray animal's bridle was decorated with pink, yellow, and orange tassels and the padded saddle was covered with a colorful woven rug.

"This is my uncle, Mohammed, and his fine camel is called Hassan. They will give you the very best ride."

Meri looked askance at the boy. "I thought you said that he was your cousin," she said, as the driver directed the creature to kneel for mounting.

Ahmed looked sheepish and shrugged.

Meri fought a smile and let it pass. She frowned at the camel, Hassan, wondering what ever possessed her. Well, it couldn't be too much different from riding a horse, and while she was no Dale Evans, she rode tolerably well.

"Here's to new adventure," she muttered.

She climbed on and gripped the saddle horn, rolling and pitching as the animal rose to his feet. With the handler holding the guide rope and tapping the camel's neck with his long stick, they were off at a lumbering gait. She soon caught the plodding rhythm and relaxed in the saddle.

Laughter bubbled up and spilled over. "Hey, this is fun," she yelled down to Ahmed who was trotting along beside her.

Mohammed grinned a toothless smile and handed her the lead rope and his long stick, motioning for her to take over. After they ambled on through the sand for a while, she nudged Hassan with her heels and his gait quickened. Just like a horse she thought. She tapped him with the stick, and he took off in a gallop.

Panicked, she screamed, "Whoa! Whoa!" But Hassan obviously didn't understand English.

People yelped and scattered in all directions. Old Mohammed ran far behind them yelling Arabic oaths and shaking his fist while Ahmed's short legs churned to keep up.

Meri jettisoned the stick and clutched the saddle horn for dear life. "Whoa! Whoa, boy!" She sawed on the rope, but Hassan had the bit between his teeth.

The first Pyramid sped by. Then the second.

The wall surrounding the Sphinx was looming ahead when she closed her eyes and prayed—hoping she would be heard over the deafening drumbeats of her heart.

She felt herself slipping sideways off the saddle and screamed. Despite her efforts, her sweaty hands were losing their grip. What an ignoble way to die. "Oh, God, help me! Help me!"

Suddenly a powerful arm whipped out and pulled her down from the runaway camel onto a horse galloping alongside. She was crushed to a broad chest, and her arms clung to her rescuer as he veered left and brought the big black stallion to a halt. Her hairpins had been lost in the wild dash and her sun-streaked hair tumbled in wild curls down her back and over her face.

Strong fingers smoothed her hair out of her eyes. "Are you all right?" the man asked, his voice husky with concern.

"Yes, I'm fine. At least I think . . ." Her words faded as she found her face being tenderly devoured by a pair of flame-blue eyes that mesmerized her completely. Their astonishing sky-dyed hue was even more startling against his dark skin, thick black hair, and mustache. Fine lines radiated out from their corners. They were set above high cheekbones and a proud hawk nose.

"That's good." He flashed a broad white-toothed smile that caused the furrows along his cheeks to deepen.

Up close and in the flesh, he was the most handsome man she'd ever seen in her life. Virility, blatant and elemental, pulsated from him with every heartbeat. But when she realized who held her, she sucked in a startled gasp.

The man from the bazaar.

The man from her dreams. Crazy, she knew, but she was sure of it.

A spark of fear flashed inside her, but it was quickly doused by the familiar comfort she felt in his arms. He'd held her thus dozens of nights. But she couldn't remember the spicy, sun-warmed scent of him being so evident or the hard muscles of his chest feeling so substantial. Confusion clouded her thinking. Was she dreaming again? Had she fallen asleep in her hotel room and conjured up this entire scenario?

She touched his cheek and could feel the faint stubble of his beard. "Are you part of my dream?"

"Would you like me to be?" he asked softly, again pushing her wind-tossed hair away from her face.

"I don't know. I don't understand. I—"

He smiled again, and the words died in her throat.

Such a smile. It speared her heart and stroked her skin.

"I'll take care of you." He settled her more firmly across his lap, and his arms went around her as he took the reins.

"Always," he whispered against her temple. "Hold on. I'll take you for a ride," he said, kicking the stallion into a gallop toward the desert.

With her body cradled against his, she was overcome with the force and rightness of the man and the place. As the hooves of the powerful animal beneath them thundered against the rocky sand, she felt as if she were flying on the back of Pegasus to a magical destination.

As they rode with the wind against their faces, the panorama wavered slightly like still water rippled by a sudden breeze. When it cleared again a pulse beat later, the hordes of tourists, tour buses, taxies, and trinket sellers were gone. Only a vast sweep of sand and craggy hills lay before them.

Suddenly, instead of the Western clothes he'd worn earlier, the man who held her wore a strange white garb that billowed behind him like a desert sail. Startled, she looked into his face, and almost went into cardiac arrest.

"Jumping Jehoshaphat."

Beneath the flowing headdress, his face was darker, and he wore a beard. His eyes were black, and they bored into hers with a fierce possessiveness that sucked away her breath and frightened her beyond belief.

"Mine," he said with a guttural ferocity. "Forever *mine*."

She tried to scream, but her throat was paralyzed. She grabbed a fistful of his shirt, but the hand she used was not her own. It was smaller, and every finger wore a ring. She looked down, her eyes searching frantically for her own familiar body and clothing. But her turquoise jumpsuit had changed into a robe of scarlet silk that fluttered against her bare legs and slippered feet.

Terrified, she tried to draw away from him, but his sinewy arms held her fast. "Please," she finally managed to whisper. "Please."

Ignoring her feeble entreaty, he threw back his head and laughed, and with a scimitar raised aloft in his hand and glistening in the sun, rode over the crest of a dune, shouting a triumphant cry.

Meri struggled in his grip, trying to yell, wave her arms, attract help from the host of tourists below. But when she twisted so that she could see over his shoulder into the valley behind them, no one was there.

No one. Not a soul moved around the Pyramids which still rose majestically from the stark landscape. There were no people, no camels, no horses. Not a single taxi stood waiting. No dogs yapped. No buses rumbled and belched noxious fumes. The wall around the Sphinx had disappeared, and rolling dunes covered the lion paws.

The only thing that stirred was a small dust devil, whipping an eddy of sand across the rocky ground. Her shouts were lost in the wind.

It was as if she'd ridden through a hole in time.

Panic assailed her. Her mind screamed in disbelief. Every muscle in her body trembled with fear. She squeezed her eyes shut, tunneled her fingers through her hair, and pressed her temples. "This is a dream. It must be a dream. Stop!" She beat on his chest with her fists. "Damn you, take me back!"

The stallion slowed, then stopped. "Shhhh," he said, smoothing her hair and holding her gently against him. "I'll take you back, love. Shhhh."

Meri kept her eyes closed and her body rigid as he turned the horse. When she allowed herself to look, she gazed straight ahead, keeping her focus on the tops of Pyramids. At least they were real.

Or were they?

What was happening to her? Had she gone mad? Too near hysterics to be rational, she clenched her teeth to keep from wailing. All she could think was *escape! escape!* Yet she found her gaze inexplicably drawn to the man who held her. She saw pale blue eyes clouded with concern.

"Are you all right?" he asked.

"No. I am *not* all right," she said, measuring every word. "Let me off this horse. Now. This instant."

"Are you dizzy?"

"That is the understatement of the decade."

He set her down beside the wall at the Sphinx. "You stay here, and I'll bring you some water. Don't move. Stay right here," he ordered before he galloped off.

Don't move? God, she couldn't have moved if her hair were on fire. She started to shiver all over. Her stomach rolled, and her head buzzed. Meri knew that she was about to throw up or faint. Her knees turned to jelly, then buckled completely. For the first time in her life, she fainted.

She must have been out for only seconds, but the next thing she knew, Ahmed, chest heaving, was patting her cheeks and saying, "Oh, beautiful lady. You are safe."

Waving him away, she covered her mouth with shaky fingers and tried to breathe deeply through her nose and to calm herself. By using stern self-talk, she forced herself to look again, but the man was out of sight. Was she going mad or had she slipped into a time warp?

She looked down at her hands which seemed perfectly normal, and she rubbed her palms over the thighs of her jumpsuit. Looking quickly around her, she sagged with relief when she spied the customary activity around the ancient monuments: tourists spilling out of buses and taxis, pointing in awe and snapping photos; vendors hustling their wares; lines of camels plodding across the sand bearing squealing burdens in camp shirts and floppy hats.

Business as usual.

No one except Ahmed paid any particular attention to Meri. No one pointed or stared at her, aghast at what had just transpired. Hadn't they seen?

Obviously they hadn't.

Ahmed sank to his knees in front of her and grinned. "Wasn't that a fine camel ride? Such a good rider you are! Such an adventure to tell your friends in America!"

Meri was too shaken to appreciate the humor of his comment. Her heart still pounded; her breathing was shallow. Willing her body to stop trembling, she struggled to compose herself. But her mind's eye saw a dark smiling face that shattered her efforts. She jumped to her feet. "I have to get away from here before that man comes back."

"What man, beautiful lady?"

"The one who rescued me. He was riding a big black horse and . . ." Her voice trailed off when she caught the odd look Ahmed was giving her. "You didn't see a man on a horse?"

"I saw no one, but maybe—"

"Forget it. Just find me a taxi. Quickly."

By the time she reached the hotel, Meri had almost convinced herself that the heat had addled her senses. Disheveled and sticky, her nerves raw and her energy totally depleted, she opened the door to their suite to find Welcome sitting on the couch waiting for her.

Her friend's blazing riot of long tight curls, curls which seemed to have a dynamic life of their own, was held in place with an Indian-style headband with small feathers dangling from one side. Always the epitome of glamour, Welcome was dressed in a clean cool tunic and harem pants of soft apricot gauze.

Meri grabbed her friend and hugged her. "Welcome, I've never been so glad to see anyone in my life. I think I'm going crazy."

Welcome laughed as she hugged her back. "You've always been crazy. I knew it the minute you walked into our dorm room. That's why we're best friends."

"No, I mean *crazy* crazy. Hallucinations and delusions crazy."

Welcome cocked one perfect eyebrow. "Sounds serious. Want to tell me about it?"

Meri collapsed on the couch. "Later. All I want now is a drink. Something potent."

Two

*So hurry to see your lady,
like a stallion on the track,
or like a falcon swooping down to its papyrus marsh.*

Love Songs of the New Kingdom
c. 1550-1080 B.C.

Meri sipped her drink and tried to make polite cocktail party talk, but she had a hammering headache and was sorry she'd let Welcome talk her into the function at the American Embassy. Leave it to Welcome to know someone and be in the thick of things wherever she lit. This time it was Philip somebody or other whom she'd known in Paris. He had one of those strange jobs at the embassy that sounded like a CIA cover, but for all Meri knew, he was merely some political bigwig's nephew. Tall, blond, and handsome in a polished Boston Brahman fashion, he spoke with the charm of a professional diplomat.

"So you're a photographer," Philip said.

"Yes," Meri replied.

"I am too, but strictly the Sunday sort. I thought at one time I might like to go into it professionally, but—" he shrugged, "—things change. What will you be shooting in Cairo?"

"Tomorrow we'll be doing some of the usual tourist attractions in the area, and the next day we'll focus on the new

Horus Giza and capture the sunrise over the Pyramids from one of the hotel balconies."

"If I promise that I'll stay out of your way, would you consider allowing an amateur to tag along and observe? I've never watched Welcome work, and I think it would be fascinating." He glanced across the room at Welcome. His captivation with the model was evident in his expression.

Meri hesitated. "What about your embassy duties?"

Philip turned on his most engaging smile. "They're flexible. I can be your assistant and tote all your gear. I'll even pick you up in my car. I'd appreciate a chance to see a professional shoot."

The man could charm the horns off a billy goat. She agreed to let him tag along, and he acted as if she had presented him with the keys to the royal treasure. He introduced her to a group nearby and left to circulate. She tried to get into the spirit of things and circulate, but cocktail parties—especially among strangers—were a strain.

Only a few women were present, but the room was crowded with dozens of male representatives from various Middle Eastern countries who wore native garb and flowing headdresses.

From the moment the pair of them entered, men gathered around Welcome—who wore a green sequined halter dress— like butterflies to nectar. Meri, who had never considered herself in the same league with her glamorous friend, had to contend with several effusive males herself. Their superficial politeness only thinly masked a lasciviousness lurking near the surface that made her skin crawl.

Finally she dragged Welcome aside and said, "I can't tolerate this. Do you know what one of those potentates offered me if I'd go out to dinner with him?"

Welcome grinned. "Was it better than a Rolls Royce?"

Meri's eyes widened. "You, too?"

"I think these wolves in bed sheets have more oil money than they have sense. Let's go tell Philip good-bye and split."

Meri reached for her evening bag and happened to glance across the room. Her breath caught.

"Jumping Jehoshaphat," she whispered.

"What's wrong?" Welcome asked.

It was *him*.

No doubt about it.

Dressed in a dinner jacket as black as his hair, he stood beside the grand piano, sipping a drink and watching her over the rim of his glass. The party chatter faded into the background as their eyes locked. For a brief moment Meri could feel tendrils of his essence invade her mind, wrap around her like soft shoots of a spring vine, ensnaring her, drawing her toward him.

Blood pounded in her ears, and her knees went weak before she managed to tear her gaze away and frantically clutch Welcome's arm. "Casually glance over my shoulder. Do you see that man by the piano?"

"The short fat one or the one with the beard?"

Meri whirled around. He was gone. She downed her gimlet in one gulp and grabbed Welcome's hand. "Let's get out of here. Quick."

In the taxi back to the hotel, Welcome leaned over and asked in her throaty voice, "Want to tell me why you look like somebody's goosed you with a corncob?"

Meri couldn't help but laugh. "You always manage to cut right to the heart of things, don't you?"

"I've been accused of being plain-spoken once or twice. What happened back there? See a ghost?"

"Maybe. I thought I saw *him* again."

"Him, who?"

"The man from this afternoon." Meri had confided in Welcome about her experience at the Pyramids. "Do you think it was my imagination?"

"Sweetie, I thought we'd decided that you'd only had your britches scared off by that camel and gotten addled by the heat. But, hell's bells, if the hunk you've rubbed up is real, maybe we'd better turn this taxi around, go find him, and hogtie him. He sounds like a trophy catch."

Meri shook her head. "I'm beginning to feel like an idiot. I'd rather just forget about it."

"You're no idiot. You're probably the sharpest woman I know, but consider it forgotten."

Feeling anchored and reassured by Welcome's presence, Meri rested her head against the seat back. "Lord, I've missed having you around. I wish you'd move back to Texas. Don't you ever get homesick?"

"Sometimes. But now that I'm over thirty, my modeling days are dwindling down to a precious few, and my Paris agency is starting to go great guns. I can't give it up just yet. A few more years, and I can retire in style."

"Welcome, don't try to kid me. With the investments you've made, you have enough money to retire in style right now."

"True. But . . . well, there's Eduard to consider."

"Ah, yes, Eduard. Are you ever going to marry that man and put him out of his misery?"

Welcome looked thoughtful. "Eduard has everything any woman could ask for. He's considerate, handsome, rich, a marvelous conversationalist, the perfect escort . . ."

"But?"

Welcome cocked an eyebrow. "But can you imagine him eating barbecued ribs with his fingers?"

Meri laughed. "Not really. But that's hardly a reason not to marry him."

"Maybe not. But the truth is, Eduard is kind of a wimp. Nice, but a wimp. Have you ever noticed that strong women like us tend to attract weak men?"

"Welcome, you attract everything in pants. Strong, weak, and in between."

"Come on, I'm serious. I'm not talking about a few propositions and a pinch here and there. I'm talking about a significant relationship."

"I suppose you're right. I guess that's why I'm not much

interested in dating anymore. Maybe I'm too picky, but it seems to me that at our age, the pool has dwindled to the leftovers and the rejects. Do you think we're destined to be old maids? I shudder to think that I'll end up like my mother."

"God forbid. At the risk of being a traitor to feminism, I always figured that a little nookie would take some of your mother's edge off. Sex is not my problem. But as for marriage, I'm beginning to wonder if I'll ever marry." Welcome shrugged. "Most of the time it doesn't bother me, but the truth is, even strong women still dream sometimes of the romantic knight on a white charger who will sweep them off their feet one day." She chuckled. "Of course our knights would have to fight us kicking and screaming every step of the way. I figure that we both need better men than we are."

"You may be right. I wonder if there are any." For an instant, a disturbing picture of a dark, blue-eyed man on a black stallion flashed through her mind. She shook it off and was relieved to find that the taxi had stopped in front of their hotel.

They returned to a room filled with several baskets and vases of extravagant flowers. Meri laughed. "Looks like one of your admirers has moved quickly."

Welcome plucked a card from one of the baskets, then grinned and winked a cinnamon-colored eye. "Not unless you would describe me as a 'Golden goddess with hair like moonlight on the desert sand and eyes like the depths of a changing sea.' I think they're for you. From a Ramson Gabrey. Who's he?"

Meri looked heavenward. "Oh, good grief. How should I know? He's probably that fat sheik with the beady eyes who pinched my bottom twice. Who else would feel he had to buy a date? He looked like he could afford to—and worse, had to. Why didn't I listen to my mother? She warned me that I'd get into trouble."

"Sweetie, with all due respect to your mother, Nora is a dragon lady who would dearly love to have you joined to her hip, with your nose to her corporate grindstone. Forget about her and enjoy doing your own thing for once."

"Easier said than done."

"How many times has she called since you've been here?"

Meri sighed. "Twice."

"Why didn't you tell her to butt out?"

"I did, politely. She won't listen."

"Polite doesn't work with Nora. The woman's a steamroller. You'll have to use dynamite."

Meri laughed. "Believe me, I've considered it."

But Meri knew that her mother was a formidable adversary. Nora Elwood, by single-minded determination and lots of hard work, had carved herself a piece of the good life as the CEO of a major public relations firm in Dallas. She would like nothing better than for Meri to join her company. There was no way in hell that she could spend her life butting heads with her mother every day. Nora refused to accept that Meri was a mature, independent woman fully capable of choosing her own path.

"I think she stays up nights worrying that I'll become like my father," Meri said.

"You could do worse. A little feyness is interesting. What's Brian up to these days?"

"He's still living off the land in northern California—with considerable help from his inheritance, my mother reminds me. He takes nature photographs for various magazines and grows herbs for health food stores."

"Herbs? Is that *all* he grows?"

Meri smiled. "With Brian, one never knows. But he's a wonderful photographer."

"As are you. Maybe it's in the genes."

"That's what Nora's afraid of. Sometimes I feel like a wishbone between the two of them." Meri yawned. "We have to get up early in the morning. Did Philip tell you that he's coming with us?"

"Yes. Do you mind?"

"Not really. Is something going on between you two?"

"We're just friends."

Meri grinned. "You said that awfully quickly. From the way

he was looking at you, I'd say that Eduard ought to be worried." She yawned again. "How about we hit the sack?"

After they said good-night and went to their rooms, Meri hurriedly undressed and fell into bed.

She hadn't told Welcome about the dreams or about how the bounds of fantasy and reality had blurred until she was honestly beginning to doubt her sanity. The doubts were chilling.

Completely exhausted, she tried to sleep, but the events of the day whirled in her head like a surrealistic carousel. Welcome's arrival had diverted her attention from the strange encounters with the blue-eyed man; her friend's pragmatic personality had kept her grounded. But now, alone in the dimness of her room, her thoughts were filled with him, with the curious blend of fear and fascination that he roused in her.

As terrified as she had been those few minutes that afternoon, in retrospect she realized instinctively that he'd never meant to hurt her or frighten her.

Oh, God! Here she was thinking about him again as if he were real. He was only a fantasy. She had to remember that. Still, she could almost hear his hypnotic voice whispering to her, enticing her to sleep, to come.

With the sheer curtains billowing around him, he stood at the door to the balcony and watched her sleep. She was magnificent. Her hair fanned out over the pillow, shimmering in the bright moonlight like silver swirls in soft beige silk.

Perhaps he shouldn't be here, but he had to convince himself that she was genuine. From the moment he'd first spied her in the coffee shop that morning, he'd been spellbound, obsessed, following her, watching her, trying to determine if she was a mirage. He'd dreamed of her like this a thousand times, and his fingers ached to touch her smooth skin. He wanted to kiss her and hold her and lay the moon, the stars, and a pharaoh's treasure at her feet.

Quietly, he crept closer, then stopped as she shifted and her lashes fluttered. She opened large, languid eyes that sparkled in the moonlight like chips of emerald, bits of amber, and slivers of aquamarine. He stood very still, concerned that he would frighten her as he had earlier. Instead, she smiled and held out her arms to him.

He was lost. He could no more resist her entreaty than Odysseus could resist the Sirens' song. Moving to her side, he gathered her to him, inhaling the sweet scent of her, savoring the softness of her body against his.

He'd only meant to hold her for a moment, but she threaded her fingers through his hair and brought his mouth to hers. Her lips were warm and alive and moist; her tongue was hot rich velvet. Her skin felt smoother and cooler than the satin gown she wore, but her hands trailed fire where she touched him. Like a man possessed, he kissed her and stoked her and murmured endearments that flowed from his heart like a living wellspring.

"My dearest heart," she whispered. "Make love with me."

Three

*I like to feel the stars turning over me,
especially when the dew falls, ever so softly;
making your garments soft, soft.*
                              Khushaymi poem

The alarm jarred Meri awake. She moaned and fought against the raucous din penetrating her brain, preferring to remain snuggled in the subliminal sensation of her lover's arms.

Lover's arms? Her eyes popped open.

Relieved to discover that she was tangled in the coverlet and had a strangle hold on her pillow, she relaxed and slapped off the alarm.

The dream again. She touched her lips with the tips of her fingers and could almost feel the lingering softness of his mouth. A vague heaviness, a sensual aching pulsated in her—

"Meritaten Vaughn, enough!" she said aloud, shocked by her state. She had to forget about her dream lover and join the real world, anchor herself, before things got completely out of hand. Determined to put the entire business from her mind, she threw the covers aside and climbed out of bed.

Her eyes widened as she discovered her state—stark naked. Her blue nightgown was casually draped over a nearby chair. She sucked in a startled, noisy breath and slapped her hand against her chest to hold in her racing heart. Her eyes widened even more, then closed as she felt the warm metal against her palm. She was afraid to look, knowing without looking what was there, but some perverse curiosity pulled her hand away and forced her gaze downward.

The gold falcon pendant.

She whimpered. "Oh . . . my . . . God."

"Welcome!" Meri screamed, grabbing her robe and tearing toward her friend's room.

Welcome was just getting out of bed when Meri burst through the door and flung her arms around her friend. "What in the world's the matter, sweetie? You're trembling worse than a dog passing a peach pit. And you look as if you've just seen a spook."

"Worse," Meri croaked, clinging to Welcome. "I think I may have been making love with one. I woke up without my gown on."

"You *think?*" Laughing, Welcome patted Meri's back. "Sweetie, if he were flesh and blood, you'd *know* if you'd been making love."

"Are you sure?"

"I'm sure. You probably just got hot and pulled your gown off in your sleep."

"Then how do you explain this?" She grabbed the pectoral and held it up for Welcome to see.

"Uhhhh. Teleportation?"

"This is *not* 'Star Trek'!"

"Sweetie, I haven't the foggiest, but I'm sure there's some perfectly logical explanation."

"Name one."

"Sleepwalking, maybe. Let me think on it. In the meantime, we'd better get our butts in gear. Philip will be here in twenty minutes."

Dressing and forcing herself to keep their work schedule required an enormous amount of courage for Meri. After the strange sequence of events that had shredded her composure since she'd arrived in Egypt, she wanted nothing more than to pack her clothes and go home to Texas.

Welcome didn't seem to appreciate how threatened she felt,

how off-kilter her perception seemed. Perhaps, Meri thought, it *was* the-heat. *Something* had affected her. Welcome simply laughed it off and attributed her hallucinatory experiences to everything from PMS to an accidental ingestion of "funny" mushrooms.

But Meri couldn't remember eating a dish with mushrooms, and she *never* suffered from PMS.

The phone was ringing as Meri and Welcome unlocked the door to the suite. They were both hot and tired from a long day of shooting around Giza and Cairo. Things would have probably been worse if Philip hadn't been along. True to his word, he'd been unobtrusive, but he'd also been a godsend. He'd carried her equipment and taken them from one location to the next in a chauffeured, air-conditioned car. She hadn't minded giving Philip, who seemed very knowledgeable, a few pointers on composition and she was happy to accept his offer to assist them the following day. She didn't kid herself that learning more about photography was his primary interest. It was obvious that if Welcome hadn't been along, he wouldn't have been nearly so attentive, but she wasn't about to look a gift horse in the mouth.

Welcome answered the phone while Meri dumped her gear and crashed on the couch. The work had been grueling, but Meri had appreciated the distraction. Not once had she seen anything or anyone out of the ordinary. Not once did *he* appear. It seemed that the aberration, whatever it was, had passed.

"For you," Welcome said, holding out the phone. "Ramson Gabrey."

"I don't want to talk to him. I'll bet he's a lecherous old man," she retorted. "He had that look in his eye at the embassy party. I'm going to take a shower."

A few minutes later, Meri was drying her hair when Welcome came in her room with a small package wrapped in gold foil and tied with a pink ribbon. "The bellman just delivered this," Welcome said. "For you. Ramson Gabrey again."

"I'm not accepting anything from that pervert. Send it back."

"He doesn't sound like a pervert on the phone. He seemed very polite."

"Polite? Tell that to the pinch marks on my fanny."

Welcome rattled the package next to her ear. "I'm dying to know what it is. You know how curious I am."

"Then you open it while I finish my hair."

Welcome let out a low whistle as Meri turned off the dryer. "I thought the flowers were grand, but, honey, it looks like this guy is bringing in the heavy artillery." She dangled a glittering bracelet in Meri's face. It was a magnificent piece of jewelry made of heavy gold filigree and encrusted with a small fortune in pearls and diamonds.

"Oh . . . my . . . God." Meri shuddered as visions flashed through her mind of that fat old sultan, sitting amidst his harem and sinisterly stroking his beard.

She had to get out of there. Between the incessant ringing of the telephone and the parade of delivery men, Meri was losing her mind. How nice it would have been to spend a relaxing evening in her room curled up with a sandwich and a good book, but Welcome had gone out with Philip Van Horn from the embassy and without her friend around to answer the telephone . . . well, she was not going to talk to that beady-eyed degenerate who'd tried to hustle her at the party. There was no way to disconnect the phone short of jerking it from the wall, and she was sorely tempted. The third time she complained, the desk clerk had patiently explained that he couldn't control the calls because they were made in-house.

Totally exasperated, she finally threw on some clothes and was about to make a quick exit when her eye caught a flash of light on the dresser. The pendant. She'd almost forgotten about it. Almost.

Frowning, she picked it up and studied it carefully, running her fingers across the bits of colored glass inlaid in the gold of the outstretched, upturned wings. The falcon seemed to warm and hum against her palm like the purring of a stroked cat.

If her dream lover wasn't real, how could she explain the pendant which lay in her hand? Yesterday she'd given it to a little girl in the marketplace. How had it gotten from the child back to her? She didn't buy teleportation as an answer. *Someone* returned it to her while she slept.

But *who?* Or *what?*

She shivered. If she had a lick of sense, she'd throw the damned thing out the window and be done with it. But at the thought of parting with it again, an overwhelming sadness flooded her. Half-formed emotions began to unfurl deep inside her, triggering vague, shadowy memories that lay just beyond her conscious reach—unnamed memories and emotions that made her heart swell and brought tears to her eyes.

As if entranced, she slipped the chain around her neck and pressed the pendant to her chest. It was warm, comforting.

The phone rang and the spell was broken. She cursed, grabbed her purse, and ran from her bedroom. She yanked open the door just as a startled young man raised his hand to knock.

"What do you want?" Meri asked sharply.

"A package for you, Miss Vaughn."

"I refuse to accept it. Send it back. And you can take all this other stuff with you." Leaving the stricken youth standing at the open door, she charged into the bedroom and grabbed the bracelet and several other packages which had been delivered with alarming regularity. When she returned to the door, the young man was gone, and another foil-wrapped box lay on the table.

"Oh, good grief!" she exclaimed in disgust as the phone began to ring again.

She flung the other things on the table before she marched out and slammed the door. She strode through the lobby and out to the circular drive. The skirt of her amethyst dress billowed and swirled about her long legs, and her high-heeled sandals clattered as she hurried toward the next building.

Her anger had abated somewhat by the time Meri arrived at Al Rubaiyat, the hotel's main dining room. Perhaps she could find a peaceful dark corner here.

A smiling maître d' stood beside the immense, intricately-carved double doors of the restaurant while a number of people lounged in large plush sofas in the elegant foyer. Bowing politely at Meri's approach, he asked, "May we be of service?"

"I would like to have dinner—a quiet table for one, please. I'm afraid I don't have a reservation."

He glanced at the others waiting before replying, "Of course. There will be a short wait. May I have your name?"

"Meri Vaughn."

His eyes widened slightly, quickly taking her measure, then he snapped his fingers for a waiter. "One moment, Miss Vaughn. Ragab will show you to your table immediately. We are delighted to have you dine with us this evening."

Feeling bewildered by the maître d's solicitous behavior, she followed the waiter through the large dimly lit room with its high ceiling and graceful archways. She felt a bit guilty at being seated before others waiting, but she was too tired and hungry to question her good fortune. Ragab seated her in an arabesque alcove near the stage and the dance floor. Meri looked wistfully at a quiet corner in the back.

"Couldn't I sit over there?"

Ragab looked alarmed. "Oh no. This is the very best table we have—for the show, for the dancing."

"But I . . ." She hesitated. No need to push it too far. "This is lovely. Thank you."

A bevy of waiters hovered about pouring fine wine, taking her order, and then serving courses with a flourish. The lamb was superb as were the succulent young vegetables. She had just lifted a forkful of tender baby peas toward her mouth when someone stopped beside her.

"Good evening. May I join you for dinner?" a deep, velvety voice asked.

Meri looked up—her fork paused in its progress—to find *him* standing by the table. Dressed in a conservative charcoal suit and subdued tie, his white shirt contrasted sharply with his dark skin and black curly hair. Those astonishing eyes, so light a blue that they almost seemed transparent, were lit with a broad smile.

Her heart gave a lurch. She cut her eyes to the right and to the left, wondering if she were dreaming again. "Uh... Uh..." she stammered. That odd combination of fear and fascination rose up to engulf her. Her first impulse was to flee, but she was determined not to make a scene. The time had come to face this situation and make some sense of it.

Trying to look more confident than she felt, she took a deep breath and said, "I don't understand what's happening between us, Mr.—"

As he seated himself across from her his eyes never left her. Their soft blue flame caressed her face, and his smile broadened. "I'm Ramson Gabrey."

Meri's eyes widened. "Oh... my... God." The tender baby peas on her fork rolled very slowly and, one by one, dropped onto her plate, then bounced onto the tablecloth. She felt a hot flush start at the base of her throat and creep up her face.

His full black mustache twitched as he said, "Why don't you call me Ram instead."

She leaned over and touched his chin with her fingertips. "Are you real or are you simply another figment of my imagination?"

He flashed that breathtaking smile again. "One hundred percent, grade-A real. I've been wondering the same thing about you."

She frowned. "You have?"

Trying to digest the situation, Meri busied herself by picking up the errant peas and depositing them in an ashtray before she looked up. His eyes had never left her face. He raised his hand slightly, and a waiter hurried to pour wine while another appeared with food; a third whisked away the ashtray.

She grabbed the third waiter by the sleeve. "Do you see this man?" She pointed to Ram.

The waiter looked at her strangely. "See him? Yes, miss."

She slumped back in her chair and sighed. "Thank heavens. I thought I was going crazy."

He laughed. "It's only fair. I've been going crazy trying to talk with you."

"You certainly are persistent, Mr.—"

"Ram."

"Mr. Gabrey. I'm Meri Vaughn."

He was silent for a moment as his gaze captured and held hers with a simmering, undulating dynamism that beat on the door to her soul. His eyes seemed to glow with an extraordinary awareness, and she felt as if she were caught up with him in a strange bond of intimacy somehow transcending time itself. She couldn't speak. She could hardly breathe.

"Yes, I know."

The impact of their encounter had caused her to lose the thread of their conversation. She startled and broke from the magnetism of his gaze. "Know what?"

"That I'm persistent and that you're Meri Vaughn."

"Oh," she said feeling foolish. Of course. He had been inundating her with calls, with flowers, with jewelry. Her irritation began to return. "Mr. Gabrey, about—"

"Ram."

"Very well. Ram. About the gifts. You must know I can't accept such things."

He frowned. "You don't like them? Of course I didn't have much time for selections, but I thought they suited you well. No matter. We'll find some things more to your taste."

"No, no. That's not the issue. I can't accept such expensive gifts from a perfect stranger."

"Even my mother will tell you I'm not perfect, and . . . we're far from being strangers." His gaze slid over her like a sensual caress, and his smile spoke of shared intimacies.

She thought of her dream the previous night, and a hot blush crept up her throat. Could it possibly be— No, no. That was insane.

"Mr. Gabrey—"

"Ram."

"Ram. Don't be obtuse! I will not accept expensive gifts from you. And there are enough flowers in our suite for a wedding."

"I'm ready anytime you say."

Puzzled, she asked, "Ready for what?"

"Our wedding."

"Our *wedding?* Oh, good grief." Meri rolled her eyes and slapped her hand against her chest. She felt the pendant bite into her palm and looked down at it. "And this thing. I don't know how you did it, and I'm not sure that I want to know, but you can have it back as well."

She reached to take it off, but he smiled, and his hand stayed hers. "It's not mine. It's yours. It was made for you. Keep it."

She started to argue, but his smile befuddled her thoughts, and his casual touch seemed strangely reassuring, as if magical power flowed from his fingertips. She didn't understand what was going on, not a damned bit of it, but she decided to follow her father's favorite platitude and "go with the flow."

"Now let's finish our dinner," he said. "I know you must be hungry."

They ate in relative silence, or rather he ate and she nibbled and sipped her wine. It was hard to chew and swallow with someone staring at you. She felt like a field mouse being circled by one of those proud Egyptian hawks—sure he would swoop down and devour her at any moment. She tried to ignore his penetrating scrutiny by concentrating on the soft music of the orchestra, by watching people at nearby tables, by counting the holes in the intricate latticework of the alcove.

When the meal was finally over, and they had drunk their thick sweet espresso, she picked up her bag and stood, planning to make a quick, polite exit. Ram rose, plucked her purse from her arm and tossed it back on the table. Grasping her hand, he pulled her toward him.

"Come dance with me."

She was on the floor and in his arms before she could protest. He molded her body to his own and, moving with a slow sensuous grace, nuzzled her ear and whispered, "Finally, my love, you're here. You've come to me."

Meri's knees buckled as an eerie feeling slithered up her back, raised chill bumps as it raced and radiated through, and then beyond, the boundaries of her body. For the second time in her life, she was afraid she might faint. Her spine stiffened and her legs turned into wooden pegs as he led her around the dance floor.

There was no mistaking it. She'd heard that whispered voice scores of times. Either she was in the middle of another one of her dreams or there was something very bizarre going on here. Her mother always accused her of wandering through life with her head in the clouds, but that wasn't exactly true. Meri was a very logical person when the occasion called for it. There was nothing logical about this situation.

She tried to remember something from a parapsychology course she'd once taken that would explain what was going on, but her brain was in such a muddle that she couldn't think clearly. She seemed to vaguely recall research on people who could consciously influence thoughts and dreams. Information. She needed more information.

"Uh," Meri said, her mind racing wildly as she pulled back from his embrace and looked up at him, "tell me, how did you know I would be here tonight?"

"Hassan told me."

Oh, Lord, she thought. On top of everything else he talks to camels. "A camel told you?"

His brow furrowed. "What camel?"

"*My* camel. Hassan. From yesterday."

His puzzled look was replaced with laughter as he pulled her to him and whirled her around. "He's about the only one I didn't talk to about you. I meant Hassan, the maître d'. He called me as soon as you arrived."

Again she made room between them. "Why should he call you?"

"Because I paid him very well to watch for a stunning blond lady named Meri Vaughn. I also bribed the desk clerk, the bell captain, the waiters at the coffee shop—" He stopped and searched her face, then frowned. "Damn my stupidity! In my elation over finding you, I've neglected to realize that I've frightened you." Hugging her to him, he said, "Oh my love, I'm sorry. You don't know me, and you must think I'm a lunatic."

"The thought crossed my mind."

Either he was crazy or she was. She preferred the former to the latter. Or she might be in the middle of a lucid dream. Of course. That was it. She was having a dream but aware that she was a participant in a dream. She remembered reading a book about it.

Oh, damnation! This wasn't a lucid dream.

Was it?

If it were, she could control it. She could conjure up anything she wanted to. Like an elephant on the dance floor. She concentrated very hard on making a great gray beast materialize. Nothing happened.

"Ohhhh, dear." If she wasn't asleep, why had *this* man been in her dreams for years?

"A problem, *sukkar?*"

"I'm on sensory overload, and it's frightening and confusing. Exactly who *are* you? For all I know you may be some modern version of Svengali or Jack the Ripper."

She noticed Ram scanning the crowd before he said, "Come," and headed, Meri in tow, toward a table and two distinguished looking couples. He introduced her to the governor of Cairo, a professor of economics at the American University, and their wives. After chatting for a few minutes, the governor's wife patted Meri's hand and said, "My dear, we are so happy to meet you. Ram is such a fine young man. We are all very fond of him and his family."

After bidding the two couples good-bye, Ram led her to another table and introduced her to a trio of Egyptologists who interrupted a spirited conversation to meet her. She'd never heard of any of the men, but she supposed that they were important in their fields. They looked important despite the fact that their eyes seemed focused more on her bosom than her face.

Next Ram led her to yet another table where she met an army colonel and his family. As they were leaving, the colonel said something to Ram in Arabic.

Ram's smile faded and a expression of cold fury narrowed his eyes. He was silent for a moment, as if marshaling control. After a few seconds he drew a deep breath, hugged Meri to his side, and smiled down at her before he shook his head and answered, *"La."*

Obviously the man had made some comment about her. Meri hated it when people were discussing her and she couldn't understand. After they were back at their table, she asked, "What did he say to you?"

"Still wary of me?"

"I'm so dazed that I don't know what I feel. Something strange is going on here, and I darned sure don't understand it, but you're obviously respectable. What did the colonel say?"

"Colonel Al-Nahaas offered me ten thousand camels for you. I turned him down." In response to her quizzical expression, he added, "It was once the custom in this country for a man to offer camels or other goods for a woman he wanted." He reached over and clasped her left hand. Gently, he traced her knuckles and her bare ring finger with his thumb. "How many camels would you like?"

"Camels?"

He smiled. "Perhaps diamonds or emeralds would be an appropriate substitute."

Meri jerked her hand away, and her eyes blazed. "You're no better than the fat old pincher! I'm not an object to be bought. I'll leave the gifts you sent in the hotel safe for you to pick up. Please don't bother me again. Good night, Mr. Gabrey." She stood and grabbed her purse. "And I'll thank you to stay out of my dreams!"

She wheeled to leave, but a strong arm grasped her waist.

"Oh, no, my proud lioness, I won't let you get away again. My intentions are strictly honorable. Camels were offered for wives." He paused. "Don't leave me," he whispered, then he turned her toward him.

Those haunting blue eyes were filled with such tender pleading that their force disarmed her. What magic did he possess to sweep away her anger with a glowing gaze or melt her resolve with simple soft words?

"I'll slow down and try not to rush you. Please be patient with me. Let's talk and get to know one another. Later I'll tell you the stories of my father and grandfather; then you'll understand why I'm acting like a madman over you." He smiled at her and touched her chin. "I'll be the perfect gentleman. Scout's honor." Holding up his right hand he let the index and little fingers escape from his fist.

Even though she tried, Meri couldn't contain the laughter. "That's not the scout sign. That's Hook 'Em Horns, the victory sign from the University of Texas. You were never a boy scout."

Ram grinned at her. "No, but I went to UT. That's the next best thing."

"UT? You're kidding. I went to the University of Texas too."

"See how much we have in common," he said. "What years were you there?" When she told him, he shook his head. "I can't believe that I only missed you by one year."

They talked for a few minutes about living in Austin, memories of special places and events connected with their university days. Meri felt herself relax as they spoke of things familiar to her.

"Why did you go to college in Texas? I thought you were Egyptian."

"I am. Born and bred. But my mother is from Dallas."

"My mother is from Dallas."

He smiled. "Maybe we're cousins."

"I doubt that."

Taking her bag, he tossed it back on the table. "Let's dance again."

Ram pulled her onto the floor and once more molded her body to his. Still puzzled about this enormously appealing man, but no longer afraid, Meri shrugged and thought, *Enjoy yourself for a few minutes.*

She relaxed and allowed him to move her to the slow melody of an old forties song. He was an excellent dancer; their strides were evenly matched. Because she was almost five-eleven in her high heels, Meri was often as tall as, or taller than, most men; but Ram towered at least four inches above her. It felt good. She sighed and snuggled against him. It had been a long time since she had been in a tall man's arms. He brought her palm to his lips, and the tip of his tongue drew warm moist circles on it before he softly kissed it and placed it against his chest. She began to melt like warm chocolate until she recognized what was happening and stiffened slightly.

As if sensing she was about to pull away, he asked, "Do you live in Dallas?"

She shook her head. "Houston."

"Tell me about Meri Vaughn from Houston."

"My mother describes me as a dilettante."

Ram threw back his head and laughed.

"You think that's funny?"

Holding her close so she couldn't struggle away, Ram kissed the tips of her fingers and replied, "I think that's delightful. I've been called that myself. I like to dabble in lots of things. I have a broad range of interests."

"You do? Do you take courses too?"

"Courses?"

"College courses, leisure learning courses, continuing education courses. I love them, and I've taken dozens—everything from origami to scuba diving. I'd still be in college taking an interesting hodgepodge if my mother hadn't put her foot down and made me choose a major. She was furious when I chose photography instead of business."

"So you're a photographer?"

She nodded. "I taught in a junior college in Houston for five years—it was great for taking all the free courses that I wanted to—until a friend and I decided to form our own company last year. V&V Creative Consultants. We do advertising and travel brochures, that sort of thing. We're small but growing. The Egyptian travel brochure for the Horus Hotels is our biggest account."

Ram let out a quick bark of laughter.

Meri cocked her head up at him. "Something funny?"

"It *is* a small world. I'm . . . involved with Horus Hotels as well. I'm the architect for the Horus-Giza."

"I'm impressed. We took photographs there today. It's going to be magnificent when it's finished next fall. So you're an architect?"

"Among other things."

She smiled and let herself relax against Ram, let the music wash over her as they moved in perfect harmony. For some reason she felt totally secure in his arms, more secure than she had felt in years. No dream, lucid or not, could be this real. She nestled her forehead against his broad shoulder and put her right hand on his chest. With both arms around her waist, he hugged her close and they moved silently to the slow tempo of the orchestra.

He whirled her around as the music ended. Noticing the orchestra preparing for a break, they returned to their table.

"This time I really must say good-night," she said.

"It's a shame you'll miss the entertainment. It will start in a few minutes."

"I'm sorry, but it's been a long day, and I'm very tired." She rubbed the back of her neck and shrugged her shoulders.

His hands replaced hers, kneading the tight muscles. "You're exhausted. How thoughtless of me. Come, I'll walk you to your room. We can see the show tomorrow night."

Outside, Meri breathed in the cool fresh air and looked up at the stars. They seemed different here—closer, more vibrantly alive. "They're like diamond dust," she said.

DREAM OF ME

"Would you like one?" Ram asked as his gaze followed hers.

"Sure. Bring me a handful." She smiled. "You never did tell me the stories of your father and grandfather."

"That can wait until tomorrow. I'll play Scheherazade and keep you interested with the promise of a story."

Moonlight washed the multitude of garden petals with an iridescent sheen. Flowering trees scented the air; now and then, as the breeze rippled through the leaves, a blossom floated and fell. The domes and spires of the old hotel stood in silver relief against an indigo sky.

"This place does look like a castle from Arabian Nights," Meri said.

"The old part," he said, nodding toward the building they had just left, "was built over a hundred years ago as a royal hunting lodge. Then, some time later, it was converted into a hotel. The garden section, where you're staying, was added about twenty years ago." A hint of nostalgia colored Ram's words as he stood with his hands in his pockets and gazed at the Islamic structure. "Much of the original decor has been preserved, particularly in the restaurant and in the coffee shop . . . where I first saw you yesterday morning." He smiled down at her and brushed her cheek with the back of his fingers.

"Yesterday morning? I didn't see you there."

"Ah, but I saw you. I went there often with my grandfather when I was a little boy, and he would tell me how he first saw my grandmother in that very spot. It used to be a veranda, you know. The British colonists would sit and sip their tea while they watched the sun set behind the Pyramids."

"Is your grandfather still living?"

"No, he's been dead for many years now. He died just a few months after my grandmother," he replied. "Come," he said taking her arm, "let's get you to bed."

When they reached her door, he took her bag, removed the room key from it and slipped a small package inside before he snapped it shut.

"Please, no more gifts—"

"Shhh." He touched her lips. "It's just some hairpins—to replace those you lost on your wild camel ride." He sifted a few strands through his fingers. "Although, I must say that I like it down like this."

"Hairpins I will accept, but if you'll wait a moment, I'll get the other things for you."

"No, I won't take them. They're yours. Give them away or throw them away if the things don't please you. You need your rest now. Sleep late in the morning. I have an early meeting, but I'll be back to take you to lunch, and we'll plan to do or see whatever you like."

"But Welcome and I have to—"

"Welcome? Oh, your red-haired friend. I'll take you both."

He unlocked the door, opened it, and handed Meri the key and her purse. Turning to her, he lifted his hand to her face, smoothed her hair away from her cheekbone and lovingly traced a small scar there with his thumb. He kissed it and whispered in her ear, "Dream of me."

When Meri opened her eyes, he was gone.

Still caught up in the midst of Ram's enchantment, she almost floated into the suite, moving languorously toward her room, shedding her clothes as she went. Such a man. Did he really exist, or was she caught in the spell of some ancient Egyptian magic?

In her bedroom she opened the package Ram had put into her purse. She found a handful of stars—gold hairpins tipped with twinkling diamonds and glowing pearls. Laughing, she laced them through her hair and slipped between the sheets to savor, to sleep, and to dream.

Four

*Every lion comes from its den,
All the serpents bite;
Darkness hovers, earth is silent . . .*

The Great Hymn to the Aten
c. 1350 B.C.

Smoke from a Turkish cigarette spiraled upward in the darkened room, the pungent wisps curling through the rectangle of moonlight illuminating the room. Behind a lavishly carved rosewood desk, the man swung the high-backed chair around to face the window.

"I tell you, I saw it with my own eyes," he said softly to someone on the telephone. "Al-Sayed and two of his colleagues saw it as well. Half of Cairo will know about it by tomorrow. Those who know of the myth will be astounded to learn of its existence."

"Are you sure that it's authentic?"

"How can I be positive without examining it more closely? But, yes, I'm very sure. It's smaller and more intricately wrought, the gold and the workmanship finer, but except for a few variations, the pectoral could be the model for the Re-Horakhte falcon of Tutankhamen."

"How did this woman—an American, you say?—come by the piece?"

"I have no idea, but she flirts with danger. To wear it so blatantly, either she's exceptionally reckless or has no idea of its value. But with an American, who can tell?"

"Mmmm. She's staying at the Mena House, you say?"

"Of that I made sure. And she seems to be a . . . close friend of Ramson Gabrey. Are you acquainted with him?"

"Mmmm."

"What shall I do?"

"Nothing for the moment. I'll telephone you in the morning."

The man replaced the receiver in its cradle. As he stubbed out his cigarette, his hand trembled. In the dim light, his eyes gleamed with avarice.

By all that was holy, he would almost barter his soul to own such a treasure.

Five

Their walls are in ruin,
Their places are no more,—
As if they had never been.
None cometh from thence,
That he might tell us of their state;
That he might restore our hearts,
Until we too depart to the place,
Whither they have gone.

The Song of the Harper
c. 27th century B.C.

A ringing phone jerked Meri from a deep sleep. Her heart pounding, she groped for the receiver.

"Hello."

"Where have you been?" Nora Elwood asked sharply.

"I have been asleep, Mother."

"You couldn't have been asleep very long. I've been calling every two hours and worried sick."

Irritation flashed over Meri, and she counted to ten before she replied. "Mother"—she took a deep breath—"I am an adult woman, fully capable of looking out for myself. I see no reason to report my every move to you. Welcome and I haven't had any problems."

"That woman *is* a problem. I can't say I'm happy that you're with her. She doesn't strike me as the cautious type, and a girl like you *must* be cautious there. I've read horrendous things in the newspaper about—"

"Mother . . . *not now.*" Meri slammed the phone down and pulled the covers over her head.

Ram picked up the phone in his office and leaned back in his chair. "Hello, my lovely," he said to his mother. "How is the book tour, and what may I do for you this fine morning?"

Charlotte Clark Gabrey, better known to her mystery fans and childhood chums as Charlie Clark, chuckled. "The book tour is going well, thank you. And how did you know I wanted you to do something for me?"

"My secretary said that you called four times yesterday. Sorry I didn't get the message until this morning."

"I do have a teensy problem. Rather Nora Elwood does. You've met Nora, my publicist in the States, haven't you?"

"I don't recall that we've met, but I've heard you speak of her. Isn't she the one who has the daughter that you've been trying to match me with for years?"

"She's the one. She and your Aunt Ruth went to school together and our families have been friends forever. Well, it seems that the daughter is visiting Egypt, and—"

"Sorry, Mother, I'm still not interested."

"Ramson, don't be such a boor. I'm not matchmaking. Nora is very concerned about her only child's safety. Since you have a security firm, I promised that I would talk with you about providing some men to sort of watch out for her while she's in Egypt."

"J.J. is in charge of the security business, but I'll speak with him. I'll see that your friend's daughter gets the VIP treatment."

"Thank you, dear. I spoke with J.J. myself yesterday, and he already knows all the details. But there's a bit of a problem. Nora feels that Meri would resent her interference, and the security you provide must be . . . somewhat surreptitious."

Instantly alert, Ram sat up straight. "Meri?" he asked casually.

"Yes. Nora's daughter is Meri Vaughn. She's in Egypt on a project that your father and I—well, that's neither here nor there. The question is: Will you personally see to her safety? Nora is a nervous wreck."

A huge grin had spread across Ram's face. He tried to keep the laughter from his voice when he said, "Certainly, Mother. I'll take care of her safety personally. Tell Ms. Elwood not to worry about a thing."

"Thank you, Ramson. I knew we could count on you. Remember, be subtle with your security measures."

"Subtle. I understand." He choked back a laugh. "She'll never know that we're watching out for her. I'll see to it that she's completely safe every hour of the day."

After a few more exchanges about the book tour and family news, they hung up. Ram fell back in his chair and laughed uproariously. What a cosmic joke! For years Charlotte Gabrey had been suggesting that Ram look up Nora's daughter when he was in Houston on business. He'd simply tuned out her intimations. If only he'd known sooner that the woman of his dreams had been under his nose all this time! But his stubborn refusal to succumb to maternal matchmaking had kept them apart. What a fool he'd been.

If he'd had any doubts that he and Meri were destined to be together—which he didn't—they would have been completely dispelled by this latest development. Fate had conspired to bring them together too often. Now they were together, at last.

He rang his secretary. "I need to speak with J.J. immediately."

Meri had slept fitfully after the conversation with her mother. Nora Elwood was a formidable woman—some would consider her downright intimidating—but Welcome was right. Sooner or later there would have to be a serious confrontation. Meri disliked confrontations, especially with strong personalities like Nora, but she was growing weary of her mother's interference in her life. While she appreciated Nora's success, and she was mindful of all the advantages her mother had given her, she resented her mother's overbearing and overprotective attitude.

Damn, she thought as she dressed, she was in a lousy mood.

Without even a cup of coffee to take the edge off, Meri and Welcome met Philip in the lobby and left the hotel while it was still dark. She wanted to catch the sunrise in the final shoot.

Working occupied Meri's total attention, but with the last click of the Hasselblad, her despondency returned. Something other than her problems with her mother seemed to trouble her as well. She suspected that Ram Gabrey was at the root of those odd feelings, but she refused to let herself dwell on her fascination with him. After all, she and Welcome were leaving for Aswan the following morning, and she'd probably never see him again.

Life was so complicated. There were days when she wished she'd been born an orphan and lived on a deserted island.

When they had arrived back at their hotel suite, Welcome said, "I don't know about you, but I could use a few more hours of beauty sleep. Dawn is for birds."

Even though she was tired from her restless night, Meri knew that she'd never be able to go back to sleep. "After I take care of this film, I think I'll go get some breakfast and walk around or something."

"You look a little down in the mouth. What's wrong?"

"Nora called again last night."

Welcome rolled her eyes. "What's on the dragon lady's mind now?"

"Kidnapping. Rape. Murder."

"Whose?"

"Mine."

Welcome laughed. "Didn't you remind her that you've had karate lessons?"

"No. I hung up on her."

"Well, good for you. I'm headed for some more sack time. See you later."

After Meri logged and labeled the film, she grabbed her bush jacket, her shoulder bag, and her trusty old Leica for personal photos and picked up a hat on her way out the door.

It was still early morning, and the hotel and grounds were quiet. A lone gardener trimmed his shrubs in the cool of the new day and nodded to her as she made her way to the cafe across the lawn.

The waiter led her to a table by a bead-draped window and filled her coffee cup. She cradled the cup in her palms and sipped, studying the imposing Pyramids and wondering about the peculiar effect they had on her, about the odd sensations that everything in this country seemed to generate. The three huge monuments almost seemed as if they were trying to speak, trying to impart their mystery to her.

She had always known there was magic in this land. There was a *reason* she was here—something she didn't begin to understand, but sensed deeply. Of course she'd come with Welcome to shoot the material for the brochure, but there was more—something, somewhere. It was as if she had been drawn to Egypt where civilizations long past had built great and enduring monuments to the dead. She could feel it, but she couldn't name it. The word that kept coming to mind was destiny. Her father often spoke of things like destiny and karma, and Meri had laughed and attributed it to part of his wacky charm. But now she wondered.

And she wondered what part Ram Gabrey played in this curious scheme. Or if he had a part. Or if—

Oh, hell, she was getting a headache from trying to make sense of it. She pushed it from her mind and ordered breakfast.

After Meri had eaten and signed the check, she glanced at her watch. Almost ten o'clock. Ram had said he would be here for lunch. Although she couldn't deny a strong attraction to him, she was sick of spooky stuff, and every time she was around him, things got weird. While she had to admit that the night before had been delightful and seemingly normal, now that she had time to reflect on the odd occurrences, she'd just as soon avoid him altogether.

Maybe she could take the hotel limousine downtown to the museum or find a tour someplace and avoid him. She walked back to the lobby and checked with the desk clerk. A bus was leaving in a few minutes for a day of sightseeing at Sakkara and Memphis. Perfect. She went back to their suite and left a note for Welcome.

As she stepped into the hall and closed the door behind her, a short, dark, gray-haired man approached her.

"Miss Vaughn?"

"Yes?"

He held out an envelope to her. "I am Omar. Mr. Gabrey said that I was not to disturb your rest, but he asked me to deliver this if you went out early."

Opening the envelope, Meri found a small gold camel on a chain with a key. There was a note which read:

> *May I offer this in lieu of 10,000 camels? Omar is at your disposal until lunchtime.*
>
> *Love, Ram.*

"What is this? I don't understand?"

Omar smiled and motioned with a slight bow, "If you would follow me outside."

When they reached the circular drive in front of the hotel, he pointed to a white Mercedes sedan. "This is for you. If you like, I will drive you. The traffic is very bad for those not used to it."

"A *car*? Just like that? You're kidding."

"I assure you than I am not, Miss. It is yours."

"No way. I refuse to accept it!" Meri thrust the key into

Omar's hand. "And you can tell Mr. Gabrey to take his car and stuff it where the sun don't shine."

"Pardon?"

She took a deep breath. "Tell him—no, thank you." She wheeled and ran toward the waiting tour bus.

Most of the people were part of a German group, and since Meri's German was limited to *nein* and *Wiener Schnitzel,* she kept to herself while they laughed and talked with each other. As they rode alongside the river, she gazed out the window at the lush green fields extending from each side of the Nile. Entire families worked in the fields with donkeys, camels, and occasionally oxen. Only once did she see anything as modern as a tractor. Now and then, clusters of mud brick huts sat crumbling back into the river banks that spawned them.

The bus ground to a stop and waited for a truck to dump its load of shell and for a grader to spread it. Their driver merely shrugged at the delay and stepped out to light a cigarette. Meri joined a few others who got off to stretch and walk around a bit.

Feeling a tug on her jacket, Meri looked down to see a small crusty-faced girl with tangled hair and a ragged, over-sized dress.

"Stylo?" the child asked shyly. *"Stylo?"* She scratched a finger in the palm of the opposite hand.

Not understanding, Meri looked helplessly to the bus driver who stood nearby.

"She wants something to write with. They are very poor here. If you give her a pen, you will be covered in begging children."

Meri hesitated and then looked into sad, pleading eyes. Her heart simply melted. How could she refuse such an entreaty? She found a ballpoint pen in her purse and gave it to the little girl who smiled and scampered away.

Two other ragged, dirty children appeared clamoring, *"Stylo! Stylo!"*

Laughing, Meri dug in her bag and managed to find another pen and a pencil for them before she retreated into the bus saying, "No more," to the other children who had begun to gather like ants to a sugar spill.

Soon they continued on to Memphis and honked their way through a herd of black and white goats to reach the front of the small museum. Once inside, Meri waited until her eyes adjusted to the darker interior, then climbed to the balcony with the other group members. She stood looking down at the gigantic recumbent statue of the great egotist and builder, Ramses II. Magnificently carved in alabaster, its hand could have held the modern folding chair sitting beside it.

Aiming her camera, she snapped a picture just as a man entered the doorway and looked up. The flash caused him to throw up a hand to shield his face from the glare, then he quickly retreated from the building. Later she spotted the same man, a casually dressed Egyptian with thin lips and a drooping eyelid, but before she could get to him and apologize for blinding him with the flash, he melted into the crowd.

Winding their way across desert dunes toward Sakkara, the City of the Dead, Meri again felt a nebulous, unformed anticipation molding itself inside her. The familiar *déjà vu* feeling that had plagued her since she'd first arrived in Egypt grew stronger as they neared Sakkara, stronger and with overtones of great sadness. She didn't understand the feeling any more than she'd understood any of the other unnerving experiences she'd had.

Still, she sensed an inner kinship with this hot and desiccated land, where with time and sun and wind, rock became sand and sand became powder, yet so many things endured and had meaning.

Perhaps destiny *had* brought her here on a blue Misr Travel bus, yet a vague sensation of dread made her hesitate when the driver stopped and opened the door. At the same time, something inexplicable pulled at her, beckoned her.

Meri was the last one off the bus. She pushed past the hawkers of postcards and mummy beads and camel rides, past the small doe-eyed dogs and piles of animal droppings toward the gate. There, out of that continuous beige monochromatic monotony of undulating rock and sand, rose the necropolis.

Pulling on her hat in a futile duel with the midday sun, she trudged on through the sand following their swaggering young guide with his bright green Polo shirt and gold watch. He led them to the remains of a colonnaded temple, said to be the oldest of its kind in the world. Forty immense, ivory-colored pillars formed the walkway. Twenty of the fluted pairs rose fifteen feet to become intricately stylized lotus blossoms and the other twenty, papyrus. One represented Upper Egypt and the other, Lower. Meri never discovered which was which because, as the guide was explaining in his heavy accent with its faint British inflection, she became fascinated with the stone-grinder.

He was sitting in a niche formed by the limestone blocks of the temple walls and two of the lotus columns—sitting there in the sand with his knees drawn up and a limestone block lying between his legs. The stone was about two feet long and ten inches wide and thick—the same color as the ivory blocks which formed the walls. As he sat he scooped up handfuls of sand and sprinkled them over the surface. Using what looked like a brick, he slowly scraped it back and forth, back and forth, making a hollow rasping sound as he smoothed and shaped the stone. He worked in the same manner as had his ancestors generations before. They built, he restored.

A long length of dirty, once-white rag was wrapped around his head and trailed over bony shoulders hunched beneath a brown robe of cotton and grime. It was as if he were caught up in some eternal task with the hollow rasping rhythm as he slowly scooped and sprinkled and scraped and smoothed the stone to restore Pharaoh's temple.

For a mesmerizing moment, Meri was caught up with him in the timelessness of his scooping and sprinkling and scraping and smoothing. She stood there for several minutes and watched his gnarled dusty fingers continue the endless tedious sequence. Some elusive flickering darted through her mind. It was a faint, phantom awareness that teased and retreated.

He continued his slow scooping and sprinkling and scraping and smoothing. She continued staring, lost with him in time, waiting for something.

"Betts, look at the size of this son of a gun!" a deep male voice beside her bellowed as he slapped the side of a five-thousand-year-old column. "It's bigger around than I am," he snorted. "Here, hon, take my picture in front of it."

Wincing at the shattering intrusion, Meri closed her eyes and sighed.

"This way, ladies and gentlemen. This way," directed the guide. "Hurry, hurry."

Meri hesitated, then turned and reluctantly followed the parade of polyester-coordinated invaders toward six crumbling rock layers of dead-brown mastabas and petrified pilings that were the Step Pyramid. She lagged further behind, then stopped. That elusive flickering darted through her mind again. Stronger now, it pulled at the core of her consciousness. Some imminent sense of meaningful experience enticed her to turn and retrace her steps through the sand, and pottery shards to the colonnade temple and to the stone-grinder.

Moving toward the hollow rasping sound, Meri saw him again. He was still sitting there slowly scooping sand, sprinkling and scraping and smoothing. She sat down cross-legged in the sand in front of him with her elbows on her knees and her chin propped on her hands and watched silently.

Using a combination of English and sign language, Meri persuaded the stone-grinder to allow her to work the stone. She scooped up a handful of sand and scattered it over the surface, then slowly began scraping and smoothing. Mastery of the task came easily to her, as if she'd done it countless times before.

When he was satisfied that she was skilled, he moved to find another stone. She sat there for a long time, entranced with her own hypnotic slow scooping and sprinkling and scraping and smoothing. The rhythm and the feel of the work with her hands seemed hauntingly familiar.

A hawk called and circled overhead.

Flickering memories, vague and unsettling, darted through her mind again. Quickly she glanced up at the workman. His eyes turned an ocher and dun color and became as vacant and lifeless as the surrounding tombs of the ancient nobles, then he faded into nothingness.

She continued staring at the space where he had been, lost in time, waiting for something.

A soul-searing pain ripped through her.

Loneliness.

She was agonizingly alone. Separated from that which completed her. She had come, but she was alone. She scooped a measure of sand and cast it over the stone.

Her hands, brown and work-worn, their knuckles knotted, their creases caked with endless days of powder and grime, continued their mindless task under the relentless sun and made stones for Pharaoh's temple.

A hawk called and circled overhead as her gnarled hands continued to scoop and sprinkle the sand on the stone to scrape and smooth it. Day after day, year after year, grinding stones, trapped in a meaningless limbo of life. Alone.

Her heart ached with overwhelming intensity. Deep despair racked her body. Her soul cried out, "Where are you?"

No answer came.

The anguish in her heart was so excruciating that she began to weep. A deep keening wail ripped from her throat. "Where are you?"

A hand fell on her shoulder.

"I'm here," a voice said softly.

She looked up through her tears to see him sitting beside her, pain twisting his face. He pulled her onto his lap and cradled her head to his broad chest and held her.

"I'm here," he said.

Joy leapt in her heart as she savored his nearness. "I couldn't find you."

He laughed. "Did you look for me?"

"Everywhere. Oh, God, I've been so alone without you." She smiled and touched his cheek, but the fingers she used were no longer gnarled and brown.

Dazed, she looked around at the ancient ruins, then at him. "Ram?"

"Yes, love?"

With a trembling hand she felt his face. "Ram?"

"Yes, love?"

She grabbed a handful of his reassuringly modern shirt front and buried her head against his shoulder. "What's happening to me? Am I losing my mind?"

He held her tightly. "Want to tell me about it?"

She shook her head. "I don't even want to think about it. It's too scary. I just want to get away from this place. I hate it here."

"Come," he said taking her hand and gathering up her things. "I have water in the car. We'll wash your face."

He led her away and helped her into the white Mercedes parked by the gate. Wetting his handkerchief with cold water from a thermos, he tenderly bathed her face and dusty hands, poured a cupful and held it for her to drink.

"Are you all right?"

"Would you be all right if you thought you were losing your mind?"

He smiled. "Probably not. Are you sure you don't want to tell me what happened?"

"Positive. Just get me away from this place. Drive."

Six

. . . From the summit of yonder pyramids forty centuries look down upon you.

Napoleon Bonaparte
In Egypt, [July 21, 1798]

Ram drove away from the desert toward the river. Meri leaned her head back against the seat and closed her eyes. Her emotions abraded and raw, her sense of sanity threatened, she tried not think about what had happened at Sakkara, but like a moth to a flame, her thoughts returned to the incident.

What had happened to her? What world had she been in? Was it the sun again? Or— She shook off the thought.

A few years before, she'd had a bout of vertigo when she'd had an inner ear infection. Losing her sense of balance and physical orientation had been a terrible feeling. She felt much the same way as she had then, except she had mental vertigo instead of the physical kind. Losing her sense of orientation to reality was scary. Very scary.

Schizophrenic.

She shuddered and locked her fingers together tightly as if to hold onto her sanity.

"Are you all right?" Ram asked.

She shook her head.

"Want to talk about it now?"

"No. I want to forget about it. I must have had too much sun and gone a little goofy."

"The sun here can be merciless. It takes some getting used to. And because the humidity is so low, you can become dehydrated and have a heat stroke before you know it. Always take a bottle of water with you and drink often."

"Can dehydration make you hallucinate?"

"Of course."

With his answer, Meri felt her tension ease. She almost laughed aloud. *Thank God.* Dehydrated. She'd become dehydrated and conjured up all that flaky stuff. Her relief was enormous.

"Let me have some more of that water." She grabbed the thermos and took several big swallows. Maybe it was her imagination, but she was beginning to feel better. Much better.

After a few miles, he pulled into a secluded spot under a eucalyptus tree growing beside the Nile. "We missed our lunch. Are you hungry?"

Meri opened her eyes. "I don't know. I think I might be."

Ram got out of the car, opened the door for her, and retrieved a basket and a thickly woven cotton throw from the back seat. He spread the rug in the shade and indicated a place for her to sit. Kneeling beside her he opened the basket.

"I have here a special feast for you," he said with mock gravity and produced two red and white boxes.

She smiled. "Kentucky Fried Chicken? In Egypt?"

"But, of course," he answered, wiggling his eyebrows. "We're very modern here."

Tenderness rose up inside her. Impulsively, she leaned over and kissed his cheek. "Ramson Gabrey, you're a dear, sweet man."

"If I can have another kiss, I'll bring you a queen's feast for dinner."

She grinned. "I'd settle for a bag of M&M's. I'm having withdrawal symptoms."

"Plain or peanut? I like the plain, myself."

"The real connoisseurs do."

They laughed and bantered while they ate chicken, coleslaw, corn on the cob, and drank chilled fruit juice from a thermos.

Ram wiped the corner of her mouth with a napkin, her fingers with the moist towel from the box. "Let me take you back to the hotel so that you can rest for a while before you make yourself beautiful for me tonight."

Her hand flew to her face. "Good Lord, I must look a sight!"

He pulled her hand away and kissed her fingers. "You'll always look like an angel to me."

She opened her mouth to make a snappy rejoinder, but when she looked into his eyes, the words died in her throat. Something burned there. Something ageless and elemental. Not allowing herself to speculate on the message there, she quickly averted her gaze and began gathering up the remains of their picnic.

After they had stowed the basket and the rug in the trunk, Ram held up the camel key chain and asked, "Would you like to drive your car?"

"This is *your* car. You drive."

When they were back on the road to Cairo, Meri shifted until she was curled up on the seat facing Ram. With her left arm draped over the seat back and cradling her head, she quietly studied his profile as he drove—the chiseled angle of his jaw, the deep furrow of his cheeks the slight hook in his hawk nose, the lines radiating from those incredible eyes. Against his dark skin, his blue eyes seemed so light, so penetrating, it was startling. The wind had ruffled his thick black hair into tousled waves and curls. She could see faint threads of silver scattered through it.

Ramson Gabrey was a handsome man—and a man of paradoxes. Strong, yet gentle; stubborn, but giving. So different from anyone she'd ever known.

And she was reluctant to part with him just yet. Although she'd accepted the logical explanation of dehydration as the cause of her hallucinations, an underlying disquiet from the eerie experience at Sakkara still clung to her, and being with him seemed to soothe her.

"Ram?"

"Yes, love?"

"It's still early yet. Would you do something for me?"

He grinned. "You name it. You got it."

"Can you believe that I haven't seen the Sphinx and Pyramids? I mean, I've seen them, but I haven't had time to really explore and enjoy them. And I thought—"

"Say no more."

As they walked through the sand toward the Sphinx and the Pyramids, Meri stopped to view the panorama of the complex. The solemn wonder of the sight was a worn travel cliché, but neither the pictures that she had seen nor the descriptions that she had read could portray the overwhelming impact of their physical and spiritual presence. Not even the busloads of tourists, the strings of horses and camels and peddlers, or the modern asphalt roads could corrupt this majesty.

In awe, she looked up at the Sphinx with its lion body and human head, then to the area between its paws. "That's where I was conceived."

Ram frowned. "Conceived? In what way?"

She laughed. "The usual way. As students, my parents spent several weeks here on an archeological project with their university. They were young and idealistic, and making love at the foot of the Sphinx seemed very romantic at the time. At least that's what my father says. My mother doesn't discuss that period of her life. Even before I was born, they named me Meritaten."

"Ah, so Meri is from Meritaten. If I recall my history correctly, she was the oldest of Akhenaten's and Nefertiti's six daughters."

"Yes. As I said, my parents had some very romantic notions

at the time. But they parted a couple of years later, and I ended up with a name I've always had to explain."

"What if you'd been a boy?"

She shook her head. "God forbid. I don't even like to think about it." She gazed up at the Sphinx, and sensed a stirring deep within her. "I've always been fascinated with Egypt and its history, and I've always felt . . . something drawing me here." She laughed. "Maybe it's the same urge that compels salmon to return to where they were spawned."

"I prefer to think you've come . . . for another reason. You don't bear a resemblance to any salmon I've ever seen."

She smiled and turned her attention back to the wondrous stone monument. "It's mind-boggling to think that countless generations have stood in the same place I'm standing. Cleopatra. Alexander the Great. Napoleon. Right here. Probably in this very spot."

"It's not as grand as it once was," Ram said, pointing out the restoration work that shored up the crumbling neck and filled broken sections. "Some say that Napoleon's troops shot off the nose during target practice, but I doubt that it's true. Blowing sand has eroded many parts but it's modern pollution that's taking its toll on many of my country's treasures. Exhaust fumes and acid rain are more damaging than a few musket balls."

"Scarred or not, it's still extraordinary."

As the wind whipped her hair and sent stinging particles of sand against her skin, the present faded and disappeared. The past emerged from the mists of time and brought its eerie splendor. A channel of the Nile replaced the road; lush green grass supplanted sand; the Sphinx was arrayed with fresh paint of white, red, black, and blue. Its paws rested near the water's edge; the gold leaf of its snaked crown gleamed in the ancient sun. The fresh-laid stones of the funerary temple and the causeway were smooth and clean. She looked to the Great Pyramid and instead of immense raw blocks, she saw a polished limestone casing rising to a golden capstone.

With a blink of her eyelids, the vision disappeared.

Meri's breath caught. "Did you see that?"

"See what?"

"Just for a moment I saw—oh, never mind. But Ram," she said, "it was *magnificent!* Absolutely magnificent!"

It felt so *right* to be here. Joy bubbled up inside her. She wanted to throw open her arms and shout to the world, *I'm here. I've come!* Laughing, she wheeled and exuberantly hugged Ram. He, too, laughed as he caught her in his arms.

She wiggled out of his grasp and grabbed his hand. "It's wonderful! Let's see everything!"

Caught up in her infectious mood, he pulled her forward. "Come, I will show you all. I am the finest guide in all of Cairo."

She giggled. Where had she heard that before? It must be the standard line. But he was, indeed, a fine guide. They took pictures by the Sphinx and bought scarabs from vendors who proclaimed that they were very old and very fine.

Meri studied a necklace made of ancient-looking turquoise scarabs that Ram had just haggled for—in Arabic. "Do you think that they're really old?"

Ram laughed. "Only as compared to bread. They were probably made last week. I won't tell you how they frequently achieve that patina of age." He draped the piece around her neck.

"Why not?"

"Because you'd probably wrinkle your pretty nose and wouldn't wear it."

"Now you have to tell me. Is it gross?"

"Fairly gross."

"I'm tough. I can take it."

He grinned. "Sometimes they feed them to geese."

It took moment for the significance of the process to sink in. She looked down at the scarabs and made a face. "Do you mean that these may have been in goose poop?"

Ram burst into laughter. "Possibly."

"That *is* gross."

"I doubt if anyone went to that much trouble for these simple trinkets. They've probably been rubbed with dirt and tallow. Want to toss it?"

She splayed her hand possessively over it. "Not on your life. I told you I was tough. Let's go see inside the Great Pyramid."

At the entrance to the thirteen-acre monument, Ram held a spirited conversation in Arabic with the attendant and slipped him several bills.

"What was that about?"

He shrugged. "As soon as the group inside leaves, we have the place to ourselves for half an hour."

"How did you manage that?"

He rubbed his fingers together. *"Baksheesh."*

In a few minutes a trail of chattering Japanese tourists exited and the attendant motioned for Meri and Ram. They ducked into an opening hacked into the north face of the Pyramid, descended briefly, then with Ram leading the way, they began climbing a steep wooden ramp crossed with small slats to secure their footing.

Meri marveled at the two-and-a-half-ton blocks that formed the walls and ceiling of the narrow corridor, quarried and fitted together without mortar thousands of years before.

In the United States, such a national treasure would have been lighted with glowing torches rigged out to look like something from Hollywood or Disneyland. As it was, their path through the two million precisely placed stones was lighted with crude strings of bare bulbs.

"What happens if the lights go out?" Meri asked, her words echoing in the stone tunnel.

"It gets very dark."

"Does it happen very often?"

"Occasionally would be more accurate. If we have a power failure, just grab hold of me. I have a penlight on my key chain."

"I'm glad I'm in good shape," Meri said as they continued climbing the steep passageway. "Are we almost there?"

"About halfway. We're coming to the Grand Gallery. The corridor is larger."

On they climbed into the inner recesses. After a few minutes, they ducked down, bending low to enter the King's Chamber. Once inside she looked around, and even knowing what to expect, Meri was surprised. Except for graffiti by early explorers—even noted academics couldn't resist carving their names in the walls—the small room was remarkably bare. No colorfully painted scenes graced the chamber. No statues, no carvings, no niches. The only thing in the musty room was a plain granite sarcophagus, lidless and empty.

"Wow," she said, running her fingers over the rough edge of the sarcophagus. She looked at Ram and grinned. "I know it's hokey, but I can't resist." Handing him her camera, she swung a leg over and climbed inside.

As she was about to lie down, he said, "Are you sure you want to do that? Men have been using this place as a urinal for centuries."

"That's even more gross than goose poop. Are you kidding me?"

"Nope."

She hesitated a moment. "Oh, what the hell. I've had my shots. Pee or no pee, I'm going to do it."

Struggling to keep a straight face, she stretched out with her hands over her chest in a mock death pose while Ram snapped her photograph.

"Want me to take your picture?"

He chuckled and helped her out. "I'll pass."

She sat down cross-legged, leaned against the sarcophagus, and marveled at the huge stones set with such precision that not even a piece of paper could pass between them.

"I wish I had some razor blades," she said to Ram as he sat down beside her.

"Pyramid power," he commented.

"What do you know about pyramid power?"

"It's said that if you place dull razor blades in a pyramid, they'll become sharp. And food is supposed to stay fresh as well."

"I wonder if anyone has tried it here in the Great Pyramid."

"Oh, yes. Not too long ago a group from one of the universities in the States placed some razor blades, some flowers, and some fruit in here for a week."

"What happened?" she asked.

"I heard that the razor blades rusted, the flowers died, and the Pyramid rats ate the fruit."

"Rats?"

"The place is full of them."

"Now that makes me nervous. Come on, my fine guide, let's get out of here." They descended the dark narrow corridor and escaped into the late afternoon light.

As Ram drove back to the hotel, he could barely keep his eyes off Meri. He had been irritated when Omar had reported Meri's escape to him. As soon as he could get out of his meeting, he'd gone chasing after the tour bus. She wasn't getting away that easily. But when he had seen her weeping in the sand, the torment in her eyes, he could only think of comforting her. He wanted to wrench the pain from her and endure it himself. Never had he felt so helpless. Nor had he experienced such profound feelings for another human being. He wanted to crawl into her skin and assimilate every cell. He wanted to fight dragons for her, scale the stars and shout that she was his.

He also wanted to tell her how long he'd loved her, how their spirits and destinies were indelibly entwined, but he knew that she wasn't ready to accept what he knew. He would wait.

Reaching for her hand, he squeezed it. "We're almost there. Why don't you rest for a while, and I'll pick you up in a couple of hours. If you like, we can see the sound and light show at the Pyramids, then have dinner and see the performance you missed last night. We can take your friend with us if you'd like."

"Knowing Welcome, I'm sure she has plans, but I'll check."

"Welcome?" Meri called.

"I'm here." Welcome strolled in from her bedroom toweling her hair. "I was beginning to worry about you. Where in the world have you been? You look as if you've spent the day rolling in a sand pile."

Meri laughed. "You're not far wrong. I get dirtier in this place than anywhere I've ever been, but I love it here." Wiping her hands on her pants, she said, "You wouldn't believe how nasty I feel. I need a bath."

"I'll vote for that. We've been invited to dinner at the embassy tonight. Interested?"

"Nope. I've got a date." Meri started stripping off her clothes on the way to the bathroom.

"Who with? Did your Romeo finally wear you down?"

Meri leaned around the door and grinned at her curious friend. "A bath first, and I'll tell you all about it. Why don't you fix us a drink?"

"By the way I checked up on him today, or rather I asked Philip to."

"What did you find out?"

"A bath first, and I'll tell you all about it," the redhead mimicked. She ducked the dirty T-shirt Meri hurled from across the room.

Meri showered, washed and dried her hair, and pulled on a soft blue terry caftan before she joined Welcome on the couch.

"Okay, give," Welcome said as she thrust a drink into Meri's hand.

"You first."

"It's really not much. I did find out he's very wealthy—owns several businesses. He's influential in the community, comes from an old and respected family, and he's never been married. He's never been known to pursue a woman the way he has you. Usually it's the other way around. Over the years a lot of mothers and daughters have been after him. Is he your date tonight?"

Meri nodded and gave Welcome an edited version of her day's activities. "Would you believe that the latest thing he's trying to give me is a white Mercedes?"

"Honey, I think you'd better grab that man before he gets away."

"Oh, Welcome, we're from two different worlds. He's an aristocratic Egyptian, and I'm just a plain gal from Texas. It's a fun, fantasy fling. It'll be a lovely memory, but I can't see it going anywhere."

"Can you imagine him eating barbecued ribs with his fingers?"

Meri thought back to him gnawing on a KFC chicken leg and smiled. "As a matter of fact, I can. But that's neither here nor there. We're flying to Aswan in the morning, and I'll never see him again."

Welcome cocked her head and shrugged her shoulders. "Maybe . . . but I wouldn't bet on it. I've got to get dressed. Don't forget we have to be at the airport early. Philip said he'd pick us up at six-thirty, and our flight leaves at eight."

Seven

*Your love has gone all through my body
like honey in water,
as a drug is mixed into spices,
as water is mingled with wine.*

Love Songs of the New Kingdom
c. 1550-1080 B.C.

The world was marshmallow . . . and fairy dust . . . and fine warm sand. Meri awoke from her nap and stretched like an awakening cat—lazily, languorously. Slowly she sat up, hugging her knees to her chest.

This land *was* magic. She felt wonderful as she strolled to the bathroom, splashed her face, and brushed her teeth. Meri, who rarely spent more than a few minutes getting dressed, took her time pampering and preening for a change. Her dress was a luxurious dusty rose velour to match her mood. It would be warm enough for the cool evening but was downy soft and sensuous against her skin.

She reached automatically for the falcon pendant lying in her jewelry case, then hesitated. She changed her mind a dozen times before she picked it up, held it in her palm, and studied it. It was warm. She touched other pieces of jewelry, testing them. They were all cool from the air-conditioned room, but the pendant hummed warmly against her skin as if the gold and stones had an inner fire, as if the falcon were alive.

"What the heck?" she muttered, drawing the chain over her neck.

With a new abandon she added the earrings and bracelet Ram had given her and smiled as she touched her throat and wrists with exotic Scheherazade. The opulent perfume had come in a package Welcome had placed on her bedside table while she napped. *For 1001 nights and more* Ram's note had said.

Meri selected a delicate cashmere shawl in muted patterns of rose, blue, and cream, and picked up her purse as a knock came.

Laying the wrap and bag on a chair, she hurried to open the door. Ram. For a moment, they stood quietly taking one another's measure. He exuded a charisma that was a living, moving force that caught and embraced her in his spell.

He was impeccably attired in a dark gray suit tailored to emphasize his broad shoulders and chest, and his leather shoes were polished to a high black gloss. The blue of his silk dress shirt and patterned tie were the same soft hue as his eyes, which were devouring her once more.

"You look beautiful," he said. His eyes went to the falcon pendant and brightened. "Perfect." He brought her hand to his lips, nuzzled her wrist, and breathed in the scent of her. "Delicious."

"Thank you for the perfume. I love it."

"It reminded me of you. Flowers and fruit and spice . . . and promises."

Clasping both her hands in his, he brought them to his mouth and touched each with a light kiss. He continued to caress her with his mesmerizing eyes and captured her gaze with his. She could almost hear the flute of a snake charmer and could feel herself begin to sway with its tune. Laughter from down the hall startled Meri back to reality, and she pulled her hands from his.

Taking a deep breath, she moved away to pick up her shawl

and purse. *Careful, careful,* she told herself. He was like some prince charming from a fairy tale. This was a delightful, but temporary, fantasy. Tomorrow she would be gone and this would end—there would be no happily ever after for them. *Enjoy tonight.*

"Shall we go?" she asked, handing him her wrap.

He fingered the light fabric. "This is lovely, but don't you have something warmer? It will be very chilly on the desert tonight for the sound and light show."

She shook her head. "This is the warmest thing I have, unless—I suppose I could wear my windbreaker, but it's not very heavy. Egypt's being cold didn't occur to me when I packed." She searched her memory for something warm that she or Welcome might have. "Oh, I know. I'll get a blanket from the bedroom. We'll pretend it's a football game."

"I have a better idea," he interrupted as she started from the room. He disappeared from the doorway and returned with a large white box which he held out to her. "I brought this in case you might need it tonight."

What had this crazy man done now? She was almost afraid to open the box, but open it she did. There, swathed in layers of tissue, was a full-length mink coat.

He draped it around her shoulders. "There, that will keep you warm."

Exasperated, she said, "Ramson Gabrey! I will not have any more of this. I can't accept it. Here!" She thrust the soft champagne-colored fur at him. "I'll get a blanket."

He grabbed her arm as she turned to go. "This is warmer than a blanket and it matches your hair exactly." He marched her to an ornate gold wall mirror and draped the coat over her shoulders once more. As he held her in front of him, he bent his face close to hers and touched his cheek to hers. "See how beautiful you make it?" he asked her reflection. "In any case, it had your name in it, so it must be yours." He folded it back to expose her name stitched into the cream-colored lining.

"My father would be horrified to think that I would consider wearing such a frivolous thing made from the skins of innocent animals."

He winced. "It didn't occur to me." He sighed. "But the deed is done."

"I understand." Her fingers wistfully stroked the sumptuous fur.

Wrapping his arms around her, he pulled her back against him and their eyes met again in the mirror. He lifted his dark eyebrow in a devilish pose and grinned. "Would you believe I got it on sale, and I can't return it?"

She shook her head. "Nope. My mother would demand to know what the catch is."

"I heard what your mother's and father's reactions would be. What about Meri's?"

"I feel a little of both, I suppose. Mostly it makes me wonder if you want something from me I'm not prepared to give."

"Would you believe that I would offer you a hundred of these simply to see your smile and your beautiful eyes sparkle?" Turning her toward him, he searched her face. "You don't understand yet, do you? I'm so happy to have found you, I want to lay the world at your feet—to give you beautiful things—to bring you joy and laughter. Egyptian men always give gifts to their ladies; it brings us great pleasure to be generous. If I could harness the wind and the sea, they would be yours."

A smile lit her face. "Truly?"

"Truly."

They stood quietly, lost in the moment, as the sky of his eyes fused with the sea of hers. Meri was aware of nothing but Ram—the vital force emanating from him and drawing her in. Even the air she breathed was filled with him—the faint mingled fragrance of wool and mint, wood and spice, and a certain virile essence exclusively his.

She licked her lips while he watched. His hands tightened around her arms and his mouth slowly descended toward hers. Wanting to be kissed, needing to be held, yet guarding herself against some fruitless involvement, she pulled back, almost imperceptibly. He released her and lightly tweaked her nose.

"We must leave or we'll be late." He collected her things and led her to the door.

They drove to the sound and light program in his low-slung black sports car. When they arrived at the gate, he presented tickets and moved Meri through the crowd to an open-air balcony. Most of the seats were filled, but he guided her to the front row and nodded to two men who caught his signal and quickly relinquished their seats.

Turning up the full collar of the coat, she felt only a tiny bit guilty as she snuggled into the fur. The wind was biting cold as it rolled in from the dark desert beyond.

"I didn't dream it would be so chilly at this time of year. This coat feels good. Very practical."

He grinned and winked at her, then handed her a pair of fur-lined kid gloves he pulled from his overcoat. "There's a scarf in your pocket if you need it."

"You think of everything, don't you?"

"Apparently not." He scowled as he noticed her nylon-clad legs and soft pumps. Despite her protests, he peeled off his topcoat, draped it over her lap, and tucked it around her feet. Looking up from where he knelt before her, he asked, "Warm enough?"

She nodded. No man had ever treated her like this. She wasn't sure how to react. Usually men understood from her manner that she could take care of herself. "But now you'll be cold."

"Not likely," he murmured as he slipped into the chair beside her. "I'm burning up."

Meri's heart lurched, but before she could comment, a voice boomed from the darkness and a light fell upon the face of the Sphinx below. She was lost in the drama unfolding as the ancient creature spoke.

It told of the many travelers who had passed, the sights it had witnessed over the ages, the wearing of time. Lights played on the Pyramids; muted chanting and a haunting, jingling rhythm transported her back in time. She was part of the gathering celebration throng. People were talking as they waited; and now and then she could catch a phrase or laughter from the mixed sounds of the crowd, could hear the slap of the oars as the pharaoh's barge neared.

She was so caught up in the saga that when the last sound echoed into the quiet of the desert and the lights dimmed, then died, she discovered herself clutching Ram's arm and his hand over hers. She turned to find him staring at her, drinking her in.

"Don't do that," she said, pulling her arms away.

"Do what?"

"Look at me as if you were going to pounce on me. It makes me nervous."

Ram chuckled. "Sorry. Did you enjoy the show?"

"Very much. It was spectacular. Thanks for bringing me." She retrieved his coat and brushed at the sand clinging to it. "Oh, no. Look how dirty it got."

He took it from her. "Don't worry about the coat. Would you like dinner now or would you rather go for a ride in the city or the desert?"

"Dinner please. I'm ravenous."

"Would you prefer the Al Rubaiyat again or another place?"

"The Al Rubaiyat, I think. I seem to remember that you promised me the show after dinner."

They were seated at the same table as the night before. During dinner Ram kept her laughing with anecdotes about his family, and some of the escapades of his two younger sisters. Meri smiled wistfully when he told of the time his youngest sister, Aziza, had brought her pet goat into her bedroom, and Ram tried to help her get it out before it ate the bedspread and their mother discovered them. They sounded like such a loving family. It seemed strange to think of this debonair man as a little boy sitting still while Suzan, his other sister, bandaged him with her doctor's kit or his taking the blame when she blew up the bathroom with her chemistry set. It made him more endearing.

"You sound like the perfect big brother. Don't you have any faults at all?"

He laughed. "Sometimes I think I tend to be overprotective. Suzan always said that I was dictatorial. I'm only two years older than she, and she resented my ordering her around."

"I can sympathize with that. How did she handle you?"

"When we were children, she kicked me in the shins," he said with a lopsided grin. "Nowadays we've both learned to be a bit more diplomatic, and she simply ignores me. Surely you didn't kick your big brother in the shins."

Meri shook her head. "I was an only child. What about Aziza?"

"She's ten years younger than I, and I spoiled her unmercifully. Aziza thinks I'm perfect."

He did seem perfect. Almost too good to be true. It made her suspicious. "Surely you have some other faults."

"Must I tell you all my secrets? Well, what I call persistence, my mother calls stubbornness. My father insists I inherited it from my mother, and on the other hand, my mother says I'm just like my father. She smiles when she says that."

"Where are your sisters now? Is Suzan still blowing up bathrooms?"

"No, she has two of her own to do that now. She and her husband are both physicians. They live in Paris where they do oncological research."

"And Aziza? Is she married too?"

"No, she and I are the holdouts. Aziza is in graduate school at Harvard. We're very proud of her."

"Do your parents live in Cairo?"

"Here or in Alexandria. They're . . . uh . . . traveling out of the country now."

"You have an incredible family." Listening to him caused a twinge of envy and a longing for the kind of family life she had missed. "You were going to tell me the story of how your parents and grandparents met."

"Ah, but only one story a night. Which would you like to hear first?"

"I'm intrigued by both of them." She propped her elbows on the table and rested her chin in her hands. "Tell me about your parents first."

Ram motioned for the waiter to clear the table and serve their coffee. After he took a sip he said, "Much to the chagrin of my mother's rather staid Dallas banking family, she became a journalist. She was assigned to her newspaper's Paris office and came to Cairo on a holiday. My father was having lunch one day here, in the Mena house, where my mother was staying. She walked into the restaurant and fainted at his feet. He fell in love with her before she ever regained consciousness. He picked her up and took her to my grandmother's clinic where it was discovered that she was severely anemic. After she was given a transfusion—my father's blood, by the way—he took her to my grandparents' house, and they cared for her until she was recovered."

"Did she fall in love with him right away?"

"Yes, but she was determined to go back to Paris and resume her career. My father was just as determined she would stay and marry him."

"How did they work it out?"

"After he had tried all manner of things to convince her, finally he locked her in her room and wouldn't let her out until she promised to marry him."

"Did your grandparents allow that?"

Ram chuckled. "My grandfather helped him. He understood about independent women, you see."

"From your grandmother?"

"We'll have to save that tale for another night. As it turned out, my mother and father were married, but two weeks after the wedding she went back to Paris. He followed her, and they lived there until she became pregnant with me. They returned to Cairo barely in time for my birth. They're still very much in love and have been happily married for thirty-seven years now."

"What a delightful story! I can see where you get your stubbornness."

"Persistence," Ram corrected.

"Did your mother ever return to her writing?"

"A few years ago. She . . . uh . . . is into a different sort of medium these days. Come dance with me. I want to hold you in my arms."

With Meri's head nestled against his shoulder and his cheek rested on her forehead, he held her close to him while they moved as one to the soft tempo of a love song. He massaged and stoked her lower back as if he wanted to absorb her into him. He drew her hand to his mouth and tasted the tip of each finger with his tongue. Chill bumps raced across her skin. Wisps of warmth rose up and intensified into trailing misty tendrils of longing.

Of their own volition, the fingers of her left hand threaded themselves through the dark curls above his collar, lightly caressed the side of his neck, and toyed with his earlobe.

Ram crushed her to him and moaned softly, "How I want you, love. I can't get you close enough to me. You were destined to be mine from the beginning of time. I'll never let you go."

For a brief moment her longing echoed his, and she molded herself closer to him. Then she caught herself. What was she doing? She hardly knew this man. She couldn't let herself get involved with him. As incredible as he was, this situation was too complicated.

She pulled away. "Let's sit down. Please."

"What's wrong? You're beginning to understand. I could feel it."

"Please."

He led her back to the table but refused to let the matter rest. "Tell me what's wrong. You draw away when I try to touch you—to reach you." With her hand clasped in his, he looked deeply into her eyes, as if by will alone he could impart some special awareness. "I have to make you understand. I want you to stay with me and be my love. Marry me and I'll give you joy and laughter. I'll try my best to get the sun and the moon for you."

For a moment Meri was caught up in an impetuous mood his words had sparked. Then as reason returned, she shook her head and jerked her hands away. What was the matter with her? "Stop all this crazy talk. I can't marry you. I only met you yesterday. You don't know anything about me."

"We've known each other forever." When he noted her skeptical look, he sighed. "I can see I have my work cut out for me. Tell me all about yourself. Don't leave anything out. Were you an adorable little princess as a child? I'll bet you wore ruffles and had silver curls."

"Hardly. I was a skinny tomboy with pigtails." Grateful when the lights suddenly dimmed, she said, "Oh, good. The show is about to begin."

When the house lights darkened, Ram turned his chair and placed it beside hers facing the stage. As the curtain opened, musicians in native dress played horns, drums, and stringed instruments that were unfamiliar to Meri, but the sound was the same one that reminded her of every movie she had ever seen of the mysterious Middle East. The muted whine of the horns and flutes were mixed with the jingles and thumps of the percussion as a small troop performed a folk ballet. Meri was more aware of Ram's arm across the back of her chair than she was the dancers.

As the group took their bows, he leaned close to her ear and whispered, "I think you'll enjoy this next act."

The room was thrown into complete darkness as the musicians began to play a soft, slow beat. A spotlight fell on the dance floor and revealed a woman curled over on her knees. Thick, waist-length hair and its flowing red veil covered her. Red and gold sequins and crystals reflected a dazzling, pulsating fire.

Slowly her hand and arm began to rise in a weaving snake-like motion; the *ping-ping* of her finger cymbals joined in the throbbing, whining rhythm. The other arm slithered up to add its *ping-ping,* and Ram's hand slipped over Meri's shoulder.

The dancer's body unfurled with a sensuous, stretching motion until she was standing. A full skirt of beaded red gossamer hung low on her hips; jeweled cups held her full breasts. Led by the brass beat of her fingers, the tempo increased, and her whole body began to undulate, bare skin and muscles rippling as she moved.

Ram's hand kneaded Meri's neck and shoulder to the same sensuous rhythm. As he stroked the soft velour of her dress, her skin caught fire. Her womb pulsated with an aching beat and quickened with the faster flash of whirling skirts and wild undulation of the dancer's hips and belly.

Meri's breath came fast and shallow; a soft glow of perspiration covered her upper lip. Ram laid his other hand lightly on her thigh, his fingers moving almost imperceptibly against the velour's grain. His heat seared through the fabric. She glanced at him out of the corner of her eye and found that he was watching her, not the dancer.

For an unsettling instant, she felt herself in a dancer's body, his eyes locked on her as she danced for him. She could hear the snap of wind against the tent, smell roasted meat and ripe fruit. She could feel the cymbals on her fingers and the rug beneath her feet. Twirling and twisting, skirts swirling, her breasts, hips, and belly rippled as she gyrated to the fevered beat.

Blood charged through her veins as he increased the tempo of his stroking. With a frenzied, whirling crescendo she dropped to her knees in a posture of supplication.

The music stopped. The lights died.

She sucked in a deep breath and shook her head.

As the houselights slowly came up, Meri glanced toward Ram. He gazed at her with undisguised longing. White-hot streaks of desire surged forth to meet the force beckoning from him.

Quickly, she averted her flaming face, took another deep breath, and willed her pulse to slow.

"Meri?"

She turned back to Ram, who was obviously waiting for her response. She cleared her throat. "I'll say one thing for her: She certainly has good muscle control."

He threw back his head and laughed. "Granted. Did you enjoy it?"

"I'm not sure if *enjoy* is the proper term." She felt overwhelmed and somehow vulnerable. Vague memories of having danced that way before him many times clung to the edge of her awareness. Her body seemed so intuitively familiar with the intricate movements—the ripple of the belly, the gyrations of the torso, the swing and thrust of the hips—that it squirmed with tiny motions straining to be unleashed. At that moment she was absolutely sure that she could have stood, raised her arms, and begun dancing perfectly. She didn't understand the sensation, and it unnerved her.

She couldn't use dehydration as an excuse this time. Maybe it was Ram, his heady proximity, and of both a rampant imagination and a monumental case of projection. Must be. Had to be. She was decidedly damp. She fidgeted.

"Would you like another drink?"

"I think I'd rather have some air. I feel like I've just gone through seduction by proxy. Let's go outside and walk."

He chuckled. *"Sukkar,* I don't do anything by proxy. And certainly not seduction."

Lord, you wouldn't say that if you knew what you've been doing in my dreams, Meri thought.

Guiding her from the room, he led her through the white marble hallway to the stairs and down to the grounds. As they strolled through the gardens by the pool, she breathed in the night air. Its coolness soothed her flushed face and overwarm skin. After a few minutes in the chilly evening, she shivered. Ram draped the mink around her.

"Would you like to take a drive into the city?"

She shook her head. "This has been a trying day for me. I think I'm suffering from sensory overload. What I need is to go to bed."

A roguish gleam came in his eyes. "I'm for that. I have a big bed in my suite. Would it do?"

It was tempting—very tempting, but it was not her style. "No, you scoundrel," she said with a levity she didn't feel. "I need my own bed. Alone."

Pulling her to him, he kissed her forehead. "You can't blame me for trying. You are the most beautiful, enchanting creature in the entire universe, but I'll be patient a little longer."

She suddenly felt shy, and she had never been shy in her life. She tried to speak, but no words came.

Lifting her chin with his finger, he asked, "Don't you know how lovely and desirable you are? I can't keep my hands off you."

"I don't ever think much about it. I guess my mind is on other things." Was she really lovely and desirable? Even if it weren't true, it warmed her to think he saw her that way. Made her feel cherished and . . . feminine.

"My God, woman. I don't believe it. Every man at the restaurant tonight had his eyes on you."

"I think they were watching the belly dancer. How does she move like that? I'd be too sore to walk."

Ram laughed and hugged her to him. "It takes practice—lots of practice."

When they reached her door, he took the key from her purse and turned the lock. "I have an important business meeting in the morning that I can't cancel. But I'd like to meet you and your friend for lunch, and tomorrow afternoon I'll give you the deluxe tour of the Cairo Museum. Would you like that?"

Meri hesitated. By lunchtime she would be in Aswan or Abu Simbel. As much as she was enchanted with this man, she knew that, for a score of reasons, there could be no future to a relationship with him. But she'd also learned that he simply wouldn't take no for an answer, and she and Welcome had a job to do.

She decided to take the easy way out. "Sounds fine."

She felt rotten about deceiving him. When he found her gone tomorrow, he'd be angry—and rightfully so. But knowing he would try to stop her or go with her if she told him of her plans to leave, she had taken the coward's way out. She would leave him a note.

Standing on tiptoe, she kissed his cheek and hugged him. "Ram, I can't begin to tell you how special being with you has been to me." Tears came to her eyes. "Thank you." She kissed his other cheek and clung to him for a moment before she stepped back. "Good night," she murmured.

"Good night, love. I'll see you at lunchtime."

She went inside, closed the door, and leaned back against it. All dreams ended sooner or later. She had collected wonderful memories to warm her on a cold, lonely night. Her fingers caressed the soft fur; she nestled her cheek in Ram's smell that still clung to its luxury, then sighed as she took it off and carefully folded it in the tissue-lined box. Gathering the other gifts he had given her, she placed them on top—all but the perfume and the hairpins—she couldn't part with them. She would keep the stars and the essence of promises. And the essence of goose. She smiled at the cheap scarab necklace he'd bought from a vendor at the Pyramids and tucked it in her suitcase.

And the falcon pectoral? What about it? She slipped the chain over her head and held the pendant in her palm. She wasn't sure exactly how he'd pulled it off, but she knew that he was responsible for its being in her possession. Some subliminal flickering made her wonder if there was a connection between the falcon and the bizarre experiences she'd been having.

Silly, she told herself. Heat, stress, dehydration she could buy. An inanimate piece of jewelry? No way. Ridiculous. She added the pectoral to the pile of gifts, then hesitated. She picked it up, cradled its warmth in her palms, felt the faint hum against her skin. Her throat tightened at the thought of never seeing it again, never holding it, never feeling its heat against her breast.

Get a grip, Meri.

Before she went all maudlin, she crammed the pendant between the folds of the coat and slammed the lid on the box.

After she packed her bags and was ready for bed, Meri sat down to write a note to deceive Ram once again. Deception wasn't her style, and she felt like a dirty dog for being so underhanded, but it was the lesser of two bad choices. She didn't like confrontations either.

As she tapped the pen against her chin—trying to find the right words, regret cast a dark cloud over her. She would never hear the story of his grandparents.

She sniffled. A tear trickled down her cheek.

Good God, Meri Vaughn, you're such a dweeb. She grabbed a tissue, blew her nose, and began to write.

His coat and tie discarded, his shirt unbuttoned and pulled loose, Ram stood on the dark balcony of his suite, the balcony that adjoined Meri's, though she didn't know it. Leaning against the railing and staring through the starry night, he imagined Meri getting undressed, preparing for bed.

He hadn't wanted to let her go to her room alone. He'd wanted to take her to his bed and whisper endless love words into her ear, taste the sweetness of her full lips, touch her soul with his fingers. His love and longing for her was almost a palpable, painful thing. God, how long he'd ached for her, waited for her, loved her in his dreams. He could almost taste her creamy skin on his tongue, and he licked his lips, savoring the sensation.

Soon, soon she would be his again. In the flesh. Permanently. Or at least for this lifetime.

If his impatience didn't make him reckless.

Nervously, he raked his fingers through his hair. He knew that if he didn't watch it, he'd be acting like his father or grandfather—locking her up or kidnapping her to make her his. He chuckled at the thought. His little Texan would give him the very devil if he tried it.

This waiting was pure hell; he wouldn't sleep much tonight. He wanted to spend every hour with her. Damn that meeting in the morning. He would have to wait until noon to be with her again. It was tempting to cancel the appointment, but Tewfik Fayed, the head of the *Mabaheth,* had told Ram's secretary that it was urgent that they talk as soon as possible. If Tewfik had said it was urgent, Ram had no choice but to meet with the man. Roughly Egypt's equivalent to the director of the FBI, Tewfik wasn't given to exaggeration. What could be wrong?

Eight

Ah, but men look like gem-birds. Squalor is throughout the land. There is none whose clothes are white in these times.

The Admonitions of Ipuwer
c. 2180-1990 B.C.

His eyes grown accustomed to the dark, he stood in the shadow of a jasmine bush and watched two areas on the upper floor of the Mena House. The lights went out in the first, the one he knew to be Meri Vaughn's room, the room that held the key to his fortune—the falcon pectoral.

He had known that it was valuable, but when Nabil Taher had told him what a buyer would pay for the piece, he was astounded. Even with Taher's quarter commission deducted, it was an amazing sum. Of course Taher, that wily old jackal, was probably getting even more than the price he had quoted, but he had decided not to be greedy and haggle with the dealer. Through his world-wide network of contacts, Taher had both the buyer and the means of smuggling the pectoral out of Egypt.

No, he would not be greedy. The sum Taher had offered would support him in style for the rest of his days. If he claimed the pectoral before someone else did. He was not so naive as to believe that others wouldn't have the same notion.

Curbing his musing, his gaze again went to Meri Vaughn's room. How long before she would be asleep? Dare he enter while she slept? He knew the layout of the room from his search earlier in the evening when the occupants were absent. For one as experienced as he, the lock had been a simple matter. A shame that the pectoral had not been there then. The other jewels he found had been tempting, but he had restrained himself, knowing that the pectoral was vastly more valuable.

His gaze slid to the second area. Gabrey still lingered on the balcony of the suite next door. No, this was not the time. He would wait. He patted the notebook in his pocket. He knew where Meri Vaughn would be; he would be there too. Waiting.

Patience.

He smiled and slipped away into the darkness.

Nine

My heart is disturbed when I think of him.
Love of him has seized me captive.
"But he's out of his mind!"
"Yes, and so am I—as much so as he!"

Love Songs of the New Kingdom
c. 1550-1080 B.C.

Meri yawned and held her coffee cup for a refill from the flight attendant.

"I'm glad to see I'm not the only one with tail feathers dragging this morning," Welcome said. "You're usually so chipper in the mornings that it's vulgar. Late night?"

"No, I came in fairly early. I just didn't sleep too well." That was an understatement—she'd hardly slept at all. She felt guilty about lying to Ram, guilty about leaving a note with his gifts, guilty about being such a sneak.

It had hurt to write and tell him that she was leaving the country, but she had a strong premonition that she would have ended up locked in a room like his mother if she'd told him the truth. Frankly, she wasn't too sure one part of her would have minded; the other part of her abhorred the idea of such caveman tactics. In the end, she'd taken the easy way out and left the package and the note with the desk clerk. By the time he received them, she and Welcome would be long gone.

She'd done the right thing she was sure. But if she'd done the right thing, why did she feel so miserable?

"You look like you've been yanked through a knothole backwards," Welcome said. "Must be man trouble. You haven't fallen for that Egyptian playboy, have you?"

"Who?" Meri asked, trying to feign wide-eyed innocence.

Welcome rolled her eyes. *"Who?* she says. Who were you out with—Omar Sharif?"

"How could I have fallen for Ram? I met him only two days ago. Or at least I think I did."

"Want to run that by me again?"

"Welcome, do you believe that we've lived other lives?"

"You mean reincarnation? I've read a little about it, and I always figured that it made as much sense as anything else. I'm not sure I believe in it, but I'd say that I'm open to the idea. I was hypnotized once and regressed back to another life. I was hoping that I'd discover that I was a Russian princess or something, but I lived in a squalid little hut with a passel of snot-nosed kids. God, it was ghastly." Welcome rolled her eyes. "Why do you ask? Think you've known Ram Gabrey before?"

"I don't know. Sounds kind of stupid, doesn't it? But with all the weird things that have been happening to me, I'm beginning to wonder. I've never thought too much about it before. Pop is the one who's into the karma and past life stuff. I just figured it was a holdover from his hippie days."

"Sweetie, your father is still a hippie. Want to tell me what's been going on?"

Meri related the latest of the strange happenings, and, to give her credit, Welcome didn't so much as raise an eyebrow. "The dreams, the visions, it's all incredibly bizarre. I've tried to chalk it off to stress, the heat, dehydration, any sort of reasonable explanation I could think of, but somehow it doesn't wash. Ram and Egypt seem to have a strange effect on me, and it's damned scary."

"From what you've told me, the whole thing sounds incredibly romantic to me. I should be so lucky."

"Lucky? With men like Philip and Eduard panting after you, I wouldn't say that you're deprived."

"Panting is the operative word. The only thing Philip has proposed is a roll in the hay, and Eduard—well, I've explained about Eduard."

Meri giggled. "He's a wimp. But Philip strikes me as being *all* man. At first I thought he was a veddy, veddy cultured diplomatic type, but after being around him more, I've discovered that under all that polish is a hard edge. *He's* no wimp. And I think he's definitely interested in more than a roll in the hay with you. I saw you two whispering at the airport."

"Trust me. I've known Philip for a long time. Any kind of serious relationship isn't in the cards. We're merely friends."

"If you ask me, I think you might be missing a bet there. Wasn't he a sweetheart to scrounge up a lens for my Leica? You know how I love that old camera Pop gave me, but after the lens broke, I was sure that I wouldn't be able to use it for the rest of the trip. And I don't know that we'll need the letters of introduction that he gave us, but it was a nice thought. He's very handsome, and—"

"Meri, he's married."

"Oh."

"Yes, oh."

Meri sighed. "Well, so much for our love life."

"So much for *my* love life. Ram Gabrey isn't married, and he's one hell of a man."

"He is one hell of a man. Under the right circumstances, Ram would be easy to fall for, but all the 'Twilight Zone' business freaks me out. Besides that, I have sense enough to know I'm just a simple gal from the USA. We're from different countries, different cultures; we have different backgrounds and different goals. You don't simply meet someone on the street, point, and say, 'I'm going to marry you.' Things could never work out for us in a million years."

"Who are you trying to convince, sweetie? Me or you?"

Meri sighed and settled back in her seat. "Myself, I guess. The whole thing's too weird. I'll never see him again anyway."

"If he's as determined as you say he is, I wouldn't count on it."

"He'll never find me. In the note I left I told him we were flying to Rome."

Ten

Do not say, "Today is like tomorrow," for how could these things end?
When tomorrow comes, and today is gone,
the flood may have become a sandbank,
the crocodiles uncovered of water,
the hippopotamuses on dry land,
the fish gasping for breath . . .

Proverbs of Amen-em-Ope
c. 900-650 B.C. or 1580-1320 B.C.

"And how are your father and lovely mother?" Tewfik Fayed asked, stirring his coffee.

"Well, thank you," Ram said. He sipped from his cup as they sat on the balcony off the director's office. "They are in the United States at present. My mother is on a publicity tour for her current book."

"Ah, yes. *Rubies at Noon*. Fine work."

Ram raised an eyebrow at the director of the *Mabaheth*. "You read my mother's mysteries?"

"But of course: I love a good murder." He laughed at his own joke, and the gold crowns on his teeth flashed. "Especially when it's not my responsibility. Have a pastry?"

Ram declined the proffered plate, sipped his coffee, and waited patiently for the director to state his business. Tewfik

Fayed was a wily old coot, innately perceptive and Oxford educated, who knew everything of consequence that went on in Egypt. And some inconsequential things as well. The demands of his office were such that he was entirely too busy to fritter away a morning making small talk. His loose jowls and slightly protuberant eyes with their accompanying bags always made Ram think of a hound—which was exactly what he was. And he was on the scent of something.

Fayed selected a muffin, slathered it with butter, and proceeded to devour it slowly. Ram waited, knowing that Fayed would get to the point of this meeting when he was ready.

"I understand that you've recently been escorting a lovely American lady about. Meritaten Vaughn, I believe her name is."

Ram tensed. "I didn't realize that my social life came under the scrutiny of the *Mabaheth*."

Fayed laughed heartily. "It is *her* social life under scrutiny. Tell me what you know of Miss Vaughn and her friend."

Ram frowned. "I can't imagine what interest you would have in these women. Meri, Miss Vaughn, is a professional photographer from Texas. Her mother and mine are old friends, and she is here at the invitation of Horus Hotels to make photographs for a brochure. I haven't met her companion, but she is the model for the pictures. I believe her name is Welcome."

"Ah, yes, the lovely Miss Venable. I understand that she is something of a celebrity and ordinarily commands very large fees. This brochure must be very costly."

"Not exceedingly so. As I said, Welcome, Miss Venable, is a friend of Miss Vaughn's. I believe that they are partners in the company that's producing the piece."

Fayed leaned back and folded his hand over his ample girth. "Ah."

Ram waited. When nothing more was forthcoming, he asked, "What is your interest in these women?"

The director shrugged. "Maybe nothing. Maybe something." He reached for another muffin, buttered it, then said, "I understand that Miss Vaughn has been seen wearing an unusual necklace."

Ram prickled. "How does her jewelry concern you?"

Fayed ate the muffin slowly and licked his fingers. "Need I remind you that the penalty for taking antiquities from the country is five to twenty-five years?"

His jaw tightened, and his eyes narrowed. "The pendant she wears is from me. I've owned it for many, many years."

"Ah."

Ram fought the urge to squirm under the director's watchful inspection. His answer was, after all, truthful. He saw no reason to go into detail about matters the pragmatic Fayed would be hard pressed to accept. Hell, sometimes even he had a hard time understanding the situation.

Fayed sipped his coffee. "You might caution the lady to be very careful of such . . . an unusual necklace. There are many who would covet such a fine piece—believing it to be an antiquity, of course."

"Of course. I'll remind her. Now if you'll excuse me—" Ram stood.

Fayed waved him back to his seat. "Another question or two, please."

"Yes?"

"Do you know a Mr. Philip Van Horn?"

Frowning, Ram searched his memory. "The name seems vaguely familiar."

"He is attached to the American Embassy here. I understand that he was previously in Paris—where Miss Venable resides. Tall man, blond-haired."

"Ah, yes," Ram said. "I recall meeting him at a party at the Embassy a few nights ago. Why do you ask?"

Fayed blotted his lips with a napkin, slowly wiped his fingers with it, then placed it on the table. He leaned back, laced his fingers over his belly again, and studied Ram. "I ask because we have strong suspicions that Mr. Van Horn is an agent of the American CIA."

"So?"

"So, he has been seen frequently in the company of Miss Vaughn and Miss Venable."

Ram forced his expression to remain calm. "I see. I wasn't aware of that." He chuckled. "But I can't imagine Meri being a spy. As I said, my mother and hers are very old friends, and we are all but engaged. I'm sure their meetings with this man were completely innocent."

"Perhaps. But before they boarded the airplane this morning Mr. Van Horn was observed handing documents to both women and a package to Miss Vaughn."

Panic, sudden and overwhelming, surged through Ram. "What airplane?" he asked, gripping the arms of his chair.

Fayed flicked a crumb from his necktie. "The airplane to Aswan. It departed at eight twenty-three."

"Damn!" Ram muttered.

"Am I to understand that you didn't know of their departure?"

"Correct. Something must have come up since I spoke with her last night." He stood. "Now if you will excuse me, sir, I have pressing matters to attend to."

The director stood as well, a small smile playing around his lips. "Certainly. Thank you for coming." He offered his hand. "I'm sure that, as you say, this is all very innocent, but I trust that you will be sure to inform my office if you discover anything . . . of national interest."

"Of course, sir."

Ram wheeled and hurried from the office and to his car, muttering blistering oaths all the way. He hoped his security force wasn't as sloppy as he was.

Royally pissed that he'd been caught with his pants down, he drove like a madman toward the Mena House.

Eleven

I have come and I have drawn nigh to see thy beauties . . . And I have entered in unto the place of secret and hidden things.

The Papyrus of Ani
(Egyptian Book of the Dead)
c. 1500-1400 B.C.

At the airport in Aswan, Welcome handed Meri an envelope. "What's this?"

Welcome grinned. "A surprise. I know how much you wanted to see Abu Simbel and how tight our schedule is. I'll go on to the hotel, check in, and scout our locations. If I do that, you can join a tour flying out to Abu Simbel in about half an hour. How does that sound?"

"Wonderful! I was sick that I was going to have to miss it. Are you sure you don't mind?"

"Not a bit. Tramping around dirty ruins doesn't excite me the way it does you. I prefer a shady veranda and a cool drink. Come on. You're supposed to meet the group over here." Welcome bumped against a man standing at her elbow and murmured an absent, "Excuse me," then hurried Meri toward a group of about a dozen senior citizens, mostly women, and their leader who was holding a sign proclaiming GOLDEN YEARS TRAVEL CLUB.

When Meri raised her eyebrow at her friend, Welcome snickered. "It's the best I could do on short notice. Don't worry, at the rate you're moving this morning, you'll be lucky to keep up with them. I'll take your bags to the hotel. You should be back here about two, and I'll be waiting." Welcome gave Meri a quick peck on the cheek. "Have fun, sweetie," she called, wiggling her fingers as she raced off.

There was barely time for her to introduce herself to their guide before they were herded onto the plane for the quick flight to Abu Simbel.

A short, plump woman with cotton-white curls and a light pink gauze tent dress eased herself into the seat beside Meri. Her warm smile spread to crinkling gray eyes. "Hello. I'm Nona Craft."

"Meri Vaughn." It was impossible to keep from responding to her sunny smile. She was somewhere between a cherub and a fairy godmother.

"We're so glad you're joining us today. It's good to have a young person around." She leaned closer and whispered, "I asked to sit with you to get away from Esther. She's my cousin as well as my roommate, you know, and such a stick-in-the-mud. Has been for over forty years—ever since her husband ran off with his secretary. Good riddance, I said, but Esther, who was always so beautiful and vivacious—she just dried up like a prune. Why, she wouldn't even climb up in the Great Pyramid. Can you imagine coming to Egypt and not going in it? Afraid, she said. Ridiculous! You can't live life like that. You've got to seize it with both hands," she said, her voice growing louder and her plump fists gesturing fiercely.

"And Leah Henry over there"—Nona pointed to a woman two rows up—"she's been planning this trip for a year. But when her son and his wife—they're biologists at Kent State—decided to do research for a year in the Amazon and dump their child with her, she was going to cancel. No way, I told her. Bring the little scamp along. Most of us have grandkids.

Nobody will care. But let me tell you, that Bradley is a piece of work. That's him sitting by Leah. Twelve years old, smart as a whip. But he's a corker. Curious and high-spirited his parents call him, but I could call him a few other things. If Leah weren't such a good friend, I'd turn that scamp over my knee—" She stopped with a chuckle. "Listen to me go on. Now, I want to know all about you and what you've seen."

They laughed and chatted for the rest of the flight and the bus ride to the temple site. Nona, as she asked Meri to call her, introduced her to the other energetic group members from Atlanta. Before long they adopted her as sort of a mascot—except for Esther Barrington, who was more formally dressed than the others and kept herself aloof from the fun-loving friends.

When they arrived, Dr. Stockton, a distinguished-looking and courtly gentleman who was a retired dentist, helped most of the ladies down from the bus. Meri had warmed to him instantly. There was something in his soft manner, his quiet strength, the gentle cadence of his Southern speech that reminded her of her Uncle Jasper, who had always been her favorite relative.

When he assisted Esther his smile brightened, but she quickly disengaged her hand with a sniff and walked away. The tall, slender man looked wistfully at her stiff back. When he noticed Meri watching, he said sadly, "She's a fine figure of a woman. It's too bad . . ."

Meri looped her arm through his and said, "I guess you'll just have to settle for me." They walked to the edge of the rocky cliff and the steps leading down to the temple. "How long have you loved her?" Meri asked quietly.

He gazed out over the calm, blinding-blue waters of Lake Nasser. A small steamer skimmed its surface. "From the first moment I saw her over thirty years ago."

"For thirty years?" Meri was astonished. "Does she know?"

"She knows." Dr. Stockton was silent for a few moments,

then added, "You see, she was hurt very badly many years ago, and she never could let herself forget."

"Nona told me." A wave of sadness washed over her as she thought of the empty, wasted years of these dear souls. The lonely feeling was akin to what she'd felt at Sakkara.

Dr. Stockton touched her arm and brought her attention back to him. "Don't look so disturbed, my dear. I've learned patience through the years. Where there is life, there is hope. A cliché, I know, but true, true. I believe it was Pliny who said, 'Hope is the pillar that holds up the world. Hope is the dream of a waking man.' There is always hope."

Meri patted his hand. "She doesn't know what she's missing."

"Enough of this maudlin talk, young lady. Let's see the temple." As they descended the steps, he added, "Did you know that Walter Rush, who I met on the plane, was one of the group involved in the moving of this site? He's worked all around this part of the country for years. British, I believe he is. Interesting fellow. He's the one giving the impromptu lecture."

They joined the others standing at the foot of the four colossal seated statues of Ramses II and listened as wiry, leather-skinned Walter Rush described the enormous feat involved in moving the temple, which was carved out of the side of sandstone cliffs. Searing sunlight glared off his round, gold-rimmed spectacles, and a hot breeze stirred thin sandy-gray wisps of his sparse hair. He told how these monuments of Nubia, which faced the sun as it rose over the southernmost part of the Upper Kingdom, were dismantled and reassembled on top of the cliff to save the site from the rising waters when the dam was built.

Rush waved his hand toward the four sixty-five foot Ramses statues which sat at the entrance. "This is a man-made mountain behind the monuments. The temple was duplicated exactly inside it. Even the broken pieces of this Ramses are lying at the same angle where they fell centuries before."

Meri snapped his picture as he stood before the mammoth

carvings. "Why weren't they restored when they were moved?" she asked.

Rush glared at her, then drew himself up and answered curtly, "We considered it but decided our mission was to duplicate, not restore."

A Nubian guide led the group through the innermost chambers and to the sanctuary where he explained that twice a year, at the equinox, the rays of the rising sun illuminated its altar and statues.

"Cool!" said Bradley, who proceeded to climb on the altar to check out the angle.

Leah Henry, the boy's harried grandmother, dragged him down. "Bradley, please behave."

"But Gram—"

"No buts."

Bradley looked disgruntled and kicked at a pottery shard on the dusty ground.

Meri wandered away from the others to take pictures and examine the carvings and paintings on the walls. She turned around to take a photo of the group, just as an Egyptian man with a drooping eyelid ducked behind a pillar. Strange, she thought. Hadn't she seen him before? She shrugged. He must be sightseeing too.

Anxious to see the inside of the false mountain, Meri decided to do a little exploring on her own and told Nona she would meet them back at the bus. She searched out the entrance and went up the steps. Pulling open the heavy door, she was astounded by what she saw when she stepped inside.

The metal door slammed behind her with a loud hollow echo that reverberated through the huge inverted bowl of steel and concrete. Shadows of supporting girders loomed from the dimly lit quiet. Standing on a catwalk about halfway up, she leaned over the railing and peered down to its floor and then up to the ceiling which rose several stories. It was like a smaller version of the Houston Astrodome, empty except for beams and layers of walkways crisscrossing its interior. It was an engineering marvel. She had to get a picture of this.

An eerie silence filled the cavernous space. The only sounds she heard were her own breathing and the faint hum of a generator. Even the rubber soles of her shoes rebounded with a *thump-thump* as she climbed the metal steps to a higher span for a better angle. Leaning against a thick post, she reached for her camera.

Suddenly the huge dome was plunged into total darkness.

She sucked in her breath, and her heart began pounding furiously. She was stranded on the narrow walkway high above the gaping concrete pit.

Don't panic! she told herself. *It's just a temporary power failure. The lights will be back on in a minute.*

She slid down the post and sat on the cool metal span. A fine sheen of nervous perspiration seeped into her clothing and covered her upper lip. Blindly, she felt through her canvas tote for matches. She knew that there were none, but it gave her something to do while she waited.

And waited.

She waited for what seemed like hours, but according to her digital watch had been only a few minutes.

Finally she heard the soft echo of the door being opened. She breathed a sigh of relief and was about to call out, when some strange sixth sense held her tongue. Leaning around the post which hid her, she looked toward the open door and saw a man silhouetted in its bright light.

As the door closed behind him, he flicked a cigarette lighter, paused to light a cigarette, then held up the flame and scanned the interior as if he were looking for someone. The puny flame of the lighter illuminated only a small area around him; it didn't make a dent in the vast darkness of the structure.

Adjusting the telephoto lens of her camera, she zoomed in on his face.

She sucked in a gasp when she saw a darting brown eye and one hidden by a drooping lid.

Quickly she ducked back behind the post and held her breath as her heart began to pound even faster. Beams of a flashlight played over the hollow hulking bowl.

It was *him* again! He was following her. Visions of all her mother's dire predictions flashed through her head—rape, kidnapping—

Murder.

She stayed glued to the spot, controlling her breathing with iron determination until she heard the heavy metal door clank shut. With its closing the building was once again totally dark and silent.

Slowly she peeked around the column toward the entrance. No one was there. At least no one that she could see. She almost giggled hysterically. He could be three feet from her, and she couldn't see him.

Cocking her head, she strained to listen with every fiber of her body. All she could hear was the faint hum of the generator, her own rapid breathing, and the blood vessels pumping on the sides of her neck.

She had to get out of that place. But how? If she tried to make it out in the dark, there was a strong possibility she would end up as a large grease spot on the concrete bottom of this false mountain.

Surely somebody would look for her. Sit tight. Wait.

Why hadn't she thought to bring a flashlight? There was one in her suitcase. A fat lot of good it did her here.

She heard a faint scrape and almost wet her pants.

Was that a footstep?

Nerve endings standing at attention, she held her breath and listened.

Another scrape. Distant, but definitely a scrape.

Dear God, he was coming after her!

She had to escape.

Don't panic. Think!

An idea wiggled out of her desperation. The flash on her camera. Of course!

DREAM OF ME   109

Carefully she stood, hitched her tote over her shoulder, and aimed the camera in front of her. Flash. Two steps. Flash. Two steps. She hadn't gone more than a dozen feet when the dim lights of the dome flickered on. Letting out a big "Whew," she hastily clamored down from her perch and made tracks for the far exit. Glancing back over her shoulder, she yanked open the door and slammed into a human mountain.

She shrieked and jumped back, but two ham fists held her upper arms. She tried to break away and run, but the viselike grip lifted her off the floor until she was looking eye to eye with a broken-nosed giant. Wildly she kicked and pounded against the block of granite.

"Easy, little lady. Easy. Be calm. I'm not going to hurt you," he said. "Everything's okay now. Somebody accidentally flipped the master switch, and the lights went off for a couple of minutes."

Meri splayed her hand across her chest and breathed deeply, feeling like a limp noodle after the adrenaline deserted her and she turned to mush. "Holy cow. I was scared to death. Sorry I whacked you."

"Don't blame you a bit. I'da been scared myself."

She looked at the size of him and smiled. "Somehow I doubt that."

"Believe it. I'm not fond of the dark. You look as pale as a ghost. Come over here and sit down. Can I buy you a Coke or something?"

"I'd love it." She sat on a rock under a scraggly tree and waited until he returned with two drinks. "Thanks." She took a sip and rolled the cold bottle across her forehead. "I really appreciate this."

"Ain't no big thing. Glad to do it."

"You sound like somebody from my part of the world," she said to her rescuer.

He grinned. "George Mszanski, ma'am. Tulsa, Oklahoma."

"Sooner, huh?" She cocked her head. "That name seems very familiar."

"I played a little football a few years back."

"Dallas Cowboys, right? You're *that* George Mszanski? I'd say you played more than a little." She stuck out her hand. "Meri Vaughn, Houston. I'm very pleased to meet you. Are you part of a tour group?"

"Naw, my friend and I have been knocking around by ourselves until now." He raked sweat off his forehead with a finger and flicked it to one side. "Tomorrow we're going to take one of those cruises on the Nile. How about you?"

"I'm with a friend, taking photographs for a brochure. We flew to Aswan from Cairo this morning. I just joined a group for this excursion. My friend had some other things to do. We're leaving on a cruise tomorrow too."

"Where are you staying in Aswan?"

"The Oberoi, the hotel on the island."

"That's where we're staying. Say, that's great. Maybe we'll be on the same ship." He broke into a big grin that made his tough face almost handsome. Then he knitted his brow and ran a hand through his short, light brown curls. "Uh, your friend. Male or female?"

"Very female," Meri answered with a chuckle.

His grin was back. "Great, that's great! How about if we all have dinner together at the hotel tonight?"

"Sounds like fun. I'll have to check with Welcome first. Call me later." Meri looked up and waved when she saw Nona and the others approaching. "Here comes my group. Are you going back on this bus?"

"We're on the next one. Hey, I'll call you later," he said, as he loped off back toward the temple.

George was a nice man—more in her league than Ram. Of course he didn't affect her the same way Ram did, but he was nice—and safe. When she thought of Ram, she could almost smell him—could see his smiling face, his blue eyes as they caressed her, could feel his virile body molding hers as they danced. These things were carved into her memory, but she pushed them aside as she walked toward the bus.

George was a nice man. And Tulsa was closer to home than Cairo.

Her group was chattering excitedly as they boarded the old army-green bus. As Walter Rush ground out his Turkish cigarette with the heel of his boot and helped the ladies up the steps, Nona said, "Meri, you come sit here with us," taking her by the arm and guiding her to the back. "Walter's going to tell us more about how they cut everything up and used giant cranes to move the pieces."

It was fascinating to hear the tales. Still laughing at a comment Mr. Rush had made, Meri turned and glanced at Dr. Stockton. She followed his longing gaze toward the front of the bus. There she saw Esther Barrington, head erect, back straight, sitting three seats behind the driver—alone. Meri turned again to the lighthearted group, but a pang of conscience brought her thoughts back to Esther. She could identify with the proud woman, knew the pain that had bound her, was drawn to the deep misery hidden behind the facade.

After arguing with herself for a moment and losing the familiar battle between hedonism and compassion, Meri heaved herself from her seat. As the bus bumped along the narrow blacktop that bisected the desolate fifteen mile expanse of hot rocky sand between Abu Simbel and the airport, she made her way down the aisle. Her body swayed from side to side as she moved forward using the backs of alternate seats to steady herself.

"May I join you?" Meri asked as she eased into the empty seat beside Mrs. Barrington. "Wasn't that the most magnificent place you've ever seen? To think they moved those gigantic statues piece by piece to keep them from flooding. And building a whole mountain! It boggles my mind."

"Yes," Esther replied keeping her eyes straight ahead. "It was quite lovely."

"And hot," added Meri as she fanned with her straw hat. She was determined to keep a conversation going.

"It was warm," agreed Esther as she delicately fluttered a white, lace-edged handkerchief near her face.

Esther patted the impeccable French twist holding her gray hair, smoothed an imaginary wrinkle from the skirt of her two-piece mauve dress, and clutched her purse tightly in her lap. Except for the concession of a pair of sensible tan walking shoes, the stately matron might be dressed for her regular Tuesday bridge luncheon. She probably even had on a girdle, Meri thought.

The bus jarred as it hit a pothole. Esther sipped in a breath of air, pursed her lips, and clutched her pocketbook more tightly.

"Are you all right?" Meri asked, noting the pained expression on her companion's face.

"Well, I do need to wash my hands," Esther whispered.

Meri reached down and picked up her canvas tote bag which was sitting on the floor at her feet. Holding it on her lap, she rummaged around through it for a moment before she pulled out a small foil packet and handed it wordlessly to Esther.

"What's this?" Esther asked.

"A moist towelette. For your hands."

"I don't want a towelette," she whispered again. "I need to powder my nose."

Biting back a chuckle, Meri said, "Oh, I see."

Mrs. Barrington straightened her back more stiffly, crossed her legs, and blinked back tears gathering in her eyes.

"There's the airport just ahead. It won't be long now." Seeing the real distress in the woman's face, Meri prepared to make a quick exit as the bus pulled to a stop in front of the small limestone building with its single airstrip.

Taking the proper lady in tow, Meri pushed past the other passengers and moved swiftly through the crowd inside the small terminal to the open door of the ladies' room. They both gasped as they stepped into the dingy room, crowded with both flies and people. Several women were already lined up to use one of the three stained booths. Alongside one wall were two sinks encrusted with years of grime and fly specks. A robed elderly Arab man, whose grin displayed several wide gaps between his four long yellow teeth, was presiding over the activities with great efficiency.

"Here, madam. Here, madam," he directed Meri and Esther, gesturing toward the end of the line.

With a great flourish he distributed three sheets of toilet paper to each lady in the line from the single roll held under his left arm. There was a great deal of twittering and eye-rolling among his charges. Many of them studied the soggy, sand streaked-floor or the flaking paint of the wall, and they were all trying to breathe as little as possible.

As a booth was vacated, he ceremoniously held open the door and indicated with a bow, "Next, madam." When the previous occupant tried to escape too quickly, he shamed and scolded with a twist of his turbaned head, "Here, madam," indicating the sink which had never encountered Comet or its Egyptian equivalent. The chastised lady held her hands under the faucet while he turned the water quickly on and off—just enough to wet her fingertips. He then offered the single filthy community towel, which he kept slung over his shoulder, and brazenly held out his hand for *baksheesh,* a tip.

Meri clamped her hand over her mouth to stifle a giggle before she turned and followed her stately companion who had fled the room. She found Esther sitting in the waiting area, red-faced and furiously fluttering her linen handkerchief.

"I'll wait," Esther announced as she composed herself. "Our flight will be leaving shortly."

Nona joined them as they waited. "Is something wrong?"

Esther nodded and Meri added, "There's a problem in the ladies' room."

"What problem?" Nona asked.

"There's a man attendant and Mrs. Barrington won't go with him in there," Meri whispered.

The taller woman kept glancing at her watch and clutching her purse as time for departure came and went. Her need was becoming greater and her pained expression more severe. A short, dark man with a black mustache and an airline uniform announced first in Arabic and then in English that due to a minor mechanical problem, the departure would be delayed for half an hour.

Esther blotted the drops of perspiration popping out on her forehead and turned to Nona in despair.

"What am I going to do? I can't use that filthy room with that man in there, but I can't wait much longer. Do you think they would let me use the accommodations on the plane? Nona, help me, please," she whispered as she frantically grasped her friend's hand.

Nona glanced around, then scurried off toward one of the young stewards she recognized from their flight. After a few moments of animated conversation, she returned to Esther shaking her head.

"Dear, I'm sorry. It's against regulations. You'll just have to use the facility here. Come on. We'll go with you."

Pulling Esther to her feet, the white-haired woman led the way back to the ladies' room with Meri following. They paused at the entrance and noticed the old man was still directing the ritual. Growing desperate, Esther Barrington motioned the attendant over.

"Sir, could you please leave the room for a moment?" pleaded Esther with as much dignity as she could muster under the circumstances.

"Oh, no, madam. It is my job. I must take care of my ladies. You wait here, madam." He indicated the end of the line and resumed his duties.

"I just can't do this," she whispered, turning to leave. "I could tolerate the filth, but not even my husband in the years we were married, ever came into the bathroom with me."

"Esther, convention be damned! This is stupid. You'll never see this man again and—"

"Oh, Nona. Oh, Nona," she whimpered grasping her cousin's hand. "I can't wait another second. I'm about to embarrass myself."

The wizened Arab, noting the stricken look on the matron's face, halted the procession and hurried over to her. "This way, madam. Quickly! Quickly!" he ordered as he rushed her into an empty booth. Then he turned and continued directing as before. Suddenly remembering something, he scurried over to Esther's cubicle, tore off a very long piece from his precious roll, and held it under the door.

"Here, madam."

The paper disappeared, and the door did not open for several minutes. When it did Esther came out, back straight, head high, and with what appeared to be a girdle rolled tightly under her arm. She marched over to the grimy sink, waited until the old man wet her fingertips, then daintily touched the dingy towel he held out to her. Pulling a five-pound note from her purse, she pressed it into his waiting hand.

"Thank you very much, sir, for your kind assistance," she said, bowing slightly.

Noting the size of his tip, he beamed a snaggle-toothed grin and bobbing repeatedly replied, "Delighted to be of service, my dear madam. Goodbye, *ma-salama.*"

Esther joined Nona and Meri who stood waiting at the door. The stately matron took the bundle from under her arm and slipped it into the big green tote bag Nona held.

"Hold on to this for me will you, Nona?" she asked. Her lips twitched as she hurried out of the room with Nona and Meri following.

When they were outside, Esther's shoulders began to shake. Meri became alarmed and rushed to her. Esther bowed her head, stifling a sound with her hand, and Nona patted her. The stately matron's head flew up and her eyes were dancing.

She was laughing! She tried to control herself, but one snicker after another exploded from her pursed lips. Then Nona started to giggle. Soon Meri joined in, and finally they were clutching each other laughing and wiping tears. As soon as there was a lull, they would look at each other and burst into a new wave of giggles.

Finally they calmed, and Esther wiped her eyes with her lace-edged handkerchief. There was a new sparkle in her face when she said drolly, "Well, when you've gotta go, you've gotta go."

She locked arms with her short companion and with Meri and added, "Now let's go have a cold drink. I'm terribly thirsty."

Dr. Stockton, looking alarmed, rushed over to them as they entered the waiting area. "Is anything wrong?" Mrs. Barrington flushed. "Esther, are you ill? Is there something I can do?"

"I'm fine!" she responded sharply. When he turned to leave, shoulders slumped, Esther touched his arm. "Thank you for asking, John. I suspect it's the heat. Would you please get us something cold to drink?" Her voice had softened, and she had the beginning of a smile.

Dr. Stockton's face registered surprise, then crinkled with a grin. He winked at Meri. "You ladies have a seat and I'll be back in a moment."

It was a small thing, Meri thought, but Esther's experience seemed to have caused a change in her. Perhaps John Stockton's persistence would pay off, even after thirty years.

Although he had protested vehemently, everybody suspected that Bradley had been the culprit who messed with the master switches and left her in the dark. When the attendant went to check the box, Bradley had been found intently studying the circuitry.

On the flight back to Aswan, Leah Henry apologized profusely for Bradley's misbehavior and made the little monster with the angelic dimples and wire-rimmed glasses apologize as well.

"Since I didn't do it, it doesn't seem appropriate to apologize," he announced, then sidled a glance toward his stern-faced grandmother. "But I'm truly sorry that you were stranded in the dark," he mumbled.

"Thank you, Bradley," Meri said. "I appreciate your concern."

Bradley marched back to his seat, plopped down, crossed his arms belligerently, and sulked.

Their flight would be landing at Aswan in a few minutes. Time to make repairs for her meeting with Welcome and the hotel rep. As she moved toward the back of the plane, Meri noticed John Stockton and Esther Barrington seated together talking quietly. As she passed, she winked at Dr. Stockton. Esther still looked a bit stiff, but it was a start.

She thought of Ram. She would miss him and what might have been. But something simple and uncomplicated was what she needed now. Like George. George was a good old Okie who didn't have a complicated bone in his body. She had seen him again briefly at the airport, and he had reminded her about dinner.

In the cramped restroom of the plane, Meri brushed her long blond hair and rewound it into a loose coil. She washed her hands and face, then applied fresh makeup. Nona had loaned her a shoe brush from the vast green tote bag that must have held everything. From her own canvas bag Meri retrieved a chunky wooden necklace and bracelet to dress up her beige cotton sweater and fringed hopsacking skirt. She skewered her topknot with two ivory chopsticks.

There. She looked presentable again. And professional enough to meet with the Horus Hotel representative later. She tried to smile into the mirror, but she couldn't quite pull it off. She felt strangely sad and empty.

Ram. Thoughts of him kept intruding into her mind. Where was he now? she wondered. Was he very angry with her? She knew the answer to that. He would be furious. But—

Shortly after she returned to her seat, they landed. The

Golden Years Travel Club was staying at the Oberoi and planned a Nile cruise as well.

"Maybe we'll all be together," Nona said as they walked across the tarmac toward the airport building, her white curls bouncing and her tent dress billowing in the hot breeze. "I can hardly wait. They say it's so romantic. Just like 'Love Boat.'"

Meri laughed and turned to say good-bye to the others when they were inside. Waving and calling farewells, she took a couple of steps backward and bumped into someone. "Sorry," she said and turned, still smiling, to look up into a pair of ice-blue eyes.

Her smile died.

"You missed lunch again."

Twelve

> *I say when I think of him,*
> *"Don't cause me silly pain, O my heart—*
> *Why do you play the madman?*
> *Just sit cool and he'll come to you,*
> *and everyone will see!"*

> Love Songs of the New Kingdom
> c. 1550-1080 B.C.

Ram was *here!* The initial shock of seeing him dissolved before a bright rush of unexplained joy. Meri's first instinct was to laugh and throw herself into his arms.

A jolt of memory stopped her.

She had lied to him.

A surge of shame flushed her face. A terrible feeling of impending doom gripped her stomach. She wished the floor would open up and swallow her.

She had been caught. There was nothing to do but brazen it out. The best defense was a good offense.

Drawing herself up to her full height, she faced him squarely. "What are *you* doing here?"

His eyes narrowed to blue slits. "I believe that's my question. The last I heard Rome is in the other direction."

"Well, uh . . . well, uh . . . we changed our minds at the last minute. Welcome is waiting for me. If you'll excuse me,

I have to find her." She felt as if she would suffocate if she couldn't escape.

"Not so fast," he said, grabbing her as she tried to brush past him. "I think you have some explaining to do."

Anger sprang forth to defend against the threat of further confrontation. She pursed her lips and glared at him. "I don't have to explain myself to *anyone,* Ramson Gabrey." She slammed her hat on her head and gripped her purse in front of her like a shield. "Now let me go and step aside."

His lips twitched.

"What are you grinning about?"

"Your hat."

Lifting her chin she asked haughtily, "What's wrong with my hat?"

"It doesn't fit down on your head with those sticks in your hair." His grin widened, and he thrust a large white package with a red bow in her hands. "Hold this and I'll fix it. You want to keep the hat or the sticks?"

Disarmed by visions of herself looking like an antler hat rack Uncle Jake used to have, she sighed. "The sticks."

He plucked off her hat and readjusted her hair ornaments. "There. That looks cute."

"It's not supposed to look *cute.* It's supposed to look chic." She held out the package to exchange for her hat.

He nodded toward the box. "That's for you."

Rolling her eyes, she said, "Oh, good grief! Don't tell me that we're going to start *that* again." She tried to hand him the box but he refused it.

"I promise you'll like it. It's not something expensive."

"What is it?"

"M&M's."

"M&M's?" Tenderness melted her irritation. How could you stay angry at someone who brought you M&M's? "Where on earth did you find them?"

"New York. Mark brought them when he flew in this morning. Don't worry about it. He was coming tomorrow anyway."

"Who's Mark?"

"One of my assistants. You'll meet him in a moment. He's waiting for us outside with the car."

"Yoo-hoo! Meri, Over here!" Welcome called from across the crowded terminal.

For a moment Meri had forgotten her meeting with Welcome and the hotel's representative. She had to get rid of Ram quickly.

"I have to attend to some things with Welcome this afternoon. Why don't I meet you later?" She waved to Welcome who was slicing her way through the throng with a dark, portly man following in her wake.

"You have a way of disappearing. How do I know you won't skip out?"

She shoved the box against his chest, "Hold the M&M's hostage. We're staying at the Oberoi. Call me later." She grabbed her hat from his hand and ran toward Welcome.

Now this was *style*. Welcome's wild red ringlets were encircled with a bright yellow headband. It matched the wide sash of her passionate purple dress and patent gladiator sandals. She certainly stood out in a crowd. On anyone else, her garb would look clownish; on Welcome, it was charming.

"Hi, sweetie." Welcome kissed the air beside both her cheeks. "Have a good trip?" Before Meri could answer, Welcome pulled the enthralled man following her forward and wound her arm through his. "Meri, this very nice man is Mr. Mohammed Abou-Basha. He's been soooo helpful." She patted his shoulder. "He's going along to point out some areas to photograph. He's providing a car, and all your equipment is in the trunk."

Biting her lip to keep from giggling at the man's besotted expression, Meri nodded politely. "We appreciate your help, Mr. Abou-Basha."

Welcome looked past Meri. "Who's your shadow, sweetie?"

Meri froze. Surely not. She heard deep throat clearing behind her. Damn him!

"I'm Ramson Gabrey. You must be Meri's friend Welcome. I'm delighted that we finally get to meet. She talks about you all the time." He stepped forward and gave her a dazzling-white smile, then extended his hand to the portly man. "It's good to see you again, Mohammed." He broke into a spate of Arabic.

While Ram and Mohammed conversed like long-lost brothers, Meri fumed. How could she have been attracted to this stubborn, insufferable man? She caught Welcome's eye and shrugged helplessly. Welcome only grinned.

Finally Meri tugged at his arm. *"Mister* Gabrey, if you will excuse us we have some business to tend to with Mr. Abou-Basha."

"I think I'll stay with you."

Through clenched teeth, Meri said in an undertone, "Why don't you take the box to the hotel before the you-know-whats melt? We'll meet you later."

Ram grinned and hugged her to his side, "I'd rather stay with you. I can be your assistant. Mark can take the you-know-whats to the hotel."

Meri rolled her eyes. "Oh, good grief."

As much as Meri hated to admit it, Ram was helpful. He seemed to know all the best places to photograph and quickly usurped Mr. Abou-Basha's role as supervisor. Which was a good thing. The portly Egyptian was obviously awestruck by Welcome, and his mind was on her instead of his business.

Meri had shot several rolls of film when Ram stopped at a spot in the marketplace. "Look," he said. "That would make a great picture."

In a small clearing along the dusty street, a wizened man wearing a faded gray robe and headdress sat cross-legged in front of a basket. As the man played haunting strains on a flute, a hooded cobra rose from the basket and swayed slowly back and forth. Bradley, Leah Henry's precocious grandson, sat cross-legged opposite the man, engrossed. Elbows on his knees, chin in his hands, the boy, dressed in T-shirt, shorts, and sneakers made an interesting contrast with the snake charmer. Ram was right. The scene would make a great picture, but she shivered at the notion of getting closer.

"I hate snakes," Meri said. "And Bradley's grandmother would have apoplexy if she knew what he was doing."

"You know him?" Ram asked.

"He and his grandmother were part of the group that I joined for Abu Simbel."

She gestured wildly for the boy to come away. He ignored her. Watching the snake made her skin crawl, but she gritted her teeth and shot a few frames. She wasn't leaving until she dragged Bradley away, but she had better sense than to cause a commotion while the snake was in striking distance of him.

She shuddered, then fidgeted nervously until the performance was over and the cobra was safely inside the basket with the lid fastened. Charging toward the boy, she jerked him up by the arm.

"What are you doing here? Where is your grandmother?"

"She's taking a nap."

"And you sneaked off. Don't you know that you were in danger? What if that cobra had bitten you?"

Behind his glasses, Bradley peered at her with disdain. "There was hardly any danger of that. I know a great deal about snakes. This one is of the genus *Naja*. I'm considering becoming a herpetologist, you know. A herpetologist is—"

"I know what a herpetologist is, Bradley. But you're not one now. Now you're a twelve-year-old boy who's somewhere he's not supposed to be. Come with us. We're taking you to the hotel."

He balked. "You have no right to tell me what to do. I'm not your responsibility."

"Thank God for that, but you're coming anyway."

"I'm not!"

Ram stepped up. "Let me handle this." He took the boy

aside and held a brief conversation with him. When they returned, Bradley dragged his feet, but he agreed to return to the hotel with them.

Ram smiled at her and caught Meri's hand. "You've done enough work today. Let's all go to the hotel. There are some beautiful sights I want to show you here." He called to Welcome and Mohammed.

After good-byes to Mr. Abou-Basha, they boarded a small ferry to take them to their hotel on Elephantine Island. Her frustrations over Ram's presence and Bradley's behavior were cast aside as Meri caught sight of the fabulous building and its lush tropical gardens rising from the sparkling cobalt waters of the Nile.

From the rail, she snapped pictures of the hotel and of another structure on a distant golden hill. An ancient domed monastery stood in relief against the late afternoon sky, looking lonely and abandoned on its high desert perch. She shot frame after frame. How this land fascinated her with its beauty and contrasts, with its mysterious past, with its constant excitement!

As if he could read her mind, Ram stood behind her, pulled her back against him, and whispered in her ear, "This is where you belong. Here. With me."

Strangely enough she felt content to stand there as the small ferry chugged toward the shore—the warmth of his body and his arms wrapped around her were a peaceful shelter. She wanted to curl up like a child and have him hold her—comfort her, close out the world.

As she relaxed against his strong chest, she could feel the vibrations of his husky murmur, "Don't run from me again, my love. We were born to be together."

It felt so *right*.

But doubt crept in once more. It was an impossible situation. There couldn't be a future for them. The fantasy would soon end. But his nearness generated a simmering sexual current and an aching tenderness that were impossible to ignore.

As the boat docked, she pulled away, instinctively steeling herself against Ram's magnetic spell. She looked around for Welcome and found her standing aside, watching them quietly.

Welcome smiled and winked.

After disembarking from the ferry, Bradley ran on ahead. The three climbed the terraced path flanked with heavy clusters of cascading fuchsia bougainvillaea. The place was like an enchanted fairyland pulsating with a magical aura.

She tried to ignore Ram and walk ahead with Welcome, but he wedged himself between them, slipping a hand beneath each of their elbows as he guided them toward the hotel lobby. All the while he recounted the history of the area. Meri didn't hear a word. His slightest touch or his very presence created such a turmoil for her that she was reduced to a mindless puddle.

When they reached the door to their room, Ram held on to Meri and oozed charm as he said good-bye to Welcome, who quickly let herself in and left them alone. Meri stared at the stone floor until he lifted her chin and searched her face.

"Love, what's wrong?"

Why did his eyes affect her so? Why did she want to throw herself against this beautiful man and burrow into his warm strength? Why did she ache for him to hold her and caress her and never let go? She was getting in over her head, and she couldn't tolerate much more.

Weighing future heartbreak against her desire of the moment, she finally said softly, "Ram, go away."

Lightly he smoothed the scar on her cheekbone and, never taking his eyes from hers, brought her hand to his lips. "We must talk so I can understand what's wrong. Whatever it is, I'll make it right."

"Just go away. I can't deal with this anymore."

"I'm not going away, and don't try to run from me again. I'll find you wherever you go. You're mine."

His tone was gentle, but she heard the resolve behind the words. He meant it. How dare he put her through this ordeal! She jerked her hand from his grasp. "I am not yours! I am mine! I'll go where I please when I please. Dammit, I said, go away!"

She struggled for the knob, but his hand held it fast, and she was caught in a pen of his arms.

Ignoring her efforts to peel his fingers from the knob, he said, "I'll be back in one hour. We'll have drinks and talk, and I'll take you and Welcome to dinner."

"I'm not going anywhere with you. Now let me go, you dictatorial, hardheaded jackass!" Exasperated with her futile struggle, she kicked him in the shin.

Immediately she was open-mouthed with mortification at her childish reaction. What had she done?

Instead of the anger that she expected from him, he roared with laughter. "God, my family will love you. See you in an hour, sweetheart." He wheeled and left her gaping beside the door.

Once inside the room, she slammed her purse and hat on the coffee table and kicked off her shoes so hard that one of them bounced off the patio door. Plopping down on the bright orange striped couch, she muttered, "That man will be the death of me yet!"

Welcome walked in from the kitchen with two glasses of ice water and handed one to Meri. "Sweetie," she said with a knowing smirk, "I think you've met your match. He's quite a hunk."

Meri gulped the cold water which was a balm to her parched throat and jangled nerves. "I thought you were the one who told me to watch out for him."

"That was before I saw him look at you like a lovesick calf. He's got it bad for you, honey. If he looked at me with those gorgeous baby-blues the way he looks at you, I swear you'd have to scrape me up with a spatula."

"Trust me, I know the feeling." She propped her feet on the table and leaned her head back against the plump cushion. "But Welcome, he keeps talking about *marriage*. Can you believe it? *Marriage*. The whole thing's crazy. He won't leave me alone, and we've still got a job to do. You know how important this project is to me, and he almost messed things up this afternoon. I doubt if I got one decent shot."

"Don't sell yourself short. I'm sure you got scads of good pictures. The hardest part will be picking from them for the brochure."

"I hope so."

"How was your trip to Abu Simbel?"

"Wonderful for the most part." Meri described the entourage and the sites they'd seen. She recounted the tale about Esther and the bathroom, dramatizing the incident with gestures and funny facial expressions until Welcome was in stitches. "Those senior citizens were a delight—except for Bradley."

"Who's Bradley?"

"Leah Henry's grandson. A precocious twelve-year-old brat. He's probably the one who cut the lights in the mountain and nearly scared the pants off me."

"What mountain? What lights?"

"Oh, I forgot to tell you about that." After she'd given Welcome a blow-by-blow account of the episode, she wrinkled her brow. "You know, now that I think about it, I've seen that man with the droopy eye several times. You don't suppose—No, that's silly."

"What's silly?"

"Well, I've had the oddest feeling for the last couple of days that somebody has been following me."

Welcome seemed suddenly disturbed. "Tell me about it."

"There's really not much to tell. I saw Droopy Eye at Memphis and maybe one other time, but I can't remember exactly when."

"Has he approached you or made any threatening moves?"

"No. He's probably just a tourist, and I'm making entirely too much of the whole thing. Maybe my mother's dire warnings have me spooked." Meri got up and poured them another glass of water, then slapped her head as she remembered something. "I forgot all about George."

"Who's George?"

"George Mszanski. He used to play football with the Cowboys. I met him today at Abu Simbel and promised him we would have dinner with him and his friend tonight. Is it okay with you?"

"Fine with me, but what about Ram? I have a feeling he has other plans for you."

"That's tough. I'm not going to see him again. You saw how he was today—just like a steamroller. He's as bad as my mother. And . . . and . . . it's just all too complicated."

"Meri, he's not at all like Nora. What's the real reason you're avoiding him?"

"When he's around, strange things happen that absolutely scare the bejesus out of me. He's dangerous. I feel it in my bones. He's too darned perfect, and he's so . . . so . . . *incredibly* sexy. God, Welcome, my tongue practically hangs out when the man's in spitting distance." There, she'd admitted it.

Welcome poked her cheek with her tongue and smirked. "Lawdy, lawdy. Looks like somebody finally shook Miss Prim and Proper's tree."

The phone's ring interrupted Meri's unladylike retort.

Hanging up after a short conversation, Meri said, "That was George. I told him we'd meet him and his friend in the bar for a drink in fifteen minutes. Let's hurry."

Meri had to give Welcome credit. She hadn't even broken stride or raised an eyebrow when they saw George and his unusual friend already waiting in the posh Elephantine bar with its dark carved wood and plush burgundy velvet chairs. George stood like an overgrown puppy beside the slight Jean Jacques.

Jean Jacques—no last name. "Last names are so plebeian, don't you think?" he said later in his heavy French accent, tossing his bleached platinum mane for effect.

To say that he was avant-garde was putting it mildly. Five

mismatched gold earrings hung from one ear, four from the other. He was dressed in pale pink: loose pink cotton tunic and jacket, baggy pink cotton slacks pegged at the bottom with the wrap-around ankle straps of his gold sandals. To a person, every patron in the bar was watching him. Some were staring with obvious open-mouthed wonderment; others were quietly stealing curious glances.

After the introductions were made, and the little Frenchman kissed the women's hands with flattery and flourish, he escorted them to a table. Although both Meri and Welcome towered several inches over his head, he strutted between them with regal grace. George followed behind with an adoring smile.

When the four were seated, Jean Jacques ordered the finest champagne available. After approving the selection and supervising its pouring, he raised his glass. "A toast to the two loveliest ladies in all of Egypt." He smiled toward Meri and Welcome. "And to my dear companion." He patted George's shoulder.

So much for George.

It was just as well, Meri thought. She was much more comfortable with platonic relationships. With that out of the way they could relax and enjoy each other's company.

"Welcome," Jean Jacques gushed, "but, of course, I am familiar with your fabulous work. Recognized you at once. Tell me, *chérie*, I have always wondered, where did you get such an interesting name?"

Welcome nodded in acknowledgement of the compliment. "My name?" She laughed. "My mother gave it to me when she found me on her doorstep. She said she always wanted me to feel welcome. Though my birth certificate says Mary Alice, I've never been called anything but Welcome."

"How delightful!" he cried clapping his hands together. "And lovely Meri, are you a model too?"

"Nothing quite so glamorous, I'm afraid. Just a photographer from Texas. How are you enjoying Egypt?"

She missed his reply when Welcome kicked her under the table. Meri looked up to see her friend gesturing with her eyes toward the door.

Ram. Bigger than life and headed their way.

"Well, hello there," Ram said jovially. "Fancy meeting you here. Who are your friends?" He stood behind Meri with his hands clamped on her shoulders.

Smiling feebly, she made the introductions and watched helplessly as he dragged a chair from another table and placed it conspicuously between her and George. She almost giggled. There was no reason for jealousy. Little did he know that George might prefer Ram to her.

"Say, are you the George Mszanski who played for the Cowboys?" Ram asked as he sat down. When George grinned and nodded, they started swapping football tales of, "You remember when . . ."

Jean Jacques and Welcome were trading gossip about European celebrities, and Meri sat there feeling like a fifth wheel. How dare he horn in and just take over! She would leave.

Then Ram's hand was on her thigh, gently kneading and stroking. For all her irritation with this infuriating man, his touch did strange things to her.

"Did you hear that, *sukkar?*" Ram asked Meri. "Jean Jacques and George are going to be on the same cruise that we are."

She sputtered into her wine glass. "That *we* are? But—but—"

Ram grinned and winked. "Yes, I'll be joining you. I knew you'd be pleasantly surprised, love." Grabbing her hand and pulling her to her feet, he graciously addressed the group. "Now if you would excuse us, please. My fiancée and I have a previous engagement."

Thirteen

*Her bearing is regal as she walks upon the earth—
    she causes every male neck to turn and look at her.
Yes, she has captivated my heart in her embrace!
See how she goes forth—like that one and only
    Goddess!*

Love Songs of the New Kingdom
c. 1550-1080 B.C.

Meri waited until they were in a quiet corridor outside the bar to explode. Whirling she faced him with her feet planted firmly apart, hands on her hips and breathing fire. "Your *fiancée?* Where do you get off calling me your *fiancée?* And how *dare* you drag me away from my friends. I ought to kick you in the shin again!"

Ram only stood there and grinned. "Do you know how adorable you are? You remind me of my grandmother."

"Your grandmother? Gee, thanks," she said sarcastically and stomped off.

"Hey, wait a minute," he said, catching up with her and turning her to face him again. "That was a compliment. My grandmother was one of the most beautiful and feisty ladies I've ever known. She led my grandfather a merry chase, but they loved each other deeply. My family has always said I'm just like him, and that I'd get mine someday." He chuckled.

"And I believe I have. But how can I court you if you won't hold still? Every time I turn my back, you run away."

"Courting me? Is that what you're doing? I could have sworn that you're imitating a renegade tank."

Lifting her chin, he gently touched the scar on her cheek and bathed her face with blue-eyed caresses. "Love, stop running from me and give us some time. Let me have the next few days to prove how special we can be together."

As his eyes bore into hers, Meri could feel her anger and resolve melting. Despite her best efforts, she was being drawn back into a web of enchantment, of longing for dreams of the impossible. She tore her gaze from his spell and walked slowly to a large window overlooking the Nile. She was stalling, but she needed a few minutes to collect her stampeding emotions.

There was a restlessness in her soul. Eerie. Alien. Unsettling. Maybe she was looking for excuses to avoid dealing with her feelings and with the spooky things that had been happening, but there were serious issues between them. He was handsome, romantic, dashing; she was an ordinary person. And while Egypt was a nice place to visit and she loved it, she was American through and through. They were worlds apart she told herself for the dozenth time. And, in any case, things were moving way too fast.

But, oh, he made her heart sing.

Even now, incredible warmth and energy radiated from him as he stood silently behind her. It beckoned an answering source at the core of her being.

"Meri, love, please," he whispered. "I promise I'll try to give you some room. I'll let you set the pace."

When she heard the intense pleading in his words, she felt terrible making this proud man beg. Turning, she started to speak, then stopped. Unexpected tears sprang to her eyes, and she gazed at him through a misty blur.

In the far, far corners of her mind and her heart, an overwhelming love for this man burgeoned, grew to enormous proportions and filled her with wondrous joy, a joy so powerful and so intense that the pleasure of it was painful. As quickly as it had come, the feeling retreated behind a heavy curtain. But for that instant, she *recognized* him. She *knew* him, as if the fingers of their spirits had touched.

Now the memories were gone. Only the traces of emotion remained.

Fiercely, he hugged her to him. "You feel it too, don't you."

She nodded her head against his shoulder. "I don't understand the strange things that happen when we're together. Nothing makes sense any more. I'm afraid."

"Afraid of what?"

"Afraid of being overwhelmed. Afraid of being hurt."

He scooped her closer to him. "I would never hurt you. I would protect you with my life. Will you trust me? You can, you know."

As she looked up at him, her heart answered instead of her reason. "Yes, I know."

"Will you stop running and let me in? Let me prove to you what can be ours."

In the space of a pulse beat, she decided to throw caution to the wind and allow herself to be swept along by fate. She would live for today, and to hell with tomorrow. "Yes."

Ram pulled back, eyes gleaming with delight. "You won't be sorry. Heaven on earth will be ours. Come, let's walk outside to the water. I have a surprise for you."

Her chin went up defiantly and she dug in her heels. "First there are some things we have to get straight if this relationship is going anywhere. One, stop ordering me around. As I'm constantly reminding Mother, I am an adult."

"Yes, dear."

"Two, when I say back off, I mean it, Ramson Gabrey."

"Yes, dear."

"This is serious, dammit. Stop grinning like a Cheshire cat. Three, don't be so smug and possessive. You suffocate me, and I've chafed against smothering all my life. I don't like it, and four . . . four . . . oh, hell, I forget four right now."

"You'll think of it in a minute," he said, giving her a peck on the cheek and hugging her to his side. "I'm yours to mold any way you want me."

She rolled her eyes. "In my dreams."

He smiled enigmatically. "That too."

"Fat chance. But as I told Welcome, I'm sick of being paving material, and sometimes you act like a steamroller."

"Oh? Have you been discussing me with your friend? What else did you say?"

"It wouldn't do your ego any good to know. Now I remember four. Where are my M&M's?"

He patted his pocket. "I've got a package right here. If you're a good girl, you can have some on the felucca."

"On the what?"

"The felucca. It's a sailboat. Come on while we still have some light."

Hand in hand, they strolled down the path to the river where Ram motioned to a graceful young Nubian standing ready for them. Ram helped her into the wooden craft which looked similar to a large rowboat. When they were seated on soft cushions, the barefoot boatman deftly hoisted the sail and took the rudder. A breeze billowed his long white robe and filled the canvas. Silently they skimmed the surface of the ancient lapis water, around and between smaller islands of time-carved gray rock.

Ram gathered Meri close and pointed toward a distant silhouette on the shore. "Up there is the villa of the late Aga Khan. He loved this spot so much he asked to be buried here. That's his mausoleum standing on the hill beyond."

"It's exquisite. And you? Would you like to be buried in this spot?"

He chuckled. "Not right away." Then he touched her cheek with the back of his fingers, and his voice became husky. "But someday, in the far distant future, I want to be buried in whatever spot that will be closest to you."

A sudden shadow clutched her throat and she shivered.

"Are you cold?" he asked, cuddling her closer.

"No. It's all the talk about death."

"It's death that made my country famous. It's what we're all about—life and death and life and on and on. But," he said, changing his solemn tone, "let's enjoy the beauty of life. There, ahead, is Kitchener's Island and it's filled with life. It's a botanical garden."

Giant stately palms rose from a profusion of flowering trees and shrubs that covered the whole island. As the boat touched the landing, a riot of color and sweet smells blended with the twittering of birds and playing children.

"It's beautiful." She climbed from the felucca and hurried up the walk. Laughing, she turned back to Ram who was following close behind. "Oh, Ram, it's beautiful!"

His face shone with pleasure. "I thought you'd like it. Let's take a quick tour before dusk."

They wandered through the lush grounds, reading labels of the exotic plants and eating M&M's. When they argued over their favorite colors of the candies, he gave in and let her have all the orange and yellow ones.

At sunset, they returned to the felucca, and she nestled against Ram's warmth as the boatman maneuvered the small craft through the rippling current of the Nile. As he held her snugly against his side, she tingled with a myriad of magical sensations. The very air around her vibrated with sensual awareness.

An erotic breeze fingered the wispy tendrils of her hair. Upriver the lights of their hotel flashed on. Its triple towers stood like a gigantic phallic symbol pulsating against the evening sky.

The bright water was rife with gentle lapping and the hint of murmured love words as the boat plowed through the mysterious river. Sail billowing, straining, their craft seemed to soar along the shimmering surface.

The last rays of the sun burst in a final eruption of glorious color, then sighed and slipped over the edge of the earth, leaving a soft afterglow behind the trailing clouds.

Where were these blatantly sexual images coming from? A sensual wildness stirred inside her. She was no quivering, breathless innocent but an intelligent, fully mature woman, yet the potent sensations she felt around Ram were something beyond her experience. She felt out of control, buffeted by some force she didn't recognize. Rejecting her feelings frantically, she raised her eyes to his and saw raw desire blazing openly.

With their eyes still locked, he lifted her hand to his mouth and, with agonizing deliberateness, nibbled and tasted each finger as now and then, in the gathering twilight, a star kissed the sky. With his tongue, he flicked and licked and thrust into the valleys between her fingers, trailing heat as he moved from one to the next. After endless electric moments, he nestled his cheek in her palm, then lowered her hand to his thigh and held it there. Slowly he moved his lips toward hers, then stopped.

The waiting was like an alluring, warm pulling tide.

When she instinctively made a tiny movement toward him, he hesitated for a heartbeat, then growled, "Oh, hell!"

With lightning swiftness he yanked her hard against his chest and kissed her with a fierce, savage hunger.

A spark from a deep, hidden corner inside her flared and leaped and surged forth to meet his frantic urgency. Consumed by wildfire, she was sucked into a whirl of unexpected sensation. Pleasurable beyond her dreams. Familiar as her own skin.

He groaned and thrust his tongue into her mouth, and her heart went into a frenzy. He tore his lips away and rained quick kisses over her upturned face, then clutched her to him in a possessive embrace.

"Meritaten, my sweet everlasting love," he murmured into her ear.

The felucca bumped against the hotel dock.

They looked up to see a broad white grin on the dark face of the boatman. When Meri, embarrassed, ducked her head against Ram's chest, his deep chuckle vibrated against her cheek.

"He's only jealous," he whispered. "Want to sail around the island again?"

She drew a ragged breath. "I think we'd better go have dinner or a drink or both."

"Sure?"

"I'm sure." She stood on shaky legs and waited for Ram to help her out of the boat. Mercy, could this man kiss. It took a mountain of self-control to keep her from flinging herself back into his arms, grinning boatman or no.

Good sense intruded and shook her by the scruff of the neck. Hold on. Back off. Careful, careful. Slowly, slowly. As exciting as this virile man was, casual sex was not her style, and their relationship had a way to go yet. Dreams were one thing, reality quite another. She drew a deep breath as she waited for Ram to pay the boatman.

As they strolled back to the hotel and through the lobby, bright with vivid-hued modern furniture, replicas of ancient paintings, and verdant tropical plants, Ram held her close against his side as if he were afraid she would bolt and run at any moment.

"Hungry?" he asked.

"Very. M&M's don't stay with you very long, do they? I didn't get much lunch, and my stomach is saying strange things to me."

"Mine, too," he said with a knowing leer, "but I don't think dinner will help much."

Ignoring his comment, she said, "I would like to take a shower and change first. I've been in these clothes all day. Mind?"

"Of course not. Come on, I'll help you." He grinned and tugged her toward her room.

Stopping dead still, she exclaimed, *"Ram!"*

His thick, dark mustache twitched as one corner of his mouth lifted. "Is that a two?"

Her brow furrowed with a puzzled frown. "A two?"

"You know. One, don't order you around. Two, back off when you say. Three, don't be smug and possessive."

"That's a definite two."

When they arrived at her door, she said, "Why don't I meet you in the dining room?"

"Oh, no. I'm waiting right here. You have this strange habit of disappearing the moment my back's turned."

"That's a three."

He hung his head and raised his eyes sheepishly. "Sorry, princess. I'm working on it. Forgive me?"

With one unruly curl of his wind-ruffled hair hanging across his forehead, he looked like a repentant little boy caught in mischief. She smoothed back the errant lock. "Pick me up here in an hour. Okay?"

"Promise you'll be here?"

"I promise." She smiled as she went inside and closed the door.

Billowing fragrances surrounded her as she flipped on the light. Vases and bowls and baskets of brilliant-hued flowers filled the room. A large box with a red bow sat pertly on the coffee table.

"Oh, good grief!" That crazy, wonderful man. Meri smiled, shook her head, and went to take her bath.

Humming all the while, she quickly showered, washed and dried her hair into shining, wavy swirls, touched Scheherazade to the pulse points of her warm skin, and made her face. Feeling just the tiniest bit wicked, she slipped on a bra and bikini panties that were gossamer wisps of black lace and she selected her boldest dress. Of deep teal blue, the soft silk dipped low in front and even lower in back. She was filling an evening bag when a knock sounded.

When she opened the door, Ram was leaning against the jamb, his hair still damp but now under perfect control. He wore a finely tailored suit, in the gray he seemed to favor, and a subdued tie.

"You're early."

"I couldn't wait any longer." Grasping both her hands, he held them wide to look at her. *"Gamil!"*

"I'm a *camel?*" she asked indignantly.

He laughed and dropped a kiss on the tip of her nose. "No, my precious one, you are not a camel. What is this preoccupation you have with camels? *Gamal* is camel; *gamil* means beautiful. You are lovelier than Isis herself."

"Thank you, kind sir." She dropped a curtsy. "Now let's eat. I'm starving."

He bowed, then offered his arm. "At your service, my lady."

A few minutes later, they were seated at a quiet table overlooking the river. The lights of Aswan flashed like fireflies in the rippling reflection of the water. Flickering candlelight danced over the glistening crystal and silver on the white linen cloth. It shone with the same warm, blue fire as Ram's eyes.

While they waited for the wine Ram had ordered, he reached across the table and loosely grasped Meri's chin with his thumb and forefinger. He studied her face, turning it from side to side.

Feeling self-conscious, Meri asked, "Do I have a smudge on my nose?"

"I'm trying to decide what color your eyes are. Every time I see you they're different. A moment ago they were the same shade as your dress, but I could have sworn that this afternoon they were a greenish-brown."

"They're hazel and very unpredictable."

"Like their beautiful mistress. And this scar," he said, tracing the small line high on her cheekbone, "How did you get that?"

"An automobile accident when I was young. Ugly thing, isn't it?"

"Nothing about you is ugly. I find it charming. Lends an air of mystery and adventure. You sometimes get a faraway look and then you rub it. It makes me wonder what you're thinking and how you got the scar."

Shrugging, Meri said, "From a piece of flying glass."

The waiter appeared with the wine, and they discussed food selections. When Ram suggested the calamari, she wrinkled her nose. "Squid has never seemed very appealing to me. I'll have scampi."

While they ate, they chatted about the day. Ram was disturbed by her harrowing experience in the dark at Abu Simbel. "That young man is a menace," he said, scowling. "I'm sorry he ruined your outing."

"Oh, he didn't ruin it. I only had a temporary fright. Abu Simbel was wonderful. I've fallen in love with Egypt. Sometimes I feel as if I've come home."

"You have."

His slow smile, knowing and evocative, made her heart lurch, and she dropped her fork with a clatter. She took a quick sip of wine. "Uh, as I recall, you were going to tell me how your grandfather and grandmother met."

Obviously aware of her ploy to change the subject, he chuckled. "So I was." He signaled for coffee before he started the tale.

"My grandmother was a bonnie Scottish lass with flaxen hair and eyes the color of a robin's egg," he began with a thick burr. "A beautiful and feisty lady. Like you, like my mother." He smiled. "Aurora Macleod she was called—Dr. Aurora Macleod. Even though she was from a wealthy and titled family, she was not content to serve in a conventional role, so she went to the University of Edinburgh and became a physician. Graduated at the top of her class, too.

"As you can imagine, there was not much demand for women doctors in that day, so she secured the only post she could find. A British officer, who was to be stationed in Egypt, wanted to bring his family along. One of his five children was very sickly, and his wife was pregnant and refused to come without a personal physician. Grandmother came with them to Egypt and began a one-woman crusade to upgrade the medical care of the country.

"One day my grandfather was having tea with a friend, a British official, on the veranda at the Mena House. My grandmother came in breathing fire and shouting at his friend about medical supplies. Grandfather was totally spellbound, knew he had to have her, and pursued her relentlessly. Although he paid her lavish court, she would have none of it—said she didn't have time for such nonsense.

"Finally, when he was totally frustrated, he kidnapped her. Tied her on a horse and took her to a tent in the desert."

"Ram! You're making that up. Things like that only happen in old movies."

"It's true. He kept her there for two weeks until she agreed to marry him. She did, of course, and nine months later my father was born." He took her hand and traced her knuckles with his thumb. Candlelight reflected in his eyes as they bore into hers. "So you see, my love, we Gabrey men know what we want and go after it."

A vague disquiet became a prickling sensation on Meri's skin. She could feel her muscles tightening, and her mouth went dry. A sudden thought drained the blood from her face.

"Ram, you wouldn't do something like that would you?" Her voice was a quiet rasp.

A low chuckle reverberated deep in his throat. "Only as a last resort."

She tried to jerk her hand away, but he held it fast. "Ramson Gabrey, that's not funny! That's sick!"

"Settle down, love. I'm only teasing." He kissed her hand and released it.

A modicum of her apprehension dissipated as he winked and called for the check. Of course he was only teasing her, but— No, she didn't want to think about it. Talk of abduction was crazy—like everything else since she'd met this man. Relax. It was merely a joke.

Fourteen

*Ah, but the face is pale . . . The wrongdoer is everywhere.
Ah, but the Nile is in flood, yet no one plows. Doorkeepers
   say: "Let us go and plunder!"
Ah, but the crocodiles are glutted with what they have
   carried off.*

> The Admonitions of Ipuwer
> c. 2180-1990 B.C.

Flicking his cigarette toward the river, he continued his stroll along the winding walkway past the two-story suite occupied by the American women. Full darkness had fallen and no light shone from the windows or from the glass doors to the veranda which lay not twenty meters up the slope from the path.

He chuckled softly, the rusty sound blending with the rustle of acacia and palm trees lining the grounds, then slipped into the shadowy cover of an oleander bush and crouched there several minutes, vigilant, listening for footfalls of other evening strollers.

All was quiet.

He struggled to rein his growing excitement. In a short time, the falcon pectoral would be in his hands. He had seen the woman leave with Gabrey and could tell from the cut of her frock that she was not wearing the pendant. It would be in her room. The sliding glass doors would be a simple matter; he had practiced on those of his own room and had opened them in mere seconds.

He was about to leave his cover for one closer to the veranda when he saw movement from the corner of his eye. He glanced to his right in time to see a figure draw behind the trunk of a palm. Cursing silently, he waited, dividing his attention between the tree and the doors.

As he waited, another figure moved from the shadows of a shrubbery thicket at edge of the veranda and stole to the glass doors. In seconds the door slid open.

Fury flushed bile into his mouth. The bloody bastard! He wanted to charge after the man, bellowing his rage and sink his knife between the usurper's ribs. But reason held his temper in check. The wrong move would doom his own chances for the pectoral.

Think, man. Think.

When an idea flashed, he quickly stole from his hiding place and hurried the short distance to his own veranda, raced through his room and into the hallway. He encountered a bellman and a family group, but he ignored them and strode to the door of the American women. He knocked loudly and rattled the knob.

Hoping that he had startled the intruder into a speedy exit, he retraced his path and again took up a post near the river walkway. No longer concerned with concealment, he lit a cigarette and continued to stroll, casually but vigilantly, walking sentry for the glass doors. As he chain-smoked to keep the interlopers at bay, he was aware of two others tarrying in the shadows. He would not hold the pectoral in his hand that night, but neither would the pair of jackals who lingered with their anticipations as well.

When a light came on in the room two hours later, he flicked his cigarette into the dark waters of the Nile and sought his bed.

There would be another opportunity. But it must be soon.

Fifteen

*For the heavens are sending us love like a flame spreading
through straw
and desire like the swoop of the falcon!*

Love Songs of the New Kingdom
c. 1550-1080 B.C.

"Had you rather go dancing or watch dancing?" Ram asked as he guided her from the restaurant. When Meri looked blank, he explained. "We can go dancing at the nightclub here in the hotel, or there's a theater just down the street featuring Nubian dancers." Checking his watch, he added, "There's a show starting in a few minutes."

"The Nubian people are so beautiful. Could we go see the dancers?"

The ferry was about to leave as they reached the dock. They ran the last few steps and jumped aboard just as it pulled away. Laughing, they clung to the rail to catch their breaths. Ram hugged her to him as the boat, its smoky diesel engine chugging, churned a wake through the glow on the moonlit river.

When they docked, they strolled half a block to the theater. While Ram bought tickets, Meri waited nearby, quietly watching the activity of the streets. Horse-drawn carriages were intermixed with cars. There was an equal assortment of long *galabiyahs* and Western clothes. Aromas of searing meat and spices wafted in the air and mingled with river smells as vendors hawking their wares by the waterfront cooked their evening meal on open braziers.

When she noticed a greasy-looking man in a white suit and loud tie watching her, she became uncomfortable. He was stripping her naked with a languid, sloe-eyed leer. He sauntered toward her, and her anxiety increased.

Ram, a fierce expression on his face, stepped to her side and spat out a heated and rapid Arabic admonition. The man paled, then scurried away.

Ram smiled down at her, protectively slipped her arm through his, and led her into the dim theater.

When they were seated, she whispered, "What did you say to that awful man?"

"It loses something in the translation."

"Well, give me the general idea."

"I told him if he didn't take his eyes off you I would blind him with a hot poker; and if he touched you, I would cut off his right hand and feed it to the dogs before I, uh, did some other things to him."

"What other things?"

"Let's just say that it had to do with his manhood."

"Why did you have to frighten the poor man so? You wouldn't do that."

"I would."

"Ram!"

"You're mine and nobody touches you."

"I think that's a definite three," she said sharply.

He grinned. "I'm trying, love. I'm trying."

Warmth was back in his eyes again, but Meri shivered when she thought of the ruthless, cold-steel glint that had been there a moment ago. This was a side of him she had glimpsed, only fleetingly, once before. It frightened her. Despite his Americanization and sophistication, there was a strong Middle-Eastern streak in his make-up, a fierceness that she'd noted in Arabic men along with their attitude of proprietorship toward women. It made her feminist hackles rise.

She was *not* his property to possess, to command, or to fight over. She was not, nor would she be ever be *anybody's* property. She was about to open her mouth to give him a minilecture on the subject when the house lights flashed, then dimmed.

A rhythmic, aboriginal beat thundered and rolled through the auditorium as the curtain opened to reveal eight magnificent Nubian women in colorful native regalia. Tall and slender with proud carriage, they were beautiful with their ebony skin, delicate features, and high foreheads. No wonder Ramses II was so enamored of his beautiful Nubian Queen Nefertari.

The dancers' bare feet moved with a *shuffle, stomp, shuffle, stomp* in time with the entrancing thump and rumble of tomtoms and other hide-covered drums. The beat was primal, compelling. It filled the room and vibrated deep in her belly.

Ram's hand rested on her thigh and lightly tapped the primitive tempo of the drums and the *shuffle, stomp, shuffle, stomp* of the dancers. With every beat of the drums and every tap of his fingers, she felt her heart pounding and her blood surging to the same rhythmic beat. Her breasts swelled, and her womb pulsated.

She shivered.

Dear God, was everything in this country geared to stimulate the gonads? The show had barely started, and she was already hot and bothered. Was it the music arousing her so, or was it the man sitting beside her? She glanced at Ram and found those magnificent eyes on her. His lips parted, then lifted to a slow, sensuous smile.

"Watch the dancers," she whispered.

He squeezed her thigh. "I'd rather watch you."

At the rate she was going, she would never last through three days of close quarters on the ship with him without jumping his bones. And *that,* she knew, would be a monumental mistake—she might enjoy the experience much too much. She had the feeling that if they ever made love, she would be branded his for life.

Like a cow. Or a horse. Property.

She shook off the thought and refocused her attention. Soon the hypnotic beat, the *shuffle, stomp, shuffle, stomp* of the dancers lured her back to a more elemental consciousness where physical, hedonistic awareness supplanted reason. Entranced, she gave over to it.

When the final curtain fell, she sat quietly for a moment, spellbound by the assault on her senses of the drums, the movements, and Ram. She could still feel the rhythmic beat. It stayed with her as they wordlessly left the theater, strolled beside the banks of the Nile toward the waiting ferry, and chugged across the river to the island. Rather than being cooled by the breezy boat ride, she grew warmer as the engine vibrated beneath her feet and sent reverberations zinging up her body.

As they walked along the path to the hotel, Ram put his arm around her waist. His gait changed to a *shuffle, stomp, shuffle, stomp*. She joined in and matched his rhythmic steps which were as provocative as a fertility dance. When they reached the hotel's entrance, she burst out laughing.

"You rascal! You know what you're doing, don't you?"

He feigned wide-eyed innocence. "I don't know what you're talking about."

"The heck you don't."

"What would you like to do now? Go dancing? Have a nightcap? Make love?"

"Ram!"

"Just testing."

"I think we'd better say good-night. Welcome must be wondering what happened to me."

"She looks like a bright lady. I'm sure she figured it out," he said, as they walked along the atrium corridor to her room.

When they reached the door and she'd extracted her key, he seemed reluctant to let her go.

"You're so lovely tonight. The color of this dress is perfect for you," he said, rubbing his fingers against her sleeve. "You should wear it all the time. What's it called?"

"Teal."

"It changes the color of your eyes. They're like the depths of the Nile at twilight."

His words might have sounded corny coming from someone else, but at the time and place they seemed very right from him. There was no denying that he was the most incredibly handsome, exciting man she'd ever met. She could easily drown in the gaze that caressed her as she stood waiting for him to take her into his arms.

Instead, he slowly raised his hand and, with his forefinger, lightly traced the low-cut neckline of her dress. With a maddening slowness, it trailed across the gentle rise of her breasts above the silk.

"Do you know you have the most enchanting mole right here?" He touched a spot on the swell of her left breast, then bent and dropped a light kiss on the spot where his finger had been.

Her nipples instantly sprang to hard peaks, obvious through the whisper-thin fabric.

His eyes crinkled above that proud, hawk nose, and the furrows bracketing his mouth deepened. His tongue licked the thin scar on her cheekbone, and he nuzzled her ear. "Soon, *habîbati,* my darling. Soon." He placed something around her neck and whispered, "Dream of me."

And he was gone.

She slipped inside, closed the door, and leaned against it with a sigh, lost in another world. Her hand went to her breast, and she looked down to see the falcon pendant around her neck. She closed her fingers around its warmth and smiled.

"You must have had some night," Welcome said. Dressed in a faded orange football jersey, she sat on the sofa, polishing her toenails. "I see we're back to the funeral parlor business. I'll bet the florists love to see that guy coming."

Still in a suspended state of enchantment and wearing a silly smile, Meri looked vaguely at her red-haired friend. Languidly raising her arm, she wiggled the tips of her fingers and breathed, "Hi."

"Oh I had a wonderful time, thank you. The boys and I did the town."

"That's nice," Meri responded absently as she glided across the carpet and headed for her room.

"Yes, but what was really fun was when we brought the crocodile and hippopotamus into the hotel lobby."

"That's nice."

"Lawdy, lawdy." Welcome snickered as Meri drifted to her bedroom and closed the door.

Over and over the thought came to Meri, *I'm falling in love with that man. Head-over-heels, honest-to-God in love.*

Somehow she managed to undress and wash her face, musing over her evening with Ram. It had been perfect except for the incident with the man at the theater. Just thinking about Ram's cold, venomous expression caused her to shudder. Being with him made her forget that there was a great deal that she didn't know about him.

But now she remembered. For all his charm and professions of devotion, she had seen a ruthless streak in him. And he could be controlling, possessive, and—despite what Welcome said—as manipulative and intrusive as her mother. Did she need that? She damned sure wasn't about to become a chattel and wear a veil in public.

Damn that virile, arrogant, crazy Egyptian! Every time he looked at her with those gorgeous eyes and murmured a few honeyed words, her good sense went on vacation. She had to keep this thing in perspective.

Ramson Gabrey, for all his endearing appeal, was a pleasant interlude, a momentary fantasy; she couldn't allow herself to think of anything like love or lasting commitments. Her life, her loyalties lay half a world away. She was not here to engage in girlish dreams or fanciful romances. She was here to work. *Get real, Meri,* she told herself.

She brushed her hair vigorously and pitched the brush onto the vanity when she was finished. Rummaging around in her bag, she found the comfortable oversized jersey that matched Welcome's and slipped it on.

A moment later she tossed a small brown package into Welcome's lap. "Want some M&M's?"

Looking up from blowing on her toenails, Welcome said, "This is like manna from heaven. Where did you get these?"

"From Ram. He had them flown in from New York."

"That man's got it bad. You, too, from the looks of you when you came in tonight."

"Just a moment of temporary insanity. It passed. If I start acting like a cow-eyed teenager again, pinch me." She ripped open another bag and popped a handful of M&M's into her mouth. "I think I've watched too many old movies."

But for all her protestations, her head was filled with thoughts of Ram. The feelings he'd stirred up just wouldn't go away. She stared forlornly into the darkness beyond the patio, wondering what she was going to do.

"Want to talk about it?" Welcome asked.

Meri shook her head.

After a few moments of quiet, Welcome asked, "Did you leave the sliding glass door open earlier?"

"No," Meri said vaguely, only half listening. "Why?"

"I found it unlocked." Welcome shrugged and tore open the pack of candy with her teeth. "It's probably nothing." She tossed a bunch of M&M's into her mouth and between munches she blew on the wet polish. She wiggled her toes and said, "It's dumb to do this at night, but I always do. They're never dry when I go to bed, and I get sheet prints on them. They'll look like miniature waffles in the morning. Want me to paint yours?" She grabbed the bottle and shook it.

"Sure, why not?" Meri grinned and stuck one foot on Welcome's knee. "The mark of a true friend. Someone who'll paint your toenails."

Sixteen

*Do not attempt to harness the quarrelsome one with a hot
   mouth, nor spur him with words.
Rather be sluggard before an enemy,
   and bend back before an attacker.*

The Proverbs of Amen-em-Ope
c. 1580-1320 B.C.

"Welcome," Meri wailed as she stood in front of the mirror, "I can't wear *this* swimming."

"Why not? It looks fantastic, and I'll have you know it's an Henri original," her friend said as she picked up a bathing suit discarded earlier. "You certainly can't wear this Mother Hubbard with the seat ripped out. How long have you had this thing anyway?" Welcome wrinkled her nose and tossed the faded garment in the trash.

"Four or five years, I guess. How was I to know the seams were split? It was okay last summer." Vainly Meri tugged at the purple maillot which couldn't have weighed half an ounce and looked as if it had been painted on. When she tried to pull the suit down, her breasts threatened to spill out of the plunging top; when she tried to pull it up, the French cut of the bottom exposed even more of her hips and made her legs look a block long. "I can't go to the pool like this. It's indecent!"

"Oh, bull! Some women would kill for legs and bazooms

like those. If you've got it, flaunt it, and hon, you're a knockout in that suit. Henri should only see you now. He'd be in ecstasy over what his creation does for you."

"It may get me arrested. This is a conservative country. Some women still wear veils, for heaven's sake. I'll wait until the hotel shop opens and get another one."

Welcome sighed. "I've already told you the boutique doesn't open until after lunch today, and we have to board the steamer early this afternoon. Had you rather wear this one?" she asked, indicating her own, which was little more than black strings and silver buckles.

Meri gasped at the thought. "That one's even worse."

Welcome chuckled. "You ought to know these little numbers cost six hundred bucks apiece."

"You should've waited for your change."

"Henri gave them to me after the showing. Here, put on this cover-up and let's go." Welcome thrust a flowing purple robe at Meri and donned its black mate. Both ignored the phone that started to ring as they headed toward the door. "I want to get some of this glorious sun."

Meri grumbled all the way to the pool.

After she kicked off her slides and dumped her bag and towel on the padded chaise next to Welcome's, she glanced around and was relieved to find only a few bathers soaking up the sun and none in the pool. Good. Maybe she could slip into the water without anyone noticing her outfit. A cool swim was just what she needed to shake off the lethargy of a restless night.

"Sweetie, would you put some of this on my back?" Welcome held up a bottle and flipped over to her stomach.

Meri smoothed the coconut-scented lotion onto the flawless olive skin. "I thought redheads were supposed to have freckles. Are you sure you need to be out in the sun?"

"The suit looks fine, Meri. Stop playing games. Want me to do your back?"

Taking a deep breath, she stood and resolutely peeled off the purple robe. "No, I'm going for a swim first."

Wish You Were Here?

You can be, every month, with Zebra Historical Romance Novels.

AND TO GET YOU STARTED, ALLOW US TO SEND YOU

4 Historical Romances Free

A $19.96 VALUE!
With absolutely no obligation to buy anything.

YOU ARE CORDIALLY INVITED TO GET SWEPT AWAY INTO NEW WORLDS OF PASSION AND ADVENTURE.

AND IT WON'T COST YOU A PENNY!

Receive 4 Zebra Historical Romances, Absolutely Free!
(A $19.96 value)

Now you can have your pick of handsome, noble adventurers with romance in their hearts and you on their minds. Zebra publishes Historical Romances That Burn With The Fire Of History by the world's finest romance authors.

This very special FREE offer entitles you to 4 Zebra novels at absolutely no cost, with no obligation to buy anything, ever. It's an offer designed to excite your most vivid dreams and desires...and save you almost $20!

And that's not all you get...

Your Home Subscription Saves You Money Every Month.

After you've enjoyed your initial FREE package of 4 books, you'll begin to receive monthly shipments of new Zebra titles. These novels are delivered direct to your home as soon as they are published...sometimes even before the bookstores get them! Each monthly shipment of 4 books will be yours to examine for 10 days. Then if you decide to keep the books, you'll pay the preferred subscriber's price of just $4.00 per title. That's $16 for all 4 books...a savings of almost $4 off the publisher's price...and there's no additional charge for the convenience of home delivery!

There Is No Minimum Purchase. And Your Continued Satisfaction Is Guaranteed.

We're so sure that you'll appreciate the money-saving convenience of home delivery that we guarantee your complete satisfaction. You may return any shipment...for any reason...within 10 days and pay nothing that month. And if you want us to stop sending books, just say the word. There is no minimum number of books you must buy.

It's a no-lose proposition, so send for your 4 FREE books today!

YOU'RE GOING TO LOVE GETTING
4 FREE BOOKS

These books worth almost $20, are yours without cost or obligation when you fill out and mail this certificate.
(If the certificate is missing below, write to: Zebra Home Subscription Service, Inc., 120 Brighton Road, P.O. Box 5214, Clifton, New Jersey 07015-5214

Complete and mail this card to receive 4 Free books!

Yes! Please send me 4 Zebra Historical Romances without cost or obligation. I understand that each month thereafter I will be able to preview 4 new Zebra Historical Romances FREE for 10 days. Then, if I should decide to keep them, I will pay the money-saving preferred publisher's price of just $4.00 each...a total of $16. That's almost $4 less than the publisher's price, and there is no additional charge for shipping and handling. I may return any shipment within 10 days and owe nothing, and I may cancel this subscription at any time. The 4 FREE books will be mine to keep in any case.

Name _____

Address _____ Apt. _____

City _____ State _____ Zip _____

Telephone ( ) _____

Signature _____

(If under 18, parent or guardian must sign.)

LF0595

Terms, offer and prices subject to change without notice. Subscription subject to acceptance by Zebra Books. Zebra Books reserves the right to reject any order or cancel any subscription.

A $19.96 value. FREE!

No obligation to buy anything, ever.

ZEBRA HOME SUBSCRIPTION SERVICE, INC.

120 BRIGHTON ROAD

P.O. BOX 5214

CLIFTON, NEW JERSEY 07015-5214

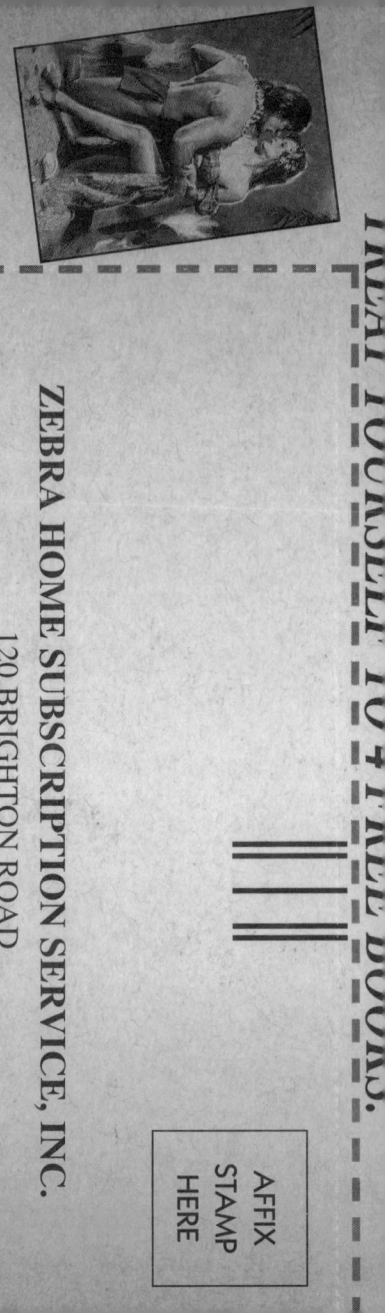

AFFIX STAMP HERE

"Terrific," said a deep voice behind her. "I'm just in time."

As Meri whirled to face Ram, it was hard to tell which of their jaws dropped lower as they scrutinized one another. His broad muscular shoulders, arms, and torso were bare, covered only by a patch of curly black hair on his bronzed chest that thinned enticingly down to a black bikini riding low on his slim hips. Her eyes traveled downward to thick corded thighs and calves to his feet. All the while butterflies were beating wildly in her stomach. He was a magnificent specimen.

Not daring to raise her eyes, she studied his feet. How interesting. His second toe was longer than his big toe, she thought as she watched them curl and uncurl against the concrete. She was aware of the smell of coconut oil on warm flesh, chlorine from the gently lapping water, and her blood pressure rising. An insect buzzed near her ear. Finally she allowed her gaze to retrace its earlier path until she was looking into his face. For once the soft blue flame of his eyes did not meet hers. They were focused lower. Much lower. Her breath caught as she could almost feel their caress on her body.

Suddenly, he glanced up, eyes narrowed, nostrils flared, and jaws clenched. He grabbed the purple robe and shook it out.

"Put this back on," he said. "I'll not allow you to parade around in that."

Her eyebrow went up. "Allow? *Allow?*"

He didn't budge from his stance.

Meri's chin lifted. "What's wrong with this suit? I'll have you know it's an Henri original. And it's the only one I have."

"Then I'll buy you another that covers you better. I'll not have every man in Egypt lusting after my woman. Put this on." He held up the robe and wrestled one arm into a sleeve.

Her temper flared. Jerking free, she stood with her fists on her hips. "Cover yourself if you're such a prude! I'm not *your* woman. Get that through your thick head. I'll wear what I want when I want! Do you hear me?"

Welcome giggled. "Lawdy, lawdy."

Ram swung Meri around and screened her with his body. "Love, be reasonable. People are staring."

"Reasonable? *Reasonable?* You're the one who needs to be reasonable." She shook off his hold. "I'm going for a swim. And *you,* Ramson Gabrey, can drop dead!"

Head high, she strode to the edge of the pool and cut the water with a shallow racing dive. Stroking furiously to the other side, she heard laughter and a smattering of applause from the audience they had attracted. But she was too angry to care that she had made a spectacle of herself. Damn Henri's six-hundred-dollar bathing suit anyway!

She swam laps until she was tired and her fury was spent. Rolling onto her back she floated lazily, staring at the cloudless sky. A dark head bobbed up beside her.

"Sweetheart, will you forgive me? I didn't mean to embarrass you or to make you angry. I acted like a damned jealous fool. That was a one, a two, and a three. I'm sorry. I just go a little crazy around you."

Something in the tenderness of his smile and woebegone look in his eyes as water dripped down his face and beaded on his thick black lashes and mustache caused Meri to melt. She returned his smile and placed her hand gently on top of his head—and shoved him under.

He came up laughing and sputtering. The war was on. They chased one another through the water, ducking, playing, splashing, and swimming together until Meri was breathless.

When she started to climb the ladder to get out, he quickly hoisted himself up and had a big towel waiting when she emerged. Although he didn't say a word, he glared at two men nearby and deftly positioned himself to shield her as much as possible until she had on her robe. Wise to his motives, she grinned. He shrugged and looked innocent.

It was like a convention in the narrow hallway of their small ship, *Nile Destiny,* as everyone excitedly boarded for the early afternoon departure. Porters, hurriedly distributing luggage, weaved around people trying to locate their cabins. Nona and Esther were sharing a room next to Welcome's. Several other members of the Golden Years Travel Club, including Dr. Stockton, were nearby. Looking harried, Leah Henry squeezed through the cluster with a sullen Bradley in tow.

George's and Jean Jacques's quarters were across from Meri's. Ram, who had escorted Meri and Welcome to their compact connecting cabins, was next door to Meri, while Ram's young associate, Mark Macleod, was across from him.

Meri tried her best to make introductions while Nona fluttered and giggled as Jean Jacques, clad in a chartreuse version of yesterday's pink, kissed hands; and porters scurried through the mass confusion. An embarrassed silence fell as Walter Rush argued loudly with the purser.

"I'm supposed to be *here*. There must be a mistake. I demand to see the captain," he shouted, his eyes bulging behind his wire-rimmed glasses and his adam's apple bobbing up and down. "I was confirmed for *this* cabin." He slapped the door of Ram's room.

As the purser made soothing noises and tried to lead the irate man away with promises of excellent accommodations on another deck, Meri looked askance at Ram. "Exactly how did you get this particular room?"

"Just lucky, I guess." His lips twitched as he shrugged his shoulders.

Before Meri could comment, John Stockton, ever the gentleman diplomat, approached the irate Rush whose face blazed as he struggled with the purser. Dr. Stockton said calmly, "Walter, I would be happy to exchange—"

The struggling man's wildly flailing fist missed the purser and slammed into John Stockton's face. He crashed against the wall and crumpled to the floor. Blood gushed from a gash over his right eye.

Ram started forward, but Esther was there first. She smacked Rush with her oversized purse and shrieked in his face, "You vile, vile man! Now see what you've done?" She hurried to Dr. Stockton, dropped to the floor and cradled his head in her lap. Dabbing the bleeding cut with her lacy handkerchief, she moaned, "Oh, my darling John. You're hurt. That nasty man has hurt you."

Dr. Stockton patted Esther's hand and said, "There, there, Esther. Don't fret. I'm a tough old bird."

The displaced passenger, clearly horrified by what he had done, slumped his shoulders and stared at the group. He mumbled something akin to an apology and made a fast exit. An attendant came running with a first-aid kit, but Esther Barrington wouldn't let anybody touch the wound. She insisted on tending "darling John" herself.

After the cut was cleaned and bandaged and it was determined that his injury was not serious, Ram said to the group, "Why don't we get unpacked? We can meet on the observation deck at three o'clock and watch the ship's departure." Everyone agreed and adjourned to their cabins. Turning back to Meri, he said quietly, "I'll call for you in about half an hour, princess."

Once inside the small stateroom with its neutral colors and temple prints, Meri tossed her purse and key on the desk and collapsed on the day bed. The ugly scene had unnerved her. Thank goodness Dr. Stockton was not badly hurt. Then she had to smile. Esther was not as indifferent to the courtly old gentleman as she would have everyone believe. And John Stockton had enjoyed every minute of her attention. Meri hadn't missed his little wink as he allowed Esther to lead him to his cabin.

When she kicked off her sandals and got up to wash her face, she glanced to a corner table flanked by a pair of bright blue chairs. Two large packages sat on the table.

She frowned. "Now what?"

One contained the fur coat and all the jewelry Ram had given her. She sighed and rolled her eyes heavenward. *Here we go again,* she thought. The other box was wrapped in bright foil paper and tied with gold cord. Taking the second package back to the bed, she opened it warily. At least a dozen bathing suits and matching robes in a variety of colors and patterns were nestled in the tissue lining.

All of them were more demure than the purple Henri original.

"Oh, good grief!" She slammed the lid on the floor. "I'm going to strangle that man yet!" A soft tapping on the connecting door interrupted her tirade. Still scowling, she yanked open the door to admit Welcome.

The redhead's eyes widened. "What in the world's wrong, sweetie?"

Meri gestured toward the bed. "Look. Just look! Do I need this? I may kill Ramson Gabrey before the day is over."

Welcome rushed to the opened package, checked the contents, then burst into laughter. Holding up a swirl of blue and green, she pointed out the designer label. "Well, the guy's got good taste. You have to give him that."

"I'll give him a piece of my mind." Meri fumed as she pulled the suit from Welcome's hands and tossed it back into the pile. Slapping the bent lid on the box, she gathered the package, colorful fabric spilling out the sides, and stormed out into the hallway. Silently raving all of the things she would say to him, she pounded on Ram's door.

There was no answer. She stalked back into her room and dumped the jumbled mess back on the bed.

Standing with her fists on her hips, eyes narrowed, and mouth drawn in a thin determined line, she considered and abandoned one plot of revenge after another. Finally, a plan caught her fancy. Her eyebrow lifted and a devious smirk curled one corner of her mouth.

"Uh-oh," Welcome said, "I know that look. What scheme have you hatched?"

"The swimming pool's on the observation deck, isn't it?" When Welcome nodded, Meri asked, "Where's Henri's purple bathing suit?"

* * *

Topside a few minutes later, Meri stood clad in the flowing purple robe, one hand gathering the fabric to her in a battle with the wind.

Maybe this wasn't such a good idea.

Several members of the Golden Years Travel Club had already congregated on deck. Nona was chattering away about something to Welcome. Esther Barrington, dressed in a sensible loose cotton dress and sandals, was actually smiling at Dr. Stockton who, wearing his bandage like a badge and peering through binoculars, was leaning against the rail beside Esther.

Meri wasn't ordinarily impulsive or vindictive, and she felt like a fool now that she had cooled off. She couldn't parade around in this skimpy suit and shock these sweet people just to vent her anger at Ram. In the last three days she had lost her temper more times than she had in the past three years. What was wrong with her? With a resolute sigh, she started back to her cabin to change.

Dr. Stockton stopped her. "Isn't that your gentleman friend over there?" He pointed toward a building up the street and handed her the binoculars. "He'd better hurry back. We're about to get underway."

Brushing hair away from her face, she adjusted the focus and peered through the glasses. There was no mistaking that profile or the muscular shoulders in the white knit shirt. A newspaper was tucked under one arm, and Ram was standing in front of a magazine stand in deep conversation with Mark and another man.

"Yes, that's him, but I wouldn't worry. Knowing Ram, they'll hold the boat." Then she gasped as Mark moved and gave her a clear view of the third person.

It was the droopy-eyed Egyptian! The one she'd noticed several times before. At Memphis. At Abu Simbel. And now here. Coincidence? It was becoming less likely. And why was he talking to Ram? Was the guy following her? Why?

The possibility that she was being tailed made her extremely anxious. What if he were some sort of terrorist? Oh, Lord, if one of those militant extremists kidnapped her, her mother would die. And Meri would never hear the end of it from Nora—if she lived to talk about it.

Feeling sick to her stomach, she handed the binoculars back to Dr. Stockton and went to her room to change into more modest white slacks.

A knock came as she pulled on a pink shirt and slipped into a pair of white leather thongs. Knowing who was at the door, she quickly brushed the tangles from her hair and dashed on a bit of lipstick.

Seeing the fellow with the droopy eye so frequently had made her exceedingly apprehensive. But she hadn't forgotten that she was still irked with Ram.

The knock became more urgent, and she heard Ram's deep voice calling her. Let the bastard wait. She took her time sorting the contents of her shoulder bag, adding her favorite camera and plenty of film. At the last minute, she wrapped the jeweled hairpins and the falcon pendant in tissues and tucked them in an inside zippered pocket for safe-keeping.

When she finally flung open the door, Ram stood there grinning, a newspaper still under his arm. "Where were you, love? I was getting worried."

As he bent to kiss her cheek, she averted her face. "The question is, where were you? I tried your room a few minutes ago."

"I went to get a newspaper," he said, holding it up. "You can read it if you like, but it's in Arabic. Did you miss me while I was gone?" His eyes brightened, and his smile widened as he moved toward her.

"About like I'd miss the plague." She retreated from him once again. "Who was that man you were talking to?"

Ram frowned. "Talking to? Mark went with me. We talked."

"No, I mean the other one. I was on the observation deck with the others, and I watched with binoculars while you and Mark were talking to that other man." Queasiness built in her stomach. "Who was he? The one with the droopy eye?"

He laughed and caught her to him in a hug as the newspaper fell to the floor. "Princess, why are you so concerned about such a thing? He's just a man I ran into at the newsstand. I'd much rather be with you than with him. You're more fascinating." Nuzzling her ear, he chuckled. "Watching me through binoculars, hum?"

Meri stiffened in his arms, then shoved him away and turned her back. "Damn it, Ramson Gabrey, listen to me. I have a serious problem. I'm very upset."

"Love, what's wrong?" He turned her toward him and searched her face. Glancing over her shoulder he saw the tangle of bathing suits on the bed and smiled. "Is that what's wrong? Are you upset about the swimsuits? Throw the damned things out the window if you want to."

"Yes, I was angry about them, but this is about something worse. Dammit, I'm frightened."

His smile faded. His eyes turned to steel slits, and his hands tightened around her upper arms. "Who has frightened you? Has someone hurt you?"

"Yes. No. I don't know. But I think he plans to kidnap me!"

He frowned. *"Kidnap* you? Who?"

"That's what I've been trying to tell you. That man you were talking to, the one with the droopy eye, he's been following me. I've seen him several times. He nearly frightened me out of my wits at Abu Simbel. For a moment I thought he was coming to murder me in the dark. He probably plans to cut my throat while I sleep."

Amusement twitched his mustache, his shoulders shook, and then he laughed aloud. "Love, you have a vivid imagination."

"Ramson Gabrey, this is not funny!" Hot tears burst their restraints and spilled over her cheeks. She brushed them away with the backs of her hands. "I'm scared."

He clutched her to him. "My life, don't cry. It tears me apart when you cry." He lifted her chin and gently kissed her eyelids. *"Rôhi,* I would never allow anything to harm you. My only concern is your safety and your happiness. I'm sorry I laughed, but I know the man. And his wife. And his five children. Believe me, he's no threat to you."

Meri's eyes, still luminous with tears, met his warm blue ones. "You really don't think he was following me?"

He chuckled. *"I'm* following you. Do we need a procession?"

She scanned the dark, rough-hewn face that was becoming so dear to her. There was something ruthless and mysterious in his nature, and she sensed . . . something. "You know, for a moment, the idea crossed my mind that maybe you had someone following me."

"Why would I do such a thing?"

"I don't know. But you'd damned well better not try it." She took a deep breath and said, "Okay. Now about those bathing suits . . ."

He hooted with laughter and swatted her on the seat. "Go wash your beautiful face while I have a word with Mark, and we'll join the others. We'll discuss the suits later."

Mad enough to chew nails, Ram didn't stop to have a word with Mark, he went straight to J.J., the manager of Horus Security. The two of them had been friends since they were fraternity brothers at U.T., and Ram had always trusted him implicitly, but if J.J. screwed up this one, he'd ship him back to that swamp he came from.

"Damn that one-eyed idiot, Mustafa!" he exploded. "What in the hell is he doing here? I thought I told you to fire him."

"I did, boss. Three weeks ago. I canned his ass, just like you told me to," he said in a soft drawl.

"Then why is he hanging around Meri?"

"You got me. I haven't seen him."

"Then you'd better start looking. Meri said she's spotted him three or four times, twice today. Even I saw him skulking behind a newspaper at the dock. He's such an idiot that he couldn't pour piss out of a boot without directions on the heel."

"Did you talk to him?"

"Sure I talked to him. He gave me some stupid story about his sister."

"He doesn't have a sister."

"Hell, I know that. I also know that the sleazy little son-of-a-bitch is up to no good. He'd sell his own mother for ten pounds. Be warned, J.J., if anything happens to one hair on Meri's head, I'll have your balls for breakfast."

"Mercy, man, you got it bad for this lady, don't you?"

"Yes, I've got it bad. And for godsake, stay heads up on this one. I want her safe, but I also want to keep her in the dark that we're protecting her."

"Or I'll be up to my ass in alligators."

Ram laughed. "In Egypt, it's crocodiles. And you wouldn't make a decent meal for one. Another thing, you might keep an eye out for the *Mabaheth*. I had a meeting with Tewfik Fayed yesterday, and he has some paranoid notion that Meri and Welcome are spies."

"*Spies?* Those two? You've got to be kidding."

"Hell, I know it's crazy." Ram filled him in on his conversation with Fayed. "Tewfik probably has a couple of men hanging around."

J.J. laughed. "Meri has more men watching her than the World Series. I hope we don't all trip over her."

"Just play it cool."

"Man, I couldn't get any cooler. I'll be as unobtrusive as a fly speck."

Ram snorted. "That'll be the day," he said, as he left the room.

Once outside he took a deep breath and blew it out.

God forbid what Meri would say if she ever found out that he *was* having her watched. Actually, he didn't consider the security measures that had been instituted as having her followed; he considered them protection. But he knew that he would have a difficult time convincing her of the difference.

For a moment he cursed the interfering Nora Elwood for placing him in this uncomfortable position of having to deceive Meri. Then he relented. Even if his mother and Meri's hadn't asked for help, he would have assigned agents to protect her. These were unsettled times, and Méri was too precious to him to ignore safety precautions. Thank God his security force had been more vigilant than he. One of his men was on her tail when she left Giza and had stayed with her until others could catch the plane for Luxor.

The thought of something happening to her made his blood run cold. She was his joy, his life, his soul. He would wrestle all the jackals in the desert rather than allow one of her fingernails to be harmed. But would she ever forgive him if she found out the truth?

He could only pray.

Still puzzling about Mustafa, he went in search of Meri.

They never did discuss the bathing suits. Instead, when they arrived on the top deck, Meri became enchanted with the view and the excitement as the *Nile Destiny* slowly steamed northward on the ancient blue water. Graceful feluccas, white sails filled as they traveled downstream on the current or upstream with the winds, navigated the river carrying passengers, cargo, or robed fishermen and their nets. Tall palms swayed beside the muddy banks and dotted the green fields beyond.

Meri leaned over the rail and returned the waves of laughing barefoot children scampering along the shore until the ship outdistanced them. "It seems strange to be sailing downriver with the current and yet be headed north."

Ram nodded. "Another of Egypt's mysteries. The Nile is the only river in the world that flows from south to north to empty into the sea. That's why we're now in Upper Egypt, in the south, yet everything north of Giza is part of Lower Egypt."

Laughing, Meri shook her head. "I can never keep it straight. It reminds me of the old Abbott and Costello routine: 'Who's on first.' "

"You're too young to remember Abbott and Costello."

"That's true. Still, I love old movies. My favorite thing to do on rainy weekends is to make a big bowl of popcorn, snuggle up in bed, and watch the black and white classics on cable TV. How do you know about Abbott and Costello? You're not old enough either, and I doubt that they have reruns in Egypt."

"As a matter of fact, they do have reruns of many American films on Egyptian television, but they're mostly recent ones. I have a large video collection of old movies: Abbott and Costello, Laurel and Hardy, W. C. Fields, Errol Flynn, Humphrey Bogart."

"Casablanca? Do you have *Casablanca?* It's one of my favorites."

"Yes, I have it. When we get to my home in Luxor, we'll watch all your favorites. I don't think I can manage a rainy day for you, but I can probably furnish some popcorn, and I have a very big bed we can snuggle in."

"Ra-am," she drawled, sending a warning.

He grinned. "Just trying to be accommodating. You said it was your favorite thing to do."

She chuckled and shook her head. "What am I going to do with you?"

He took her hand and, with his eyes never leaving hers, touched it to his lips. "Anything you want."

For an instant, she swayed hypnotically toward him feeling as if time were suspended and the very breeze held its breath.

"Oh there you two lovebirds are." Nona Craft's bright chatter intruded, and the moment was lost. "We were afraid you had missed the sailing—or is it the steaming? Can you sail on a steamship? We've all been up at the front—I mean the bow—and we're about to have a drink to toast our departure. Won't you join us?"

Her cotton curls bobbed as she continued without waiting for an answer. "It's so wonderful to have you along, Mr. Gabrey—being Egyptian and all. Funny, you don't look Egyptian—most of the ones I've seen are short and have dark eyes—but Welcome says you are. You can explain all the sights to us."

Ram looked at Meri, gave a small shrug, and courteously offered an arm to each lady. "I'd be delighted—Mrs. Craft, isn't it? What would you like to know?"

"Oh, just everything. And please call me Nona. I'll call you Ram. Ram—that's an unusual name. So strong. Did your mother call you that because you're hardheaded?" Her eyes twinkled, and her plump cheeks dimpled as she laughed at her own joke.

He grinned as Meri exploded into snickers. "Not at all, Nona. My full name is Ramson. It was my maternal grandmother's maiden name."

Ram easily charmed the group as they sat on cushioned deck chairs around the pool. He pointed out the sights along the way and explained the farming and irrigation methods of the peasants living by the Nile's banks.

These simple people, whose lives were intimately bound to the land along the river, lived and worked their crops in the same manner as had their ancestors for generations, even back to pharaonic times. The only difference was that they no longer depended on the annual flood to soak their fields and deposit rich silt. Now the dam regulated the sacred flow and modern fertilizers aided growth.

After a few minutes, Jean Jacques quietly excused himself from the group that had gathered. "I just love to listen to your handsome brute," he whispered to Meri as he stepped around her, "but if I don't get out of the sun, I'll turn as red as a lobster, *chérie.*"

Even while Ram was weaving his enchantment with the others, his eyes seldom left Meri for long. Unobtrusively he saw to her comfort, kept her glass filled and her back to the sun. Now and then he lifted his black eyebrows and smiled as if asking, "Are you okay?" When she answered with a slight smile and nod, he would continue.

"The building of the dam has been a real boon to this country, hasn't it?" Dr. Stockton asked as he fanned himself with his floppy golf hat.

"Yes and no," Ram answered. "There are the obvious advantages, of course. Over half of our population is made up of very poor farmers, and they no longer have to depend on the caprice of the annual flood. Now they can harvest as many as five crops a year, and more land has been reclaimed for agriculture. We have the electrical power it generates. But as so often happens when man interferes with nature, there have been serious problems. Now the sea is beginning to encroach into the Nile delta, which is one of our most fertile regions. It's becoming salty; the ecological balance is disturbed. Chemical fertilizer is adding an unknown factor.

"Although we have a vast area of land, for all practical purposes, Egypt consists of the long narrow strip of land bordering the Nile. Tourism is our greatest industry now, but if we are to grow and prosper as a people, as a nation, we need to move from an agricultural country dependent on tourists toward greater modern industrialization." He stopped and laughed. "Forgive me. Occasionally I get on my soapbox about this issue."

Welcome stood and said, "I don't know about you folks, but I'd like to find some air-conditioning. God forbid that I'd have to plow fields in this sun all day."

"I believe they're serving tea in the lounge now," Nona said.

"Sounds good to me." Welcome and several of the others went in search of refreshment.

Ram turned to Meri and asked, "And you, *sukkar,* would you like tea? The British custom remains with us."

"I'm not such a hothouse flower as Welcome, but tea would be nice."

They spent the rest of the afternoon chatting over tea and exploring the ship's gift shop. Meri had to be careful not to admire anything or Ram would insist on buying it for her. Already he'd bought her a string of lapis beads, a pair of sandals, and a gold cartouche necklace with her name in hieroglyphics was on special order. She would slip back later to purchase some of the custom-made pendants for friends back home as well as the colorful *galabiyahs* that filled the racks. If she had admired them openly, he would have bought a dozen, and Meri had long ago run out of luggage space.

"It pleases me to buy things for you," he'd said when she protested.

Meri still had to finish unpacking and wanted to bathe and wash her hair before dinner, so Ram left her at her door with a peck on the cheek and a promise to call for her. "Just knock on the wall when you're ready," he said, lightly tracing the outline of her lips with his finger, "and I'll come running."

Two steps inside her cabin, Meri stepped on a shoe. "What in the wor—"

Horrified, she looked at her room.

It was in shambles. Everything in her luggage was dumped out and scattered over the floor and the bed. The linings in her suitcases were torn out. Even the packages of M&M's had been ripped open, and their contents littered the cabin like candy confetti.

Seventeen

The storm cloud thunders, and evil are the crocodiles!
O Moon-god, raise up his crime against him!

The Proverbs of Amen-en-Ope
c. 1580-1320 B.C.

Shock paralyzed Meri for a moment as she encountered the chaos. Her shock soon gave way, first to horror and then to fear. Her initial impulse was to fling open the door and call to Ram. Then she stopped abruptly. No, if she did that, he'd come charging in like an avenging angel and probably want to whisk her off the boat. He always over-reacted to everything.

Her first thought was that she hoped to God that her mother didn't hear about this. She could just see Nora smirking and smugly saying, "I told you so."

She felt as if a rock as big as a cannonball sat in the pit of her stomach, and she tried to control the monumental case of the shakes that rattled her teeth. *Calm down,* she told herself. *Think. Check it out.* This was a simple robbery. After all, she hadn't been in the room, so it couldn't have been someone bent on murder or kidnapping. Somehow the notion didn't do a thing to lower her pulse rate.

Frantically she scratched through the jumbled pile of clothing and was relieved when she located the expensive fur coat.

Her relief evaporated quickly, however, as Meri searched the deep pockets where she'd crammed the jewelry.

It was gone.

She searched every nook and cranny. No jewelry.

Meri banged on the connecting door yelling for Welcome.

"Hold your horses! I'm coming. I'm coming," Welcome shouted as the lock rattled and the door swung open. "Where's the fire? Sweetie, what's wrong? You're white as a sheet."

Waving her arm wildly in the direction of her room, Meri managed to croak, "Just look. I've been robbed!"

The redhead charged into the littered cabin to investigate the damage. In a shaky voice, Meri explained what was missing. As she stood beside her friend, Meri's earlier fright dissolved into outrage. How dare someone invade her private domain, go through her personal things—touch them, trash them—steal from her! Fury boiled up in her as she thought of someone's hands rummaging through her clothing. And to rip open all the candy was sick—wanton destruction reeking of anger and hostility.

Welcome phoned for the captain and helped Meri search through the mess to determine what was missing. Thank heavens the hairpins and the pendant had been in her purse. At least they were safe. It hadn't occurred to her to do anything with the rest of the jewelry. Surprisingly enough, Ram had told her when Mark Macleod had supervised the handling of their luggage before they boarded, theft was uncommon in Egypt. Well, maybe not so surprising when one knew the swift justice meted out to thieves. She wouldn't steal anything either if she knew that her hand might get lopped off.

Meri shook her head. "I can't seem to find anything else missing. Damn! My film. I meant to ask you about that. Did I put my personal rolls of film in your suitcase with the ones for the brochure? I noticed when I packed today that every exposed roll is gone."

"I don't think I have it, but let's check."

They pulled the film case from Welcome's closet and searched through the rolls.

"Nope," Welcome said, "it's not here."

"Where could I have put it?"

"Do you think the thief got it?"

"No. I missed it earlier. I just assumed that I must have put them in your stuff. And why would a burglar steal exposed film anyhow? He didn't take the cameras or the unexposed rolls. It makes no sense."

Before Welcome could comment, a knock came at Meri's door. They hurried through to her connecting room and admitted the captain.

The captain was distraught about the break-in and destruction.

Ram was called in when Meri didn't know if the pieces were insured or not. She had never seen him so furious as when he first surveyed the disorder. Then he dressed down the captain in a rapid, raging Arabic that had the poor man bowing and mumbling profuse apologies.

"I shall alert the authorities at once," the captain said, bowing his way from the cabin.

"Don't worry about the baubles, sweetheart," Ram said lovingly as he ushered Meri into Welcome's cabin while a bevy of maids, ordered by the captain, straightened hers. "We'll get you some more."

Meri only shook her head and sank into one of the blue chairs, identical to the pair in her stateroom. Ram filled three glasses from a large brandy bottle that appeared mysteriously, offered one to Welcome, and squatted at Meri's feet when he handed one to her.

"Take a sip of this," he coaxed as he scanned her pale face and grasped her free hand. "Your hands are like ice. Are you okay?"

She tossed back a big gulp of the liquor. It went racing down her throat like sulfuric acid and prompted a fit of coughing. Tears came to her eyes. Meri grinned self-consciously and gasped, "I forgot to sip."

"Sip the rest slowly," he said, as seriously as if he were instructing a child. "Will you be all right with Welcome now? I need to go straighten this out. Are you going to feel like going to dinner later, or shall I have it sent to your room?"

"Of course I'm going to dinner!" she said crossly. "I'm not a child to be pampered. I can take care of this myself."

"I'll tend to it, Miss Independent," Ram answered gently but firmly. "Let me know when you're ready for dinner, okay?"

He was a hardheaded son-of-a-gun, but right now she was in no mood to argue. Meri sighed. What the heck. "Okay. I'll knock on the wall."

Ram smiled and squeezed her hand before he rose and turned to Welcome. "I'm going to get to the bottom of this. You take care of Meri while I'm gone."

The redhead snapped a saucy salute and said, "Yes, sir!"

Laughing at himself, Ram said, "Sorry, but I go a little crazy over her. This lady is very special to me," he added, gazing at Meri with open adoration.

"She's special to me, too," Welcome said quietly. "Don't worry."

The theft and destruction unnerved Meri more than she was willing to admit to either Ram or Welcome. She replayed the whole incident a dozen times in her mind as she sipped another glass of brandy from the bottle Ram had left.

The captain had dropped by again, so effusive in his apologies that she thought he might start kissing her feet at any minute. He told her that he had made arrangements for Meri's room to be watched at all times by one of the crew.

While her room being trashed and the jewelry stolen unnerved her, she wondered about the film too. That was even stranger. Had someone gone through her things once before?

"Why in the world would anyone want my film?" she asked Welcome. "It was only the usual tourist stuff."

"Beats me, sweetie."

"When could it have been taken?"

Welcome frowned. "Remember when I asked you about the patio door? Last night I found it unlocked when I came in. That must have been when it happened."

"Who could have done it? And why? I can understand a jewel—Damn! That droopy-eyed man. I'll bet that's why he's been hanging around. Why the sticky-fingered little weasel! I'll bet he's on the ship with my stuff in his pockets. I'm going to call the captain and report him."

That done, Meri tried to dismiss the incident from her mind. Another glass of brandy helped.

Her room had been returned to pristine order and was sporting a large bouquet of flowers from the captain. Meri stood in front of the closet mentally ticking off choices of a dress for dinner. She finally selected a soft, frothy creation in pale sea-green voile with pink cabbage roses and moss green leaves, ruffled flounce, and spaghetti straps. Not a style she would ordinarily select for herself, the dress and its matching stole had been a birthday gift last summer from a great-aunt. She couldn't even remember why she'd brought it along. But this evening the feminine creation seemed right.

She decided to put her hair up in a fussy style of waves and curls. By the time she threaded her special hairpins through the swirls, she was humming a waltz.

She considered wearing the falcon pendant, but it didn't match the dress. Hesitant to leave it in the room—even if a crew member was on guard—she wondered what to do with it. It wouldn't fit in her tiny evening purse with all the other stuff she needed.

Ram. Of course. She would ask him to keep it in his pocket.

She dumped her costume jewelry from a small silk pouch and slipped the pendant inside.

Playfully, she leaned over the bed and tapped "Shave and a Haircut" on the wall to Ram's room. He gave an answering rap and was at her door before she could gather her purse and stole.

He kissed her cheek, then trailed lower, nuzzling her neck. "You look good enough to eat."

Sensual chills raced over her at the touch of his warm lips on her bare skin. Placing her hands against his chest, she tilted her head, inviting more of the delicious tasting, but he pulled back when Nona and Esther exited their room and spoke to them. Meri collected her accessories and locked her room while Ram chatted with the two women.

Meri slipped the pouch into his jacket pocket. "Hold on to this for me."

The four of them walked to the dining room together and joined Welcome, Dr. Stockton, and Jean Jacques who were waiting for the second seating. George, "poor dear," Jean Jacques had confided, had a touch of *mal de mer*.

When they were amused that anyone could be seasick on the slow smooth voyage; the slight Frenchman twirled a lock of his platinum hair and added, "He's much more sensitive than he looks, you know."

Standing together in close quarters while they waited, Ram turned to Dr. Stockton to answer a question, and Meri patted her foot impatiently, listening to her stomach growl. Suddenly Ram stiffened and his eyes widened, then narrowed. He whispered in Meri's ear, "Did you do that?"

"Do what?"

"I was afraid it wasn't you," Ram said with a wry half-smirk.

"What are you talking about?"

"Somebody pinched me on the butt."

Turning to look behind them, she noted Jean Jacques, decked out in tight black pants and a black pirate shirt cinched at the waist with a silver chain that matched his sandals and earrings. He was talking innocently with Nona and Esther, who were sedately dressed in their Sunday best.

Meri giggled. "Which one do you think it was?"

Ram tugged on his navy blazer and straightened his tie. "I wouldn't dare speculate."

She laughed and teased him as the maître d' led them to a place for eight overlooking the water. The elegant room was softly lit; tall tapers flickered at each large round table, formally set with crisp white linen, fine gold-banded crystal and china, and heavy silver. Centerpieces of fragrant flowers spilled over ornate épergnes dripping with fiery prisms. A wall of glass, beside their circle of diners, allowed a view of the river below and faint outlines of date palms and thick bushes dipping their branches into the dark Nile.

After wine and a soup course were served by exuberant Nubian waiters, the guests made selections from a lavish buffet. There were heaps of succulent grilled lamb chops, skewered meats on beds of steamed herb rice, great slabs of roast beef, several kinds of fish, chicken in rich, pungent sauces, and delicately cooked vegetables of all kinds as well as the ever-present salads of cucumbers and tomatoes.

"I'm going to gain fifty pounds on all this glorious food," Meri moaned.

"You don't have to eat it all, *sukkar*. Even so, I'll still love you when you're a roly-poly."

"I've been meaning to ask you," she said, ignoring the last part of his statement. "What does *sukkar* mean? Are you insulting me?"

"Hardly. It's an Arabic endearment. It means sugar. Do you mind if I call you that?"

"No, I just like to know what's being said." She spooned a dab of saffron rice onto her already-full plate and looked wistfully at the other tempting dishes she didn't have room for.

When they were seated, he said, "We'll start soon with Arabic lessons for you." He leaned over and whispered against her ear, "I'll teach you all the love words first."

She almost choked on a bite of lamb and quickly gulped her glass of wine. A conscientious waiter immediately refilled it. He refilled it a number of times during the meal.

"What would you like from the dessert table, love?"

"Oh, I don't know. What would you like?"

His light blue eyes trailed over the length of her, one eyebrow arched, and a slow seductive smile lifted one corner of his mouth. "Need you ask?"

It took her hand two tries before she found the wineglass again. "Just bring me something chocolate." *Or yourself on a plate with a big spoon.* She giggled.

Was she feeling a tiny bit tipsy or was this glorious hunk of a man finally getting to be too much to resist? A bit of both, maybe. No more wine tonight for her.

Ram returned with a dish of the most delicious concoction she had ever tasted—a bowl of miniature cream puffs with a generous ladle of warm, velvety chocolate sauce. She savored every luscious bite even though he watched her as she ate with that silent, proud-hawk look of his. She even fed one to him, laughing and jiggling the spoon when he clamped his teeth on it and wouldn't let go.

Lost in their suggestive play for a moment, she forgot everyone but Ram. She was embarrassed when she heard Nona's stage whisper. "Isn't that sweet?"

After dinner the group moved into the lounge for dancing and drinks. John Stockton immediately claimed Esther, who seemed to glow with a new inner light, for a slow foxtrot. As Meri watched the pair, she remembered her time with them at Abu Simbel and the things the courtly old gentleman had told her.

Leaning against Ram, she watched the couple on the floor discovering a new relationship. "Do you know he has loved her and pursued her for over thirty years?" *Would you follow me for thirty years, Ram?*

"I would follow you to the ends of the earth and beyond eternity, if that's what it took, *rôhi.*" His voice was soft and husky as his finger drew small circles on her bare shoulder.

She was startled. Now he was reading her mind! Quickly she reached to gulp another glass of wine and turned her attention to the others.

Nona was excited about the talent show to be held the next night and proposed that they form a troupe to participate. Most of the Golden Years Travel Club were also part of a folk-dance class in Atlanta, and Jean Jacques agreed to dance as well.

Meri asked, "Oh, do you dance, Jean Jacques?"

He sniffed and preened. "I danced professionally for several years. I'm retired now, but I try to keep in shape. What will the rest of you do in our International Terpsichorean presentation?"

"Texas *must* be represented." Meri brooded a moment before a brilliant idea struck her. "I know," she said, as she thrust her finger in the air and turned with a deliberated slowness to Ram. Propping her elbow on the table and planting her chin in her palm, she said slowly, "Tell me, *sukkar,* have you ever done any country dancing?"

His mustache twitched, but he said seriously, "But, of course, my dear. I'm a two-stepping fool."

"That's it," she announced with an exaggerated wave of her hand. "Ram and Welcome and I will demonstrate and teach everybody a line dance."

Welcome rolled her eyes heavenward and shook her head when the others asked what Meri was talking about.

When Meri's chin came down on both propped fists and her bottom lip turned down in a pout, Ram asked, "What's wrong, kitten?"

"We've got jeans, but to do this right, we need boots and hats and bandannas. Oh, heck."

"I'll take care of it."

She beamed. "Oh, Ram, could you?"

"If you want it, I'll get it."

When Welcome protested, Meri clutched Ram's arm and, although her words were slightly slurred, she announced haughtily, "My Ram can do anything."

Ram grinned as he wrote down their group's sizes for boots and hats. He grinned even wider when Meri said in a loud whisper, clearly audible to everyone at the table, "Don't tell anybody my foot is a size nine."

"I won't tell a soul, *sukkar*." He excused himself for a few minutes, whispering to Meri before he left, "Love, don't order another drink while I'm gone."

She didn't. Instead she danced with Dr. Stockton, who did an elegant waltz; Jean Jacques, who was remarkably graceful even though he barely came to her chin; and two men she didn't know but who seemed very friendly. She seemed to vaguely recall that one was Jerry from Jackson, Mississippi, and the other was somebody or the other from Canada.

Welcome grabbed her when she started to do a rock number with a third amiable stranger and hissed, "Sit down, sweetie, you're potted."

Potted? She'd never been potted before in her life. She was about to protest when Ram slipped into the chair beside her and told her that everything was taken care of.

She looked smugly at Welcome. "See, I told you." Throwing both arms around Ram's neck, she pulled his ear to her mouth. "Welcome says I'm potted. Am I potted, Ram?"

"Maybe just a little. Why don't we go outside for some air?"

"I want to dance with you first."

"One dance and then we'll go outside."

They stayed on the floor longer than that, moving with the steady sensuous beat. When Meri wrapped her arms around his neck and plastered herself against his body, Ram groaned and mumbled something she didn't catch. Filled with a warm glow, she burrowed her head under his chin and murmured, "I love to dance with you. It makes me feel all tingly." Looking up at his darkly handsome face, she asked, "Does it seem awfully hot in here to you?"

"Yes, and it's getting hotter by the minute. Let's go topside and walk for a while."

They stopped by the table to retrieve her things. She looped her stole around her neck and tossed one end over her shoulder with all the flourish of a World War I flying ace.

Ram gingerly guided her outside and upstairs to the deserted observation deck where a cool breeze teased loose wisps of her hair and the full moon shimmered across the surface of the water.

Only the faint music from below and a gentle, rhythmic lapping of the river about the ship resounded through the silence. Now and again, the transient call of a distant waterfowl rose through the hush of the night.

There was magic in the air. Meri could feel it and she responded by breathing in deeply, throwing her arms open wide and whirling around. Her joyous laughter went echoing through the shadows and silver moonglow.

She was far from potted, as Ram and Welcome had suggested. It was only that the wine had made her feel warmly relaxed and gloriously uninhibited.

She went whirling gaily about again. Ram's strong arms caught her, a second before she would have pirouetted into the swimming pool. "Not even you, my tipsy fairy princess, can waltz on the water." Laughing, he led her to another spot, leaned back against the rail, and cradled her to his side.

"I'm *not* tipsy." She pivoted from his grasp and threw her arms around his neck. "I feel *wonderful*." Nestling her body between his legs, she drew his face down until his nose touched the tip of hers. "Did you know that you've got the sexiest eyes? They're so blue, it amazes me that you can see out of them. And the sexiest lips . . ."

She drew back just enough to lazily trace the outline of his mouth with tip of her tongue. "You're the world's best kisser," she murmured, brushing her lips against his. She nibbled and nipped below his soft mustache.

He groaned and tried to pull her away. Undaunted, she ran her hands over his wide shoulders, his broad chest, and ground her lower torso closer to his. "And the sexiest body." She grabbed his head and hungrily forced his lips toward hers.

For a moment he returned her passionate kiss, then wrenched his mouth away and hugged her close, his breathing ragged against her ear.

"You've even got sexy toes." She giggled and rubbed her knee up his inner thigh.

"That does it," he burst out, trying to pry loose her arms. "I've had a hell of a time trying to remind myself that you're too smashed to know what you're doing, but, honey, I can't take any more of this. We're going to put you to bed. Now."

"Good.' '" She flashed her most beguiling smile. "Your bed or mine?"

"You're going to sleep alone tonight, love."

"Don't you want me?"

Crushing her to him he answered, "Hell, Meri, I've been begging you to marry me."

"Oh, I don't want to get married. Let's have a wild, wonderful affair instead!"

Chuckling, he said, "You can't have my body unless you agree to marry me."

Rubbing her breasts against his chest, she murmured, "Oh, Ram, I want you so much. I'm so hot. Are you sure you don't want me?"

"Nope."

"You *lie.*" She giggled, thrust her hand between his legs, and slid it upward. "I can feel you're lying. Touch me. Love me."

He groaned and captured the stroking hand, *"Habîbati,* don't do this to me. Not tonight. Not like this."

Heavy footsteps sounded on the stairs and then the deck. Ram tried to tear away her fingers which were intent on unbuttoning his shirt and slithering inside to caress his chest. He cleared his throat and said loudly, "Hello, George."

"Oh, hello, Ram. Meri. Sorry to interrupt. How's it going?" A friendly half-grin split one side of George's face.

Meri continued her exploration of Ram's bare chest and giggled. "Not too well. I'm trying to seduce Ram, but he won't cooperate. Spoilsport."

Ram seized her wrists and held them in one big hand while he quickly buttoned his shirt with the other. He picked up her purse, cleared his throat again, and said, "Would you excuse us, please?" He dragged her toward the stairs.

"Good night, George. Ram's taking me to bed now," she called loudly as he propelled her off the deck. They could hear George's loud whoop as Ram practically carried her down the steps.

"You're going to hate yourself in the morning," he muttered, steering her toward her cabin.

After he found her key and unlocked the door, she wound her arms around his neck and said sweetly, "Are you sure you don't want to share my bed?"

"I'm not even sure of my own name right now, love." He smiled and removed her hands. Dropping a light kiss in each palm, he turned her and pushed her through the open doorway.

She fumbled with the back of her dress. "Ram, would you please unzip me before you go?"

"All right, you lovely witch. Back up to me."

Strong fingers slowly slid open the fastener. She could feel his hands tremble as they touched her bare back. But they withdrew.

The door closed quietly, and she was disappointingly alone. She shivered as the flowered dress fell to the floor.

It was freezing in the room.

Using only the bright moonlight from the open draperies as illumination, she kicked off her shoes, shed her undergarments, scurried to the bed, and jumped between the warm covers.

DREAM OF ME

Pulling the blanket to her nose, she curled up into a ball. "Ram could have kept me warm."

Ram. The thought of him, his look, his touch, made her breasts tingle and an aching heat rise low in her belly and radiate downward.

Her toes curled as she stretched and arched imagining his flesh touching hers. She drifted in and out of a dreamlike fantasy, relishing the feelings as her Egyptian hero made love to her as he had on so many nights.

For long moments his lips trailed over her body, his mustache titillating, his breath warm as his mouth caressed and his fingers stroked her most sensitive, intimate parts. A fine sheen of perspiration coated her burning, begging body as she kicked off the cover, threw back her arms, and stretched her legs in silent entreaty.

It seemed so real she could hear the hiss of the sibilant Arabic love words and the swollen hard length of him slither along her thigh . . . over her hipbone . . . across her stomach . . . toward her breasts.

Moaning softly, she savored the cool gentle writhing against her hot skin.

Distant alarms sounded somewhere in the recesses of her passion and wine fogged awareness. Struggling toward reality from the misty dream, she squeezed her eyes tightly.

Why was he so cool?

Long? *Nobody* was that long!

Sure that she was fully awake now, she could still feel a weight coiled around her body.

A sudden, sobering, horrifying chill raced over her.

Heart pounding to rival a bass drum, she made herself look.

She gasped.

She was eye to eye with a swaying hooded cobra.

Eighteen

He who knows the words of power against this serpent shall be as one who does not approach his fire.

The Book of Gates
Funerary text, tomb of Ramses VI

Dear sweet merciful Heaven! Her eyes almost bulged out of their sockets. Her mouth went dry. She almost choked on her tongue.

Meri prayed. Hard. She wasn't even Catholic, but she beseeched every saint she had ever heard of and frantically racked her brain for the names of others.

This couldn't be real. It was a nightmare—or the DT's. It was punishment for drinking too much—or somebody's idea of a cruel joke. This was something from an Agatha Christie novel.

It wasn't real:

She fought hysteria rising within her like a tidal wave. Fought the urge to run screaming from her bed. Thankfully, she was paralyzed with terror.

One part of her mind even watched with sort of a calm detachment and morbid fascination as the hooded serpent, its tongue flicking in and out, bobbed and swayed in the moonlight that shone through the window. The dim rectangular glow illuminated the sinister iridescent beauty of its slowly coiling scales. Its deadly weight nestled in the soft hollow above her navel.

Her arms were still stretched above her head. One finger touched the wall, felt the rough texture of the paper. Ram was just beyond the partition, but she dared not call out. For the longest time she didn't even breathe.

Struggling with a frantic need for air, she finally forced herself to take slow, shallow breaths. Think. She had to think. And stay calm. Very calm.

Slowly she drew her knuckle back and began, very faintly, to rap on the wall.

At the sound, the cobra became agitated—once again moving and weaving in a macabre moonlight dance. She froze. The snake quieted but remained poised in its upright arc, head flared, tongue flicking. She clamped her teeth together to keep from screaming.

She closed her eyes and pictured Ram. Silently she entreated, *Oh, Ram, help me. Help me. Please. Ram, it's a cobra, and I'm terrified of snakes. Oh, dear God, Ram, please come and held me. Please.*

Over and over she repeated her mental plea. She dared not move. She could only wait and call silently.

She felt a soft caress run through her mind and the words, *I'm coming.*

Ram? Had she imagined it? She felt the caress again, whispering amid her frenzied thoughts.

Eons passed. Her muscles began to quiver in faint uncontrollable spasms as tension drew her nerves and sinew into taut vibrating threads threatening to snap at any moment. By a monumental force of will, she held herself together and waited.

Ram was coming. She must not move.

She heard faint ringing from a telephone in another cabin, steady humming of the air-conditioning, blood pounding in her ears, and finally . . . the knob of the connecting door from Welcome's room turning very slowly and quietly.

More eons passed.

Out of the corner of her eye she saw Ram, clad only in a pair of dark slacks, cautiously making his way to her bed. She could smell him as he hesitated beside her.

Meri died a thousand deaths as he stood, still as the Sphinx, for what seemed like a millennium. Suddenly, his right hand whipped out, grabbed the swaying cobra, and thrust the thick, writhing serpent into a pillowcase he'd snatched from his waistband.

As soon as the weight left her body, the last thread of control snapped with a piercing, hysterical scream. Wailing and trembling, she bounded out of bed and flung her naked body against Ram.

"Shhhh, love," he crooned, holding her tightly with one arm. "It's okay now. You're safe."

Breathing rapidly and fighting to calm herself, she burrowed her face against his sweating, bare chest.

Lights came on. He shoved the pillowcase toward someone behind her. "Give this to Mark and call the captain." Now both arms held her to him as he continued to soothe, "Shhhh, love. It's okay. It's okay."

"Oh, Ram, I was so scared," she whimpered, her arms locked around him.

"I know, love, but it's over."

When he pulled away for a moment, she cried out, "Don't leave me."

"I'm not leaving, *sukkar*." He jerked the spread from her bed and wrapped it around her before he drew her close once more.

"Oh, my God, Ram. I don't have a stitch on."

"I know, love. Believe me, I know." When her knees buckled and she sagged against him, he said softly, "You need to lie down," and moved toward the bed.

She stiffened, then shuddered. "I don't ever want to lie in that bed again."

Ram picked her up and carried her to Welcome's room,

which was blazing with lights and beginning to fill with curious people awakened by the noise and activity. Welcome hurriedly fluffed pillows against the headboard, and Ram gently laid Meri against them.

A brandy bottle appeared, and Ram sat on the side of the mattress and held a glass for her to sip.

Nona and Esther, in bathrobes, curlers, and shiny faces, clucked about asking questions and looking perplexed. Leah Henry, minus her dentures, and John Stockton, with his pajamas poking out of his pants, came to inquire into the uproar. Big George, barefoot and in hastily donned jeans, stood like a mountain at the foot of the bed looking worried. Even Jerry from Jackson, Woozits from Canada, and several people she didn't know poked their heads in to see what was going on.

Jean Jacques, in white satin pajamas and a hairnet, wrung his hands. *"Sacré bleu!* There are snakes loose on the ship. What are we to do?" He scampered toward Meri's room waving his arms. "Snakes! *Merde!* Shoo! Shoo!"

"Snakes?"

"Did he say snakes?"

"Snakes? Oh, dear. Oh, dear."

The captain hurried in. His white jacket was buttoned crookedly and his thin gray hair stood in disordered tufts. "What has happened?"

Ram tried to rise, but Meri grabbed his hand and held him beside her. Ram's bitter tone was a cutting but controlled fury when he said, "Ms. Vaughn found herself in bed with a cobra. It's a miracle that she wasn't bitten. Do you often have snakes attack your passengers?"

Jean Jacques slapped his cheeks and cried, *"Merde!"*

Nona's eyes widened, Esther gasped, and Leah Henry clutched the bosom of her bathrobe and said, "I have to check on Bradley immediately."

The captain paled and anxiously ran a hand through his sparse hair. He said to Ram, "Such a thing has never happened before. And I can assure you that I have had a man watching this corridor at all times since this afternoon's break-in. No one has been in this area except for the passengers whose cabins are here. I will investigate the matter at once."

"See that you do. And I have some *investigating* to do as well," he said angrily.

Meri took another swig of the brandy which seemed to be calming her considerably. But at the rate she'd been guzzling it, she was afraid she'd be an alcoholic by the end of the cruise.

While the captain made arrangements for members of the crew to search the other staterooms and soothe the congregation of passengers back into their beds, Ram and George disappeared into Meri's cabin.

Welcome sat on the side of the bed and patted Meri's hand. "Are you okay, sweetie?"

"Hell, no, I'm not okay. I was scared to death. Do you have any idea what it feels like for someone who's as afraid of snakes as I am to have to stare one in the eye for two weeks?"

"I think you are exaggerating just a tad, sweetie. It couldn't have been more than a few minutes."

Meri took another swallow of brandy. "It felt like two weeks. And I don't think it simply slithered into my room by accident. Either it was looking for its mate or someone put it there."

Welcome frowned. "Who would put a snake in your room?"

"I don't know. Unless—"

"Unless what?"

"Unless it was that strange man with the droopy eye who's been following me around."

"Sweetie, I think you're letting your imagination run away with you. I'm sure that there is a perfectly logical explanation, and it wouldn't happen again in a thousand years. It probably crawled onto the ship somehow and got into your room by pure chance."

"How?"

Welcome shrugged. "I don't know how. Maybe through the air-conditioning duct."

DREAM OF ME

Meri's gaze zeroed in on the outlet above her head. "Why am I not comforted by that idea?" She poured another glass of brandy.

Ram and George rejoined them.

Smiling at Meri, Ram said, "You must be feeling better. Your room is locked tightly and totally snake free. Let's all get some sleep." He scooped Meri, still clutching the brandy bottle and glass, into his arms.

"Put me down," she protested. "I'm not going to sleep in that bed tonight."

"I know, love. I'm taking you to my room. You'll be safe with me. I'm not letting you out of my sight until we get off this damned ship."

Whacking his bare back with the sloshing brandy bottle, she kicked her feet against the tangled, trailing bedspread which was still draped around her. "Put me down, I said. I can't stay with you in your room."

"You were anxious to get into my bed earlier. Stop wiggling."

Welcome snickered, and George ducked his head, fighting to keep a straight face as Meri continued to sputter. "You arrogant dolt. Put me down, now!"

They kept arguing, but Ram took charge and held firm. He would not let Meri out of his sight. When it was finally settled, George returned to his own quarters, Welcome was relegated to Ram's cabin for the night, Meri stayed in Welcome's bed, and Ram took Meri's room. The connecting door was left open and Ram maneuvered himself so that he could see Meri, who lay wide awake, muttering vile threats and sipping brandy straight from the bottle.

She was too keyed up; she would never get to sleep. Even the liquor didn't help. As a matter of fact, she was getting a bit nauseous and plunked the nearly empty bottle on the bedside table. Thoughts were zipping through her head like a Japanese express train.

Who would have thought that less than a week ago she was

living a quiet, simple existence? Yet, strangely enough, she had never felt more vibrantly alive than in the past few days. Most of that was due to the sexy, obstinate, wonderful crazy man who had chased her all over Egypt.

Thank heavens that he had or she would be full of cobra venom and stiff as a board right now. Her mother would have been able to stand over her coffin and say, "I told you that you would be murdered in your bed."

Turning onto her side, she peered through the open doorway to the shadow of Ram, outlined in the soft moonlight, in her bed. She shuddered when she thought again of being there with that snake.

A disturbing idea flashed through her head.

How had Ram known she needed him? Had he really been able to pick up her thoughts?

No. Surely not. But yet . . .

Ram! she screamed silently. *Help me. I need you.*

"Meri?" he called anxiously through the shadows. "Meri? Are you all right?"

"I'm fine," she lied, trying to control the tremor in her voice, stalling for time to think. Dear Lord, he *could* read her mind! This was too weird for words. She tried to go to sleep, to block out all the turmoil in her head, but she couldn't close her eyes without seeing snakes.

Welcome. She needed to talk to her friend. She understood about stuff like this.

When she tried to sneak from the bed, there was a loud thud.

"What was that noise?" Ram called.

"Uh . . . I just knocked the brandy bottle over."

Ram chuckled. "Love, you're going to have a magnificent hangover in the morning. Go to sleep."

She had to talk to Welcome. Waiting for what seemed like hours until she thought Ram must be asleep, Meri stole from the bed, wrapped the spread around her naked body, and tiptoed toward the door.

"Where are you going?" Ram growled from the other room.

She froze. "I have to—I have to go to the bathroom." He was watching her every move, probably eavesdropping on her thoughts. She'd never make it out of the cabin.

"I'm not surprised," he muttered. "Are you going to run around all night?"

Haughtily, she retorted, "If I'm bothering you, Mr. Gabrey, I'll—just close the door."

"No! The door stays open."

Once inside the small bathroom, she flipped on the light, slammed the door, and stared at herself in the mirror. "You look like warmed-over death," she mumbled.

After washing her face, she stripped the pins from the drooping hairdo and used Welcome's brush to loosen the tangles. Wishing for her own toothbrush, she finally settled for using her friend's green mouthwash before she turned out the light and went back to the darkened bedroom. Discussing this with Welcome would have to wait.

Standing beside the bed, she raised her arms and stretched in a pool of dim moonlight, and the makeshift toga fell to her feet before she climbed between the sheets once again.

Muffled muttering came from the room beyond.

Sleep was elusive. It became impossible when she realized no one had thought to search this room for snakes. Her imagination began to work overtime. There could be another cobra silently undulating its way to her bed this very minute—drawn to her body warmth. Swallowing repeatedly to dislodge the giant lump in her throat and frantically trying to control the mounting dread erupting in a cold sweat, she tried to think of something else. But like a boomerang, her thoughts returned to hooded, hissing, swaying phantoms. She had always been terrified of snakes.

The drapery fluttered, and she almost lost it. Dear God the window was open. In her mind she could see a snake crawling up the side of the ship, through the window, and slithering toward her. Goose bumps popped out on her body, and she crammed her fist against her teeth to keep from screaming.

"Meri? Are you okay?"

"I'm fine," she croaked. But she wasn't fine. She was scared shitless. She didn't want Ram to know what a ninny she was, but if she had to stay in this room by herself another minute, she'd be a basket case.

"Ram . . ."

"My God, Meri," he groaned. "Go to sleep."

Tears filled her eyes. The sheets were drenched with the dampness and scent of fear as she fought a growing nausea. She whimpered and, holding her hand over her mouth, bounded out of bed and ran for the bathroom before the retching began.

Then Ram was there holding her head, bathing her face, helping her rinse her mouth. "Oh, *sukkar*, I'm so sorry. I didn't realize . . . I'm so sorry." He held her clammy body closely against the length of his warm dry one until her trembling ceased.

"Ram?"

"Yes, love?"

"We don't have any clothes on."

"I know, love. I know." He continued to hold her, not moving.

"Ram, I was so scared. Nobody thought to check Welcome's room for snakes. I feel like such an idiot, but I'm terrified of snakes. What if there's another one?"

He released his hold just enough to lift her face. "There was only one, and it's gone. I promise. Are you okay now?"

She couldn't bring herself to look at him. Totally humiliated that he had witnessed her fear, her nakedness, her upchucking, she squeezed her eyes shut. "I'm fine. But would you *please* check? And close the window. And lock it."

He smiled. "One is not likely to get in your window, *sukkar*. We're on a ship with no outside walkways, and our Egyptian cobras are not aquatic."

"I know it must seem silly to you, and I'm sorry to be such

a bother, but would you please do it anyhow?" Embarrassed by her irrational fear, she hung her head. She wanted to hide.

Hugging her fiercely, his voice broke slightly as he said, "*Rôhi,* my spirit, you could never be a bother. I could cut my heart out that I didn't think to check the room before." Ignoring their nudity, Ram closed the lid of the toilet and gently sat her down before he knelt at her feet.

"Meri," he said softly, taking her hands in his. "Look at me."

When she hesitantly lifted her eyes to his, it was like looking into the blue depths of a flame. An ethereal longing of his spirit beckoned to some mystical answering source within her that she didn't understand, but obeyed.

"Don't ever be embarrassed with me. Between us there's no shame, only sharing and caring. I've waited this entire lifetime to find you, to find that which goes beyond reason, beyond infinity. You complete my soul. I'm yours and you're mine. Meri Vaughn, I love you."

Moved, in some unexplainable way, beyond words, she could only clutch his hands tightly as a single tear balanced on the edge of her left lid, then spilled over and slowly made its way down her cheek.

"Trust me," he said and smiled so tenderly that she relaxed her grip and answered with a feeble smile of her own. "Now, *sukkar,* I have to make a quick snake-check so you can get some sleep, or you'll never be up to teaching the country dancing." He tweaked her nose and stepped out of the tiny bathroom.

Loving Ram would be so easy. Besides his obvious attractions, he was immensely likeable. She'd never met a man who created such turbulent emotions within her or had shown such tenderness, such concern. Despite what her mother thought, Meri had always been strong, in control, but in the past few days her whole world had slid off center. To be confused and a little scared was perfectly normal. Used to being alone, independent, and responsible, she felt strange leaning on someone else—but it felt good.

He'd said he loved her. Was it possible? Everything still

seemed like something from a fairy tale instead of real life. It made her suspicious. Yet all Ram's actions were loving—even when he had seen her at her worst. What would it be like to be married to someone like him?

"All clear." His voice intruded into her thoughts. "And the window is closed and locked."

Looking up, she saw that he was once again dressed in dark slacks with his muscular torso bare. For the first time she noticed the gold pendant he wore. His was very much like hers, very similar, yet different in some way. She reached for hers automatically, but only touched bare skin. Suddenly aware of her own nakedness, she blushed and grabbed a bath towel to wind around her.

He chuckled. "I think it's too late for modesty."

Her own chuckle was nervous. "I think you're right."

"We have a bit of a problem. Your bed is soaking wet, and I can't seem to rouse anyone to change the linens. I put the sheets from your cabin on Welcome's bed. Do you think you could sleep on them? Just for tonight? If not, we can let Mark stay in here and we can use his room."

She blinked against a sudden rush of tears at the thoughtfulness of this man. At that moment she desired him with an intensity the like of which she'd never experienced before. Instinctively, she pushed the feelings aside and stood. "But where will you sleep?"

"Don't worry about me. I'll manage."

Their path illuminated by the bathroom light, he led her to the awkwardly made bed and held back the cover. Clutching her towel sarong, she slipped between the sheets. He tucked her in gently but seemed very careful not to touch her. "Get some sleep," he said thickly. "Dawn will be here in a few hours, and you need to rest. You must be exhausted."

"Ram."

"Yes, love?"

"Aren't you going to kiss me good-night?"

There was a long pause.

"I don't think so."

When he turned to go, she couldn't bear the void his leaving would bring. "Ram." Her voice was barely a whisper. "I'm afraid to sleep alone tonight. Stay with me."

There was a long silence.

Ram returned to the bathroom, flipped off the light, and stood in the darkness with his fists clenched. The memories of her lovely face and the feel of her naked breasts against his chest had long since robbed him of reason. God, he loved her, and he wanted her. But he wanted more than her body. Could he lie with her and not claim her? Hell, he could try. He had to.

Finally he sucked in a deep shuddering sigh and returned to the side of the single bed. With a false bravado, he said, "Move over."

When he climbed in, still wearing his slacks, she giggled and cuddled near him, resting her head on his shoulder and her hand on his chest. She touched the falcon pendant around his neck. "This is very similar to mine, isn't it?"

"Yes. Very similar."

"I forgot to get it back from you. It was in the pouch I put in your jacket. Where is it?"

"I have it in my pocket. Now go to sleep." As he gathered her close, she burrowed deeper against his warmth.

"Sukkar, don't wiggle so."

"I like to snuggle," she murmured, tangling her fingers in the curls on his chest. Her hand drifted down through the hair to his belly.

Capturing it before it went any lower, he cleared his throat and said, "Go to sleep."

"No," she answered, straining to loose her hand and pulling his face close to hers. "I don't want to go to sleep yet. I want you to kiss me."

Her towel had been lost somewhere in the tangle of sheets, and the length of her sleek nude body molded itself against his. Ram longed to taste every sweet inch of her. Using all the willpower he possessed, he gently touched his lips to hers.

It was not enough. She deepened the kiss, teased and tormented him with her tongue, nudged his hand like a cat wanting to be stroked. As his fingers slowly traced the contours of her body, he could feel every fiber in her straining, calling to him.

Meri ached for him to surround her softness with his power—to pull him around her like the warm colors of a desert dawn. She felt a consuming need to be held closer, tighter, until they were no longer two separate people, bound by the laws of the earth, but fused into one.

She tugged at his slacks and whimpered at the cloth barrier between their skins.

"Easy, easy," he whispered hoarsely, stilling her hand and using up the last of his self-control. "Are you sure you want this, *habîbati,* my darling? Once we make love, you're mine. We can never go back."

Thinking was the last thing she wanted to do, but he was forcing her to consider the consequences. His words were both comforting and frightening. Once her assent was given, she was committed. It was like blindly stepping off a precipice and expecting him to catch her.

But she couldn't think about tomorrow; she didn't care about the future or the past. There was only now. She wanted to feel, to touch, to be washed in his golden warmth.

"I'm sure," she murmured. The tip of her tongue outlined his lips and her fingers trembled over the planes of his face. "I'm sure. Teach me the love words."

Ram was lost. His slacks were shed and tossed aside.

They gloried in the gliding dance, like an underwater ballet, of skin upon skin, of hungry touching, of secret tasting, of dipping into molten magic. Each anticipated unnamed longings of the other. The underside of Meri's breasts tingled, and he cupped them; her rigid nipples beckoned, and he savored them; her lips whispered entreaties, and he plunged his tongue between them.

He worshiped her, consumed her softly, lit her with pieces of sunlight until she opened, dewy with desire, and he entered, filling her aching emptiness. It was as if the sun had come from behind a cloud—drenching her with its golden glow, and she leapt into its brilliant light.

"*Hayati,* my life. *Ana bahebbek,* I love you," she heard him call from among the showers of cascading stars as she went soaring through timeless, endless space toward the sun, her sun, her source.

"Ram, hold me!" she cried as she turned into a dazzling burst of liquid crystal, fragmented, and flew apart into a trillion shining pieces pulsating in the universe. Shards of sunlight and glass prisms vibrating with new life shone full on her face and illuminated her soul, then rejoined into a new person. Bits of her and pieces of him. They were one—yet two.

Even as they shuddered and sighed, slipping together back to earth, born anew, the overwhelming intensity lingered—staggered them. The surrealistic power of their encounter was beyond anything either of them had ever experienced.

"This isn't real," she gasped, her body trembling as she clutched Ram like a lifeline. Tears of wonderment spilled down her cheeks. "This can't be real."

"This is all that's real," he whispered as he tenderly smoothed the dampened tendrils away from her face. "The rest of the world is illusion."

Even their pulses throbbed to the same tempo as he held her in his arms. He found it difficult to tell where he ended and she began. Long after Meri's slow, even breath against his chest told him she was asleep, he lay awake savoring his love for her. He would kill for her, die for her, tear out his heart for her and lay it, still beating, at her feet.

Would she trust him now? Would she share her life, her love with him? Something told him she was not quite ready, and he must be patient.

As he recalled their lovemaking, he wondered if such intensity could be sustained. Then he remembered the powerful devotion of his parents and of his grandparents and he smiled, fully understanding for the first time. This was what the

Gabrey men had told him he would one day find and recognize in his very soul.

This extraordinary woman was *his,* and he was bound to her beyond eternity.

Nineteen

> *Death is in my sight today*
> *as the odor of myrrh,*
> *as when sitting under sail on a breezy day . . .*
> *as the odor of lotus flowers,*
> *as when sitting on the riverbank . . .*
>
> The Dispute of a Man With His Soul
> c. 2180-1990 B.C.

Smiling, she stepped from her bath. Zizi, her plump maid, wrapped her in soft linen and blotted the water droplets from her skin. Still smiling—her head in the clouds, her mother would say—she lay down on the stone slab for Zizi to massage her with fragrant oils scented with almond and myrrh.

"You seem very happy today, mistress."

"Oh, I am. Very happy. I had a lovely dream last night."

"With good omens, I trust."

"Very good I think. Perhaps I shall go to the priest for interpretation," she said playfully. She was silent for a long while, knowing that Zizi, who fancied herself an excellent interpreter of dreams, was impatient to hear of her story. Finally she giggled. "Would you like to hear it?"

"Only if you wish, mistress." Zizi's strong hands never paused in their ministration of perfumed balm.

She giggled again. "I do wish. Oh, Zizi, I dreamed of

Khnum. He was so handsome. I saw him coming from far away, holding a bow in his hand. Behind him were bearers carrying five large caskets filled with treasure from distant lands. As through a mist I watched him burn incense to Thoth, then come to me. He laid the treasure at my feet, then took my hand and led me to the garden.

"It was so romantic. He kissed my eyelids and my nose and murmured honeyed words in my ear. And there, beneath the sycamore tree, we made love."

"Mistress!" The maid seemed truly alarmed. Shocked.

She laughed. "Oh, Zizi, don't scold. It was only a dream. But such a lovely dream. Don't you think so?"

Zizi sniffed. "I think you should go to the priest for an interpretation."

"I don't need to visit the temple to understand its meaning. I think Khnum is coming home very soon. Maybe today. Surely tomorrow. He has been victorious, and Pharaoh will bestow a great office on him for his conquests. Then my father will consent to our marriage. That's what I think."

"I think you've spent too many hours staring into the river and letting your imagination run wild. Which tunic will you wear today?" She held up two.

"This one. It's Khnum's favorite."

"Humph," Zizi commented, but she helped her don her attire and brought her cosmetics box and bronze mirror. "The man is a mere goldsmith, and one not even favored by the royal household. Your father will never wed you to such a person."

"We shall see. Remember my dream."

Zizi shivered.

"Have you a chill?"

The maid cast her eyes downward and shook her head.

When she had darkened her eyes with kohl and applied her red ochre rouges, she touched the lock of dark hair which was tied with yellow string and tucked into a corner of the case among her sweet-smelling unguents. She smiled. Khnum's. He had given it to her before he left as a token of his promise.

He would bring back a king's treasure for her and have her for wife. They would have fine children, grow old together, rest in the West together—forever.

She closed the toilet case and went to her jewel casket. She selected several rings and bracelets. The last piece of jewelry she picked up was the most beautiful. A small falcon pectoral—not as ostentatious as those worn by most of the court, but delicate and magnificently wrought. One of the finest she'd ever seen. Khnum had made it for her from bits of gold and glass and stones he had collected for many years. He wore its mate—a piece that fitted hers with perfect precision.

As she slipped the chain over her head, she thought that Zizi was wrong in her estimation of Khnum. He was the most gifted goldsmith in Egypt. He was brilliant and strong and very, very brave. When he returned with great riches, everyone would see. Even Hepu.

Hepu. She wrinkled her nose when she thought of her brother. How she and Hepu could have sprung from the same womb, the same loins mystified her. He was such a sourpuss. Sneaky, vicious as a wild dog. He didn't like to see anyone happy, especially her. Jealousy, she supposed. Because her father favored her. It had been Hepu who had followed her when she met Khnum secretly by the river.

It had been Hepu who ran to their father with the information.

Oh, her father hadn't beaten her—he was much too kind a man for that—but he was very, very angry. Father, she knew, was hoping for a match between her and Harkhuf, one of the king's favored sons.

Harkhuf. She wrinkled her nose. She couldn't abide Harkhuf. He was two years younger than she, interested in nothing but wild-fowling, and stammered every time he was in her presence. Even worse, he and Hepu were great friends. Besides, it was Khnum that made her breath catch and her heart pound. It was Khnum that she wished to wed. She had known at the moment their eyes met that their spirits were entwined from the days of the ancient ones. If her parents would not bless their union when Khnum returned with his riches, she would flee with him in the middle of the night—to Mesopotamia if need be.

She went outside to the gardens, sat on a bench beside the pool, and watched the butterflies that flitted and hovered amid the fragrant lotus blossoms. A gentle breeze swayed the heads of the papyrus reeds. Bees droned about the flowers, and birds sang in the tamarisk trees. It was an altogether lovely day, blessed by Ra, and made more precious by knowing in her heart that Khnum would soon be home. His visage stayed always before her inner eyes, and her love for him swelled her belly. She clasped the Horus image in her hand, felt the warmth of the gold and stones, and prayed to Isis that he would soon come safely home.

Something dropped at her feet. She looked down to see what it was. A fig. Another plopped in her lap. She heard a deep masculine chuckle behind her and glanced quickly over her shoulder.

Her heart leapt in her breast.

Khnum sat on the high garden wall, a broad smile on his handsome face. Laughing, she jumped up and ran toward him, but a tangle of bushes and vines kept her from drawing too near.

"Khnum, you've returned!"

He laughed. "Yes, I know."

"Did you . . . have you . . . uh . . . will you . . ." Curses, she was stammering worse than Harkhuf.

Khnum only laughed again. She could swear by Hathor that he'd grown more manly and handsome in the moons since she'd seen him last.

"Yes, my love," he said. "I did. I have. I will. I have returned with a king's treasure and tales that will entertain you for many, many nights. As soon as I've washed off my grime, I'm bound for your father's office, but first I wanted to see your beautiful smile and give you this."

He pulled a small package from his waistband and tossed it down to her. She caught it and clasped it to her breast. He laughed, touched his fingers to his lips, and was gone.

She stood there watching the place he had been and sighed.

"What have you there?" a voice snarled.

Hepu. Curses! "It's none of your concern, brother."

He wrestled the package from her and tore open the wrapping. A ring. A beautiful gold ring set with pearls and large crystals that sparkled like fire in the sunlight.

She tried to take it from Hepu, but he only sneered and held it high over his head and out of her reach. "Why would you want such a silly trinket from that baseborn scum?" He threw it into the bushes.

"Hepu!" she screamed. "Damn your Ka for eternity!" She ran to the place where the ring had fallen, dropped to her knees, and searched through a thick tangle of vines that clawed at her arms.

A flash on the ground caught her eye. She parted the twisted branches and stuck her head into the opening for a better look. She felt a foot in her back and went sprawling into the vines.

"Hepu, you scorpion!" she shrieked.

She heard a soft hiss and raised her eyes. Less than two hand spans away lay a coiled serpent, its head upright and flared, its eyes malevolent slits.

She turned to stone.

When her wits returned, she whispered, "Hepu, help me."

He only laughed wickedly and threw a pomegranate at her head.

The cobra struck.

She felt its sharp fangs pierce her temple.

She cried out, screaming and screaming over and over.

Deadly poison raced through her body, searing her insides with raging flame and sucking the breath from her chest.

Her limbs commenced to quiver. She gasped for voice to pray to Isis, but she knew her prayers were futile.

Her back bowed. Her sight dimmed. She felt her spirit slipping away.

Clutching the gold falcon with her last bit of strength, she whispered, "Khnum. Oh, Khnum, my beloved. Come to me. Come to me."

Twenty

Come to me, come to me. O my mother Isis! Behold, I am seeing things which are far from my dwelling place!

Here I am . . . ; let there come out what you have seen so that the afflictions pervading your dreams may go out, and fire spring forth against him who frightens you. Behold, I am come to see you, and to drive forth your evils, and root out all that is horrible!

A Magic Spell for the Exorcism of Bad Dreams
c. 2000-1800 B.C.

"Khnum! Khnum!"

"Yes, love, I'm here."

Meri slowly opened her left eye and, by squinting, could make out a blur of blue and white through the tumble of her hair before the blinding light went screaming through her head. Quickly, she snapped her eye shut and tried to locate the source of the piercing pain.

Somebody was using her brain as a dart board.

Groaning, she worked her mouth and rolled her tongue. It felt and tasted like the floor of a circus tent after a busy night. She tried her eyes again.

"Good morning, love," the blue and white blur whispered with a deafening roar. "How do you feel?"

"About like I look, I imagine," she mumbled. "God, I had

the most awful dream. I was bitten by a snake, and I was dying. And—" She frowned. "It's gone. I can't remember the rest of it. What time is it? What day is it?"

"You look beautiful. It's just after nine, and it's Thursday." He chuckled and bent to kiss her swollen lips.

"Mmmpht." Averting her face, she lay quietly for a second, trying to get her bearings, trying to remember last—

Oh, God, no! Unfortunately, in between the beats of the "Anvil Chorus" pounding in her temples, her memory was embarrassingly clear. She covered her head with a pillow and groaned. Had she actually seduced Ram and promised all sorts of things? Fool! She was furious with herself.

True it had been magnificent. She could still feel—

Stop it! How in the world could she face him this morning? Ignore the whole episode. Yes, that was best. Brazen it out. That always worked. For sure she was certainly not going to marry him. That crazy Egyptian probably had a minister right outside the door. Or was he Muslim? In Egypt, probably. What was the Muslim equivalent of a parson? She didn't even know.

Religion was another reason a relationship between them would never work. Muslims and Methodists didn't exactly have compatible belief systems. She was liberal, but she wasn't *that* liberal. Or rather she couldn't be that conservative.

"Here's some coffee and aspirin. I told you that you'd have a magnificent hangover, *sukkar.*"

She sat up slowly, dragging the sheet up to cover her nakedness, swallowed two aspirin, and washed them down with a sip of coffee he'd poured from an insulated pot. When her eyes began to focus she glared at Ram who was freshly showered, shaved, and dressed in a powder blue knit shirt and crisp white pants. "I hate people who say that."

"Say what, love?"

"I told you so. It was the brandy you poured down me that did it, anyway."

"Of course," he said.

"Don't do that!"

"Do what, love?"

"Try to humor me. I despise being patronized."

He smiled. "I'll try to remember that." He flicked open a white linen napkin, spread it under her chin, and turned to the tray beside the bed.

"What are you *doing?*" She scowled, snatched away the napkin, and tossed it aside.

He retrieved the cloth and repositioned it. "I'm trying to feed you breakfast. Are you always this grumpy in the morning?"

Flinging the napkin away, she replied sharply, "I don't want breakfast right now. I want to brush my teeth."

"Oh. Very well."

But he merely stood there, grinning while she continued to glower. "Well?" she said, waiting.

"Sorry, love, did you want me to carry you?"

"Oh, good grief! You know very well I want some privacy. Back off, Ramson Gabrey."

"Is that a two?"

She only glared and crossed her arms.

He kissed the end of her nose. "You're beautiful even if you are a grump. I'll leave and let Welcome in. She's having a fit—something about her wanting her makeup. The tour for Kom Ombo leaves in about an hour if you want to go. I'll stop for you, and while we're gone we'll have your things moved into my room."

When Ram let himself out and Welcome in, Meri waved at her friend as she made a mad dash for her own bathroom. The nerve of that man! She wasn't moving in with him. They make love once, and already he's trying to run her life.

We'll see about that, Mr. Pompous Gabrey!

While she was showering, Meri noticed the familiar falcon pendant around her neck. She didn't recall having it on the night before. She shrugged. With all the furor, maybe she was mistaken.

When she came out of the bathroom, dressed in a kimono

and drying her hair, Welcome was waiting for her. The redhead glanced at the bare mattress and grinned. "Looks like you had a wild night, sweetie. I'll bet he's a fantastic lover."

Meri draped her wet towel over Welcome's head. "No comment."

Welcome laughed and tossed the towel aside. "God, the man's got it bad. Watches over you like a hawk. He wouldn't even let me in my room to get clothes and makeup. Said I might disturb you. I had to borrow an outfit from your room to go to breakfast and buy a toothbrush from the gift shop."

"Welcome, I need to ask—"

A knock came at the door. It was George and Jean Jacques, anxious to check on Meri and effusively offering their connecting rooms to the two women. They agreed to change cabins, and before they left, Leah Henry came by with a sulking Bradley in tow.

Bradley glared at George and Jean Jacques, who nodded politely to them and left.

Leah took a deep breath. "Bradley has something to say to you." She dragged the boy forward.

Bradley kept his eyes on the floor. Leah nudged him. "It was my cobra that got in your room. It was an accident that he got away. Honest."

Leah nudged him again.

"I'm sorry," he said, but Meri didn't hear sincere remorse in his apology. "But he wouldn't have hurt you. He doesn't even have fangs."

"I can't tell you how terrible I feel," Leah said. "I'm so very sorry that this happened. I had no idea that Bradley traded his high tops to a snake charmer for that—that disgusting creature. You can be sure that he'll be punished for this escapade. Except for meals, he's confined to his room for the remainder of the excursion."

Bradley glared at Meri as Leah dragged him from the cabin. No sooner had the door closed when Nona and Esther dropped by.

"Ten to one the little snot did it on purpose," Welcome said.

"No bet. He's probably still ticked because Ram and I hauled him away from the snake charmer in the market place."

"What? What?" Mona and Esther wanted to know.

Dr. Stockton knocked and joined the group.

"You explain," Meri told Welcome, escaping to the bathroom to dress. It was like Grand Central Terminal in this place.

She slipped on a blue jumpsuit, fixed her face, and twisted her hair into a topknot. As she opened the bathroom door, Ram barged in with a maid and started giving orders for Meri's belongings to be packed and moved into his room.

Meri, hands on hips and barefoot, yelled at Ram, "Just a damned minute! I'll decide when and where my clothes will be moved." Esther looked shocked, and Nona giggled. Eyes narrowed and standing toe to toe with him, Meri poked her finger in his chest and said emphatically, "Welcome and I are going to switch rooms with George and Jean Jacques. It is not up for discussion. Do you hear me?"

"Everyone can hear you, *sukkar.*" He dismissed the maid and added, "We'll discuss this later."

Turning away to search for her shoes in the bottom of the closet, she was too angry to be embarrassed or intimidated. She had only to remember the manipulation she had endured from her mother to make her more determined. No matter that she turned to tomato aspic when Ram's soul-searing eyes caressed her, or that she felt like someone held a blow torch to her toes when he touched her.

She and Welcome had a job to do, and come hell or high water, they were going to do it, even if she had to wade through sexy playboys, snakes, and all the tour groups in Egypt. Her work and the success of their company must be her number one consideration. She would not be deterred, and she would not be intimidated. She had photo shoots today and tomorrow afternoon when they disembarked in Luxor. In two days all the necessary photographs would be made. She would deal with Ram and her feelings then.

If the truth were told, she knew she was falling in love with that stubborn, magnificent specimen. Wasn't he the embodiment of every woman's fantasy? But if she spent another night in his arms like last night, she wouldn't be able to tell which end of her camera was up.

Damn and double damn! Where were those blamed shoes?

"Looking for these, love?" Ram held a pair of blue espadrilles that he'd retrieved from the top shelf of the closet. She nodded, and he said, "Sit down, Cinderella, and I'll put them on you."

Sometime during their exchange, the room had cleared. She heaved an exasperated sigh, sat down, and held out her foot. Some things just weren't worth arguing about.

Ram stuck like glue while Meri shot film of Welcome and the temple ruins of Kom Ombo. A number of their regular troop trailed along behind them, thinking Ram made a better guide than the one assigned to them from the ship. Jackson Jerry and the Canadian tagged along as well. So did Walter Rush, though he didn't look as if he were enjoying himself nearly as much as some guy from Alexandria who practically salivated every time he looked at Welcome—which was frequently. Mohammed, she thought his name was, but then three-fourths of the men in Egypt were named Mohammed.

The hot, bright sun was making Meri's head pound so badly she couldn't get interested in Sobek, the crocodile god, or much of anything. From somewhere in the distance, a noisy helicopter churned, and a group of boys shouted and splashed in the muddy river, having as much fun as a gang at Water World. It would be a miracle if those kids didn't die from dysentery or something equally dire. But perhaps they were immune to the local bacteria.

Dr. Stockton gingerly helped Esther, who seemed to unbend more each day, over the fallen stones to peer into a dank, musty room filled with crocodile mummies. Nona had adopted

George for the morning. Jean Jacques had stayed behind to prepare for his performance that night and had called a full practice of their group after lunch.

Meri wasn't sure that she would live until noon, much less be able to dance. Sweat dampened the curls around her face, and her blouse stuck to her back. The ancient carvings of river gods seemed to be closing in on her. When she stumbled, Ram looked sharply at her.

"Love, you look a little green. Why don't we return to the ship?"

Her shoulders slumped with relief. "I've about had it." They excused themselves from the group and started back down the path toward the river.

Shading his eyes with his hand, Ram looked up toward the sound of the rotors. "That must be our boots and hats arriving. We need to see if they fit." Grinning, he hugged her and added in a stage whisper, "Yours are size nine."

She groaned. "Don't remind me—please. I'd rather forget last night."

"Not everything, I hope," he said softly.

She remained silent until he deposited her on deck with a gentle kiss and instructions to take a cool shower and rest until lunch. "Shall I come aboard and make a snake check first, *sukkar?*"

"I think the danger has passed."

"Rest for a while then. I'll bring your photo equipment along and call for you in about an hour or so."

"Ram, I can carry the equipment myself. I've managed it alone quite well for several years now." She reached for the bag.

He held it away and gave her a quick kiss instead. "But now you have me to carry things for you. Don't worry your pretty head about it. I'll bring it along later, or I can take it to your room now if you prefer."

His tone rankled. Her eyes narrowed. "Dammit, give me the frigging bag!"

His brows went up, but he only seemed amused. "Yes ma'am."

He held it out. She snatched it from his hand, wheeled, and stomped off. All the way to her cabin, she muttered vile deprecations about his parentage and his overbearing, overprotective ways.

As she opened the door to her room, Meri glanced at the neatly made bed and shivered. No way could she rest in that bed. The sooner she packed and moved, the better. She was about to set down her camera bag and head for her suitcase in the closet when she heard a noise and startled. A strange racket came from the bathroom.

She tiptoed closer and put her ear against the door.

Over the sound of the shower someone with a nasal twang was singing loudly about poling a pirogue down the bayou. And it wasn't Welcome's voice.

What in the world? She clutched her bag, raced to the hall door, and flung it open to yell for someone.

Mark Macleod was standing in the corridor. He looked horrified to see her. "Oh, my God, you're back. Ram will kill me! I didn't expect you so soon. Oh, my God, I'm sorry."

"Calm down, Mark. Of course Ram won't kill you. What's the matter?"

"I was supposed to watch for you and tell you that Jean Jacques has already had your and Welcome's things moved." The distraught young man fumbled in his pockets until he came up with a key and held it up like a prize.

She laughed. "So that's who was in the shower—Jean Jacques. It nearly scared the living daylights out of me."

Mark's face turned ashen. "Ram will kill me for sure when he finds out. I just left for a minute to go to the bathroom."

"Then we just won't tell him, will we? May I have the key?"

Mark looked relieved but insisted that he unlock Meri's cabin, which was identical to her old one, and searched both it and the connecting room before he was satisfied.

"Everything's fine," she said. "Ram will never know. Is he always such an ogre?"

Mark grinned. "Only when it comes to you. Beats anything I ever saw."

"You leave Mr. Gabrey to me." She winked and closed the door.

Feeling much better after a cool bath, Meri decided to visit the gift shops instead of resting. She dressed in white slacks and a powder blue T-shirt. She braided her blond hair into a long, thick pigtail which hung over one shoulder, added a dash of makeup, and slipped on white thongs.

Before she set out, she unzipped the large camera bag she'd used earlier and retrieved the film she'd shot at Kom Ombo. She labeled the canisters and went to put them in Welcome's room with the other film for the brochure.

She looked in Welcome's closet, but the film box wasn't there. She checked drawers, inside luggage, everywhere she could think of. Nothing. Where could it be?

Thinking that when their rooms were changed, perhaps it had been put in her cabin, she went back through the connecting door and searched her own room thoroughly. Not there.

Damn! She'd try Welcome's room again.

She was on the floor of the closet, butt in the air, when Welcome came in and sprawled supine onto her bed.

"God, if I never see another dried crocodile, it will be too soon for me," Welcome groaned. "I couldn't take another hour of traipsing around in that heat." She raised her head and frowned at Meri. "Sweetie, what are you doing down there?"

"I'm looking for the film case. Do you have any idea where it is?"

"Isn't it there?"

"No. I've searched both our rooms, and I can't find it. God, Welcome, if it's missing, do you know what that means?"

"Yep. It means we're in deep doo-doo."

Still sitting on the floor, Meri rested her forehead on her

knees and wrapped her arms around her head. "Oh, God, please no."

"Maybe it got left behind when our rooms were switched. Let me call."

Meri crossed her fingers and prayed while Welcome spoke to George on the phone. When she hung up, Meri looked up expectantly.

"It's not there."

"Oh shiiiit," Meri wailed, wrapping her arms around her head again.

"Sweetie, it's not the end of the world. We'll just have to take a few extra days and shoot it again. We'll manage."

What Welcome said was true, but the more Meri thought about it, the madder she got. "No, dammit! I'm sick and tired of people making my life miserable. First they trashed my room and took my personal film, then that little weasel stuck a snake in my bed, and now this. I've had it! If that film is on this ship, I'm going to find it."

"How are you going to do that?"

Meri rose from the floor. "I know where I'm going to start! With that little brat, Bradley." She strode from the room, slammed the door behind her, and marched down the hall with blood in her eye.

She banged on the door to Leah Henry's room. Bradley, who was still confined to quarters, opened it. When he spotted Meri, his mouth curled down, and he started to shut the door in her face. She stiff-armed it open and barged in.

"Bradley, we need to have a little talk."

"I have nothing to say to you."

"Tough shit, kid. I have a few things to say to you." She shoved him backwards until he plopped down on the bed, and she stood over him, hands on her hips. "First, I know that cobra didn't slither into my cabin accidentally. You purposely put that snake in my bed."

He only sat there and glared up at her, but she noted the tremble of his chin.

"Didn't you?" she demanded.

"It didn't have any fangs. It wouldn't have hurt you."

"Why did you do it?"

He pressed his lips tightly together and hung his head.

"Answer me, dammit!"

"Because I don't like you."

"I won't lose any sleep over it. I'm not too fond of you either, Bradley. Is that why you trashed my room and stole my things?"

His head shot up. "I did not!"

"You didn't trash my room?"

"No."

"You didn't swipe any jewelry or film?"

"No! I'm not a thief!" Tears came in his eyes, and the little tremble in his chin became a quiver.

She studied him for a minute. You know, she believed the little bugger. She squatted down in front of him and took his hands in hers. "I'm sorry that I accused you, Bradley. I can see that I was wrong. But after the thing with the snake, I—" She shrugged. "I'm sorry."

"The snake was defanged. Harmless actually. It wouldn't have hurt you. It was no big deal."

"Perhaps not to you, but you see, I'm phobic about snakes."

His eyes widened. "You are?"

"Yep. They give me the screamin' meemies."

"Wow, I didn't know that. I'm really sorry."

Meri squeezed his hands. "Now that we're both really sorry, maybe we could be friends."

He cocked his head. "Well, maybe."

"If I talk to your grandmother, perhaps we can lift your grounding. Would that help?"

Bradley brightened. "Yeah."

She smiled, ruffled his hair, and was about to leave when something occurred to her. "Bradley, how did you get in my room to leave the snake?"

"I borrowed a key from the desk when nobody was looking." He looked sheepish. "But I put it back," he added quickly.

Outside, she saw Mark at the end of the corridor talking to one of the crew members who was on guard duty. She waved and let herself into her cabin. She sank down into one of the blue chairs and drummed her fingers on the table, thinking. If Bradley was innocent, who was guilty? And why would anyone take her film? The jewelry she could understand, but *film?* It made no sense. But the fact was, it was gone, and she was pissed.

The motive eluded her, so she concentrated on the means. She could see how a thief could have gotten into her room the first time—he could have lifted a key the same way Bradley had or have simply picked the lock. But how had someone stolen the brochure film from Welcome's room? Surely the guard who was posted would have noticed if anybody tried to get in the door.

An idea struck her. She ran into Welcome's room, calling her. The shower was running, so she stuck her head in the door of the tiny bathroom. "Welcome," she shouted to be heard over the water.

Welcome poked her wet head through the curtain. "What do you need, sweetie?"

"Did you leave the window of your room open anytime yesterday or last night?"

"No."

"Are you sure?"

"Positive. I didn't even know the windows would open. The ship is air-conditioned. Why?"

Somebody had opened that window. Which meant that somebody, if they couldn't get in the door, got in by the window. How? There weren't any walkways.

A rope.

"Just an idea I have. I'm going out. See you later."

As she started down the hall, pacing off the distance from

the door of 216, Welcome's previous cabin, Mark met her. "Is everything okay?"

"Everything's fine. If you'll excuse me," she said, trying not to lose count, "I'm going exploring for a while."

"I'll go with you." He fell into step beside her.

Rats! She didn't want him along. He would put a crimp in her plans. *And* report her every move to his boss. She didn't want Ram interfering in this; she was perfectly capable of handling it herself. "That's not necessary, Mark. I'm just going to the top deck for a drink and maybe to the gift shop for a bit."

He hung his thumbs in the empty belt loops of his jeans and grinned. "I just finished switching rooms with Ram so he could have the one next to yours. Something about you being able to bang on the wall. Anyway, while he's talking to his helicopter pilot, I'm to see after your needs. Orders from headquarters. By the way, I confessed my foul-up."

"Was he angry?"

Mark ducked his sandy head and shuffled his feet. "It wasn't so bad. I deserved it, I guess. Ram's a terrific guy, and he's been great to me. I owe him a lot. I'd do almost anything for him," Mark said, a bad case of hero-worship evident in his expression. "I'll stick with you till he gets back, if you don't mind."

She did mind. She would relish a little solitude. Damn Ram and his overbearing ways! The next thing she expected was for him to shackle her to his ankle. She wasn't about to put up with his baloney for one minute.

When they had climbed topside, she decided to ditch her watchdog. "Mark, would you get me a ginger ale from the bar, please?"

While he was gone to the little striped cabana at the far end of the deck, Meri paced off the distance from the stairs to the spot just above where the window to room 216 would be. She examined all the rungs of the railing carefully.

Nothing.

It was freshly painted, and the weight of a person on a rope would have made some kind of scratch or scrape. Rats! So much for that idea.

But wait. There was another possibility. The ship had three decks. Theirs was the middle one. What if—

She had to find out who was in room 316. She was about to head for a house phone when Mark returned with her drink.

Grabbing it, she drained it quickly, leaned against the railing, and smiled sweetly. "My goodness, I was thirsty. Would you get me a refill?" She held out her glass.

Mark looked at her strangely, but said, "Sure."

As soon as he was out of sight, she scooted to the stairs, scrambled down them, and took temporary refuge behind a potted palm on the landing below.

"May I help you, miss?" said a soft voice behind her.

Her stomach dropped to her knees, and she whirled to find a white-jacketed attendant squatting at her elbow. She smiled sheepishly, grasping frantically for an excuse for her bizarre behavior. "Oh, thank you. I . . . uh . . . I was just looking for my contact lens." She smiled brightly and patted the floor. "There! I've found it." She scooped the imaginary lens from the carpet, wiggled her fingers, and said, "Be seeing you."

She scurried down the stairs to the phone just inside the gift shop.

When the operator answered, Meri asked, "Could you tell me, please, who is in room 316?"

There was a short pause, then, "There is no one registered in that room, miss."

Well, hell. So much for that idea. It would have been too easy. Wait. An empty room. "Are you sure?"

"Very sure. There was a problem with the plumbing and the carpet is wet. It is closed off until it can be repaired. May I help you with something else?"

"No, thank you." She quickly replaced the receiver. Empty, huh? She'd bet her last pair of pantyhose that somebody had used that room—wet carpet or not.

She wanted a look at it. She was going to pull a Bradley and filch the key from the desk on the lower deck. Sticking her head out the door of the gift shop to see if the coast was clear, she nearly had a stroke when she spotted someone coming down the corridor. She jerked back inside.

It was the little Egyptian fellow with the droopy eye. Had he seen her? She quickly ducked down behind a rack of *galabiyahs* and hid among the folds. What was *he* doing on board? She didn't care if he *did* have five kids, he gave her the creeps.

After a few minutes she parted the hanging garments and peeped through them. He was gone. Was it her imagination again, or had he followed her on board? The hairs on the back of her neck prickled. Was he the one who broke into her room?

She didn't have time to speculate about that now. She had to get that key. The coast clear, she hurried down to the lower deck.

The desk was deserted. This was child's play. No wonder someone could get in to search her room so easily. She quickly ducked behind the desk, grabbed the key to 316 from the box, and stuck it in her pocket.

"May I help you, miss?" said a soft voice behind her.

Meri whirled to find the same white-jacketed man at her elbow. Thank God she hadn't had lunch or she would have lost it. "Oh, thank you. I . . . I was just checking my box for messages. I didn't have any." She giggled and tried to imitate Welcome's flighty act. "I guess my friends have all forgotten about poor lil' ole me." She wiggled her fingers and added, *"Ciao,* ya'll."

Her knees were knocking so badly as she climbed the center stairs from the belly of the ship, Meri stopped and leaned against the wall even before she reached the middle level. Maybe she ought to go get somebody before she went any further.

No, that's silly, she told herself. It's just an empty room. Besides, if Ram got wind of what she was doing, he'd come charging in like an avenging angel, spouting some more of that male-chauvinistic garbage. She could handle this alone.

Taking a determined breath, Meri put her foot on the next step, then froze as she heard a commotion in the corridor above and to her left. Loud voices were coming from the direction of her cabin. Crouching low, she sneaked another step up and then another until she could slowly peer over the edge of the stairwell.

She heard footsteps from above and looked up. Oh, God, someone was coming! She got a quick glimpse of the little Egyptian fellow with the droopy eye. He was after her. She almost had a heart attack as she hightailed it back down the stairs and huddled, trembling, behind another big potted plant on the deck below.

With her body curled in a tight ball, eyes squeezed shut, and heart thudding against her chest, Meri sat like an ostrich and waited. And waited.

And waited.

Muffled footsteps passed about three feet from her hiding place. She waited some more.

After what seemed like about two weeks of agony, Meri forced her eyes open, made herself uncoil and peek through the thick foliage. She spied Droopy-eye unlocking a door at the far end of the corridor.

She slumped back against the wall, closed her eyes, and waited for her heart to calm down.

"Miss?"

Meri yelped and her eyes shot open.

The guy in the white jacket again.

"Miss, is something wrong?"

She stretched her lips over her teeth in an effort to smile. "Not a thing. I'm—I'm meditating. Would you excuse me, please."

He bowed. "Certainly, miss."

When he was gone, once again she prodded herself to creep up the steps and sneak another look over the edge.

DREAM OF ME 219

Ram and Mark were standing in the hallway outside her room. Ram, his back to her, was gesturing wildly.

"Mark, I ought to break your neck! It ought to be a simple thing to keep an eye on one woman for a few minutes. I told you not to let her out of your sight. You're a damned incompetent idiot!"

Meri felt a pang of conscience as she watched Mark, head down, shoulders slumped, mumble to his idol, "Sorry, Ram."

She ought to stop Ram's harangue against Mark, but she had to get a look at that room. Ignoring her guilt feelings for once, she snatched off her sandals and bounded up the next flight to the third deck.

The corridor was clear. Meri put her ear against the door of 316. All quiet. With her sandals still tucked under her arm, slowly she turned the key in the lock and pushed the door open just wide enough to slip through, then closed it soundlessly.

The cabin was dark as a cemetery at midnight. And freezing cold.

A musty, sour smell of mildew and stale tobacco smoke hung in the waiting stillness. It made her skin crawl.

She leaned against the door to gather her courage from adrenaline still pumping like a Texas oil rig. She crammed the key in her pocket and felt along the wall for a light switch.

In the soft lamplight, it looked no different from the other cabins. There was the same nubby bedspread, the same striped draperies, the same blue chairs. As she walked toward the window, the soggy carpet squished between her toes.

Wait. She looked down and saw trails of footprints in the wet pile. Squatting down to examine them closely, Meri noted that one bunch seemed to be regular shoes—a man's, she suspected—while another had a distinctive tread, like hiking or climbing boot prints. Small foot for a man, she thought as she measured one sandal over it. Or a big foot for a woman. She almost giggled.

Careful not to disturb the prints leading to the window, she laid down her shoes and tiptoed toward the draped opening. More curious than cautious now, she inspected the molding around the windowsill and found several long scrapes. Could be a rope. What had it been anchored to? Glancing around the room, she settled on the built-in bed as the best possibility.

Sure enough, as she flipped up the spread and ran her fingers along the sturdy bottom railing, there were grooves worn in the thick wood. It was the same pattern that a rope looped around it and burdened with a heavy weight would make. The question was: Who had been in this room?

Look for clues. Yes, that was it.

Tiptoeing to the bathroom, she turned on the light. It was clean and neat, except—the commode seat was up. A man, for sure. They never remembered to put it down. Peering into the bowl, she saw the remnants of a dark cigarette floating on top, staining the water.

She started to open the medicine cabinet, but caught herself. Fingerprints. Glad that she remembered, Meri tore off a piece of toilet paper and gingerly opened the mirrored door. Nothing but two covered glasses and extra soap bars.

Next Meri methodically searched the drawers. In the bottom of the bureau, she found a long coil of nylon rope. It was in the far back corner of the desk drawer, behind the stationery and brochures, that she found the paper sack. It was the kind of sack used in the ship's gift shop.

At first she thought that it was empty, but when she turned it upside down and shook it, an M&M fell out. A yellow one.

That bastard!

She was about to search the closet when she heard a noise in the corridor outside. She sucked in her breath. Her eyes widened. Her heart started pounding a mile a minute.

Oh, God, she had to get out of here—now. But how? She couldn't go down the rope; she was no Shannon Miller. She hadn't gotten around to taking classes in gymnastics.

But karate—she damned well knew karate. She had a brown belt.

Sucking in a deep breath, she positioned herself near the door, ready to attack whoever came through it.

Poised and alert, she waited. And waited.

And waited.

The truth finally reached her brain. A vacuum cleaner. The noise she'd heard outside was a vacuum cleaner.

She relaxed for a moment, then realized that she could easily be cornered alone in the room. She grabbed her sandals and decided to make tracks.

Meri had just pulled the door closed when a steel hand clamped down on her shoulder.

Her heart flew to her throat. She was paralyzed. She couldn't breathe.

Twenty-one

Rise, O my heart, and bewail this land whence you are sprung! Rest not; behold, it lies before your face: rise up against that which is before you!

The Prophecy of Nefer-Rohu
c. 20th century B.C.

Prepared to meet her maker, Meri swallowed the basketball in her throat. But she wasn't going down without a fight.

She dropped her sandals and let out a yell as she kicked out behind with her foot and grabbed the thick wrist with both hands. With a deft move she slammed her attacker against the wall. Whirling toward him, she poised ready for the next assault.

Ram lay sprawled on the floor.

"What the hell are you doing?" he growled.

"Defending myself, obviously. Karate. I have a brown belt."

"I have a black belt," he said, "but it never occurred to me that you were interested in a match." He stood.

"You startled me. I reacted automatically. Sorry." She gave him a sickly smile.

He didn't smile back. "Where the devil have you been?" he shouted. "I've torn apart this ship looking for you."

"Don't you yell at me, Ramson Gabrey! I don't have to account to you. Who appointed you God? I'll go where I please, when I please. Do you hear me?" Muttering oaths about his ancestry, she snatched up her sandals and brushed past him.

"Oh, hell. *Sukkar,* I'm sorry. It's just that I was frantic when we couldn't find you."

"You didn't need to find me. I wasn't lost." She stuck her nose in the air and headed down the corridor to the stairs, then toward her cabin on the deck below.

Ram stayed beside her. Her fingers were shaking so badly that she couldn't fit her key in the door.

"Here, let me, *sukkar,*" Ram said, reaching for the key.

She slapped his hand away. "Don't *sukkar* me, I'm tired of your possessive hard-headedness." She drew herself up to her full five feet eight, squared her shoulders and said, "Look at me. Do I look fragile and helpless? I can take care of myself! And another thing, I don't need a watch dog. If I wanted one, I'd buy a German shepherd. And don't you dare scold Mark about this, Ramson Gabrey. It's not his fault that I shook him."

"If I promise not to scold Mark, will you forgive me?"

"That's blackmail."

He smiled broadly and shrugged.

"Okay, this one time. But damn it, Ram, we've had this conversation before. Remember one, two, three? You're driving me stark raving mad."

Ram felt like a bumbling idiot. All he wanted was to please her, see her smile, hear her call his name in passion, protect her from harm. He didn't want her to know that one of the radical groups *had* threatened to kidnap a tourist to emphasize their ridiculous demands of the government. Such rumblings were usually meaningless, but he didn't want her to be afraid. Nor did he want her to know that, despite her feelings, his operatives watched her constantly. If he had to deceive her a bit, so be it. Her happiness and her safety were his main concern.

He scowled when he remembered that his men had screwed up and let a jewel thief and a prepubescent boy get past them.

But to give them credit, they were focusing on Meri and Welcome more than on their rooms. That had been changed. In addition to the captain's sentry, he had somebody stationed in the corridor at all times—though when they docked at Edfu, one of those somebodies wouldn't be Mark. Two extra operatives would be coming aboard.

His face softened as he watched the fire dance in Meri's eyes. Brown belt, huh? He smiled. She reminded him more of his grandmother every day. Meri could tie his stomach in knots and make his soul soar at the same time. He sighed, trying to ignore the ache in his loins that developed when she was near, or when he thought about her, or when he even spoke her name. When he was apart from her, there was a void, something missing. Like an arm or a leg . . . or a heart.

His thumb gently massaged the small scar which grew more evident when she was angry, or sad, or tired. He bent and softly touched her lips. "I love you. I'm trying hard, believe me. Help me, *sukkar*, help me to learn. Don't be angry with me. I can't bear it."

He held her close, molding her sweet body against his. It was delicious agony. No one ever told him loving was so painful . . . or so wonderful.

He pulled away to drop small kisses on her upturned face—her cheeks, her eyelids, her nose, her cleft chin. He nipped and nuzzled his face against her neck, yearning to devour her, while his impatient hands kneaded the soft flesh of her back.

He almost went wild when he heard her sweet whimper. His mouth leapt to hers; his tongue plunged between her lips with a fervent thrust; his pelvis ground against her.

In a rush of exultation, her ardor matched his. It was like a flash fire or the rolling thunder of sudden furious storm. And she kissed him with a fierceness that should have been painful, but it was a wonderful, wild fusion—sweet, hot, bruising.

When Ram pulled his lips away, Meri moaned at their loss. Hugging her to him, he whispered, "People will be returning from the tour at any minute. I think we might shock them if they found us making love in the middle of the hallway. Let's go to your room."

Meri almost grabbed his shirt to drag him inside and jump his bones. *What are you doing, you idiot?* She stopped, drew a deep breath, and said, "I—I have a headache."

He looked amused. "A headache?"

"Yes, a headache." She rubbed her temple.

"Shall I get you some aspirin?"

"No. No, I just need to rest for a few minutes. I'll be fine."

"Very well, love. Shall I have lunch sent to your room?" He kissed the spot on her temple where she'd rubbed.

"No, no. I'll see you in the dining room."

Inside her cabin, Meri leaned against the door and took a ragged breath. That was a close call. The moment that he'd touched her, her anger had dissipated like smoke, her resolve had crumbled, her reason had gone on vacation. Though she didn't understand it, she was filled with a raging anticipation only to love and be loved by this magnificent, infuriating man.

How could something so wrong feel so right?

She heaved a frustrated sigh. And why, with all the other complications in her life at the moment, did she have an overwhelming urge to chuck it all and snuggle in his arms?

She couldn't answer that one.

"Welcome!" she shouted, anxious to tell her friend what she'd found in 316. But Welcome's room was empty.

Damn! She plopped down on the bed. She wanted to search the room upstairs more thoroughly, but she didn't want to do it alone. And they would have to pick a time when the other passengers were occupied.

Mopping the sweat off her face, Meri sank into a soft velvet lounge chair at the edge of the dance floor. She fanned with the straw cowboy hat, one of the dozens that Ram had flown in from heaven knows where, and gulped the ice water Ram handed her. Had she really suggested this? The practice for their line dance had nearly killed her. She'd have to go into training if she survived many more days like the last few.

Even Esther Barrington and the rest of the Golden Years Travel Club looked sprier than she did. Nona Craft was glowing with laughter under her ten-gallon brim. She had deftly maneuvered a red-faced Walter Rush into joining their group, and Ram had managed to outfit him with boots and a hat.

"Do your feet hurt, love?" Ram asked as he knelt on the floor in front of her and squeezed the sides of the boots as if checking for fit.

Meri wiggled her toes in the glove-soft leather. It was as if they had been made for her. They were as comfortable as moccasins.

Puzzled at the question, Meri frowned. "No, I'm fine now that I've rested a bit."

Ram persisted. "Is it because they're cobra skin? I ordered them before you tangled with one last night. Does that bother you?"

Meri held out her feet and looked at the colorful and, she knew, very expensive boots. "Is that what they are?" She laughed and said, "Better on my feet than in my bed."

"Are you sure they're okay?"

Puzzled by his questions, Meri answered, "I'm positive. Why are you so concerned?"

"You've been measuring your foot against everyone else who wears about the same size. I thought you might be wanting to trade for a better pair."

Meri's froze. She thought she had been discreet searching for a small-footed man among the dancers. "Uh . . . no. Just sensitive I guess. Where did you find all the boots and hats so quickly?" she asked before he could pursue the subject.

"I have a friend in Rome who was stuck with a warehouse full when the Western craze died out a couple of years ago. He was glad to get rid of them. I got a bargain."

Meri shook her head at the tall stacks of boxes. She hadn't intended for him to outfit the whole passenger list, but then,

Ram rarely did anything half way. At least it gave her an excuse to check foot sizes. Of the men here this afternoon, the smallest feet belonged to Jean Jacques, Walter Rush, and, surprisingly, Mark.

She recalled that a bald Italian, one of the retinue who was so enamored with Welcome, wore a small size too, but Meri doubted, remembering the girth that indicated soft living, that he could even climb stairs without getting winded.

She hadn't forgotten old droopy-eye either. In fact, he was her number one suspect; he was small and quick, and it figured that he wouldn't have a big foot. Of course there were still at least twenty-five or thirty other men on board including waiters, although she suspected that most of them could be eliminated since they would have been working during the only time when someone could have filched the film. Most of the men would be at the party tonight. She would be spending a lot of time looking at the floor. It could be anybody.

Well, except George, who wore at least a size fourteen, and Ram, who had a fair-sized foundation himself.

Still fanning with her straw Stetson, Meri stood. "I think I'll go to my room for a while."

"I'll go with you." Ram rose and slipped his arm around her waist.

"I want to take a shower," Meri said emphatically.

He cocked an eyebrow, and his mustache twitched. "Good, I'll wash your back." His hand made slow, lazy circles down her spine.

She shivered. His simple touch and seductive words disrupted the evenness of her breathing. Tiny aftershocks still lingered along the trail of his fingers. Her back had always been sensitive, and he seemed intuitively to know the right spots to tease. Each time they were together, he peeled away another layer of reserve, breached another defense. It was almost frightening. A few seconds more and she would have been dragging him down the hall with her.

Instead, Nona broke the spell. "Meri! Ram!" she chirped.

"We've arrived at Edfu. It's almost time to leave for the Temple of Horus."

Ram looked down and said softly, "Do you want to go?"

Meri swallowed. *No,* she thought, *I'd rather have my back washed, but I'd better go.* "I really do need to take some more pictures. Do you mind?"

Meri savored the last bite of her creamy chocolate mousse and sighed. Ram, who had rarely taken his eyes off her all afternoon, was captivated as her delicate pink tongue licked the spoon. He remembered the feel of her tongue on him and, almost forgetting they were in a public dining room with six others at their table, touched her lips with his two fingers entreating her to taste them.

He felt filled with her—the intoxicating perfume of promises and fascination that was hers alone, the glow of candlelight that caught in her hair like the silver moonlight on the desert's rippling sand. He adored her sensuous lips, the smooth skin of her lush body that came alive under his touch, the spirit that completed his and made him ache with longing. Before they docked in Luxor, he would convince her, somehow, to marry him immediately. All the necessary paperwork had been done and the rings were in his pocket. He was *that* sure.

"Why are you looking so fierce?" Meri whispered, bringing Ram out of his reverie. "Your fingers are very tasty, but . . . uh . . ." She nodded toward his half-eaten dessert.

He grinned and pushed his dish in front of her. He sat back and watched, planning to enjoy vicariously every flick and roll of her velvet tongue, every movement of her luscious lips.

Oblivious to the six other people who chatted among themselves at their table, Meri was totally aware of the flame-blue eyes caressing her as she ate. The idea of intriguing this man pleased her immensely, and knowing that soon she would be returning home and never see him again left her wretchedly disappointed. He was a magnificent lover—the perfect embodiment of her dreams. But like all dreams, it would soon end.

All afternoon he had made subtle, and some not so subtle, references to their marriage, but she knew marriage was an impossibility.

Still, it had been a marvelous afternoon. Horse-drawn carriages had driven them to the Temple of Horus and to hundreds of images of Ram. He had laughed when she teased him about his likeness to the hawk-headed god. They had climbed high on the ancient walls and shook their heads sadly as they viewed the crumbling mud-brick structures of the current inhabitants standing in stark contrast to the enduring stone marvel built in centuries past. Meri had shot some great pictures of the area.

Ram had bought her a switch to keep the pesky flies away and paid too much for a black stone statue of Horus because she had loved it and felt sorry for the small, bright-eyed boy who scampered beside them trying to make a deal. He had reminded her of little Ahmed in Cairo. She would always have a soft spot for him.

They had taken the last carriage back to the ship and barely had time to dress for dinner. Meri had wanted to go for a swim first, but Ram promised they would go after the show tonight—when they would be alone in the warm moonlit pool.

She almost chuckled as she finished the last of Ram's mousse. He didn't fool her for a minute. It wasn't the romantic setting that he was waiting for. He was afraid she would wear the purple suit in public again. She wouldn't.

She sat back, groaned, and cast an accusing eye at Ram. "Why did you let me eat all that? I'll never be able to get my jeans buttoned for tonight."

His hand, hidden by the tablecloth, patted her flat stomach, leaned over and nuzzled her ear as he whispered, "Feels fine to me."

Meri heard Nona twitter to Esther, "Isn't that sweet?"

She glanced up to find six pairs of eyes on her. Embarrassment heated her face. The rest of the world seemed to float away when she was with Ram.

Welcome giggled and said, "Lawdy, lawdy," as Dr. Stockton gave a mischievous wink.

Jean Jacques rose with a toss of his platinum locks and patted Meri's hand. "Isn't love wonderful, *chérie?* I must go and prepare for my performance tonight, *mes amis*. Run along everyone and get into your costumes. The party starts in one hour. Our folk dancers will be first, I will be second, and your delightful line dancing with hats for everyone will be our *pièce de résistance*. It is such fun," he gushed and clapped his hands together. "I know so little of your wonderful American country music, but I promise when I return to Paris, it will become the rage."

Meri stamped her feet so that her jeans fell neatly over the tops of her boots. She set her hat at a jaunty angle, and yelled at Welcome, "Hurry up. We need to be there before anyone else so we can check sizes as we pass out boots. Ram and Mark are going to hand out the hats. I had to do some tall talking to convince him to let us do it instead of hiring the waiters."

She had told Welcome about what she'd found in the room upstairs, and her friend had promised to slip away later in the evening to help her search it further.

Welcome grinned as she sauntered in dressed in jeans and an electric blue T-shirt with the sleeves and bottom cut into long fringe dotted with wooden beads. She stood behind Meri, who was checking her appearance in the full-length mirror. "Boots and hats for everybody? Sweetie, you could talk that man into importing sand for Egypt."

"I don't know about that. And I didn't intend for him to outfit the entire ship." Meri laughed and adjusted the tie of her red halter blouse. "Pardner, we look real Texan. These armbands were a stroke of genius," she said, wiggling her elbows and watching the beads and feathers dance around her upper arms.

"Just doing my part. Even if I did have to sacrifice my

favorite headband and a very expensive belt. We look très Texas chic." Welcome turned solemn. "I still think you should tell the captain or at least Ram about what you found in the empty room upstairs."

"We've been over that ground already. My main concern is finding the film. I don't want to shoot it all over again, and if it's there the canisters might be confiscated as evidence, and God knows when—or if—we might get it back. I've read horror stories about the way police operate in foreign countries. We can handle this ourselves. And after we comb the place, whether it's there or not, I'll discuss it with Ram."

"Promise?"

"I promise."

"And will you promise too that you won't go up to that room by yourself again?"

"Do you want me to sign a blood oath?"

"It might not be a bad idea. Sometimes you can be as pigheaded as Nora."

"God forbid."

Welcome laughed and hugged Meri. "I just don't want anything to happen to you, sweetie. Best friends are hard to come by."

"I won't go without you." Meri drew an X across her chest. "Cross my heart and hope to die."

Before they left, they checked the windows, turned out the lights, and made sure the doors were locked behind them. Arm in arm they strolled down the corridor and tipped their cowboy hats to the burly crewman who was standing guard.

Meri, bubbling with excitement, jumped to her feet and clapped as the folk dancers came back for a second bow. The audience loved the spirited senior citizens in their hastily improvised costumes. The men wore white shirts and suspenders with a variety of Bermuda shorts and long socks, while the ladies had fashioned aprons and caps from napkins, scarves and handkerchiefs.

"Weren't they wonderful?" she exclaimed to Ram as she sat down beside him at their ringside table. She took a long swallow of a delicious fruity concoction he had ordered for her—nonalcoholic she would bet.

Ram squeezed her hand. "Nervous?"

"Just a little. Oh, here's Jean Jacques. I'm dying to see what he does."

The lights dimmed and the dance floor was covered in total darkness.

A flute sounded. Then silence. When it trilled a second time a spotlight fell on Jean Jacques, a graceful statue in white tights and a flowing white tunic. An arm fluttered, then was still. The spot momentarily caught the brilliant fire of a diamond in the single earring he wore. His arm fluttered again with the flute's lilt as if he were slowly awakening. Gradually the lights came up, and as the other instruments of the orchestra joined, the tempo increased, and Jean Jacques' movements became more animated until Meri sat spellbound, almost gaping at the beauty and power of the dance unfolding before her.

He leapt like a gazelle as cymbals crashed, he whirled with the timpani rolls, and strutted with the sassy brass of the recorded music. His performance was the epitome of jazz ballet. By the time he ended with a series of high leaps, when he seemed to hang suspended in midair, the audience was on its feet, applauding and shouting.

Standing straight, with his arms thrust above his head, Jean Jacques gave a quick bow, the floor went dark, and he was gone.

Meri and Ram stood clapping with the others while the agile little Frenchman took several bows. When the audience finally let him go and settled down, Meri leaned over to Ram and said, "Do you mean we have to follow that?"

He laughed and said, "I thought Texans could do anything."

She didn't have time to think before Ram pulled her up to join the others in front.

"Ladies and gentlemen," Meri began with a bright smile, "we can't teach you to move like Jean Jacques, but we're going to teach you how to dance like they do back in Texas. Grab your hats and let's boogie!"

She and Ram started everybody clapping and stamping in time to the music while they demonstrated the steps. After several bars the others who had learned at the afternoon practice joined in. They split up and began pulling others to their feet and teaching them, amid much laughter, the infectious foot-stomping, hip-bumping line dance. It was a rousing success. The International Terpsichorean Troupe won the talent contest hands down.

After they collected their ribbons from the judges, the group started weaving its way toward a large table Ram had somehow managed for a victory celebration. Meri found herself next to Jean Jacques, still dressed in tights and tunic with his cowboy boots and straw hat. She laid her hand on his arm and congratulated him on his outstanding performance.

He flashed a brilliant smile in answer to her own. *"Merci."* He bent low over her hand and kissed it.

Ram scowled, elbowed the little Frenchman aside, and led Meri to the table.

"Ram! You didn't have to be so rude to Jean Jacques."

"Let him get his own girl. You're mine."

She grinned. "I don't think you have to worry about *him*."

She thought she heard him mutter something about being surprised about a peacock, but before she could ask him to repeat his comment, John Stockton stood and rapped a spoon against his glass.

"My friends, I have an announcement to make." He smiled lovingly at Esther, who dropped her eyes as demurely as a young girl, before he continued. "After thirty years, Esther has finally consented to become my wife. You're all invited to the wedding, which will be as soon as we can make the arrangements. I don't intend to let this lovely lady get away from me again." His face glowed as he sat beside his fiancée and gave her hand an affectionate pat.

Tears brightened Meri's eyes as she added her congratulations to the clamor of good wishes and surprise rising from their table. Ram ordered champagne to celebrate, and everybody was soon talking gaily about the wedding.

Later as Meri danced with Dr. Stockton, she said, "I'm so happy for you. Your patience paid off, didn't it?"

"Yes. I'm not sure what happened, but I think it was the knock on the noggin that did it. You're not going to make your young man wait for thirty years, are you, my dear?"

It was too complicated to explain to the courtly old gent, so she just smiled and said, "We'll see."

As soon as Meri sat down she looked around for Welcome and spotted her sitting between Walter Rush and the bald Italian at a table nearby. With all the passengers occupied with the party, now would be a perfect time to search room 316. When she caught Welcome's eye, she motioned to the door with her head.

Meri stood and said to Ram, "Would you excuse me, please?"

Ram sprang to his feet and grabbed her arm again. "Where are you going?"

"To the ladies' room, if you don't mind."

"I'll go with you."

Meri rolled her eyes in aggravation. "Oh, good grief! You can't go to the ladies' room."

Ram grinned broadly. "I just meant I'd walk you to the door."

Meri sighed. "Honestly Ram, you're driving me up the wall. Back off."

"Is that a two?"

"Bingo!" she said, shrugging off his hold. "I'll get Welcome to go with me. I'll be right back."

Giving her a peck on the cheek, he whispered, "I'll miss you, love."

Meri walked up behind Welcome who stood near the door talking to some of the senior citizens. "Let's go to the ladies' room," she said to Welcome in an undertone.

Nona's curly white head bobbed up. "I'll go too. Esther, would you like to powder your nose?"

The four of them trooped out together. Meri hadn't meant for it to be a group experience. At the door to the ladies' room, she said, "Uh . . . uh, I just remembered that I need to get something from my cabin. Welcome, would you come with me?"

"Sure."

They excused themselves from Nona and Esther, and as soon as the two older women went through the door, they hot-footed it up the stairs to the third deck.

As Meri fumbled the key in the lock, Welcome stood behind her and said over her shoulder, "Are you sure you want to do this?"

"I'm sure." The door swung open. "Come on." She dragged Welcome inside, quickly shut the door, and flipped on the light.

"God, it stinks in here," she whispered.

"Wet carpet. Hurry. I'll check the nightstand and under the mattress; you take the closet. Use your shirttail to open it. We don't want to leave any fingerprints."

Meri had just yanked out the drawer when she heard a strangled noise from Welcome. She glanced over her shoulder to find Welcome slumped against the wall next to the closet door, her eyes big as gongs.

"What's the matter?"

Welcome worked her mouth, but nothing came out.

Meri hurried to her. "Welcome, what's wrong?"

"The closet," she croaked.

"Here, let me see."

"Don't open that door."

"Oh, don't be silly." Meri grabbed the handle and flung open the closet.

Like a hewn tree, a man fell out.

Meri shrieked, jumped back, and grabbed Welcome in a stranglehold. "Ho-ly shit!"

"I told you not to open the door."

Twenty-two

The innermost chamber is opened to the man of silence. Wide is the seat of the man cautious of speech, but the knife is sharp against [the one] who forces a path . . .

The Instruction of Ka-Gemni
c. 1990-1780 B.C.

Meri and Welcome stared down at the man who lay stiff as a board, his nose buried in the carpet.

"Is he—is he—" Meri stammered.

"Deader than King Tut."

Panicked, Meri turned around in tight circles, flapping her hands and chanting, "Ohmygod, ohmygod."

Welcome grabbed her. "Now is not the time for hysterics. Let's get out of here. Now."

"Wait." She clutched Welcome's arm, her eyes glued to the body on the floor. "If he's dead, he can't hurt us, can he?" She drew a deep breath, tried to calm her jangled nerves, and let her brain kick in. "Let's look for the film."

"Look for the *film?*" Welcome's voice rose two octaves. "To hell with the film. It's probably at the bottom of the Nile. *He* might not be able to hurt us, but whoever killed him sure as hell can."

"He was *murdered?*"

"Didn't you see that knife sticking out of his chest?"

"Oh . . . my . . . God."

Welcome grabbed Meri's hand. "Let's vamoose."

Meri dug in her heels. "No, dammit. We've come this far. Let's take two minutes and look for the film. Then we can call the captain."

"Call the *captain?* And tell him what? Are you nuts? Police will swarm this place. They'll probably throw us in jail, and we won't see Texas again until we're a hundred and three."

"Ho-ly shit!"

"You said it, sweetie. Let's light a shuck."

Her eyes still morbidly focused on the body, Meri hesitated. "Who is he?"

"How should I know? I didn't get a good look at his face."

"I think we should find out who he is."

"And just how do you propose to do that?"

"We could turn him over."

"What's this 'we' crap, Tonto? I'm not touching that body."

"Oh, Welcome, don't be chicken. Dead men can't hurt you. Good Lord, we've seen mummies all over Egypt."

"Yeah, but this fellow is fresher."

"Come on, help me." Meri squatted beside the corpse and tugged at his shoulder.

Welcome rolled her eyes. "Oh, God, I can't believe the things I do for friendship."

The two of them grunted and tugged and rolled the man onto his back. Obviously Egyptian and obviously dead, the man did indeed have a knife sticking out of his chest, buried to the hilt.

"Do you recognize him?" Meri asked.

"I think I've seen him hanging around with that guy from Alexandria. Mohammed."

"His name is Mohammed?"

"No, the guy from Alexandria is named Mohammed. I don't know who this man is, and, sweetie, I don't really give a fat rat's ass. Now, let's get out of here."

"Not till I look for the film."

"Then let's look for it."

With the body on the floor, nothing was left in the closet except a pillow. The nightstand drawer was empty. A search under the mattress yielded zilch.

"Now can we go?" Welcome asked, carefully stepping around the body. "I'm about to have a nervous breakdown."

"Don't you think we ought to put him back?"

"Put who back?"

"The guy on the floor."

Welcome's eyes widened. "You've got to be kidding."

"If anybody opens the door, like a maid, they're bound to notice."

"You think they won't notice him in the closet?"

"At least he'll be . . . less conspicuous. We should leave things the way we found them."

"Oh, God," Welcome groaned.

Grunting and puffing, they levered the corpse back into the closet, leaning his forehead against the back wall and quickly shutting the door before he could topple out again.

"Oops," Meri said.

"What now?"

"We left him facing the wrong way."

Welcome glared. "Don't even *think* it." She scurried around wiping everything in the room with her shirttail.

"What are you doing?" Meri asked.

"Fingerprints, remember?"

"But you're obliterating the killer's fingerprints as well."

Welcome shot her a droll look. "Tough titty. Now let's get out of here."

Meri didn't know who was shaking worse as they hurried, arms locked, down the corridor. "Remember," she cautioned Welcome, "when we get back, act natural. None of this happened."

Welcome snorted. "Sure."

"Do you want to spend the best years of your life in an

Egyptian pokey? Did you see the movie *Sphinx?*" Meri shivered. "It was terrifying. The guards—"

"I don't want to hear about it. I'll be so natural that it'll be nauseating. The whole thing never happened."

When Meri slipped back into her chair beside Ram, he said, "You were gone so long that I was getting worried about you."

She glanced at her watch. Had they been gone only twenty minutes? It felt like hours. Days. "Sorry. Minor emergency."

"What sort of emergency?"

"Uh . . . we uh . . . uh . . . Welcome broke her bra strap. We had to sew it."

"I see."

Meri squirmed. "I'd like something to drink."

Ram raised his hand. "What would you like?" he asked when the waiter appeared.

"Scotch on the rocks. A double. No, make it a triple."

"The lady will have a small glass of wine."

"Scotch, dammit. A triple."

Ram shrugged, then nodded to the waiter who left in a hurry. "What's wrong? You're acting very strangely. Did something happen to upset you?"

"No," she squeaked, then cleared her throat. "I'm fine." When her drink appeared, she emptied half the glass in one gulp.

Ram frowned. "Love, I—"

She grabbed his hand. "Let's dance." She downed the rest of the Scotch.

Ram had slipped some country and western records to the disc jockey, and a country swing was playing. She did her damnedest to become the life of the party.

Meri refused to think about the corpse in the closet of 316. It didn't exist. She laughed and danced and ordered another Scotch. She couldn't remember drinking the second one, but she must have, since she was feeling no pain.

Meri and Ram were doing a spirited two-step when her foot faltered and she sagged against him.

"Love, you're exhausted and it's after midnight. Why don't we put you to bed?"

"I'm not ready to go to bed. It's early yet. Let's go outside, and you can rope me some stars, cowboy." She nuzzled her face against his western shirt. "Did I tell you I like your outfit? You look like a real Texan."

"But I am. Half, at least."

"That's right. I'd almost forgotten that you said your mother was from Dallas. I wonder if she knows my mother?" She rubbed her nose, which had grown strangely numb.

"Let's get some air."

The observation deck was deserted. They tossed their hats on a deck chair as they strolled through the bright moonlight to the railing and watched as the ship slowly stirred the dark, ancient waters below. A breeze teased the feathers on Meri's arm bands and lifted the damp wisps framing her face.

Ram leaned against the rail and pulled her back against him. As she nestled in the warm strength of his arms and looked up at the stars glimmering in the quiet night sky, a strange feeling of *déjà vu* rose from the deep mist of her unconscious. It was as if they had stood like this for countless nights. If she had believed in reincarnation as her father did, Meri would have sworn they had spent other lifetimes together under these same skies.

She voiced her thoughts to Ram, who nuzzled her ear and whispered, "But we have, *rôhi*. You've been my soulmate, my one great love, throughout eternity. You're remembering."

Memories pushed on the door of Meri's awareness, and she shuddered—afraid. This was madness.

It was the Scotch. The after-effects of finding the body.

She shook the eerie feeling and tried to move away, but he held her fast in his arms.

His tongue tasted the outline of her neck, and she automatically bent her head to the side and strained toward him to give him free access to the sensitive skin. His mouth trailed across her bare shoulders while his right hand slipped up to cup her tingling breast.

Burning with desire to kiss him, to touch him, she strained to turn facing him, but he wouldn't let her move. Instead, his left hand splayed lower, across her belly, and pulled her buttocks tightly against his pelvis as his tongue slid down the satin skin of her spine.

Her back arched, and her mouth fell slack as she sucked in a deep shuddering breath. She could only cover his fingers with hers as his hands kneaded and caressed; she could only moan as his tongue trailed fiery spasms down her vulnerable back.

"Oh God, woman, I love you," Ram murmured against the sensitive skin of her shoulder blade. "Promise you'll marry me tomorrow. *Promise.*" His entreaty was fierce, demanding.

She couldn't think; she could only feel a naked passion pleading with her voice for him to make love to her, to complete her, to take her soaring to see the sun.

He ceased the burning kisses and caresses and hugged her full against him. "Will you marry me?" His voice was ragged with wanting, but he waited, dead still, for her answer.

Only their heavy breathing and the lap of the water against the side of the ship echoed in the silence.

"Will you marry me?" he asked again.

"Ram, don't talk about marriage. Make love to me," she pleaded. "Can't you see how much I need you, want you?"

He asked a third time. "Will you marry me?"

Silence.

A bird screamed in the trees, then fluttered its wings and soared across the bow of the ship to the opposite bank of the river.

He sucked in a deep breath, released her, and stepped away. He held out his hand for her and said, "Come, let's get on our bathing suits. I promised you a moonlight swim."

"Ram! You can't leave me like this. Please." She was humiliated that she was reduced to begging a man to make love to her.

His throaty chuckle grated her nerves as he said, "I'm in worse shape than you, my love, but if you want me, you'll have to promise to marry me. I won't settle for anything less. Don't fight destiny. Say yes."

Tears stung her eyes. "Ram, you have to understand. There are a hundred reasons why I can't marry you."

"And they're all overshadowed by the one reason that you should." She hung her head in dejection. He lifted her chin and gently touched his lips to hers. "Come, *sukkar,* let's change. We both need to cool off."

They walked in silence to the corridor, then stopped in front of her door. She pulled the key out of her pocket and turned to Ram. "I . . . I don't want to go swimming anymore. Won't you come in with me, please? I—I *need* you."

She prayed that he would. She was nervous about sleeping alone, but she didn't dare tell him why.

"Will you marry me?"

"Ram, I can't. It's impossible. But I don't want to sleep alone. You could—"

He silenced her plea with two fingers and slowly shook his head. "Not tonight, love."

She unlocked the door, slipped inside, and closed it gently. For several seconds she stood slumped against the heavy wood, her hand still on the knob, letting the misery wash over her.

Their time together was drawing to a close. A few more days, and she would be gone. The idea of never seeing Ram again made her soul feel as dark as her room, as despairing as she'd felt grinding stones at Sakkara.

Finally, her hand reached lethargically for the light switch. Nothing happened. The lamp must have burned out.

The breeze lifted a corner of the striped drapery, and she saw a silhouette in the dim moonlight.

She froze.

Fear crept into her pores.

Twenty-three

*How sweet it is to go down to the lotus pond
and do as you desire—
to plunge into the waters, and bathe before you—*
     Love Songs of the New Kingdom
           c. 1550-1080 B.C.

Ram stood outside Meri's door, his hands jammed in the back pockets of his jeans to keep from knocking. It had taken every bit of his self-control to restrain himself from clutching her to him and giving her anything she wanted.

Last night had only been a gentle beginning; he had held in check the savage hunger clawing at his belly. Tonight when they had stood under the stars, he knew if he allowed her hands on him he would have been lost. What else could he do to convince her?

The look in her eyes as she begged him to make love to her had almost destroyed him. He had wanted to cradle her in his arms and offer her the flesh off his bones, the breath of his body.

He loved her beyond reason, and her refusal to commit totally to him rent his very soul. Their destiny was together. He had to make her understand. He *had* to.

A muffled scream and a thud came from Meri's room.

It raised the hairs on his skin and wrenched an answering roar of primal fury from his gut. He shouted her name and threw himself against the heavy door with superhuman strength. It splintered and crashed open.

The blood drained from his face when he saw Meri lying in a still, crumpled heap on the floor.

Meri opened her eyes and blinked, trying to get her bearings. Where was she? Her memory was foggy and she blinked again. The room was dimly lit. She was lying on a large soft bed with an elaborate tentlike canopy of blue silk surrounding her. A smooth spread of the same material covered her.

How had she gotten here? Closing her eyes, she frowned and forced herself to think. Now she remembered. The open window. Someone had been in her room. My God, she'd been kidnapped! Her heart began pounding, and her mouth went dry before she could calm herself. No. She vaguely remembered seeing Ram's and Welcome's faces after that. She tried to sit up but something held her feet.

Cautiously, she raised her head and saw Ram, still dressed in his jeans and rumpled western shirt, stretched across the end of the bed with one arm thrown across her lower legs. He was sound asleep.

Trying not to disturb him, she slowly eased her legs from under his arm.

Immediately Ram's eyes shot open, and he jumped up. "Don't move. Lie back down. Do you need something? Do you feel okay?" He leaned over her, searching her face. Dark stubble shadowed his jaw, and his blue eyes drooped with a weary, haggard expression.

"I'm fine," she answered quietly, touching his cheek. "But you look a little worse for the wear. Where are we? What happened? How did we get off the boat? The last thing I remember was seeing the window open and the lights not working. After that everything is fuzzy."

"Somebody was waiting for you in your cabin. From what we could piece together, it appears that he broke the window and came in from a rope tied to the railing of the observation deck. He hit you and knocked you out."

Her fingers gently touched a tender spot, and she found a small lump. "It's a good thing I'm hardheaded."

Ram scowled. "I don't find the situation humorous. It's a miracle that you weren't killed—and no thanks to me. I'm supposed to be protecting you. God, I feel like such an idiot. I should never have left you alone. Love, can you ever forgive me?"

He was so distraught that she felt his pain. "There's nothing to forgive. How could you have known?" She moved toward him and winced. She touched her head again. "How bad is it?"

"Not too bad, but it could have been. He must have hit you with his flashlight. We found it near the window. Either he only intended to frighten you or the blow was somehow deflected."

"I remember now. I saw him silhouetted against the window. I knew immediately that he'd come in by the window since—" She clamped her mouth shut. Ram would have a cat-fit if he knew all that she and Welcome had done.

"Since what?"

"Never mind."

"Since what, Meri?"

"Since . . . uh . . . since the door was guarded. Anyhow, he shined the light in my eyes and came after me. Thank heavens for quick reflexes and karate lessons. But I guess I wasn't quick enough. He whacked me. But if the light hadn't blinded me, I would have nailed that sucker."

"Don't be glib about this, Meri. You could have been seriously injured. I've been through hell."

She touched his cheek. "I'm sorry. But obviously he didn't mean to kill me, or I would be dead. He knocked me unconscious, and he could have finished me off."

"I think I scared him away when I broke down the door."

"You broke down the door?"

"I did. And I almost went berserk when I saw you lying there so still. Thankfully, the Italian who is so enamored of Welcome is a physician. He checked you over and didn't find any cause for alarm, but I radioed for the helicopter and took you to the hospital in Luxor for X-rays to be sure. There was no evidence of concussion, so after they gave you a sedative, I brought you here."

"Where is here?"

"This is my villa. We're just outside of Luxor."

She struggled to sit up. "How long have I been here? Welcome must be frantic."

"Shhh." He gently pushed her back against the pillows and brushed her forehead with his lips. "You need to move slowly." He checked his watch. "It's ten o'clock in the morning. I contacted the ship and told her you were all right. Mark will look after her until they dock this afternoon and check into a hotel. Do you feel like some coffee now or some breakfast?"

"Please. But I'd like to freshen up first."

When he bent to scoop her up from under the silk spread, she tried to wiggle from his grasp. "I can walk to the bathroom!"

"Humor me." He lifted her firmly and strode toward an arched doorway.

"Ram."

"Yes, love?"

"I don't seem to have any clothes on."

He sighed and his mustache twitched slightly. "I know. Believe me, I know. This is getting to be a habit." He grinned as he set her on her feet in densely piled carpet. "Not that I'm complaining, you understand."

After he had pointed out a fresh toothbrush, toiletries and towels, and made sure that she was strong enough for him to leave, he left to order breakfast.

As soon as the door closed, she glanced around. The room almost took her breath away. It was like something from a movie set. She ran her fingers over the polished surface of the immense, finely-veined marble counter with its deep sinks. It was the same delicate sand color as the plush carpet in which she wiggled her toes. The fixtures were gleaming gold and multifaceted crystal.

The intricately carved gold frame of the mirror, which must have stretched ten feet or more, matched the delicate gilt throne chair sitting before the dressing table. Its cushion was encased in a lush watermelon-colored moiré which also covered the walls. It was the exact shade of the roses filling a crystal vase that sat amid the bottles and rosewood boxes on the marble countertop.

A large skylight and ornate gold sconces lit the room. Thick-foliaged plants breathed life into every corner. Meri could hardly attend to her morning rituals, so astonished was she with the beauty and opulence of the room. If the bathroom was this grand, what was the rest of the house like? She was anxious to explore, but after she brushed her teeth and tried to bring some order to her tangled hair by rebraiding it, she wrapped herself in a large bath sheet and searched for the shower or tub.

How she would love to soak in a steaming bath.

But there didn't seem to be one. That was odd. She was still puzzling over the lack of a tub when a knock came at the door.

She opened it and found Ram, barefoot and still dressed in his rumpled shirt and jeans. He smiled and offered the tray he held. "I thought you might like coffee with your bath."

She lifted a steaming mug and sipped from it. "Ahhh, that's perfect. Thank you. I'd love a bath, but I can't seem to find the tub."

"I didn't want to take a chance you would slip and fall until I could get back to help you. Push that button on the bottom." He cocked his head toward the light switch by the door and set the tray on the counter.

When she pressed it, the moiré-covered walls slid back and

she gasped. "This is like something from a Turkish harem! I don't believe this."

In the center of the large skylighted garden room beyond the wall was a small pool lined with colorful mosaic tiles, dotted with floating lotus blossoms, and surrounded by urns of papyrus reeds, broad leaf greenery, and small trees. The air was redolent with the crisp fragrance of the exotic flowers, the faint scent of spice, and the clean mixture of moisture and sunlight on green leaves.

Ram chuckled as he led her down two stone steps toward the pool where a waterfall splashed into the clear blue water. "Egyptian, please. Not Turkish. And you're the only one in my harem, *sukkar.*"

"Do you mean this is your *bathtub?*"

Ram's mustache twitched as he led her toward the end with the waterfall. "That," he said, pointing toward the opposite side, "is a lotus pool. This"—he indicated a smaller section, filled with bubbling, steamy water and separated by a mosaic wall—"is a bathtub." He nodded in the direction of an enclosure in the corner. "There is the shower. Do you like it?"

"What's not to like? It's magnificent! But I can't take a bath in there. I'd feel decadent wasting so much water. Did you design this?"

He nodded. "The whole house is solar powered—we have plenty of sun in Egypt. We also have our own water source, as well as a purification and filtration system. I'm very conservation-minded, so nothing is wasted."

Hugging her to his side, he said softly, "Do you feel strong enough now for me to leave you alone for a few minutes?"

"I feel fine, honestly. Not even a headache, surprisingly enough. Just a little sore spot."

As soon as he left the room, she dropped the large towel, stepped down into the sunken tub, and sank into its bubbling warmth. This was big enough for half a dozen people, she thought, turning to allow the waterfall to splash over her tight shoulders. It seemed more like a spa than a bathtub, but whatever it was, it was heaven.

She leaned against the side and studied the murals on the stone walls. They were painted with modern renditions of brightly hued scenes from ancient temples—bits of life from long ago—of families, farmers, gods and goddesses, kings and queens, animals, ducks, and feluccas on the Nile.

Long, low couches and small tables were scattered around the room. It gave her a strange feeling almost as if she had been transported back to ages long past. She closed her eyes and her mind drifted to a faint, far-off memory of another time when she sat in a similar pool.

When Ram returned, he quietly set a basin of hot water, his shaving gear, and a mirror on the glass table beside the pool. His eyes never left the vision in the tub. He was jealous of the water swirling over her breasts and caressing the sweet secrets in its depths.

Forcing his attention to the task at hand, he stripped off his shirt, hurriedly lathered his face, and hoped his shaking fingers wouldn't cut his throat before he could join her. They ached to touch her creamy skin and explore her soft curves. He swelled with longing and cursed himself.

Dammit, fool, he told himself, *she needs rest and care. Hold off. Control yourself.* He shaved in record time and slipped unnoticed into the bubbling water.

Something tugged on her toe. Meri's eyes flew open as she jerked her foot. "Ram! What are you doing here?"

"I live here, remember?"

"But I—I'm in the tub."

He smiled. "So am I. And while I'm here, I'm going to bathe you and wash your hair. Then I'm going to give you a massage and serve you breakfast in bed. I promised the doctor that I'd take very good care of you."

"Oh, good grief! I'm not a child. I can bathe myself." Nobody had bathed her since she was five.

"Humor me." He picked up a bottle beside the tub and

poured the fragrant liquid onto a sponge. His face was totally devoid of expression as he methodically and nonchalantly soaped every square inch of her body. Only once or twice did a slight twitch of his jaw and a subtle flare of his nostrils indicate that his blasé, almost clinical, attitude hid a different feeling entirely.

Amusement playing around the corners of her mouth, she bit her lip as she docilely submitted to his ministrations. His asexual performance hadn't fooled her for a minute. He was suffering.

When her finger made a lazy trail through the thick, wet hair on his chest, it tangled around the gold pendant he wore. She examined it closely, then held up the one she wore. "Look, these are very similar."

He smiled. "I know." He fitted the two together, his and hers, back to back. "Together they make a perfect whole."

All sorts of emotion-laden images began to flash through Meri's mind. When Ram separated the two halves, the flashes stopped. Strange. "Are—are these pieces very common in Egypt?"

He shook his head. "They're very old. Ancient. And as far as I know, unique and unduplicated. There is yours, and there is mine."

She swallowed. "Some very strange things have happened with mine."

"I know." His smile was enigmatic.

"You want to explain that statement?"

"I think I'll let you figure it out for yourself."

"So you want to play games, huh?" Her fingers slid beneath the water.

He clamped his hand around her wrist and said hoarsely, "Don't do that, love." As he reached to unbraid her hair, his eyes met hers and he scowled. "Don't you dare say a word."

She giggled and fluttered her eyelashes innocently. *"Moi?"*

He cocked his eyebrow at her as he raked his fingers through her hair to loosen it. After he wet the long strands under the waterfall, he turned her around and gently worked the shampoo into her scalp. "Tell me if I hurt you."

He didn't hurt at all. "Mmmm. That feels wonderful." She closed her eyes and relaxed as his graceful fingers tenderly soaped and massaged.

When he was finished, Ram held her under the cascading water to rinse away the lather. With his back to her, he quickly climbed out of the sunken tub and wrapped a towel around his waist, then turned and helped her out.

A little snicker escaped as she looked down at his hastily donned covering. "Hiding something?"

Without a word, he twisted her hair in a rope and squeezed out the excess water. Briskly, he dried her, bundled her into the soft bath sheet, and carried her to the gilt chair in front of the vanity.

She smiled into the mirror as she watched him struggle with brushing and blow drying her hair. She didn't make a move to help, and actually, he did a pretty good job.

"Have you ever thought of becoming a hairdresser?"

This time he laughed with her. "Only for you, *sukkar*—only for you." He laid down the tools and stood behind her, silent for a moment. "I have to ask you something. Do you have any idea who hit you last night?"

"No, do you?"

"No, but if I ever get my hands on the son-of-a-bitch, I'll kill him! *Nobody* touches what is mine."

Meri shivered. "You frighten me when you talk like that." This side of him made her wonder about his true character. Was the tender charm a sham to cover some secret, ruthless nature?

"I'm sorry if I upset you, love." Bending over, he nuzzled her cheek. "I died a thousand deaths last night, *rôhi*, when I heard you scream and found you lying so still. I love you so much that I go insane when I think someone might harm you in any way. I vow that in this lifetime, as long as I draw a breath, no one will harm you or take you from me again."

DREAM OF ME

She melted at the sound of his words, the warmth of his breath, the touch of his lips against her face. Familiar, indescribable longing filled her.

Light struck their pendants, and twin golden sparks shot outward in dazzling sunbursts. Their eyes met in the mirror. His hands lifted and stroked her bare shoulders, the curve of her neck.

Meri closed her eyes, dropped her head back, and tried to keep her breathing even. His caress was as gentle as a warm twilight breeze. She trembled beneath his fingers, and he hugged her back against him.

"This time, we'll be together," he said.

She rose, turned toward him, and held out her arms. He gathered her to him, molding her against his near-nakedness as if he wanted to blend them into a single flesh with a single mind, a single heartbeat.

He whispered sibilant Arabic love words, and his tongue traced the hollows of her ear. When she whimpered and tried to pull his lips to her own, he stiffened, drew a ragged breath, and gently set her away.

Noting her bewildered expression, he said, "I don't think this is what the doctor had in mind when I promised him you would rest." He smiled and kissed her fingers. "Let's have breakfast."

She pulled her hand away and thrust out her lower lip in a theatrical pout. "But you promised me a massage first." An impish gleam lit her lovely eyes.

He shifted his weight to one leg, rested his hand on the opposite hip, and hung his head. He scratched his eyebrow, took a deep breath, then blew it out. He could almost feel the petal-soft skin under his fingers. This was going to be torture. Could he do it? Could he hang on to his self-control? It was slipping fast.

God, he wanted her.

He ground his teeth and reminded himself that he was not some rutting stallion. He could do it. Hell, he could try. A sardonic smile twisted his lips. Where had he heard that before?

Taking another deep breath, he quickly hoisted Meri in his arms and strode back to the garden bath. She giggled and nestled her head against his chest. With the fingers of her left hand, she toyed with the hair at the nape of his neck. With her right hand, she traced slow, maddening circles around his nipples.

"You're enjoying this aren't you?" he asked through clenched teeth.

"Immensely."

He laid her on a high linen-draped massage table beside the lotus pool. "Turn over."

She loosened her towel and did as he directed. He draped the fabric over her buttocks and picked up a bottle of fragrant oil from a warming tray. The exotic spice scent blended with the delicate perfume of the lotus blossoms as he poured it into his palms and began to smooth it over her feet and lower legs.

He thought he was safe, starting with her feet, but as his fingers kneaded and stroked her pink-tipped toes, the high arch of her slim foot, her trim ankles, he could feel his control slip another notch. When his hands glided up to her curved calves, she gave a sexy little moan, and it slipped again.

His fingers found a small zigzagged scar on the inside of her right knee. In an effort to take his mind off the mesmerizing sight and feel of her honey-sweet skin, as he traced the pattern he asked, "How did you get this?"

"A car wreck."

"When did it happen?" His hands moved up, kneading her thighs and buttocks with fresh oil.

"When I was a teenager."

Ram's gentle stroking moved upward to her sensitive back, and Meri was in a languid heaven as he smoothed the fragrant warm balm along her spine and over her shoulders.

She turned. He stilled. His gaze caressed where his hands

did not. "Please," she murmured. "I need you. Make love with me."

He hesitated only a heartbeat, then scooped her up and carried her to the canopied bed. Almost reverently he laid her on the silk sheets and stood looking down at her. The blue flames from his eyes warmed her skin to glowing. She held her arms in entreaty, and he dropped the towel knotted around his waist.

She smiled at the blatant evidence of his desire. "You're a hell of a man, Ramson Gabrey. Come here."

Ram yearned to devour her, to bury himself inside her with all the force of the ravenous passion rumbling inside him. But he must not. He needed to be gentle, careful because of her injury.

He knelt at her feet and touched her toes with his lips. His mouth and tongue and hands worked magic on her as he followed an upward path—licking, nipping, kissing, tasting, feeling, trailing fire as he stopped now and then to nuzzle and explore soft, special places.

Meri moaned as he kissed the scar on her knee, sucked in a noisy breath as he nuzzled the inside of her thighs. All the time his strong fingers were stroking, teasing. Aching, Meri clutched handfuls of silk sheet, then buried her fingers in his thick black hair, pulling him, urging him to bring his lips to hers, to fill the void and give her release, to take her to the sun.

"Wait, my love," he whispered. "We're not ready yet."

"Ram," she said hoarsely, "I'm on fire now."

He chuckled against her sensitive skin and went back to his seduction, all the while murmuring love words and praising her body in English and Arabic. There was no part of her he forgot as he kissed and caressed. His tongue traced her hip, her belly, and thrust into her navel as his hands slid up her rib cage and cupped her throbbing breasts. She moved restlessly, whimpering. When he slowly circled a puckered areola and pulled the nipple into his mouth like a sweet delicacy, she moaned and frantically clutched at his hips, urging.

Capturing her wrists, one in each powerful hand, he held them against the bed as he moved to the other waiting breast, teasing, tantalizing.

She threw back her head and squeezed her eyes shut. Her body writhed, glistening with a fine sheen of perspiration and fragrant, spicy oil. As his velvet tongue slid up her neck, along her jaw, and with a sensuous slowness, paused to lick the cleft in her chin, she cried his name. She was awash with mindless passion, swamped with a storm of violent craving. Never had her body been so consumed with desire. She felt like a wild thing thrashing in primitive abandon.

When his face was even with hers, he whispered, "Look at me *rôhi.*"

She opened her eyes. Glazed with craving and pupils widely dilated, his gaze smoldered with aggressive virility, but there was something more. She saw twin pools of longing emanating from the depths of his soul, pulling and pleading, weaving dreams and promises that settled around them like a gossamer mantle of golden threads and starlight.

"I love you, *habîbati,* the one I'll spend all my days with. I love you more than life or breath. You are mine forever," Ram murmured. "Mine forever. Say it, *sukkar.* Forever."

The word leapt and swelled in her heart. "Forever," Meri whispered.

A deep growl ripped from his throat as he released her wrists and claimed her lips with a wild, devouring hunger he could no longer contain. Her ardor matched his own as she uninhibitedly explored every corded tendon and muscle in his body. Her hands grasped his taut buttocks and her thighs parted, beseeching his entry.

As his tongue plundered the honeyed depths of her mouth, his fingers explored her moist, waiting core. He rolled and rose to his knees between her sleek legs. Arching her back, she strained toward his tumescence, as he slipped his hands under her hips and prepared to enter.

"Come with me, my love. Cling to me," he urged, plunging into her welcoming sweet musk.

They came together like the splendid violence of a desert windstorm with sensations and emotions so intense Meri thought she might die if they were sustained—and she didn't care. Clinging, reaching, striving together, they plunged into a sensual journey through a wind-whipped turbulence. They were sucked into the whirling eddy of no return, then released and flung past the edge of the earth to a shared splendor beyond the galaxies.

Meri screamed Ram's name as she reached the source and was filled with a piercing golden light. It pulsated through her and illuminated every cell in her body with throbbing, shattering, exquisite ecstasy. She was iridescent, growing, expanding out of her own skin. It would kill her if she continued. She embraced it and was swept into the void.

When her eyes fluttered open, Meri felt as if her spirit was awakening to a new world. Still glowing, she smiled, basking in the love rooted in her very soul and savoring the strong arms holding her to his heart.

She took his face in her hands. Love flowed from her fingertips as she looked directly into his sky-kissed eyes and said, "That was the most incredible experience of my life. I don't understand what it is that happens when we're together, but it's something magnificent." She lightly kissed the outside corner of each eye. "I say again: Ramson Gabrey, you're a hell of a man."

One side of his mouth lifted in a cocky grin. "Haven't I been trying to tell you that?"

She grabbed a pillow and smacked him with it. "I'm starving. Now that you've ravished me, you could at least feed me."

"Ravished *you?*" He hooted. "Love, I've had to peel you off like flypaper." When she whacked him again, he threw up his hands in defense. "Okay, okay. Let me call the kitchen. I think we missed breakfast. Let's try for lunch. Would you rather eat here or in the dining room?"

She looked down at her nudity. "I'd love to see the rest of your house, but I'm not sure I'm dressed for formal dining."

He laughed. "We can take care of that." He punched an intercom on the nightstand and gave instructions for lunch. A soft feminine voice answered in Arabic.

"Who was that?"

"My housekeeper. Lunch will be ready in half an hour. Now let's see if we can find a clean towel in your size."

"Oh, good grief! I can't wear a towel. Where are my clothes?"

"They cut them off when you were examined at the hospital. I brought you here in a sheet." He stroked his chin. "Let me see, where did I put that towel?" He walked to a large closet and pulled out several lovely *galabiyahs* in various colors, some of cool cotton, others of heavy moiré and delicate silk. "Will one of these do instead?"

She touched the fabrics. "They're exquisite. And all my favorite colors." Her eyes narrowed. "Whose are they?"

"Jealous? That's a good sign." He tweaked her nose. "They're all yours *sukkar*. They've been here waiting for you. Like this house. I built it for you."

She frowned. "But how could you have built it for me? We only met a few days ago."

Tenderness softened his voice as he touched the winged pendant that lay between her breasts. "Ah, but I've been dreaming of you for a long time. I knew you'd find your way here someday."

Dressed in identical white *galabiyahs* and soft sandals, Meri and Ram strolled hand in hand over the grounds of his villa. It sat on a small verdant rise beside the Nile. The gardens were filled with roses and all manner of fragrant blooming plants, a sharp contrast to the sand and rocky hills of the desert beyond. The exterior of the house was thick stone, designed to capture the Middle Eastern tradition with small domes and spires. The garages and helipad were discreetly hidden behind high walls, trees, and bubbling fountains.

Inside was every modern convenience, and the furnishings were a delightful blend of ancient and contemporary. Each room commanded a breathtaking view of the river or the desert. Meri loved it.

The two of them had decided to have lunch in the shaded courtyard. Attended by invisible servants, they had giggled like children, feeding each other strawberries, cold shrimp, and melon.

"What would you like to do now, love?"

Meri sighed. "I suppose I'd better call Welcome. She should be at the hotel by now."

"Sorry, *sukkar*, the telephones aren't working today. We'll call her in the morning."

They strolled back inside the house, drawn like a magnet to the huge silk-canopied bed. This time their lovemaking was slow and sweet, less frantic than before, but just as satisfying in a different way. It was a time for gentleness and discovery, tender caresses and languid smiles, closeness and drifting into peaceful sleep.

Meri yawned and stretched, feeling refreshed after her nap. Ram was not beside her. She rose, pulled on the white *galabiyah* and sandals, and walked to the bathroom. Judging by the skylight, it was late afternoon. She splashed her face and brushed her tangled hair. Behind her the waterfall splashed into the tub and the lingering fragrance of the lotus blossoms wafted through the damp air.

She walked to the quiet pool and knelt beside it. She touched the closed petals of the mystic flowers floating there and thought of Ram. For him, she had opened like the lotus. She loved him. Loved him with an intensity beyond comprehension. From that first day when he'd rescued her from the runaway camel, she'd known they shared something unique. No, even before that she'd known. From her dreams.

Perhaps, as Ram claimed, they were lovers in lives past. It didn't matter. They were lovers now.

She trailed her fingers through the water and watched her reflection carried away on the ripples and thought of all the reasons why a relationship between them might not work. Now, basking in the enchanted aura of the time, the place, and the man, those reasons seemed inconsequential. They were both intelligent, caring people. They could work things out some way.

Fate had drawn them together. She had accepted it. She couldn't imagine wanting anything more than to marry Ram and share a life with him. Being together *was* their destiny.

She stood and hugged herself with the sheer joy of loving and being loved and went to find Ram to remove the final barrier, to speak the simple words of love and commitment. She moved quietly, searching through the spacious rooms until she came to the open door of his study.

He stood beside his desk, his back to her, talking on the phone. Not wanting to interrupt, she waited silently for him to finish, letting her eyes feast on this beautiful man who was hers.

"How is the book tour going? Yes, Mother, she's perfectly safe. Tell Nora that there's nothing for her to be concerned about."

Meri frowned. *Nora?*

"J.J. and his men did an excellent job, and I got involved . . . personally." He chuckled. "Exactly. We ran into a problem or two, but believe me, she was watched more closely than the crown jewels. Someone followed her every minute. No, Meri will never hear it from me. I know her well enough to know that she would be furious. No, no. Tell Nora that there's no charge for the service. I received . . . adequate compensation." He laughed. "I know that you did. Yes, you will, Mother. And, no, I won't tell her about the Horus Hotels brochure either."

Twenty-four

A sickness has crept into me,
  my limbs have become heavy.
  and my body does not know itself.
  Even should the master physicians come to me,
  my heart would not be soothed by their remedies.

Love Songs of the New Kingdom
c. 1550-1080 B.C.

Blood drained from Meri's face as she stood rooted to the spot. She felt her fragile new love and trust shattered like a rock through an exquisite stained-glass window. The remaining jagged slivers dropped slowly, one . . . then another, ripping her heart, rending her soul, splintering with a tinkling crash around her feet.

Nothing was left but a gaping, scarring hole.

The warmth of love had fled.

She was cold.

Noiselessly, she turned and walked back to the sanctuary of the lotus pool. Its magic was gone.

Ram? Her mother? His mother? What vicious conspiracy had they hatched behind her back, mocking her, manipulating her? How typical of her mother to interfere in her life. But Ram? Was it all a pretense? Some sick joke played on a naive American girl?

She should have been angry. She should have been furious. She only felt empty. Empty and alone.

For long moments she sat and stared into the pool.

Destiny?

Destiny, hell. It was all a lie. A slick line good for a roll in the hay.

She had been deceived. And used.

God, how he must have laughed at her. Humiliation rolled over her in nauseous waves. She had bared her heart and soul to that Egyptian gigolo. She wanted to die when she remembered all the things she'd said to him, done with him. She'd known he was too good to be true. She should have heeded her doubts. Every time she listened to her heart instead of her head, she got into trouble.

And the Horus Hotels brochure too? Oh, dear God. Her mother from Dallas, his mother from Dallas. Of course it wasn't a coincidence. And he'd known, dammit! The job she'd worked so hard for, had been so proud of, meant nothing now. It was merely a sop bestowed by one of Nora Elwood's old cronies.

The knot in the pit of her stomach fluttered. From the cold, sick feeling that sat there, anger began to grow until it was a whirling, burning, magnificent rage. She stood up, lifted her chin, and stiffened her spine.

Ramson Gabrey, you bastard! You sexy, good-looking, smooth-talking, conniving, egg-sucking bastard!

He should win the Academy Award. She'd fallen for all his tales of undying love and destiny, believed him when he'd lied like a dirty dog about the droopy-eyed man, *Ram's* man she was sure, following her. Hell, she'd probably been traipsing around the country with a parade of men following her like a string of baby ducks.

No wonder he'd watched her so closely. She couldn't believe that her mother had the nerve to hire that cad as her bodyguard or to stick her nose in Meri's and Welcome's company business!

Yes, she could. It was exactly the sort of thing her mother would do. Damn the both of them! What a silly fool she'd been!

Her fury blazing, she started for the door, ready to tear a strip off Ramson Gabrey. When she got through with him, he'd be nothing but dry bones. Then she stopped.

Don't get mad. Get even.

Revenge. That's what she wanted. Sweet revenge.

She paced the floor trying to hatch a plot. Something diabolical. She was still pacing when she heard Ram call her name from the bedroom. She stiffened.

She drew a deep breath. Now it was Academy Award time for her.

"Oh, there you are, love. Did you have a nice nap?" Ram's velvet voice asked from the doorway. He smiled and walked toward her. She steeled herself to keep from flinching when he hugged her and kissed her cheek. "Want to take another bath? I'll wash your back."

She slipped out of his arms and tried to keep her voice normal as she said, "Not right now. I'd like to phone Welcome and let her know I'm okay."

"I'm sorry, *sukkar*, the telephone is still out of order."

Liar! she screamed silently, and the last niggling little doubt, the final tiny hidden hope that she had somehow been mistaken about him dissolved into desolation. "Maybe we could drive to the hotel. I need to get some clothes anyway."

"I'll have one of the servants pick up your things and deliver a message to Welcome." He grasped her hand and brought it to his lips. His eyebrow lifted devilishly as he added, "You won't need clothes for a while." He unclasped her *galabiyah* and drew it over her head.

She fought a rising panic. This wasn't going to be easy. She managed a feeble smile as her mind raced. *Stay cool.* Swallowing the bile building in her throat, she impishly tweaked his nose. "Sounds naughty."

His arms snaked around her, and he nuzzled her throat. "Very."

She rolled her eyes and endured his touch. "Ram?"

"Yes, love?"

"Do you ever have sexual fantasies?"

"I'm having one right now."

"Would you indulge one of mine?"

He kissed her. "Need you ask?"

She whispered in his ear, teasing the inner shell with her tongue as she revealed her desires.

He chuckled. "You're full of surprises, *sukkar.*"

"Will you do it? Please? For me?"

"Of course. But I may never be the same again."

She undressed him slowly, then rubbed her cheek against his chest. Touching him felt so wonderful that she had to grind her teeth to remind herself that she despised this lying jerk. She slid her hands over his muscular flanks, then patted his taut derrière.

"You get in bed, and I'll get the oils and other things, *sukkar.*" She almost had to bite her tongue to keep from saying "sucker" instead of *sukkar.* He'd played her for one long enough. Now it was her turn.

"You want it. You got it."

Ram lay naked and spread-eagled on the bed, his wrists and ankles each tied to a post with heavy silk drapery cords. Tasseled, no less.

As she secured the last knot on his ankle, he frowned. "Are you sure you know what you're doing, love?"

She smiled sweetly. "Certainly I do. I told you that I was always taking courses in everything. I took a jim-dandy one in knot tying." She drizzled a few drops of warm, fragrant oil into his navel, then stopped. "Did I hear a phone ring?' "

"No, *sukkar.* The phone is out of order, remember? In any

case, the walls are too thick to hear anything from the rest of the house."

"Good. I thought so." She got up, went to his dresser, selected a fine cotton handkerchief from a drawer, and climbed onto the head of the bed. "But just in case—" She crammed the handkerchief into his mouth.

Ram frowned, then began making muffled noises around the gag. She grabbed the oil cruet, upended it on his chest, and wiped her fingers on the sheet.

After she snatched on her *galabiyah,* she stood over him and yelled, "Ramson Gabrey, you son of a bitch! I heard you talking on the telephone. I heard what you said to your dear, sweet mama. You're a bold-faced liar, and I hate liars above all things. It's the worst form of condescension. When I want protection, *I'll* ask for it. And you and your mother and my mother can take your friggin' brochure contract and stick it where the sun don't shine."

He growled and struggled frantically; his eyes pleaded.

She smirked. "Gottcha, you bastard. Don't ever mess with a *real* Texan. You're outclassed." She ripped the falcon pendant from her neck and threw it in his face. "And I want you and your hocus-pocus to stay out of my dreams and out of my life! If you ever come within spitting distance of me again, I'll skewer your gizzard."

He wrenched at the bonds and made more muffled sounds, but the silk was as strong as steel, and her knots would hold till kingdom come. She'd made sure of it.

She wiggled her fingers in a wave. *"Ciao,* ya'll."

She locked the bedroom door behind her and headed for the study and a telephone.

Trying to get through to the hotel was a nightmare. She finally succeeded, but damn, wouldn't you know it, Welcome didn't answer in her room. Rats!

Someway, somehow, she was leaving this place.

First, she dismissed all the servants for the day, laughing to herself when she realized that the maid was in for a surprise when she went to change Ram's sheets the next day.

Next was a matter of transportation. There were three cars in the garage: a white Porsche, a blue Volvo, and a nice shiny black Jeep. Now if she could find the keys.

She rummaged through the study, hoping to find keys there and dreading a return to Ram's room if she didn't.

No keys.

Damnation!

But wait. She could hot-wire the Jeep. It was amazing how many things you learned to do when you took courses. She hot-footed it back to the garage.

First she grabbed a hammer and some other implements off the workbench and quickly knocked a valve stem off the Porsche and the Volvo. At least Ram couldn't follow her for a while. Grinning as she heard the hiss of tires deflating, she ran to the Jeep and, tossing the tools on the seat, climbed in.

She leaned over the ignition switch to insert a long screw. When it was tightly in place, she wiped the sweat off her brow with her forearm, picked up the small crowbar beside her, and took a deep breath. She positioned the lever, hesitated for a second, then pried out the ignition assembly.

In less than a minute she had the Jeep started. She backed out of the garage and burned rubber toward what she hoped to hell was Luxor.

Thankfully, her instincts were right. She saw the city in the distance—a mile or so dead ahead.

She was tooling along feeling damned proud of herself, and furious with Ramson Gabrey—and with her interfering mother—when a rattle-trap car pulled up beside her. He didn't pass, he only drove parallel with her and honked his horn.

"Go around, fool!" she yelled.

He kept honking. She ignored him. He had plenty of room to pass. There wasn't another soul on the road.

When he tried to cut her off, Meri got pissed. She swerved

and honked her own horn. When she saw who was driving the other car, she got scared.

The man with the droopy eye.

"Ohmygod." She shoved the gas pedal to the floor and pulled ahead.

Droopy-eye stayed right on her tail.

He pulled even with her again and once more tried to run her off the road. Royally pissed now—and scared witless to boot—she gritted her teeth and cut the wheel sharply to the left.

Metal groaned as she pushed his souped-up heap off the road and onto the rocky terrain. Meri struggled for control of the Jeep and kept it headed in the right direction. In her rearview mirror, she saw the other car fish-tail over the rocks, then slam into a fair-sized boulder.

She didn't slow down.

Just as she reached the outskirts of Luxor, she felt a thump under the Jeep. Then another. Then a *blump* and a shimmy. She stopped, leaned her head against the wheel, and prayed that what she figured was the matter, wasn't.

It was.

Her left front tire was flat, the rubber peeled away in big strips. Damn!

She wrestled the spare from the rear and jacked up the Jeep's front. Amid straining and swearing, she changed the tire. When the last lug was in place and tightened, she released the jack. The new tire touched the ground, then kept going and going and going.

Damnation! After all her work, the spare was flat too.

She kicked the errant tire and started out on foot.

Roaring muffled curses, Ram strained against the silk ropes binding him. They held as if they were made of steel. He stopped his futile struggling for a moment and let his trembling muscles relax.

God, how was he going to get out of this mess? He was

furious that Meri had left him trussed up, naked and helpless, but he was even more furious with himself. He never should have lied to her. Even though he was trying to protect her, one lie had built on another until he was in too deeply to tell her the truth. Hell, he was too scared to tell her the truth. He figured that she would react exactly as she had.

He'd bet his last pound that Meri was on her way to Luxor, alone, vulnerable, a perfect target. Trying to shield her from ugliness, he hadn't told her about the murdered *Mabaheth* agent who had been found on board the ship that morning. J.J. had spotted the agent and his partner early on in their travels. Given Tewfik Fayed's suspicions, Ram hadn't been surprised by their presence. He and J.J. had laughed over the notion that Meri and Welcome could be engaged in some covert CIA mission. They had never seen two more unlikely spies. But if the *Mabaheth* wanted to keep the pair under surveillance, Ram and J.J. welcomed the extra help.

Ram wasn't laughing now. He was terrified. He knew instinctively that whoever had killed a member of the elite, highly trained *Mabaheth* was probably the same person who attacked Meri. A pro. Dangerous, deadly. It was a miracle that he hadn't killed her as well.

What was he after? The jewelry had been taken in the first burglary. Meri had little left of great value. Except—

He cursed anew. God dammit, what a fool he was!

Meri had no idea what sort of danger she was in. A cold sweat broke out over Ram's body. Fear shot adrenaline through his bloodstream. He balled his fists, let out a muffled, primal roar, and yanked at his bonds.

The cords held. The bedposts cracked. Another mighty pull with teeth gritted and sinews straining, and the wood splintered.

Exhausted, Meri hobbled to the bench and plopped down. She took off her right sandal, brushed the sand from her foot and examined the bottom. Yep. A blister. Damnation! She didn't even have her purse, with antiseptic and a Band-Aid. Nor did she have a penny to her name for a taxi or a phone call. And it was getting dark.

She looked at the small row of shops ahead. She'd passed this same way three times. She recognized the rug in the window of the one on the corner. It seemed that the proprietor who had given her directions didn't know what he was talking about. She'd heard that the Egyptians were such an accommodating lot that they sometimes gave misinformation rather than admit that they didn't know which way to go.

She tried a different shop this time. Two, in fact. When both directions to the hotel matched, she set off again, hurrying as night fell.

"Thank God," she whispered when she saw the name of the hotel a block away. She desperately wanted a drink of water, a bath, and a bandage for her foot.

Meri figured that she must look a fright because the desk clerk wrinkled his nose and said superciliously, "May I help you?"

"Yes, you certainly may. My traveling companion has already checked in, and I need a key to our room."

"And who is your traveling companion?"

"Welcome Venable."

The clerk shuffled through some papers, then said, "I see that Miss Venable is alone. There is no mention on her card of sharing her accommodations with anyone."

Meri ground her teeth and counted to five before she lost it. "Look, bud, my name was on the reservation. Meri Vaughn."

He shuffled some more papers. "Ah, yes, I see. Meri Vaughn. Do you have your passport, some identification?"

"Uh, no." She held out her empty hands. "I don't have my purse with me."

He gave her a weasely smile. "Then I'm very sorry. Without identification I couldn't possibly give you a key to Miss Venable's suite. I'm sure you understand."

Tired, grungy, and with her blister throbbing, Meri didn't feel at all understanding. She felt irritated. And she needed to go to the bathroom. "We can solve this all very simply. Call Miss Venable for verification of my identity."

"Certainly, miss."

He picked up a phone. Meri tried to see what number he dialed, but he gave her a haughty look and shielded the numbers with his hand. She rolled her eyes in disgust and leaned her tired body against the marble desk.

"I'm sorry, miss. Miss Venable doesn't answer. She must be out."

"Out? Out where?"

The clerk sniffed. "I really couldn't say, miss."

"Then let me have another room."

"Certainly, miss." He raised his eyebrows slightly and Meri could swear that he smirked. "Do you have a passport, a credit card?"

"You know damned well that I don't! This is getting ridiculous. I have several friends staying here. Ring them, please. Try Nona Craft."

The clerk tried one name after the other. No one answered. The situation was quickly changing from annoying to frightening. She was alone in a foreign country with no passport, no money, and a blister on her foot. Plus her need to visit the ladies' room was growing more urgent.

The clerk seemed to sense her increasing desperation, and he began to fidget, worrying, Meri was sure, that she was about to become hysterical in the lobby.

"Perhaps," he suggested, "you might try the restaurant. Your friends may be there."

The restaurant. Of course. It was dinnertime. She asked for directions, then ducked into a ladies' room along the way.

When she caught sight of herself in the mirror, she understood why the clerk had behaved as he had. She looked like something the cats dragged in. Her face was grimy, her clothes were caked with dust, and her hair looked like a fright wig. She made repairs as best she could, then went searching for the restaurant.

No luck. She didn't see a single soul that she knew. Nor did she find anyone in the bar.

Dejected, she hobbled back toward the lobby. Her only option was to sit there and wait for Welcome. Or somebody.

She dropped into one of the plush chairs grouped around a fountain in the lobby. God, it felt good. She ached down to the bone. She was tempted to rip off her sandal and soak her foot in the fountain. About to give in to the temptation, she cast a furtive glance around the area.

A man sitting in a lounge chair nearby lowered the Arabic newspaper he was reading and snuffed out his pungent cigarette. When she spied him, Meri's heart surged, and she leapt from the chair.

"Walter Rush! Boy am I glad to see you." She grabbed his hand and pumped it. "I couldn't find anybody, and I can't get a room until I locate Welcome. Do you know where everybody is?"

He withdrew his hand from her spirited pumping, adjusted his glasses, and said, "I believe they're at the sound and light show at the Temple of Karnak."

"Oh, thank God. Is it far from here?"

"Not very."

"Uh . . . Mr. Rush, would you loan me taxi fare? I seem to be stranded without my purse."

Walter Rush smiled, actually smiled. Meri didn't think she'd ever seen him smile before. "No need for that," he said. "I have a car. I'll be happy to drive you."

"Oh, would you? I'd be eternally grateful. I have a humongous blister on the ball of my foot, and it's killing me. You don't happen to have a Band-Aid on you, do you?"

"I think I may have something in the glove-box kit that will suffice."

***

J.J. hopped in his car and took off toward the hotel. Damn the timing! He'd been about to sit down to dinner with a nubile young Dane he'd met on the cruise when his pager went off.

Ram naturally. And fit to be tied. Meri was loose, on the run, and unguarded. J.J. didn't take time to learn the particulars; he only bade his dinner companion a reluctant farewell and hauled ass.

Half a block from the hotel, he spotted Meri in the car with Walter Rush. He downshifted, made a U-turn, and was about to take out after them when a dented old Chevy with a souped-up engine came barreling out from a side street and clobbered him.

J.J. cursed as he rammed into a light post that creased the front end of his car. He cursed more loudly when he glimpsed the driver of the Chevy. Mustafa! Damn that bastard. But Mustafa was gone in a roar of blue smoke before J.J. was out of his car.

Water dribbled from J.J.'s radiator, but he drove the car despite it, hoping to get a fix on their direction before the engine died completely. He grabbed the mike from under the dash and radioed Ram.

As they drove along the narrow asphalt highway out of the city, Meri dabbed antiseptic cream on her foot and covered the area with three bandage strips. "Ah," she said, "that feels better already. I really appreciate this. How far are we from the place?"

"Not far," Rush said. "Do you mind if I smoke?"

She did, but now was not the time to deliver a lecture. "Of course not."

He shook the package against his mouth. His eyes never left the highway as he flicked a lighter and held the flame to the dark Turkish cigarette dangling from his thin lips.

Meri felt the bottom drop out of her stomach.

Ohhhh, shit.

Twenty-five

I have seen yesterday; I know tomorrow.

Inscription on Tutankhamen's shrine

Meri closed her eyes and her head fell back against the seat. A feeling of impending doom churned her belly and raised chill bumps across her skin. God, what an idiot she'd been.

Her eyes opened and zeroed in on the foot on the accelerator. Field boots. Small feet for a man. About the same size as hers. The pieces of the puzzle began to come together. Walter Rush's boot prints were in the wet carpet; his cigarette butt had floated in the commode. She knew as surely as she knew her own name that he'd been the one who'd broken into Welcome's and her rooms. Had he killed the man in the closet as well? If he had, she may have signed her death warrant by getting into his car.

Her first impulse was to fling herself from the speeding vehicle, her second, to confront him. She did neither. Instead she sat quietly, drawing on reserves of courage she didn't know she had.

Was she being abducted? Why? For some political purpose? But Walter was British, not Arabic. It made no sense. Neither did breaking into her cabin make sense. Especially the second time. Stealing the jewelry she could understand, but *film?* Why was he after film? And what were his plans now?

If he was going to hold her for ransom, one thing was sure. With her knowing his identity, she wouldn't live to tell about it.

The churning in her stomach grew more acute.

She searched her memory, trying to recall exactly where the temple at Karnak was. Now that she thought about it, it seemed that it was only a couple of miles from Luxor. They had driven considerably more than two miles.

Ohhh, God.

She couldn't just sit there and be meekly driven to her death. A weapon. She needed a weapon. But what?

She remembered a flashlight in the glove compartment. Not much of a weapon, but something. She casually reached for the button on the dash.

"What are you doing?" Rush asked sharply.

"I was going to get the first-aid kit and put some more cream on my foot," Meri replied as casually as she could manage.

"Leave it."

"But—"

"Leave it."

The charade was coming to an end. Testing, Meri asked, "Exactly where is Karnak?"

"The turnoff was about four miles back."

She swallowed. "Where are we going?"

"Into the desert."

"But why?"

"You have something that I want."

"What? I only have the clothes that I'm wearing. I don't even have my purse."

He gave her a Peter Lorre sort of smile. "You have the falcon pectoral."

Meri's hand automatically splayed across her chest. "Do you mean all this hullabaloo is over the pendant? Good Lord, why? I mean it's pretty and all, but I imagine that you can buy them in half the gift shops in Egypt."

"No, Miss Vaughn, you can't. I've never seen another like it; it is one of a kind. Such a pectoral has been described in one of the early Egyptian myths—or what was thought to be simply a romantic myth—on at least two papyrus scrolls that have been recovered. If the piece is authentic, as I suspect that it is, it is priceless."

"You're kidding."

"No, Miss Vaughn, I assure you than I am not."

"But I don't have it." She quickly unbuttoned the throat of her *galabiyah* and spread the flaps. "See. I don't have it." She slapped her bare skin. "Can we go back to the hotel now?"

He chuckled, an eerie, rusty sound that grated her nerve endings. "Then I suppose that I must . . . persuade you to tell me where it is."

"You don't have to persuade me. I'll tell you right now. Ramson Gabrey has it."

"Ah, good. From what I've seen, I'm sure Mr. Gabrey can be easily convinced to trade the pectoral for you."

Remembering Ram as she'd seen him last, Meri said, "Uhhhh, I wouldn't count on it."

"Pray that he's willing."

Meri prayed. She also prayed that the Marines would land and save her from this mess she'd gotten herself into. But when she opened her eyes, she didn't see Marines, only a long black stretch of asphalt ahead of them.

"You broke into my room, didn't you?" Meri said quietly.

He merely smiled—if it could be called a smile. His expression was more like a death rictus.

"And you clobbered me with a flashlight."

"An instinctive reaction."

"And you—" Meri clamped her mouth shut. She wasn't about to accuse him of murder. As it was, she had a slight chance of getting out of this mess alive. If she revealed that she knew about the body in 316, she could kiss her chance good-bye.

"I—what?" he asked.

"You . . . uh . . . took my film. Why?"

"I took no film."

"You didn't?"

"I have no interest in film."

Strange. If he didn't take the film, who did? Oh, God, what did it matter? Missing film was the least of her worries. She went back to praying.

When she heard Rush mutter a curse, she glanced over her shoulder and saw a pair of headlights, coming up fast on their tail.

She prayed some more. And crossed her fingers.

The car behind them pulled along side and honked. The droopy-eyed man, the one Ram had following her. She'd never been so glad to see anybody in her life.

"Bloody fool!" Rush said, stomping down the accelerator and pulling ahead.

It was *déjà vu*.

Old Droopy-eye was no quitter, she'd say that for him. He roared up beside them again and cut them off. Cursing, Rush skidded to a stop. Something slid from beneath the seat and whacked Meri's ankle. She glanced down and saw what looked like a small fire-extinguisher. Carefully she put her foot on it and rolled it forward and toward her door, out of sight from Rush.

Droopy-eye got out of his car and started toward them with what looked like a gun in his hand. Meri could have kissed him. He wasn't the Marines, but he'd do. "Looks like the jig is up," she said smugly. "The cavalry, such as it is, has arrived."

"Mustafa is an idiot."

"You know him?"

"Shut up and keep quiet."

Mustafa approached, saying something in Arabic and waving his gun. Rush said something back in Arabic, harshly. He unbuttoned his jacket as Droopy-eye came closer, pulled out a pistol and held it by his leg.

Meri's eyes widened, and her breathing grew so rapid that she was afraid that she'd hyperventilate and pass out. Slowly she reached down and curled her fingers around the fire extinguisher, ready to attack Rush's flank.

Before she could find which end of the cylinder to squirt, Walter Rush shoved open his door and slammed it against Mustafa, knocking the gun from his hand and sending him sprawling.

Ohhh shit.

Thinking to distract Rush, Meri jumped from the car and headed for the cover of a shadowy crag to their right. Her heart in her throat, she scrambled over the sandy rock. A shot rang out behind her. She flinched but crouched low and kept going.

"Stop!" Rush shouted.

Stop, hell. Did he think she was crazy? She hoisted the tail of her robe and kept climbing. When she neared the top of the hill, she plastered herself against the wall and paused for a breath, her body trembling as she peered through the darkness toward the cars.

The headlights were on. The beams of one caught the lower part of a man's body lying toes up on the road.

She heard the crunch of boots against rocks below. "Miss Vaughn, you've no place to go," Rush said. "Come down."

She didn't reply. In a few moments the boots crunched again. Taking a deep breath, Meri held up the fire extinguisher, ready to give Rush a face full of foam.

Suddenly, a churning sound pierced the quiet. Meri strained her ears. A helicopter! Two helicopters.

The churning grew louder until the choppers hovered overhead, flashing day-bright spotlights. Walter Rush was caught in the beam of one, and as he made a run for his car, gunfire spit across his path. He stopped and raised his hands.

Meri's knees shook too violently to hold her up. She slid down the side of the rock until she was sitting on the ground and forced herself to breath slowly and deeply. "Thank you, Lord," she gasped.

She heard the helicopters set down and heard shouts below. Praise be, the Marines had landed after all.

No, not the Marines, not here, but at least they were the good guys.

Or were they?

Good Lord, for all she knew this bunch could be a worse group. Cutthroats, kidnappers. Ohmygod! Her body tensed to full alert, ready to cut and run.

"Meri! God dammit, Meri! Where are you? Meri!"

She recognized the voice bellowing her name. Ram.

"I'm here," she called. Rising, she began picking her way down the hill.

The moment Ram spotted her, he ran and wrapped her in a bone-crushing hug. "Oh God, I've been through hell. Are you all right, love?"

"A little shaky, but I'm fine. At least I was before you cracked my ribs."

He loosed his hold, but still kept her firmly in his arms. "Sorry, *sukkar*, but I'm afraid to let go of you. What has happened?"

Meri gave him a quick rundown of the evening's events. "I was terrified until your droopy-eyed man stopped us—Mustafa his name is."

"Mustafa isn't, wasn't my man. I suspect that he had the same idea that Rush did."

"Ohhh God. I though he was going to save me. He had a gun, but Walter shot him, and I grabbed the fire extinguisher and headed for the hills. I was scared spitless, and then the helicopters came. Ram, is it true that the falcon pectoral is a priceless antiquity?"

He shrugged. "I suppose that it is. But its value to me is seeing you wear it."

"Well, I won't be wearing it anymore."

He lifted her chin and scanned her face. "Wear it or not as

you choose, but don't run from me again. I need you. My life is nothing without you."

His tone was so tender and pleading, his flame blue eyes so filled with love, his body so knee-weakeningly magnetic, Meri almost wavered—almost believed the sweet lies, almost reached for the lips descending toward hers. Almost. Then she remembered his words on the phone and jerked away. "Oh no you don't, you weasel. I'm going to Luxor. Alone," she said emphatically. "Then Welcome and I are leaving."

Ram's fingers bit painfully into her upper arm as he grabbed Meri and spun her around. "You're not going anywhere. You're staying with me." The love-washed glow had disappeared from his eyes. In its place was the glacial blue determination she had glimpsed before.

"No, I'm not."

"You are."

"Read my lips," she ground out. "No, I'm not." Meri gave a savage cry, twisted, and flung Ram flat on the ground. She yanked her skirt to her thighs and ran like the devil was on her heels. She hadn't made it ten yards until she was grabbed from behind.

Ram threw her over his broad shoulder like a sack of potatoes and carried her kicking and screaming back toward one of the helicopters. She pounded on his back while he issued rapid orders in Arabic to a group of men there. All her bucking and twisting and beating was to no avail. Ram held her firmly.

Terrified now, frantic tears mingled with sweat on her blotchy, crimson face. The blood pounded in her ears from hanging over Ram's back. Still she struggled. She might as well have been beating against the Great Pyramid, so ineffectual were her blows.

When they reached the helicopter, Ram lowered Meri into the passenger seat and strapped her in. As soon as he stepped away, she grabbed the harness and undid it. Before she could climb out, he was back, capturing both her wrists in one of his hands. She struggled and muttered vile imprecations about his parentage, but he held her firm, reached under the seat and pulled out a tasseled silk cord. It looked very familiar.

"Ram, dammit! Don't you dare!"

Despite her protests, he dared. She could have sworn something akin to pity or remorse flickered across his implacable features as he gently bound her hands together, then bathed her flushed face with water from a thermos.

"I'm sorry, love. I didn't want it to come to this," he said softly.

"Ram, for God's sake, let me go. Don't do this," Meri pleaded.

"I have to. You've left me no other choice." Ram climbed into the pilot's seat and strapped in.

"Okay, you've had your little joke. Now untie me and let me go."

"No. You're coming with me."

"Where are you taking me?"

"Into the desert. Beyond the Valley of the Kings."

"How long are you going to keep me there?"

He didn't look at her. "As long as it takes." Ram grasped the controls and started the engine.

Slowly the craft rose, hovered, then flew toward the sandy hills. The noisy churn of the rotors matched Meri's heartbeat as she sat rigidly staring out at the sky, a sky filled with millions and millions of bright stars.

The moon had risen, full and silvery, and illuminated the age-sculpted terrain below as they flew over the Valley of the Kings where pharaohs and queens long dead had rested, hidden among the arid hills with vast, coveted treasures.

A few minutes later, the helicopter fanned swirls of ancient, endless sand as it set down near a large tent standing alone in the barren desert. When the engine was quiet, Ram unbuckled his seat belt and stepped out. He moved to Meri's side of the craft and released her harness as well. This time he took her in his arms and walked toward the desert dwelling. He brushed aside the flap and went in.

Setting her down, he struck a match and lit two lamps, lending a soft golden glow to the billowing canopy and its contents.

Meri gasped at the opulence she saw. "Where are we?"

Ram grinned. "It's my sheikh's tent. Like it? I thought you might enjoy it, but I hadn't planned to bring you here quite this way." He picked her up again and strode across the intricate Oriental carpets and laid her gently on a soft bed covered with dozens of tasseled silk pillows. He untied her bonds and gently kissed each of her wrists.

She jerked away.

"Did I hurt you?"

"Not physically, but I'm totally humiliated."

He chuckled. "You think I wasn't?"

"That's what this is all about, isn't it? Well, you've had your revenge. Now take me back to Luxor."

"No. This isn't about revenge. We're going to stay here and plan our wedding." He smiled and traced the scar on her face with his thumb. "Forever, remember?"

Meri knocked his hand away, her eyes blazed, and she shouted, "You low-life, contemptible scum! Don't talk to me about weddings! I wouldn't marry a lying scoundrel like you if you were the last man on earth."

Ram only smiled and lit several candles. The flickering light danced over the rainbow of shiny fabrics and sparkled off polished brass candlesticks, bowls, and plates. "I'd planned a midnight supper for us here."

She crossed her arms and glared at him. "I'm not hungry."

"You will be eventually."

"How long do you plan to keep me here?"

"I told you, as long as it takes."

"Hell will freeze over first."

Ram chuckled. "I believe that's what my grandmother said too."

A new wave of panic assailed her. What were his plans? "Are we alone here?"

"Quite alone. And don't try to run away again. There's no

place to run." He looked sternly at Meri. "You'd die in the desert, so don't try it. Promise me?"

"I'm not a fool. There are better ways to die than of exposure in the scorching sun."

Ram touched his lips to her brow and said, "I'll be right back." He walked through the portal and dropped the flap behind him.

Meri scrambled to her feet and nearly fell. Her foot had gone to sleep. She stamped a few times to restore the circulation, hobbled to the entrance, and gingerly lifted the covering. Ram was headed toward the helicopter.

Was he really going to keep her here in this bizarre holdover from a Hollywood studio? This was the twentieth century, for gosh sakes. People didn't do things like this anymore. Or did they? She watched Ram retrieve bundles from the craft and start back. Meri dropped the flap and rubbed her forehead. She had to get away somehow. *Think!*

She was pacing—when Ram returned and dropped the bags on the bed. Distrustful of his every move, Meri asked, "What's in there?"

Ram untied one bundle. "Extra clothes for each of us and plenty of food and water."

Keel cool, she reminded herself as an idea formed from the desperation flitting in her head. "Ram," she said sweetly, pouring on her most dazzling smile, "does this place have a bathroom?"

Ram grinned. "There's a wash basin behind that screen," he said nodding toward the back of the tent. "If you have anything else in mind, you'll have to use nature's convenience."

"I had something else in mind," she said demurely. "Excuse me, please."

As Meri started toward the entrance, Ram caught her elbow. "I'll go with you."

Meri shook off his hand, "I would prefer the dignity of some privacy, if you don't mind."

Ram held her shoulders and looked her straight in the eye.

"Will you promise me you won't run off in the desert? I'm not exaggerating when I tell you how dangerous it would be."

Meri held up her fist, letting the index and little fingers escape in the University of Texas victory sign. "Scout's honor. I'm not stupid."

Ram laughed and hugged her. "I know, but sometimes you can be stubborn." He kissed her on the forehead and said, "I trust you. While you're gone, I'll fix our supper. Are you hungry now?"

Meri slowly let out the breath she had been holding and nodded. "Famished." Forcing herself not to run, Meri lifted the flap and went out into the moonlight. When she was a few paces away, she broke into a trot toward the helicopter.

Quickly slipping into the pilot's seat, she buckled in and took a few seconds to familiarize herself with the controls. She took a deep breath, prayed, and started the engine. She had just lifted off when Ram came charging out of the tent yelling and gesturing wildly.

Meri hovered for a moment and leaned out, laughing and waving. "I took a course," she yelled before she headed southeast.

Meri was still laughing with elation as she flew toward the lights of Luxor. "Gottcha again, Ramson Gabrey, you lying bastard! It was your male chauvinism that finally did you in. It didn't occur to you I could manage your fancy helicopter, did it?"

Twenty-six

You are bright and great and gleaming,
   and are high above every land.
Your rays envelop the lands, as far as you have created.
You are Ra, and you reach unto their end . . .
When you go down in the western horizon,
   the earth is in darkness, as if it were dead.

The Great Hymn to the Aten
Akhenaten, c. 1350 B.C.

As Meri and Welcome were buckling their seat belts on the plane, George Mszanski slipped into the seat across the aisle. Meri didn't feel like talking to anybody. She turned and stared out the window beside her.

"George!" Welcome said. "What are you doing here? I thought you were staying in Luxor for a few days."

"Naw, I decided to head on back to Cairo."

"Where's Jean Jacques?"

"Oh, J.J. decided to hang around a while longer."

"Lover's quarrel?"

George blushed. "You might say that."

J.J.? That was the name Ram had mentioned in the phone conversation with his mother.

Meri leaned forward and peered around Welcome. "Did you call Jean Jacques *J.J.?*"

He frowned. "Yes."

Dammit it all to hell! J.J. was one of Ram's watchdogs. Which undoubtedly meant that George was too. Damn and double damn! Wasn't anybody what they seemed? She glared at George. "You're probably not even gay!"

For two days, Meri moped around the Mena House suite, waiting for their flight home. Lord, she'd be glad to get back to Texas.

Even though she tried to push memories of Ram away as soon as they popped up, he constantly intruded into her thoughts. She couldn't recall ever having been hurt so badly in her life. Not only had her mother betrayed her, the man she thought that she loved more than breath had betrayed her.

She'd always prided herself on her savvy, lost patience with her friends who were gullible enough to fall for the smooth line of a flagrant cad. It galled her to realize that she hadn't been immune to a smooth line either. It just took the right man with the right line to hook her as slickly as a hungry catfish.

Obviously she'd only been a lark, a job, an amusing interlude. She hadn't heard from Ram since she'd flown away that night. And she knew that he wasn't still stranded in the desert tent. When they'd landed in Cairo, Meri had blessed George out and told him where to find his *boss*.

And she knew that Ram *was* George's boss. And Jean Jacques. After Welcome had done some checking with her friends at the embassy, Meri knew a great deal about Horus Security and the gaggle of men they employed. Ram owned it; J.J. managed it. And while *Jean Jacques* was an excellent dancer, he was also a martial arts expert—and no more Parisian than she was. He was a Cajun from Abbeville, Louisiana. He and Ram were fraternity brothers from UT.

And she'd found out a lot more about Ramson Gabrey and

his family too. They *owned* Horus Hotels and lots of other things in the country. Ram might be an architect all right, but he was actively involved in running the family business.

His mother wasn't just Mrs. Gabrey, she was Charlotte Clark Gabrey, a.k.a. Charlie Clark, known for her best selling mysteries. Meri had heard her mother gloating over Charlie Clark's success many times. Nora was her publicist.

The past two days had been miserable. Pure hell. *And he hadn't tried to call and offer any sort of explanation, dammit!* Because there *was* no explanation. It was betrayal, plain and simple.

Meri sat on the sofa, her knees drawn under her chin, feeling totally wretched.

"Sweetie, I wish I could do something to cheer you up," Welcome said, rubbing Meri's back.

"So do I."

A knock came at the door, and Meri's heart stumbled in undeniable anticipation. She was irritated by her reaction, her continuing hope that it would be Ram with some plausible explanation to all this mess.

"I'll get it," Welcome said, pushing herself up from the plush sofa and padding to the door. Meri was right behind her.

A bellman, holding a cardboard box and a small floral arrangement, stood outside. "For Miss Vaughn," he said.

Welcome tipped him, then grinned as she held out the bouquet to Meri. "Maybe this will cheer you up."

Meri plucked the card from the flowers. "It might if I knew who the hell Tewfik Fayed was. What's in the box?"

Welcome untied the string and peeked in. "Holy cow!"

"What is it?"

"Our film."

"Here, let me see."

Sure enough, inside the box was the case with all the film they'd shot for the brochure along with the canisters of her labeled personal film. An envelope was tucked inside. She ripped it open, and she and Welcome read the letter inside. It was a cryptic note from the man named Tewfik Fayed. He said that the film had come into his possession erroneously and that he was returning it to her. The letterhead indicated that he was the director of the *Mabaheth*.

"What is the *Mabaheth?*" Welcome asked.

"I haven't the foggiest notion. Probably one of those endless agencies spawned by the Egyptian bureaucracy. How do you think he knew where to contact me?" It was peculiar, very peculiar. But then everything that had happened to her since she'd been in the country was bizarre.

"I'll call Philip at the Embassy. He seems to know everything," Welcome said, charging to the phone and snatching it up. After she explained the situation to Philip, her end of the conversation consisted of, "You're kidding. You're kidding. You're kidding." She looked stunned when she hung up.

"Well?"

"You won't believe this."

"Try me."

"Tewfik Fayed is the director of the *Mabaheth*, which is roughly the equivalent of the FBI."

"The *FBI?* Holy cow."

"Wait. There's more. It seems that a *Mabaheth* agent was found dead on our ship, the Nile Destiny. Stabbed."

Meri's eyes grew big. "You mean our body . . ."

"Was a *Mabaheth* agent."

"Holy shit!"

"The knife sticking out of his chest was identified as belonging to Walter Rush, and it had his fingerprints all over it."

"Holy shit!"

"You said it, sweetie."

"But how did the *Mabaheth* end up with our film? Walter Rush told me he didn't take it, and at that point, he didn't have any reason to lie."

"I don't have a clue. But if you ask me, I think we would be wise to keep our mouths shut."

"I'm with you."

* * *

Meri was growing more and more impatient to leave Egypt. The country had lost its allure. She sat on her bed and stared out at the Pyramids. They were only big heaps of old stones. They weren't magic.

Welcome rapped on the open door to Meri's bedroom. "Someone's here to see you."

Meri's heart went to her throat. "Who?"

"Your mother. And another woman."

"Tell them to get lost."

Nora Elwood charged into Meri's room. "Meri, don't be difficult. We've flown halfway around the world to explain things to you." A tall, blue-eyed blond woman followed cautiously in Nora's wake.

"What's to explain? You've butted into my life again. *My* life, Mother. My professional life and my personal life. And this time you've screwed up royally. You've cut my heart out, Mother. Go away. I don't want to talk to you." Tears gathered in her eyes and spilled down her cheeks.

"Meri, don't be so dramatic. I—"

"Nora, let me handle this," the other woman said. She crossed the room, sat down beside Meri, and took her hand. "Dear, I'm Ram's mother, Charlotte Gabrey. Or Charlie, if you prefer."

Before she thought, Meri said dreamily, "He has your eyes." Her face went hot. "I mean—"

Charlotte patted her hand and smiled. "I know what you mean. And I also know that Nora and I are two interfering old biddies who may have ruined your happiness and my son's. I could never forgive myself if that happened. He is heartsick over this mess, and he demanded that your mother and I straighten it out. He loves you deeply, you know."

Meri started to speak, but Charlotte shushed her. "First, let me explain about the assignment you won for the Horus Hotel brochure. Nora had told me about your new business and I, without her knowledge, asked my husband to see that your company had an opportunity to bid. And that's all it was—an opportunity to bid. The assignment was awarded on merit."

Meri frowned. "Truthfully?"

"Truthfully. Of course I was delighted to learn that V&V had been selected."

"*I* wasn't," Nora interjected. "The papers are full of stories about—"

"Let me finish, Nora," Charlotte interrupted. She turned back to Meri. "Tell me, when did you meet my son?"

Meri gave her the date.

Charlotte smiled. "I thought so. I didn't speak with him until the following day. We were in Philadelphia, weren't we, Nora?"

"Do you mean—"

"Yes, dear. You and Ram had already met before he knew about your mother's and my connection. In fact, because Nora was so concerned about your safety, I spoke to J.J., the manager of Ramson's security firm, myself. And before I spoke to my son. I didn't realize that I was placing him in such a difficult position when I swore him to secrecy about the security measures. Can you forgive me? Moreover, can you forgive him?"

"I—I don't know."

Charlotte touched her cheek. "Think about it, Meri. Think very hard. To be loved by a Gabrey man is heaven itself."

An hour later, Meri hadn't moved from her place, sitting on her bed, gazing out at the Pyramids. She still hadn't heard a word from Ram himself. Did she want to?

She couldn't deny it. Yes. If what Ram's mother had said was true, if Ram really loved her, yes, she did.

But she imagined that he was furious about her leaving him tied up in Luxor. He might never forgive her. Dear Lord, what if his mother was wrong? What if he really didn't love her?

There was a knock at the door of the suite.

"Sweetie, would you get that? I'm in my underwear."

Meri went to the door and opened it. She stood aside in open-mouthed wonder as Omar led in a parade of delivery men. There must have been a dozen baskets of exotic flowers, several luxurious furs, intricately styled silk *galabiyahs* encrusted with jewels, and a small chest, about the size of a shoe box, which Omar presented with a bow.

It was finely carved, translucent alabaster. When Meri opened it, she gasped. It was filled with loose stones—everything from topaz and turquoise to rubies, emeralds, and diamonds.

"Oh, good grief!"

Omar smiled and handed her a key on a gold camel key chain. "Mr. Gabrey said perhaps you would like this one better. It is a Jeep, and the doorman will bring it around if you wish to use it." He bowed again and backed out the door.

Meri threw back her head and let out a whoop. She giggled and whirled and danced around the room. That crazy, wonderful Egyptian still loved her!

"Lawdy, lawdy," Welcome commented dryly as she strolled into the room and fingered the loot. Then she broke into a grin, grabbed Meri and hugged her. "Looks like we'll be having a wedding instead of a wake."

Meri knew the next move was hers. She spent a frantic hour trying to call Ram. The Egyptian phone system was notoriously poor, especially for someone whose Arabic was limited to the words she knew. "What I am going to do?" she asked Welcome impatiently. "I can't get a flight to Luxor until in the morning."

"There's no need to starve in the meantime. How about some food? I believe I could eat a horse, saddle and all."

"You go ahead. I think I'll go for a walk instead."

Meri strolled alone, head down, hands shoved in the pockets of her turquoise jumpsuit, shoulder bag bumping against her side, through the grounds of the hotel. Her feet unconsciously retraced a path toward the desert.

"Hello, beautiful lady," a small voice called. "You want to buy some postcards? You need a guide to the Pyramids?"

She looked up and smiled at the grinning little face. Some things never change. "Hi, Ahmed."

"Miss Meri Vaughn! You want another camel ride to the Pyramids?" His black eyes flashed and his grin widened.

She ruffled his hair and laughed. "Why not? Think we can find Hassan?" She pulled a bill from her purse and handed it to him. "Let's shoot the works."

Ahmed scampered ahead, pulling her behind him toward the animal stalls. Soon she was plodding along, swaying with the rhythm of the gangling gray beast as it ambled its way to the Pyramids. Bittersweet flashes of memory teased her back to another time. She closed her eyes and could almost conjure up the hoofbeats of a big black stallion. She started.

They sounded so real.

They were real! Her heart started pounding, and she swung around to search out the rider.

Galloping fast behind her was a dumpy, ruddy-faced man in a plaid shirt. Meri's shoulders slumped in defeat. It was only a fantasy, a thin hope that Ram might reappear in this significant place to take her into his arms and gallop away.

When they reached the Sphinx, the driver tapped Hassan down for dismounting. She wistfully patted the camel after she got off and tipped his owner. Ahmed seemed to have caught her pensive mood, for he stood quietly by as she sat down on a familiar stone and gazed at the enduring silent sentinel as it beheld the sun of yet another day.

Don't move. Stay right here. The words echoed through her memory. Her lashes lowered, and she was lost among the faces of Ram. . . . one, flame-blue eyes crinkled with laughter; another, ablaze with passion; yet another, pained and pleading. God help her, she loved him.

She waited and waited, hoping against hope that Ram would come to her.

He didn't come.

As the sun began to set behind the Pyramids, she sighed, rose, and walked slowly back to the hotel. Even if Ram had come, they had a world of issues to work out between them. Sometimes love didn't conquer all.

Sometimes love wasn't enough.

Twenty-seven

My heart is fluttering to the point of springing forth, at the thought that I may see my [lover] in dreams this night; How beautifully, then, would the night pass!

                    Love Songs of the New Kingdom
                              c. 1550-1080 B.C.

He came to her from the shadows, mist still clinging to his form and obscuring his features so that only his deeply penetrating eyes were distinguishable. They were blue, an arresting blue like pale crystal shot with fire.

A familiar love for him swelled and filled her with an inner glow. She smiled and held out her arms to him. He brushed her temple with his lips, then kissed her softly. His presence cloaked her in a surreal splendor as their spirits blended, like two souls meshing into one to form a timeless unity. When he drew back, she was filled with sadness and a wrenching longing to hold on to him forever.

He smiled, and an ephemeral flood of warmth spread through her like sunlight. As he placed a pendant around her neck, a magnificent golden falcon suspended on a gold chain, his features materialized, forming high cheekbones, a strong jaw, and a dark mustache.

"It is our time, rôhi," he whispered. "I've come for you."

"Ram?" Meri murmured, her voice husky from sleep.

"Yes, love."

"Where have you been for so long?"

"Waiting. Waiting for you."

He touched her, and her senses came alive; he kissed her, and her spirit soared. They made love, and their bodies intertwined, joined male and female into a flawless whole of marvelous rightness. One body, one mind, one spirit, they strove for distant galaxies, went shooting through space, and exploded in a starburst of consummate pleasure.

Breath held, time suspended, wave after wave of indescribable bliss rolled over them until at last they shuddered and stilled.

Meri's eyes opened, and she touched his face. "Are you part of a dream?"

"Would you like me to be?"

"No. I'd like for you to be real."

He smiled. "Then you have your wish. I'm very real. I'm here in the flesh, and I intend to stay. I've searched lifetimes for you, finding you, losing you, finding you once more. You're mine, and I'll never let you out of my sight again. While I draw a breath, nothing will harm a centimeter of your skin." He hugged her fiercely.

She laughed. "Ramson Gabrey, what am I to do with you?"

"Marrying me would be a start."

"Marrying you might be disastrous."

"Why? Don't you love me?"

Cupping his cheek in her palm, she kissed him gently. "I'm drawn to you in a manner I can't begin to understand, powerfully, inexplicably. And of course I love you. But sometimes love isn't enough. We're very different."

"In some ways perhaps. But we're two halves of the same whole and alike in all the ways that count. Marry me, *rôhi,* and I swear by all that's holy that you'll never regret it for a day. I love you more than life. You complete my soul."

"But Ram, sometimes you . . . overwhelm me . . . smother me. I don't think I could tolerate that."

He raked his fingers through his hair and pressed his forehead with the heel of his hand. "I know that I'm sometimes overbearing, but, God, when I think something might happen to you, I go insane. Maybe if you understood how I feel, why I feel . . . Oh, hell!"

"Then why don't you explain?"

"I don't think I can explain in words, but I can show you."

She frowned. "Show me?"

"Yes. Are you prepared to see it? Are you ready?"

"Ready for what?"

"The truth about us."

"I don't know what you're talking about."

He sighed. "I'll show you. Do you trust me?"

She nodded.

With his arm around her, he pulled her close. He lifted the falcon pectoral around his neck and turned it so that the back faced outward. "Fit the back of your falcon against mine." She did as he asked. He pressed the two pieces together until a clasp snapped them together, then touched his forehead against hers. "Relax. Clear you thoughts," he whispered, "and follow me."

Meri felt his mind touch hers and beckon like the soft fingers of a gentle breeze. She followed. They entered a vortex that carried them back . . . back . . . back . . .

A formless entity of pure joy and blinding light danced among the stars, whirled between universes, and traveled eternity's pathways. Boundless, unbelievable love pulsated at its core, generated the light that shone like a small exploding sun. It split, then came back together like beads of iridescent water blending into a single drop.

The entity circled, then touched Earth, split into two ethereal beings of light, then joined together, then split again, playing among the plants and waters. As they lingered on the planet and separated, their bodies became more corporeal, more substantial—one, yet two.

Like other light beings who visited Earth to experience its

pleasures, their spirits changed to human form; their memories of their source clouded. They became caught up in a cycle of birth and death, light and darkness, man and woman, joy and sorrow. Still their memories of being one lingered, and they each sought the other to be complete.

In the spiral of the vortex, lifetimes in many ages and many places flashed by, some filled with the joy of togetherness, others with the sorrow of separation. Many times the yin and yang came together only to have the female snatched away through death or circumstance. The anguish of those times was wrenchingly intense.

The eddy slowed to show a lifetime in the land of the pharaohs when the falcon pendants were made to preserve the memories, still strong in the male but growing faint in the female. The male had struggled with all his might to secure riches so that he could wed the female, only to have her die from the bite of a serpent before she was his. The agony of the male was indescribable. Despair filled his soul, self-blame for not protecting her pierced his heart like a searing brand, and his cries almost ripped his spirit apart.

Meri thought she would die from the pain of it.

The eddy moved, again to Egypt where the male was a desert chieftain. He had spotted the female, a captive of another tribe, and had tried to barter for her. That failing, he slew the cruel barbarian who held her and took her to his tent many days' journey away.

Leaving her unguarded one day when he went to trade, he returned to find her dead, her throat cut by unknown avengers. He cradled her in his arms and wept. Overcome with grief and self-deprecation, he staggered outside and howled curses at the moon. In his torment he rent his clothes and sliced his flesh.

Meri cried out and jerked her forehead away from Ram's. "No more. Dear God, no more."

Ram unclasped the falcons, then held her close. "Shhhh,

love. It's long past. We're together again, and this time I'll keep you safe."

"Ram, did all that really happen?"

"What do you think?"

She didn't respond for a moment. In her heart she knew that it was true. "Is that the way you feel when you think I might be in danger?"

He nodded. "It's hell."

"Oh my God. I didn't understand." She kissed the center of his forehead. "No wonder you're so obsessive. But those days are long past. You can relax a little now." She smiled. "Remember I have a brown belt in karate."

He laughed and hugged her close. "I'll try to remember one, two, and three, but be patient with me, *sukkar.*"

They made love again, and this time it was even sweeter, more poignant with shared memories.

As they lay in the afterglow, bodies still joined, Meri asked, "How did you find the pectorals?"

"When I was a boy, I remembered where I had hidden them last. Dreamed about it actually. I didn't understand all the particulars then, only that I would find a very rare treasure. My grandfather took me there, and we dug them up."

"Where?"

"Near Luxor. On the spot where I built our house."

"How did you come to know about me?"

"I dreamed of you. From the time I was a teenager, I dreamed of you, over and over."

She brushed her cheek against his shoulder. "And I dreamed of you."

The Mena House coffee shop was temporarily closed for a wedding breakfast. The ceremony was at the foot of the Sphinx just after dawn.

Nora and Charlotte stood to one side beaming. In spite of his jet lag, Brian Vaughn, his long hair tied back with a leather thong, looked proud enough of his daughter to pop. Mark, George, and Jean Jacques were there as were the members of the Golden Years Travel Club—sans Bradley.

Never, Ram thought as he watched Meri glide over the stones toward him, had there been a more beautiful bride or a happier groom. She walked behind Welcome, flaming in a copper-colored *galabiyah*. Zaki Gabrey, Ram's father, who looked like an older, gray-haired version of his son, stood beside him waiting.

"She's a lovely woman, son," Zaki said.

"I know. And she's *mine*."

"Don't try to hold her too tightly. Like a beautiful wild bird, she'll beat herself to death or smother in the grip of your hands."

"I know. I've learned that. One, two, and three."

Zaki frowned. "What?"

Ram chuckled. "Never mind."

"I wish your grandmother and grandfather could be here now."

"So do I. But I have a feeling that they're here in spirit." He turned his attention to the vision that approached.

Dressed in a royal purple *galabiyah* trimmed in gold and dotted with pearls, Meri's face rivaled the radiance of the sun rising behind her as she came to him. Her hair was drawn up in a soft cloud of curls and waves with her stars, as she called them. A golden falcon pendant hung between her breasts. Its mate adorned his chest.

As Meri walked toward Ram, the man she loved beyond time and reason, she could almost hear the laughter and rustle of an ancient celebration throng gathered there. In her memory the Pyramids were gleaming white and gold, the sand was green with lush grasses, and her old comrade, the Sphinx, was arrayed in colorful pharaonic splendor. Meri was sure she saw the stone lips move as she took her place beside Ram and looked into his sky-dyed eyes.

As they once more pledged their eternal vows under a sky

lit with renewed promise, the desert breeze sang and danced in distant whirlwinds.

When they kissed, time was suspended for a moment as destiny sighed and smiled.

> *I have found a courageous heart and I am content. All that I desire will come to pass.*
>
> Ramses II
> Invocation to Amon

Dear Reader,

When I visited Egypt a few years ago, the entire trip was a peak experience. All my life I had longed to travel to that mysterious and magical country replete with magnificent ancient monuments steeped in mystical history. The reality was beyond my wildest expectations; I felt as if I'd found my roots. I had many curious experiences as I made my odyssey through the land of the pharaohs, as did several of my traveling companions—some of them downright spooky.

When a dashing man in Cairo became enamored of one of my friends and literally pursued her all over Egypt, as a writer I thought, *What if* . . . This story of every woman's fantasy—the finding of her soul mate, her other half—began to take shape then, and I've wanted to write it for ages. With the current interest in areas such as reincarnation, time travel, and other paranormal themes, I felt that the time was right for the unusual elements in *Dream of Me*—elements of destiny and eternal love that defy time and space.

I've walked every inch of the journey described in *Dream of Me,* sailed the Nile by felucca and steamboat, climbed the Great Pyramid, ridden camels, bartered for "mummy beads," poured cupfuls of sand from my shoes, swatted armies of flies, and sweated buckets in the Valley of the Kings. I've never gotten so filthy in all my life, and I adored every moment of it. I saw Egypt's entire King Tut collection, some in situ and some at the Cairo Museum (where, when they painted the ceiling, workers simply threw grungy drop cloths over three-thousand-year-old statues and weren't too concerned if Ramses got a drip or two down his back). As a confirmed Egyptophile, I yearn to return. Despite the awesome heat (and I don't *do* heat), I fell in love with the land and its people.

Gazing up at the Great Pyramid of Giza and climbing inside those wondrous stones gives rise to the conviction that *anything* is possible. I felt that exotic Egypt was the perfect setting for a cabalistic tale of romance, enigma, and adventure—with liberal doses of rollicking humor. I hope that you enjoyed the cast of colorful characters I created and have become as enchanted by this mysterious land as I have.

Lately I've been thinking about the vivacious Welcome Venable as the heroine of another unusual story. And I've been thinking about Greece . . .

Bis salama!

Jan Hudson

Bibliography

Besides interviews with Egyptian friends and the Egyptian consul in Houston, I have drawn from the following books that might interest you for further reading on Egypt and its people:

Breasted, James H., *A History of Egypt*. New York: Bantam, 1967.

Budge, E.A. Wallis, *The Egyptian Book of the Dead*. New York: Dover, 1967.

David, A. Rosalie, *The Egyptian Kingdoms*. Oxford: Elsevier, 1975.

Elias, Edward E., *Practical Dictionary of the Colloquial Arabic* (English-Arabic). Cairo: Elias' Modern Publishing House.

Grayson, A. Kirk & Redford, Donald B., *Papyrus and Tablet*. Englewood Cliffs, NJ: Prentice-Hall, 1973.

Hansen, Kathy, *Egypt Handbook*. Chico, CA: Mood Publications, 1993.

Hobson, Christine, *The World of the Pharaohs*. New York: Thames & Hudson, 1987.

James, T.G.H., *Pharaoh's People*. London: The Bodley Head Ltd., 1984.

Kaster, Joseph, *The Wisdom of Ancient Egypt*. New York: Barnes & Noble Books, 1993.

Mertz, Barbara, *Temples, Tombs and Hieroglyphs*. New York: Peter Bedrick Books, 1990.

*If you liked this book, be sure to look for the June releases in the **Denise Little Presents** line:*

Sweeter than Dreams by Olga Bicos   (0142–9, $4.99)
". . . Finely crafted . . . will keep you mesmerized from first page to last. . . . An unforgettable, magical read!"
—*Affaire de Coeur* in a five-star review of *More than Magic*

From the moment that Leydianna Carstair, lovely bookkeeper and uncontrollable dreamer, comes into the orbit of Quentin Alexander Rutherford, Lord Belfour, nothing is impossible. Lord Ruthless, as she calls him, is handsome, wealthy beyond imagining, unpredictable, and brilliant. He's also about to have his well-ordered life turned upside down by his impish young employee. Sparks fly when the man who swore never to marry meets the woman of his dreams. It's the beginning salvo in a wild adventure where anything can happen—from kidnapping to kisses, from piracy to passion, and love is only the beginning of the dreams that come true.

Shades of Rose by Deb Stover   (0143–7, $4.99)
"Deb Stover spins an engaging tale of a love that defies time and destiny, with some of the most delightful characters to grace the pages of a book!"   —Barbara Bretton

Shades of Rose has a little bit of everything in its pages—ghosts, time-travel, a quest for hidden treasure, and a love that transcends time. From the moment that Dylan Marshall begins dreaming about a beautiful woman that he's never met (and these are some pretty intense dreams, let me tell you!), his life is changed. Awake and asleep, he's haunted by her. His only hope of retaining his sanity is to find out what's going on. Trapped between the past and the present, the only hope for then and now, Dylan finds the love of two lifetimes and the answer to his dreams!

Available wherever paperbacks are sold, or order direct from the Publisher. Send cover price plus 50¢ per copy for mailing and handling to Penguin USA, P.O. Box 999, c/o Dept. 17109, Bergenfield, NJ 07621. Residents of New York and Tennessee must include sales tax. DO NOT SEND CASH.

Nightingale, Florence, *Letters from Egypt*. New York: Weidenfeld & Nicolson, 1987.

Roberts, Paul William, *River in the Desert*. New York: Random House, 1993.

Watterson, Barbara, *The Gods of Ancient Egypt*. New York: Facts on File, 1984.

West, John Anthony, *The Traveler's Key to Ancient Egypt*. New York: Alfred A. Knopf, 1985.

White, Jon Manchip, *Everyday Life in Ancient Egypt*. New York: Perigee Books, 1980.